SARRA MANNING

Rescue Me

HODDER

First published in Great Britain in 2021 by Hodder & Stoughton
An Hachette UK company

This paperback edition published in 2021

1

A CIP catalogue record for this title is available from the British Library

Paperback ISBN 978 1 529 33658 0
eBook ISBN 978 1 529 33656 6

Typeset in Plantin Light by Hewer Text UK Ltd, Edinburgh
Printed and bound in Great Britain by Clays Ltd, Elcograf S.p.A.

Hodder & Stoughton policy is to use papers that are natural, renewable
and recyclable products and made from wood grown in sustainable
forests. The logging and manufacturing processes are expected to
conform to the environmental regulations of the country of origin.

Hodder & Stoughton Ltd
Carmelite House
50 Victoria Embankment
London EC4Y 0DZ

www.hodder.co.uk

'My little dog, a heartbeat at my feet.' Edith Wharton ·

I

Margot

Margot Millwood was a cat person. Unfortunately, no one had explained this to Percy, her cat.

It also seemed that no one had explained to Margot's ex-boyfriend George that after two months apart, they were getting back together.

George had asked to meet for early drinks after work. Margot had imagined that early drinks would lead to dinner then a declaration that, like her, George had seen what was on offer on the dating apps and realised that what they'd had together hadn't been so bad.

Wrong!

'I found a few of your things knocking about my place,' George said, handing over a bulging bag for life, before Margot could take even one sip of her gin and tonic. 'I can only stay for a quick drink. I have plans.'

'Plans?' Margot echoed as she cast a cursory glance inside the bag and saw an almost empty tube of bb cream and a pair of red lacy knickers that absolutely did not belong to her. She was tempted to hand them back to George with a scathing remark, but she didn't know if they'd been washed or not. 'These knic—'

'Yeah, sorry this is so rushed, but I'm sure neither of us want to rehash the details of why we broke up,' George continued, then downed half his bottle of fancy, locally brewed lager with almost indecent haste.

Margot could never back down from a challenge. 'We broke up because, after two years together, you decided that you weren't ready to even have a conversation about when we were going to start a family and you decided to break this to me on my thirty- sixth birthday.' Nope, she still wasn't over it.

'Only because when I took you out for your birthday meal, you told me, no, *demanded*, that we start trying for a baby that very night. I hadn't even looked at the menu,' George recalled with an aggrieved tone as Margot's phone rang. She ignored it.

'I didn't demand that you impregnate me that very night, I just pointed out that at thirty-six, I couldn't continue to take my fertility for granted,' Margot reminded George. Her phone beeped with a voicemail message at the same time as George sighed long and loud.

'Anyway, it's water under the bridge now. We've both moved on,' he said. 'Really, there's no use in holding a post-mortem, Margs.'

There really wasn't. Margot steepled her hands together so she wouldn't make any threatening gestures. She didn't want a post-mortem either, but still, George could benefit from a little advice.

'Talking of moving on, can I just say that the next woman you get involved with . . . well, it would be better to tell her right from the start that you're categorically not interested in having kids. Better to be up front than stringing her along for two years on false promises and maybes,' Margot said coolly and not at all bitterly as, once more, her phone started to ring.

Again, she ignored it, because she was far more interested in the way that suddenly George wouldn't meet her gaze.

'You're already in another relationship.' It wasn't a question. Didn't need to be.

George nodded. 'There's no law says that I can't be,' he said a little defensively. 'Are you going to answer your phone?'

'Never mind my phone,' Margot said. 'Like I said, please don't lead her on if you're not serious. By the time a woman is thirty-five, her—'

' – fertility could be halved,' George finished for her. 'Yeah, you did mention that about a few hundred times when we were together.'

But still, it hadn't been enough to spur George into action apart from vague platitudes about how Margot would make a great mother. Or how it would be best to wait a year or so and a couple of promotions down the line, so they could buy a house for this hypothetical family that it turned out George hadn't really wanted.

'I'm just saying. For the sake of your new girlfriend.' No one could ever accuse Margot of being unsisterly.

'Not something you need to worry about and neither does Cassie,' George said, probably not even realising that he was puffing out his chest, proud as the plumpest pigeon.

'I take it that Cassie isn't in her thirties.' It was obvious that she wasn't, but George's faux bashful smile confirmed it.

'She's twenty-six,' George confirmed. He didn't look even a little embarrassed to be dating a woman fifteen years younger than him. On the contrary, he looked pretty bloody chipper about it.

Margot's phone started ringing for the third time. By now it was a welcome relief. 'I really must get this, it sounds like someone is trying to contact me urgently,' Margot said, getting to her feet and quickly gathering up cardigan, handbag and the bag for life full of mouldy crap that probably wasn't hers. 'Lovely to catch up. Must go!'

Of course her handbag strap was caught on the arm of her chair, so in the time it took to extricate herself, her phone stopped ringing and George had the chance to not only have the last word but deliver a pretty damning character assessment while he was at it.

'The thing is, Margs, I always hoped we might go the distance, but you're just too much.'

Margot was completely blindsided. Also completely furious. A younger Margot might have sworn that in the future she wouldn't be so much. But older Margot refused to make herself something less than she was.

'No, *you're* just too much,' she hissed under her breath, as she fled the chichi little bar in King's Cross, her hand digging into her bag for her phone, which was ringing and vibrating yet again. When Richard Burton had met Elizabeth Burton for the first time, he'd said that she was 'just too bloody much', but that was because Elizabeth Taylor was too much of all the good things that womanhood had to offer: wit, intelligence, killer curves and a pair of violet eyes. But when George, who had a very weak chin and a weak grasp of current affairs to match (there! She could finally admit it), said that Margot was too much he meant that she was needy, demanding and desperate. Margot didn't think that she was any of those things, but she *was* thirty-six and time was marching on even if her prospects of being in a committed relationship weren't.

'Yes?' she snapped as she answered the phone to a withheld number – probably someone in a call centre on another continent wanting to know if she'd recently been in an accident.

'Hello?' the caller, a woman, queried back uncertainly. 'I've been trying to get hold of you for the last half hour. I'm calling about your cat. I believe you call him Percy.'

'I call him Percy because that's his name,' Margot said evenly, though she felt very far from even. 'Are you the person who's stolen him?'

Margot was used to Percy keeping his distance. In fact, he barely tolerated her presence. After a long night of catting, he'd come home and scream at Margot until she fed him. How she longed for an occasional dead bird or half-alive mouse – the tokens of love that her friends received from their cats. But just because loving someone, or a cat, was difficult, it didn't mean that one should just give up. He was still her Percy. Though Margot's friends called him Shitbag on account of his habit of luring Margot in with big eyes and floppy limbs as if he wanted to snuggle. He'd even begin to purr as she tickled him under his chin. Then, just as Margot dared to relax, he'd either scratch or bite her. If she were really unlucky, he'd do both. To love Percy was to always make sure that your tetanus shots were up to date.

Over the last few months, Percy's absences had been getting longer and longer and he was getting fatter and fatter. It was obvious that Percy was tarting himself around the neighbourhood, and Margot had had to resort to desperate measures. She'd been dripping with blood by the time she'd managed to secure a note around Percy's collar.

> *To whom it may concern,*
> *Percy is a very well loved, well-fed cat. Do NOT let him come into your house and do not feed him.*
> *My number is on his collar tag, if you need me to come and fetch him.*

'We haven't stolen him, he happens to prefer it round here,' the woman now said indignantly. Then she must have realised that technically she had catnapped him if he was on her premises, because she sighed. 'Look, I don't suppose you could come round?'

Margot would have liked nothing more than to go home,

change into her cosies and brood over what had gone wrong with George. She might even have cried. Not for George and his ripely fertile twenty-six-year-old new girlfriend, but because finding a man, just an average, ordinary man without commitment issues, continued to elude her.

Not tonight, Satan. Tonight, Margot was only home long enough to grab Percy's pet carrier, a pouch of Dreamies and a thick towel so she could retrieve her sociopathic cat from one of the beautiful big Victorian villas that Highgate was famous for.

Margot was ushered into a double-aspect, open-plan living room with not one but two wood-burning stoves, a Warhol print of Chairman Mao on the wall above one of them, and a huge sectional sofa, which would have taken up her entire flat. On that sectional sofa were two little girls – they couldn't be more than four and six and should absolutely have been in bed at eight o'clock on a school night – and nestled in between them, wearing a baby bonnet was Percy. He pointedly ignored her.

'The thing is, you have to stop letting him in,' Margot said to the harassed-looking woman who had answered the door and said her name was Fay and her equally harassed-looking husband, Benji. As Margot had entered, their nanny was just leaving for the day, so Margot didn't know why either of them was quite so harassed looking. 'He's a cat. He's an opportunist. But Percy is *my* cat and *my* opportunist.'

'His name isn't Percy, it's Pudding,' the smaller of the two girls piped up. Her chubby arm held Percy/Pudding round the neck in a vice-like grip. Soon there would be bloodshed.

'If he was happy with you, then he wouldn't keep coming here,' her older sister said with an opaque stare, which was similar to the venomous expression on Percy's face as he now gave Margot the full weight of his attention.

Margot's boss, Tansy, had told her not to get a tortoiseshell cat. 'All cats have a tendency to be bastards but torties are the worst,' she'd advised when Margot had been scanning cat rescue websites during kitten season a few years before. There were many times that Margot had wished that she'd listened to Tansy but now, she wasn't giving up on her cat without a fight.

There *was* bloodshed. Margot's blood that Percy shed as she tried to herd him into his carrier, an exercise that necessitated throwing the thick towel over Percy to incapacitate him which also ensured that he couldn't do much harm. Unfortunately, he managed to work a paw free and inflict considerable damage on Margot's right hand, which already bore many Percy-inflicted scars.

The little girls were crying. Fay had disappeared with the words, 'God, I need a drink' and Benji kept saying, 'Are you sure he's your cat?'

Oh yes, he was Margot's cat all right. The latest in a long line of men who thought that the grass was much, much greener somewhere else.

'Fine,' Margot said, when Fay returned with a first-aid box. 'Fine. You know what? You can have him.'

Fay and Benji were very gracious in victory and the youngest girl, Elise, came over to give Margot a consolatory hug as Fay carefully dabbed antiseptic cream on Margot's hand while Benji wondered aloud if she needed stitches.

They kept calling her Marge until at last Margot pointed out that it was 'Margot, *Mar-go*. Marge is a butter substitute and I'm not a substitute', even though her substitution status had been a recurring theme that evening.

Benji gave Margot a lift home, but that was only so he could pick up Percy's things. The cat scratching tower, the countless toys, the very expensive cat food which was all he would eat. Margot boxed it all up, refused to take payment for any of it and came to a momentous decision after she'd shut the door.

'That is *it!* From now on, I'm a dog person.'

2

Will

Roland wore black turtlenecks, cream chinos and horn-rimmed glasses. Come winter, come summer, come the in-between seasons, his black turtlenecks, chinos and specs were absolute and his face impassive.

For a whole year Will had been coming, once a week, to Roland's consulting room just off Kilburn Park Road, and yet Will was sure that without the turtlenecks and the horn-rimmed glasses, he'd never be able to pick Roland out of a police line-up.

Maybe that was the point.

'So, you're quite sure that you want to pause our sessions?'

Will realised that while his own mind had been wandering, Roland's gaze had been fixed on him.

'Not pause, stop,' Will said firmly, though there was always something about Roland's expressionless expression that made him want to squirm. 'I said right at the beginning that I was going to give myself a year of therapy to fix myself.'

As soon as he said it, Will wished he hadn't. Roland adjusted his spectacles so he could peer over the top of them. 'Fix?' he queried mildly. 'I seem to recall that at the beginning of our very first session we also discussed that this wasn't a fix but a process. An ongoing process.'

'Yes, but I only wanted to ongo it for a year,' Will reminded him. Thanks to Roland, he no longer felt uncomfortable about confrontation. 'To favour a goal-orientated approach. Well,

I've hit my targets, so now is a good time, a great time, to move on. When I lived in New York, there were people who'd been in therapy for years, decades, with no end in sight.'

Will didn't add that most of them were completely dysfunctional because the therapy had invaded every aspect of their lives, instead of improving it.

'Well, you have made a lot of progress,' Roland conceded. 'Put a lot of work in, and I don't say that lightly because it's been challenging at times, accessing memories that have been buried for so long.'

Which was another reason why Will deserved time off for good behaviour. A year ago, he'd been a shell, a husk. Burned out. Not fit for purpose. And now? Now, he might still be on a fact-finding mission to discover who he was, but he certainly wasn't any of the things that he used to be. 'I have come a long way.'

'And the panic attacks have abated?'

'Haven't had one for months.'

'And your GP agreed that you could come off the antidepressants?'

Will nodded. 'I started reducing the dose about five months ago, stopped taking them completely two months ago.'

'And you're ready to make the emotional connections that have been missing in your life?'

Of course Roland saved the most difficult question for last. 'Making emotional connections really isn't a priority for me right now.'

'But I thought the lack of emotional connections, your inability to connect with people in a deep, meaningful way, is what we've spent the last year working on?' Roland glanced down at his pad and the copious notes that he'd been scribbling.

'I've emotionally reconnected with my family over the last year. That has to count for something,' Will insisted. He'd left home over twenty years ago and hadn't felt the need to return that often. After three years at Manchester University and a first-class degree in international finance, economics and business, Will had been headhunted by a global investment bank. They'd funded an MBA at Wharton Business School in Philadelphia and after that there'd been five years working in their Berlin office, three years in Paris and a brief stint in Hong Kong before he'd been transferred to New York then subsequently poached by New York's largest privately owned investment bank.

It had been a glittering career by anyone's standards. There'd been performance-related bonuses and corner apartments with iconic views, each one bigger than the last. It was a world away from the family home and the family florist in Muswell Hill.

Of course, Will had dutifully phoned his mother, Mary, every Sunday morning. And he'd been back for hatches, matches and, more recently and tragically, despatches. Less infrequently, they'd come to visit him. So, yes, he had a family. He liked them. But it turned out that he liked them a lot more when there was a wide expanse of sea and several time zones between them.

This last year, Will had seen his family on a daily basis. And although he was meant to be on a career sabbatical, he'd somehow ended up working in the family business. Roland should give him props for that, and also for managing not to kill his half-sister, Sage, who hadn't even been thought of when Will had first left home, and who made being annoying into an art form.

'Of course, family ties are important, defining, as are the family ties we break.' Roland folded his arms, but Will wasn't going to wander down that particular path again. He folded his arms too and made sure to maintain eye contact with

Roland until his therapist sighed. 'So, Will, remind me of your last romantic relationship? The woman who hit you with her shoe?'

Roland had many admirable qualities, but his total recall of some of the more humiliating moments of Will's life wasn't one of them. 'Dovinda? She didn't hit me with her shoe, she threw her shoe at me,' he clarified. 'And we weren't in a relationship. We were just seeing each other. Dating. That's what you do in New York.'

They'd been through this. Several times.

'So, no one in New York is in a relationship? How . . . odd.' Roland, face still stuck in neutral, shook his head. 'Remind me why Dovinda threw her shoe at you?'

Will had walked right into this one. 'Because she wanted to transition towards being in a relationship and I thought we both understood that although we enjoyed hanging out together, and yes, having sex with each other, that was as far as it went.'

'This has been a recurring pattern in your relationships with women,' Roland noted, writing something in his pad.

'Again, they weren't relationships.'

They'd been through a lot in this room. Between 6 p.m. and 6.50 p.m. every Thursday evening, Will had confronted hidden truths, long-buried secrets, voiced things that he never thought he would. There'd been pain, raw emotion, even tears, but breaking up with Roland might be the hardest thing yet.

Also, Roland was wrong. Will's avoidance of deep, emotional connections with other people had nothing to do with the defining moment of his life, which had brought him to Roland's consulting room. When he'd lain on a trolley in an ER cubicle at New York Presbyterian Hospital, convinced that he was having a heart attack. And OK, he'd lived in New York for over five years and there wasn't a single person that Will had felt he could call, but that hadn't been the issue. The issue had been that he had a glittering career, a fancy Tribeca apartment, lots of money in the bank, all the latest tech, gadgets and expensive trainers, but suddenly the most important thing in his life was a gnawing, stabbing, desolate pain in his chest. The dynamic, successful, driven person he'd forced himself to become no longer existed and he'd reverted back to being a terrified, powerless twelve-year-old that—

Roland cleared his throat and Will was back in the room, back in his present, which was so much better than his recent past. 'You've come back from a very difficult set of personal circumstances and bedded down with your family this last year, so obviously you can make and need emotional connections, despite your claims to the contrary. But outside of family, I want you, off the top of your head, to name one other person in your life who you've ever felt a connection with,' Roland suddenly demanded, and immediately Will could feel panic rising in him, like bile. 'Someone who you weren't afraid to be vulnerable with. Someone *you* loved unconditionally.'

There wasn't one. But even so, there was an answer that immediately came to mind. 'Muttley,' he said without hesitation. 'Dogs count too, right?'

Just thinking of his childhood dog, a Jack Russell crossed with god knows what, put a smile on his face. Muttley had been his constant companion. He'd walk Will to school then be waiting when he got out. They'd spent hours playing endless games of fetch. And there'd been other hours, in the dark, when Will had whispered his secret worries and fears to the dog and pressed his face into his warm, dank fur when he could feel the tears starting.

That was love. That had to be love. But . . .

'I'm not getting a dog!' Will stated very firmly.

Roland raised his eyebrows by a couple of millimetres. 'No one's suggesting that you get a dog.'

'Getting a dog, even fostering a dog is a huge commitment. Huge.'

'No one's telling you to foster a dog either.' Roland sighed again. The clock was showing that it was fifty minutes past the hour and it was time for Will to say his final goodbyes.

But he didn't want to leave things unresolved, which only went to show how much he'd grown as a person. 'Maybe I could take a dog for a walk sometimes. Volunteer at a rescue?' Will frowned. 'What would be the harm in that?'

Given the solemnity of the moment, Roland frowned too. It was the most animated that Will had ever seen him. He waited for Roland's goodbye speech, which, as ever, would be insightful and thought-provoking.

Roland put down his pen all the better to give Will one last incisive look. 'I'm sure I'll be able to find you a slot when you want to resume our sessions,' he said with a slightly wistful smile. 'Until then, good luck.'

3

Margot

'I am kind. I am strong. I am positive. I attract kind, strong, positive people into my life. I am deserving of love. I am a great dog owner.'

Usually Margot tried to be more effusive with her daily affirmations, which painted a picture of the very best version of herself and sent it out into the universe to be transformed into truth. But she was in the back of an Uber – the driver had already taken offence when she asked him to swap Talk FM for Magic – and she was with her best friend Tracy, and Tracy didn't really get the whole positive affirmation thing.

As the BeeGees insisted that they should be dancing, yeah, Margot took a couple of steadying breaths. She was just as terrified as she was before one of her innumerable blind dates. Actually, more terrified, because lately the only feeling she got before heading out to meet yet another man from yet another dating app was the grim resignation that he probably wouldn't be The One. That he'd give her the old up-and-down and not bother to hide either his dismay or the lecherous belief that she wasn't his One either, but would do for his One Night Stand.

But a dog wouldn't care that Margot was a size sixteen or that she was two weeks late to get her roots done or that she'd spilt coffee on the 'Strong Girls Club' sweatshirt she was wearing and only noticed by the time she'd already left the house. A dog would know that was all superficial stuff, and the stuff that mattered – Margot's soul, her heart and her innate sense of doing right – was in perfect condition.

'I'm so nervous,' she said to Tracy. 'What if none of the dogs like me.'

'Odds on, there has to be at *least* one that likes you.' Tracy patted Margot's hand perfunctorily.

They'd been friends since they'd met at fashion college, eighteen years before, Tracy just off the plane from New Zealand where 'there's a lot of sheep, not very much in the way of cutting-edge fashion'.

Back then, Tracy had a buzzcut, a lip piercing and had been terrifyingly forthright on first acquaintance. Time and Margot had softened her. She'd let her auburn hair grow out and ditched the lip piercing, although she was still inordinately fond of a DM boot, leopard print and a strong opinion.

'Anyway, this is why I'm here. You're too emotionally unbalanced after meeting up with George to make any life-changing decisions on your own.'

'I can't believe I wasted two crucial years of my fertility window on him,' Margot said. Tracy sighed. Not just in agreement but because Margot had been revisiting that theme all week and it was wearing thin.

'You'll be fine. The doggies will love you, of course they will,' Tracy insisted, possibly to ward off any more talk of George. 'Are we nearly there yet?'

'There' was a local dog shelter. Obviously Margot was going to adopt rather than shop. She knew what it was like to be abandoned and made to feel as if you weren't good enough. Margot had filled out a rehoming questionnaire and passed her home visit with flying colours because, as she affirmed daily, she was a kind, caring, positive person. Though what had really swung it was that she had a back garden, even if it was the size of a postage stamp. A smaller than standard-sized postage stamp. It had also helped that Margot had said she was going to take the dog into work with her every day, which was slightly stretching the truth. Or rather, it was stretching the truth so far that when you held it up to the light, the truth became completely transparent because both her bosses, Derek and Tansy, had said that there was no way she could bring a dog to work with her. But Margot was sure they'd change their minds. They'd initially been very resistant to work-from-home Wednesdays but they'd come round eventually.

Anyway, time enough to worry about that. Right now, as the Uber careered around the streets of North London, bunny-hopping over speed bumps, Margot tried to manifest the perfect dog. Something cute and Instagrammable, possibly fluffy, hopefully portable and definitely house-trained. Margot was leaning towards maybe a small cockapoo as the car pulled up outside a long, low building just off the A41 in Barnet.

'I am a *great* dog owner,' Margot muttered under her breath as she got out of the car.

Her doggy destiny awaited.

The reception area was quite utilitarian because it was a charity and they clearly didn't have money to fritter away on sofas or a lick of paint on the nicotine yellow walls. But the volunteer waiting for them had a huge smile on her face and said fervently, 'I'm Sophie. Thank you so much for considering a rescue dog.'

Sophie was a young woman with bright orange dreadlocks, tattoos and a no-nonsense air, so Margot didn't dare say that she wanted a dog that would look good on the Gram. Or fill up the hole in her heart that had been carved out by every man that had passed her over, and more recently, Percy's perfidy.

Sophie pulled open a set of doors and Margot's nostrils were immediately hit by the stench of ammonia, even as she recoiled from the noise of what sounded like a hundred dogs barking. It was so much more brutal than she'd imagined. She'd pictured something more heart-warming than this . . . this . . . dog prison.

Each dog was kept in a small enclosure, a cage really, with hard stone floors and harsh fluorescent lighting. No wonder that they jumped up, scrabbling at the bars that held them captive, desperate to get Margot's attention as she walked past them.

'Kennels can be very distressing for a lot of dogs,' Sophie explained. 'Especially the owner surrenders. They don't understand why they've gone from living with someone in a comfortable house to suddenly being here on their own.'

'It's so sad,' Margot breathed, and though she was here for the cute, there was something tempting about every dog that she walked past. For a couple of minutes, she was quite taken with an elderly white French bulldog that snuffled at her hands, but Tracy pulled her away.

'Frenchies are completely overbred and riddled with health problems. Our neighbours have a Frenchie. The poor thing can't even drink water without bringing it back up.' She fixed a wilting Margot with a stern look. 'You have to be practical, Margs. The vet bills would bankrupt you.'

There weren't any cockapoos, but there were a lot of Staffordshire Bull Terriers. Margot definitely didn't want one of those. She didn't like to judge, but whenever there was a dog attack in the papers, the culprit always seemed to be a 'Bull-Terrier-like dog' and certainly the ones in these kennels lunged for Margot when she approached.

'They're just being friendly,' Sophie said, though Margot doubted it. 'I know they get a bad press, but Staffies are actually one of only three breeds that the Kennel Club particularly recommends for families with children.'

'Really,' Margot said in what she hoped was a noncommittal voice.

'Yes. Here's a fun fact for you, more people seek hospital treatment after being bitten by Labradors than by Staffies,' Sophie said, which wasn't as comforting as she seemed to think it was.

They were coming to the last kennel now and although Margot had seen lots of dogs who'd tugged on her heartstrings, she was yet to find the dog that could steal her heart.

The final kennel was empty, but even so, Margot stopped to read the card with its former occupant's vital statistics on it.

Name: Blossom
Age: 3-ish
Breed: Staffordshire Bull Terrier
Notes: Picked up as a stray and unclaimed from the council pound. Nervous around men. Highly food motivated. Can't live with cats. Blossom just wants to be loved!

'Oh my God, Margot,' Tracy hissed. 'It's your spirit animal.'

Margot put her hand on her heart to check that it was still there because now there was a distinct possibility that it might have been stolen.

'This one . . .' but before she could ask where Blossom was, Margot realised that the kennel wasn't empty. Cowering right at the back was a little white Staffy, shaking like it was a freezing winter's day rather than unseasonably warm for late September.

Margot crouched down and held out her hand. 'Hello,' she said softly. 'Do you want to come and say hello?'

This would have been Percy's cue to fly at Margot with

claws unsheathed and teeth bared but Blossom merely lifted her head.

'Oh, you are *so* pretty,' Margot cooed, and it was the greatest validation she'd ever received when the little dog slowly stood up and tremulously approached. 'What a special, precious little girl.'

Blossom had big brown eyes that looked as if they'd been ringed with thick kohl by a top make-up artist. They were fixed on Margot warily as she came right up to the bars and tentatively stuck out her tongue to lick Margot's proffered fingers.

Margot stroked the dog's cheek and Blossom rubbed against the bars of her cage as if she was desperate to get closer to her. Margot didn't want a Staffy. She wasn't convinced that they were great family pets and they were hardly fluffy and portable. But Blossom was staring up at her with soulful brown eyes and it wouldn't do any harm to take her out of her kennel for a little walk. Just so she could stretch her legs.

'I'll stay behind,' Tracy said with a frown. 'But, remember, no rash decisions.'

'Absolutely,' Margot agreed as Sophie clipped a lead on to Blossom's collar.

Blossom was very skittish as they ran the gauntlet of the other dogs, who all upped their barking at the sight of one of their number staging a breakout. She tried to hide behind Margot, her head bumping into the back of her legs, until they got outside.

The kennels were on the edge of woodlands and once they were out of earshot of the barking, Blossom walked beautifully alongside Margot, pausing occasionally to look up at her with those cartoon-like eyes. She was built like a barrel, all shoulders and ribcage, resting on short legs that seemed delicate by comparison; her slightly bandy back legs resembling a fragile wishbone. She wasn't all white either. Her snout was white but the top of her head and her floppy ears were fawn. Her back was fawn with white splodges, one of them in the shape of Italy, and her tail was fawn too, apart from the tip, which looked as if it had been dipped in a can of white paint.

But still, she was in a pitiful condition. She had bald patches on her flanks and though she was built solidly, Margot could see every single one of her ribs through what fur she had.

'What has happened to you, little one?' Margot asked. The dog didn't answer, but trotted obediently at her side until they came to a fallen log and Margot sat down. Immediately, Blossom plopped down by her feet then rested her chin on Margot's knee so she could keep staring at her. As if Margot was the one thing that she wanted to look at for the rest of her life. It had been a long, long time since anyone had gazed at Margot with such rapt wonder.

The feeling was mutual. Margot couldn't stop staring at Blossom. She really was extraordinarily pretty with her heart-shaped head and those liquid eyes.

'Oh! Oh dear!'

All those dates. All those men. All those *years* spent trying to find someone who wasn't afraid to love Margot, despite all her contradictions and complexities. And just as all those men had never felt that spark, that connection, the recognition that came from finding your other, so Margot hadn't either. Not if she was being really truthful. Until now.

Now, she felt as if she was going to burst into sudden but intense tears, even as her heart seemed to swell to three times its size. Margot wanted to throw her arms around Blossom, smother her with kisses and promise her that she never had to feel scared again.

Margot wasn't an expert, but she thought that this could be love at first sight.

'Blossom's the dog for me,' she told Sophie and Tracy when they got back to the kennels. 'We were destined for each other.'

'Blossom really deserves a loving home,' Sophie said, reaching down to stroke Blossom's snout. 'Once she feels settled and safe, she'll be a completely different dog. Shall we go and fill in the paperwork?'

'Are you sure about this?' Tracy asked. 'I thought we agreed that you wouldn't do anything rash.'

Margot nodded emphatically. 'I've never been more sure. Let's get the paperwork sorted and then I'll be back to pick her up next week.'

'You can't take her now?' Sophie queried as Blossom was put back in her hated kennel with one last forlorn look at Margot.

'I really can't,' Margot explained when she was sitting in front of Belinda, the Head of Adoption Services. 'I told you when you did the home check that I have to go away for work tomorrow.' Desperation made her voice squeak. 'I'll come straight from the airport to pick her up on Sunday morning.'

'Blossom can't tolerate another week in kennels,' Belinda said firmly. 'I'm not going to put her on reserve for you, because someone might come in tomorrow who can take her immediately.'

I am a great dog owner. The universe was not transforming Margot's affirmations into reality.

'But Blossom is meant to be *my* dog,' Margot pleaded, her hands actually clasped in the prayer position. 'There must be someone who can look after her for the next week?'

4

Will

Will pulled up outside the kennels in the work van. He didn't usually do deliveries, but somehow, over the last few months, he'd become the go-to guy for whatever needed doing in the family floristry business. Whether it was negotiating contracts for the events side of the company, overhauling the website or delivering a bouquet of seasonal flowers to Sandra in Barnet who'd finally passed her driving test on the fifteenth attempt.

He'd googled rescue kennels while waiting for his mother to put the finishing touches to Sandra's flowers because he'd just received his weekly message from Roland, even though he was no longer, officially, on Roland's books.

Just checking in. I want to reiterate that forging new emotional connections can only have a positive impact on your mental health. Signing up as a volunteer at a rescue kennels would be a great start. (Your Thursday evening slot is still free, if you want to rethink the pause.) Regards, Roland

He was going to make this quick. Find a dog in need. Be both giving and receiving of emotional sustenance. Take a picture with said dog, send it to Roland, then head off into town for a meeting with a high-end PR agency who were tendering a contract for a florist to provide flowers for all their events.

Will hadn't taken more than two steps through the door when he was met by a young woman with neon orange dreadlocks, a navy-blue T-shirt with the rescue organisation logo on it and a resolute look on her face.

'I've come to take out one of your dogs,' he said, raising his voice over the sound of frenzied barking coming from the door behind her.

'Oh, have you had a home check? What's your name?' she asked, her gaze moving to another door marked PRIVATE. 'I'll go and look you up.'

'I'm not a volunteer,' Will admitted. 'I just wanted to hang out with a dog for a few minutes.'

'Well, we don't really allow walk-ins.' The woman folded her arms. 'You'd have to be properly vetted first. We could do that now . . .'

Will didn't want to find himself suddenly committed to coming back week after week to hang out with dogs. Although objectively there was no good reason why he couldn't. This was proving much harder than he'd thought.

'I'd be happy to foster,' he improvised, because perhaps he could take a dog out then decide that actually he wasn't cut out to foster, sorry to have wasted your time and I'll just be on my way, thank you very much. Though, again, there was no reason why he couldn't foster a dog. Except fostering a dog, an actual living being, was a big commitment and he didn't want any big commitments. Only small commitments. Very, very small commitments. 'I have some experience of dogs. We had one when I was a kid. Muttley. He was the best dog in the world.'

Dreadlocks cracked a smile. 'Everyone thinks their dog is the best dog in the world,' she said.

'And none of them are wrong,' Will added. The barking seemed to increase in both intensity and volume. 'Apart from the poor dogs who've ended up here.'

Her arms were now unfolded. 'We do need to do some background checks,' she said.

But Will could tell she was softening. 'Of course, but while I'm here, can I have a quick look at the dogs?'

Once they were through the door, the noise was almost deafening and there was a stench of ammonia that caught at the back of Will's throat as he scoped out the dogs hurling themselves at the bars of their kennels.

There wasn't much cuteness on display. Mostly pain and despair at being incarcerated in these cold, inhospitable surroundings when once they must have been a cherished pet. At least, Will hoped so. He didn't like to think that these dogs had never known a soft bed, a stroke from a loving hand.

He turned away from a frantic spaniel with desperately sad, pleading eyes, to the next kennel, housing a French bulldog. Everyone loved a French bulldog, but this one was grizzled, had gunky eyes and was making such awful noises, like a motorbike that wouldn't start, that Will feared it would keel over midway through taking a selfie. 'Sorry, mate,' he said, reaching through the bars to stroke the top of its head with the tips of his fingers. He could feel himself weakening. If he stayed here much longer, he'd probably agree to foster all the dogs. Every single last one of them. But before Will could do anything hasty, his attention was caught, or rather grabbed, by a commotion at the far end of the kennels.

There was a dark-haired woman on her knees in front of one of the kennels looking up at two other women. 'This is my soul-dog. We're meant to be together,' she was saying, her voice pitching up and down. As Will drew nearer, intrigued to find out what was going on, he realised there were tears streaming down her face.

It was a pretty face. A really pretty face. She had a pretty body to match. She seemed soft and yielding, though he tended to prefer his woman to be harder and unforgiving. That way no one got hurt. Certainly, he couldn't imagine

Dovinda, or any of the many others before Dovinda, crying in public.

'I have work commitments this week and of course I don't want Blossom to be distressed in the meantime, but there has to be a solution,' she said, voice still wobbling, her forehead knitting together as she frowned.

Will and his volunteer shared a look. A look like they were two sensible people who didn't really care for histrionics.

He was close enough now to see that the woman had been shielding a dog from view; a sad Staffy with velvet eyes, though if it were sad because life had been unkind or because it didn't like being held in a chokehold while being cried on, Will couldn't tell.

'If she's still here in a week, you can take her, but until then she's on our priority list for rehoming,' said the older woman firmly. She had spectacles attached to a chain around her neck, which gave her an air of authority, so Will supposed that she was in charge. 'She's being featured on all our social media channels this afternoon.'

Will wondered why the crying woman was so drawn to that dog in particular, but he couldn't really get a good look at either of them as they'd merged into one crying, shaking whole. The woman's dark head bent over the dog, her arms wrapped round its stocky frame.

'Come on, Margs,' the second woman said softly. She had red hair and was wearing two different kinds of leopard print. 'It will work out if it's meant to.'

Margs (what kind of a name was Margs?) raised her tear-stained face. 'Can't you take her for the week?' she asked hopefully.

'Really can't. Den's away until Friday night and dogs aren't allowed on campus unless they're registered guide dogs,' her friend said. 'There was an incident with a so-called emotional-support ferret. Sorry.'

Will felt a sudden tug on his arm. 'Didn't you say you'd be happy to foster?'

'What?'

Will turned to Dreadlocks who was looking right back at him with a gleam in her eyes. 'We're desperate for fosterers. Absolutely desperate.'

'Oh! *You* could foster her!' Now all eyes were on him, especially the big blue eyes, only slightly puffy from all the sobbing, of the woman on her knees. 'I knew there had to be an answer.'

Will held his hands up. 'Hang on a minute! I said I was *thinking* about fostering.' His initial impression of this woman may have been wrong. She was straightening to full height now and he could see something uncompromising in the set of her face, the way she drew her shoulders back, and the assessing look she was giving him in return.

'One week out of your entire life,' she said to him softly, as if they were the only two people in the place, as if her words weren't sound-tracked by a cacophony of barks. 'You'll be getting Blossom out of here and freeing up a kennel for another dog, so actually you're saving two dogs. That's pretty good going for one week out of your life, don't you think?'

He didn't want to, but Will nodded, because when she put it like that . . . But he was a busy man. Except, he wasn't *that* busy, and if he could save one dog from this hell-hole then that had to be a good thing. 'But don't you have to do a home check, first?' he remembered. 'And I can't do that today because I've got a meeting in Shoreditch at three and it's eleven now.'

'We could easily do a home check now, then I don't mind bringing Blossom round this evening,' Dreadlocks pointed out. 'Where do you live?'

This whole situation was spiralling ever further out of

control and Will didn't do well when that happened. 'Muswell Hill. Look, let's put a pin in it and—'

'That's perfect because I live up the hill in Highgate,' Margs said and she smiled at Will, radiantly, like sun suddenly breaking through after a heavy rainfall. He returned the smile, or rather he lifted the corners of his mouth in an approximation of a smile because he was out of practice. 'We're literally neighbours. Don't you find that when you want something badly enough, and you put that energy out there, then the universe usually comes through?'

'Margs, don't start positively affirming again. This morning has been stressful enough.'

Will immediately wished that he could take his smile back. He knew from bitter experience to be wary of women spouting nonsense about positive energy and manifesting joy. Not a lot of joy to be found when they were shouting at him about his failure to commit.

'It does seem very fortuitous,' Spectacles agreed. She placed her glasses on her face so she could peer at the card pinned to the empty kennel. 'Ahh. I knew it was too good to be true. Blossom's not very keen on men.'

Will was no stranger to rejection, but he didn't think he'd ever been rejected quite so swiftly before.

'I can't help being a man,' Will said in his defence, and Margs smiled at him weakly, like he could at least have *tried* not to be a man.

Meanwhile Dreadlocks and Spectacles were in a huddle. 'It's worth a try,' Will heard one of them say. 'She was all right with Randeep, once she'd got warmed up. Shall I go and get the treats?'

Dreadlocks emerged from the scrum and headed back the way they'd come. Will wished that he could go with her. He could; he was a fully functional grown-up. But then Dreadlocks turned round. 'I'll get the posh treats. The duck ones,' she called out, hope ringing through every syllable. 'She really likes those.'

While all this emotional blackmail, manipulation and strong-arming had been going on, Will hadn't paid much attention to the dog at all, but when he looked at her now, she cowered from him, burrowing between the legs of her intended owner and the kennel staff to get away.

It was another punch right in his gut. He knew he had had problems establishing an emotional rapport with people. But Will wasn't unkind. He wasn't mean. He wasn't nasty. He wasn't violent. He didn't possess any of those base qualities, which would make someone, this dog, shake with fear.

'I don't want to traumatise her,' Will said.

'I won't let you traumatise her,' Spectacles said resolutely and then Dreadlocks came back with a small metal bowl, which she handed to Will. It contained some shrivelled up meaty things, which smelled vile.

'Freeze-dried duck giblets,' he was told cheerfully. Obviously being a dog owner wasn't for the faint-hearted . . . or vegans. 'Now, take one, squat down and hold out your hand but keep your head averted.'

Will did as he was told. This was not how he'd imagined his visit would pan out. So low on the floor that he was practically on his belly, a freeze-dried duck heart in his palm as he kept his eyes trained on a spot on the floor where the corner of one tile had cracked.

'Come on, Blossom,' Dreadlocks said in a gentle voice as she moved nearer to Will and encouraged the dog to do the same. 'Come on, good girl.'

Ten minutes later, Will was lying flat on the floor, his head at an awkward angle so as not to make eye contact. It was one of the most excruciating experiences of his recent memory. To have to put himself on display to four complete strangers, so they could witness his rejection, his humiliation, his abject failure to make this dog trust him. It was like a metaphor for his entire life.

But then, unbelievably, the dog crept close enough to Will that she could take the treat. Will thought she'd snatch it out of his palm, probably take the skin off with it, but instead she picked it up almost daintily and so swiftly that it didn't even touch the sides as she gulped it down. Then she shuffled back but shuffled forward again quite quickly when another duck internal organ was placed in Will's hand.

On the third go, the dog obviously decided that she was on to a good thing because instead of shuffling back, she decided to sit down in front of Will. 'Just hold out your hand, with your fingers curled, and let her sniff you,' he was ordered, and didn't dare refuse.

His muscles were now screaming in protest, but Will forced himself to stay horizontal. His eyes flickered up to where Margs was gazing down at the dog, her expression intent, her bottom lip caught between her teeth until Blossom sniffed his hand. As the dog's nostrils twitched, Margs relaxed, and when the dog let Will ever so carefully brush her cheek with one knuckle, she sighed. And when the dog lifted a paw and brought it down heavily on Will's shoulder, she laughed.

'I think she's trying to tell you that she wants another treat, aren't you, Blossom?'

Will was happy to oblige. Also happy to crouch rather than lay on the floor and feed the dog more treats. She even made eye contact with him and, for one fleeting moment, let Will caress the underside of her chin with one careful finger. Will looked into those wary brown eyes and acknowledged the pain and the sorrow that the dog had gone through in her past life. I see you, he wanted to say. I've been there too. It will get better, I promise. Blossom's long pink tongue sneaked out of her mouth to lick Will's finger and then she backed away to the safe refuge of the women who'd been watching this small, quiet exchange with their heads tilted, breath bated.

It had taken no more than ten seconds, but those ten seconds had warmed Will's frozen heart. He'd got what he'd come here for; an emotional connection with another living being, and yet he was in no hurry to leave.

They always said that dogs were good judges of character and now Will felt validated. Looking after Blossom for a week, helping her with the transition from trauma to a happy, new life, rather than being a chore, a huge commitment, might actually be rewarding for Will. Make him think about some-one other than himself. He'd never thought as much about himself as he had done during this past year in therapy and it was exhausting.

'That went much better than I expected,' Spectacles said with satisfaction. 'A week ago, she was peeing in fear when-ever a man approached her.'

Then again, the bar was set pretty low, but this wasn't about Will and his feelings. It was about Blossom. No one should go through life feeling frightened, whether they were human, canine and everything in between.

'So, when would be a good time for this home check?' he queried, because apparently yes, he was going to foster a scared Staffordshire Bull Terrier for the next week.

'Let's go through to the office and get your details,' Spectacles said, but before Will could move, Margs put her hand on his arm. She had capable hands, like they got the job done, her nails painted a chalky, pastel blue.

'I'm Margot,' she said, with another one of those sunny Sunday smiles. 'Never Marge. Margot.'

'Although you love it when people call you Margs,' her friend pointed out with a nudge.

'I merely tolerate it.'

'Will,' he said, and now they shook hands. Their eyes met and stayed met until Will dropped his gaze.

'Thank you! Thank you *so* much for agreeing to do this,' Margot said with all the fervour of a woman who believed in positive energy.

'I might not pass the home check.' Though Will could tell that short of living in a rat-infested hovel, which he didn't, he was going to be responsible for keeping Blossom alive for the next week. Panic shot through him like a sudden fever.

'We should swap numbers,' Margot said, pulling her phone out of the back pocket of her jeans, unaware that Will was silently and comprehensively having a crisis of confidence. 'I expect hourly updates with picture attachments.'

Even in the depths of his crisis, Will could tell that she wasn't joking.

Later that evening Blossom arrived at his flat. She still reeked of eau de kennel and came with half a bag of dog food and the cheery instruction that 'she has a shy bladder. She might hold in her wee for the next couple of days'.

Will shut the door behind Dreadlocks, shook his head, and pulled back his shoulders. 'Right. OK. I can do this.'

He turned round to face Blossom who was gazing fearfully at Will's hall walls, her little doggy brow furrowed, tremors racking her body. Then she cast one terrified look at Will and dived for the safety of the living room.

Will sighed so heavily he could feel it in his toes. 'Oh God, what have I done?'

5

Margot

Twice a year, Margot enjoyed five days away in a foreign country to shoot next season's fashions.

It was the last week of September and the night before she'd left London, she'd had to turn the central heating on. So who would say no to five days on the Peniche peninsula, with its sandy beaches, temperature in the mid twenties and Lisbon only an hour's drive away?

Margot had trained to be a fashion designer. But it had quickly become apparent that she was not going to be the next *enfant terrible* of British fashion. Much as it pained her to admit it (and what a long dark night of the soul that had been) Margot was more Boden than Balenciaga. More Mango than Marc Jacobs. More Cath Kidston than Christian Dior.

She could design pretty clothes that flattered women's figures, but her designs were never going to be feted on the Paris runways and worn by celebrities at the Met Gala.

It was a salutary lesson in managing her expectations at a formative age. Still, when Margot had graduated, she'd hoped her first job would harness what talent she did have. Unfortunately, she ended up designing tracksuits for a leading high-street sportswear chain.

Obviously people wore tracksuits and someone had to design them, but Margot was stuck in a sportswear ghetto for three years, unable to move forward because every time she applied for a new, more simpatico job, her portfolio was full of leisure wear made from synthetic fibres. Her greatest achievement was when one of her tracksuits was worn by a ne'er-do-well on *Hollyoaks*.

The only time that Margot felt fulfilled was when she was making clothes for herself. She was a curvy size sixteen and the more stylish end of the high street only went up to a size fourteen. And even if they did go all the way up to a size sixteen, finding that largest size before it sold out was as rare as a genuine Fabergé egg turning up on *Antiques Roadshow*.

Margot knew she could probably drop a dress size if she ate less and exercised more, but quite frankly, she didn't want to. Yes, she could eat spaghetti made from spiralised courgettes, pizza which had cauliflower crusts, and ration herself to two squares of dark chocolate a day. But life was often hard, so why should Margot deprive herself of the simple pleasure that was spaghetti made from wheat, or a pizza with a proper crust? And two pieces of dark chocolate would never, ever hit the same sweet spot that a Cadbury's Twirl did.

So, it was easier and a lot less upsetting (there had been tears once in a Topshop changing room when Margot realised that a Topshop size sixteen was like a size twelve anywhere else) to make her own clothes. Pretty dresses and tops in Liberty prints and softly draped jersey which flattered her figure. In fact, she was wearing one of her own creations – a wrap dress in a crisp black and white polka dot cotton – on the day that she met the two most important people in her life.

It had been a Tuesday lunchtime in Camden Marks & Spencer. Margot was after a BLT while Derek and Tansy Spencer-Williams had popped in to buy a Colin the Caterpillar cake for an employee's birthday.

'I love your dress,' Margot heard a woman say as she reached for the last BLT. She turned to see an elegant woman in a pristine white jumpsuit, her hair cropped close to her skull, all the better to show off her incredible cheekbones, and an ageing rockabilly, his grey quiff as big as the turn-ups on his jeans, staring at her.

Margot said the only thing she could in the circumstances, 'Thank you! It has pockets!' And stuck her free hand into one of those pockets so they could see for themselves.

'It's very hard to get a cotton wrap dress to drape like that,' the woman said, which was a tactful way of saying that it was very rare for a cotton wrap dress not to gape when its wearer was large of bust and hip. Certainly no man had ever run his eyes over Margot's figure with such forensic intensity.

For a second, Margot wondered if this approach was some kind of proposition. *Older couple seeks curvy F for discreet afternoon fun.* But then the rockabilly gathered a tiny section of the skirt between his thumb and forefinger and announced, 'The fit is great considering it's not even lined,' and she realised they were fellow fashion professionals.

'I sewed in a secret button on the opposite side from the bow,' she explained. 'I know some people put in an inner tie, but a button is a lot more secure.'

'So you made it yourself?' the woman asked. 'From a pattern?'

'Kind of from a pattern but I adapted it,' Margot began eagerly, because she loved talking patterns and fit and fabrications. For the next fifteen minutes, the three of them nattered happily away about how hard it was to find well-made clothes on the high street at an affordable price point, and generally obstructing a lot of hungry people from their lunchtime sandwiches.

It wasn't until an assistant manager was despatched to ask them to move it along, please, that the rockabilly proffered his card and asked if she'd like to come and work for them. Margot had phoned in her resignation from the sportswear company five minutes later.

That had been twelve years ago, and Margot was still gain-fully employed and creatively fulfilled at Ivy+Pearl (named after Derek and Tansy's mothers.) Before Ivy+Pearl, they'd worked at Sex, Vivienne Westwood and Malcolm MacClaren's shop, which had sold fetish and bondage wear to punks before punk was even a proper thing.

Now Derek and Tansy were more about timeless style than screen-printing the word 'fuck' on T-shirts. Twice a year, they brought out a small capsule collection of dresses, separates and loungewear that they sold in their boutiques in affluent areas, from Primrose Hill to Cheltenham, Harrogate and all points north, south, east and west. With their web business picking up and the more expensive high street fashion chains increasing their market share, they were looking to expand and Margot had been at the forefront of that expansion.

Margot had pioneered their use of prints, overseen their new ranges of nightwear and home furnishings and had even persuaded Tansy that they should do a limited-edition scented candle each summer and winter. After all, who didn't love cushions, throws and scented candles? But Margot liked to think that her greatest work achievement was insisting that the Ivy+Pearl sizing went up to a size twenty, instead of the very uninclusive size fourteen that it had been when she'd first started working there.

More than that though, with Derek and Tansy, and her Ivy+Pearl colleagues, she'd found what Armistead Maupin called a 'logical family'. Not the people who were there because they shared your DNA, but the people you *chose* as your family because some things went deeper than DNA.

Now, Margot perched on a rock and watched as three models, diverse in size and ethnicity, frolicked in the surf on a Spanish beach while showcasing a swimsuit, a bikini and a tankini, all featuring full coverage bottoms, in Ivy+Pearl's summer print: birds of paradise on either a black or a white background.

Derek, who was very red in the face even though Margot kept reminding him to top up his factor 50, was art directing the shoot and occasionally asking Margot for her input, but mostly she was free to soak up the sun and eat through her data allowance as she composed a text message to Will. With bullet points.

Bullet points were better on an email, but Margot didn't have Will's email address, just his phone number, which he'd rather grudgingly given. But he was looking after Blossom, *her* dog. And although it was only for six days, they were six crucial days for a dog that had no doubt been mistreated, abandoned, put in a council pound and then ended up in a small caged enclosure.

Blossom's new life with Margot was going to be fantastic – she'd already booked Blossom in for a shampoo and a blueberry facial at a doggy spa – but she also wanted the preceding week to be fantastic and unlikely to cause Blossom even more trauma. Will hadn't seemed entirely on board with the whole foster thing and Margot needed to know that he was now properly leaning in as Blossom's primary, if temporary, caregiver.

Their acquaintance had been brief and the circumstances unprecedented. Margot didn't often conduct her conversations while sobbing and snotting everywhere, especially when there was a very handsome man in the vicinity.

Though was he *too* handsome? Margot's mother had warned her off good-looking men. 'I've always found they have a weakness of character,' she'd once said, so she probably wouldn't have thought much of Will with his thick, straight, dark-blond hair, the colour of old pound coins, swept off his face so it wouldn't detract from his impressive bone structure.

Lips that wouldn't have lost any of their charm if they had been curved into a smile instead of pressed into a tight line. Though he had smiled at Margot briefly and their eyes had met, and she'd felt a little frisson pass between them, a gossamer flutter that was over before Margot had had time to catch her breath. And now Margot couldn't remember what colour his eyes were because she hadn't wanted to keep gawping at him. He was probably used to women desperate to get their hands on his tall, rangy body.

He'd also had an aloof air about him, as if he were slightly better than everyone he encountered. Maybe it was just the way his face was. Could men have resting bitch face? Margot decided they probably could as she recalled Will looking down at her from a great height (though she had been on her knees, and he couldn't help being tall). Still, he could have helped the side-eye and the pursing of his lips and the hollowing of his cheeks as if he was auditioning for the role of Mr Darcy in an am-dram production of *Pride and Prejudice*.

Or perhaps Margot was projecting her own issues on the memory. But whatever his perceived faults were, Margot wasn't imagining the way he'd ignored her previous message.

It had been twenty-four hours since she'd sent Will a text and yet still no reply to her many bullet-pointed enquiries. Margot's reasoning being that one big text message was much better than many, many, many separate text messages. Something that George, and even some of her dearest friends, had always been keen to point out.

- *How is Blossom?*
- *Has she settled?*
- *Is she still nervous around you?*
- *How did she sleep?*
- *Has she eaten?*

- *Is she house-trained?*
- *Would love it if you could send pictures.*
- *Have you taken her for a walk yet? How does she walk on the lead?*
- *Also, can you buy some pure coconut oil (will reimburse you) and start rubbing it on her bald patches?*
- *Is she still completely adorable?*

I'm in Portugal, so aware that there is a time difference, but can't wait for your reply. And don't forget pictures!

That had been *one* whole day ago and still no answer. It was so rude.

Margot, though it took every ounce of restraint she possessed, decided to leave another twenty-four hours between text messages. Again, something that she had learned by trial and error and Tracy repeatedly telling her, 'Just because you reply to all messages within five seconds, doesn't mean that everyone else should. We're humans, Margs. We're fallible.'

So, Margot left it another day; she had to sleep after all. She also took time to follow every Staffy with an Instagram account and pondered what Blossom's account should be called (Blossom_the_Staffy seemed a little dull) and what the look and feel of it should be. However, she could only put off the inevitable for so long, and the next morning Margot was compelled to send another message.

- *It's been forty-eight hours and I'm officially worried!*
- *How is Blossom?*
- *Nothing's wrong, is it? She is with you, isn't she?*
- *Pics to prove it, please!*

6

Will

Will shuddered as his phone pinged with another, no doubt bullet-pointed message from Margot. He'd have turned it on to silent if he could, but he was waiting for his sister Rowan to get back to him with rough estimates for the flowers for two weddings and a corporate drinks reception.

He glared at his phone then schooled his features into something calm and neutral as he checked on Blossom.

He hadn't replied to Margot's . . . screed, because Blossom was not fine. She'd been with him for thirty-six hours and hadn't come out from under his dining table in all that time. Will had used his softest voice, had got down on his hands and knees, he'd even cooked chicken and held it in his outstretched palm, but nothing would coax Blossom out.

After a morning of deep-dive dog research, Will had put together a schedule for Blossom of walks, feeding times, nap time and play time to settle her into a routine. Routines were great for establishing safe, secure boundaries but Blossom hadn't got that memo. She hadn't been for a walk either, so she hadn't had a wee or done the other thing (though the sanctity of his newly sanded and varnished floorboards was the very least of Will's worries) and she certainly hadn't slept.

All that Blossom had done was sit, her back up against the wall, her head hanging down, her body still shaking. Much as she was doing when Belinda, aka Spectacles, called to see how he was getting on. 'I'm not,' Will said, not even caring that he was admitting defeat and giving up at the first hurdle. His manly pride would survive but he wasn't sure that Blossom would. 'I'm beginning to wonder if she wasn't better off in kennels. I think she was marginally less terrified there.'

'Well, it's only been a few hours,' Belinda decided after a moment's tense silence, when actually it had been twenty-two at that point. Will hadn't even gone to bed but had spent the night before sitting on the floor where Blossom could see him, just in case she'd be even more scared if she were left on her own. 'Give her time to settle, don't push her.'

'But she doesn't even want to go out,' Will protested.

'Oh, dogs can hold their pee for over forty-eight hours in some extreme cases,' Belinda told him. 'It's not ideal, but she's probably picking up on your own stress. Try to ignore her.'

It was very hard to ignore another living being that was experiencing this level of abject despair, but Will decided to give up his vigil at the dining table in favour of stretching out on the sofa.

Thankfully he hadn't been called upon to troubleshoot any dire problems that had arisen in Bloom & Family, purveyors of beautiful blooms since 1936, as the signage in the shop downstairs proudly proclaimed. He'd told his mother that he was spending a couple of days putting the paperwork in order, which wasn't a lie. No one would miss him, unless there was a sudden mad rush for mixed bouquets.

For reasons that he didn't want to examine, Will hadn't felt the need to inform his family that he had a severely traumatised rescue dog on the premises. Instead, he reached for a ledger on the coffee table, the top one in a teetering pile of accounts books, and with a deep sigh, opened it at the first page.

There were rows of neat figures in his grandmother Maureen's precise hand. Will sighed again. Maureen Bloom, though everyone called her Mo, had died just over a year ago and nothing had been right since. Mighty Mo. By the time he was thirteen, Will could rest his chin on the top of her head, but though she was four feet eleven in her stockings ('Nonsense, I've five feet and half an inch') she had all the presence of a giantess. Saying that someone was larger than life and that their smile could light up a room were hackneyed clichés unless someone was talking about Mo Bloom, and then it was gospel truth.

She was the sun around which the rest of the family were happy to satellite. Gentle and kind but equally a woman not to be trifled with – even well into her seventies and with an artificial hip, she'd given chase to a man who came in for a bunch of red roses and tried to do a runner without paying.

'Never trust a man who buys red roses,' she'd panted when one of the fishmongers round the corner had apprehended the villain by upending a bucket of slimy, fishy water over him. 'That's a man who's been up to no good.'

She doted on her grandchildren: Will, Rowan, and later Sage, and even later than that, on Sam and Harry, Rowan's twins. She was also adored by her customers, but not half as much as she was adored by her husband Bernie. Bernie and Mo had only spent three nights apart in sixty years. Those were the three nights that Mo had spent in the Alexandra maternity hospital giving birth to Amaryllis, Will's mother, whose one act of rebellion in life was insisting that she'd rather be called Mary, if it were all the same.

So, when Mo died of stage four pancreatic cancer, diagnosis to death being three short terrible weeks, it was like a light going out. Without her, life was full of spiky edges that couldn't be gently filed down. In the shop downstairs, even the flowers had lost a little of their brilliance, their fragrance.

43

Bernie had been a shadow without his Mo, though he'd tried to put a brave face on like he still put on his three-piece suit and came to work, but he'd lost his spark, the twinkle in his eyes. Maybe that was why he'd died peacefully in his sleep three weeks after they'd buried Mo. With Bernie gone too, the heart and soul had been irrevocably ripped out of the family.

Mo's size two shoes were too big for Mary to fill. Ian, Mary's second husband, Sage's dad and Will and Rowan's stepfather, wouldn't even attempt to walk in Bernie's shadow. Rowan had her own family to worry about and Sage was only eighteen and numb with grief at the sudden loss of her doting grandparents. It was left to Will, back from New York with problems of his own and a repeat prescription for anti-depressants, to try and fumble his way through the many problems that Bernie and Mo instinctively knew how to solve.

The financials currently being the most pressing. Before she'd fallen in love with Bernie and joined the family firm, Mo had worked in the accounts department of a holiday company. She'd taken over the bookkeeping of Blooms' and had kept careful track of each penny that went in and out of the business for nearly six decades.

Mary had tried to keep up since she'd been gone, even though she preferred narcissi and nasturtiums to numbers. Added to that, their accountant had retired just after Mo had died. Mary had forgotten to file their accounts at Companies House and ended up having to pay a fine. Will, against his better judgement and also because he was used to dealing with figures that had a lot more noughts in them, had said, 'OK, all right, I will take over the accounts *but only* until you find a new accountant.'

Now, he dispensed with the last ledger to be lovingly compiled by Mo, in favour of this year's ledger, which Mary had started with great gusto in January and abandoned in

February. But she had shoved a lot of receipts and figures scrawled on odd scraps of paper into the book instead. Just to show willing.

Tomorrow Will was going to take the whole mess to an accountant in Camden Town who came highly recommended. He would probably have to bring Blossom with him too. Though how he was going to coax her out from under the table for a thrilling appointment with an accountant, when she wouldn't even go out for a wee, Will didn't know.

Then, as if on cue, he heard the faint scrabble of claws on his wooden floor and Blossom suddenly emerged from under the table. Will didn't dare to even twitch an eyelash as she navigated the lounge by sticking as close to the walls as possible until she reached the door, left the room and sat down by the front door.

Will got to his feet and followed. Her head swivelled to throw Will an imploring look – the first time she'd made eye contact with him since she arrived.

'Do you want a walk?' he asked softly, which was a redundant question as she so obviously did.

On the console table in the hall was a raggedy rope lead left by Dreadlocks, poo bags and a packet of treats. Will scooped them up and then – he couldn't believe he was doing this – dropped to his hands and knees and crawled over to where Blossom was patiently waiting.

He didn't want to loom over her and send her retreating back under the table, so it was best to approach her on her level. Still, he felt her flinch as he tried to attach the lead to her collar and inadvertently brushed her fur.

'Sorry, Blossom,' he murmured. 'I'll try and keep my hands to myself.'

But she was up and walking, gingerly picking her way down the stairs. When he opened his front door, Will prayed that no one in the florists would notice them. God was obviously smiling down on him, because nobody was standing in the open shopfront where buckets of flowers were displayed around a vintage bike that Bernie had used for deliveries when he was a lad.

Will thought that Blossom would cock her leg at the first lamp post, but no. None of the trees they passed were suitable either as she walked determinedly alongside him, her tail tucked between her legs.

'Come on, Blossom, you must be desperate,' Will muttered a little desperately himself, but it wasn't until they came to a grass verge that Blossom squatted down (apparently only male dogs cocked their legs) and peed for England. She did it with an extremely beleaguered look on her face, so Will turned his head to give her some privacy.

It wasn't until they came to a third grass verge that Blossom deigned to have a poo. Will was so relieved himself that he didn't even mind having to deploy a poo bag.

They were equidistant from Alexandra Palace and its parklands and an old railway line turned nature trail which led to Highgate Woods, and from his research, Will had ascertained that Staffies needed up to an hour's exercise every day, but Blossom had other ideas. She did an abrupt one-eighty turn, tangling them both in her lead, and pulled in the direction they'd come from.

As soon as they got back to the flat, she dived for her safe space under the table, and with a resigned sigh Will went to dig out some old towels and blankets. If that's where Blossom was happiest, then at least he could make her comfortable.

This went on for two days (Will had had to postpone his meeting with the accountant) with little progress made apart from Blossom appearing in the hall with a cautious look on her face when Will jiggled her lead. But on Friday morning he and Rowan were meeting the head of events at a venue in Shoreditch, and he could hardly leave Blossom on her own for hours. Nor could he take her with him, so he had only one option . . .

'Gawd blimey, he's a big bugger, isn't he?' Ian exclaimed when Will walked into the shop with Blossom dragging all four heels behind him. He was all in Lycra and flushed of face, his thinning fair hair damp and flattened, which meant he'd must have already finished his daily ten-mile bike ride.

'He's a she and she's not big, she's big-boned,' Will said defensively as his mother came out of the back area, her little domain, where she made up bouquets. 'Hi, Mum, meet Blossom.'

Mary Bloom blinked her eyes like she couldn't believe what she was seeing. 'Oh, Will, no!' she said. 'Where did *that* come from?'

'I'm looking after her for a few days,' Will said, glancing around at the flowers. They kept the more expensive blooms inside the shop, along with plants, several racks of cards, and a shelf of flower-centric gifts from scented candles to flower receptacles of every shape, colour and material. Amber glass vases shaped like owls, single flower phials made of enamel, pretty floral china jugs that his youngest sister Sage loved to hunt down in charity shops.

Talking of whom, Sage was always going to be an easier crowd than Mary, who was running her fingers through her wispy, pale blond hair and muttering about 'turning up with a dog without a word of warning'.

'Where's Sage?'

'She's out on deliveries,' Ian said, perched on the high-backed stool that had once been Bernie's domain. 'She'll be back in a bit. Shall we get her to call you?'

'I have to go out for a few hours and I need you to look after Blossom,' Will said, trying to gently tug her forward, but Blossom sank down on her bottom with her head in its usual downcast position. He reached down to pat her but she shied away from his hand. She was one hell of a death knell to his ego, was Blossom. 'She can just stay in the back. She won't be any trouble. I mean, she doesn't do anything.' Not that Will blamed her. 'She's traumatised.'

'In the back with me?' Mary pulled an anguished face which was at odds with her usual cheery smile. 'She might bite me. She might bite a customer! We're not covered for that in our insurance.'

Ian gingerly lowered both feet to the stone-flagged floor (he must have done a lot of uphill cycling that morning) and crooked a finger at Blossom.

'I wouldn't bother, she's not keen on men,' Will said, as Blossom inched forward to greet Ian.

'Well, he might be a big bugger but he's a handsome bugger,' Ian decided as Blossom plopped herself down again and placed a paw on Ian's leg. 'Better leave some treats for him.'

It was ridiculous. Will was thirty-nine. Like anyone just shy of forty, he'd experienced both triumphs and (mostly) disappointments of a romantic nature. He'd been rejected many, many times before, but none of these rejections had stung quite so fiercely as being constantly rejected by a small, underweight dog who, it turned out, didn't mind men so much. She just minded it when the man was Will.

Even locking down the contract with the Shoreditch venue to provide flowers for a year's worth of super-luxe, super-bougie weddings was small consolation. Back in the day, when Will had worked in the shop after school and on weekends, wedding flowers had consisted of bouquets, buttonholes, centrepieces for the reception and, if the budget stretched to it, garlanded church pews.

Now, the wedding and events side of the business had changed beyond all recognition. People wanted all manner of floral adornments for their weddings and fancy dos, from flower arches to cascading trails of greenery suspended from the ceiling of marquees and function rooms, and flower walls so their guests could pose for pictures in front of a backdrop of seasonal blooms. Two years ago, Will had invested some money into the business so that Rowan could transform two empty units in the mews behind the shop into a studio and take on a small dedicated team, which swelled in number when wedding season was upon them. William was proud of his younger sister and how she'd rejuvenated the ailing family business, but right now he had far more pressing things on his mind.

'I know she's been through a lot, but I've been unfailingly respectful of her boundaries and she wants nothing to do with me. Just two seconds with Ian, who thinks she's a he, and she's all over him,' he complained to Rowan on their way back to the shop.

'Are we talking about a dog or your latest girlfriend? It's hard to keep track,' Rowan said, nudging Will in the ribs as they walked out of the posh wine shop opposite Blooms' with a couple of bottles of Prosecco so Rowan's team could toast the good news.

'You're not even a little bit funny,' Will sniffed, yanking Rowan back as she stepped out into the road and straight into the path of a 102 bus.

'It can't be a girlfriend because you haven't dated anyone since you got back from New York,' Rowan mused as she let Will guide her twenty metres to the zebra crossing. 'I still don't even understand how *you* ended up agreeing to foster a dog on behalf of a complete stranger.'

'Why wouldn't I?'

Rowan shrugged. The afternoons were getting shorter and shorter; the streetlights were already on, their glow reflecting off Rowan's pale blond hair. Her pretty, gentle features were at odds with her teasing smile and the mischievous twinkle in her eyes – Mo had always said that she looked like an Alpine milkmaid, and if she hadn't been named after a flower, Mary should have called her Heidi.

'It's a bit of a left-field move for you, the whole dog thing. I can't believe you'd even want a dog. Not after what happened with Muttley. I still think about that and cry sometimes,' she said now in reply to Will's slightly huffy question.

'Yeah, me too,' Will admitted with a sigh.

'That's why I think it's odd that you've suddenly acquired a dog, not that you're doing someone a favour. Which reminds me, can you come over and change a light bulb?'

'Really? *Really?* Surely in the name of gender equality you should be changing your own light bulbs, or else getting Alex to do it for you.'

'Oh, bless him, he gets vertigo just standing on a tube platform,' Rowan said fondly of her husband. 'And this is the light bulb on the landing. One false move with the ladder and it's a plunge straight down a steep flight of stairs. But I can't call out an electrician just to change a light bulb, and Ian would do it, but he helps out so much on the practical side – the other day he designed and built a four-poster bridal canopy – and he refuses to let me pay him.'

Ian used to own the hardware shop across the road from Blooms' (it was how he and Mary had first met) and was the most hands-on person they knew. But he'd recently retired so he could ride his bike, mend his bike and talk about riding and mending his bike with his biking friends. When he wasn't helping out in the florists and designing and building flower-supporting structures for his stepdaughter.

They'd safely got across the road without any mishaps. 'I don't know why it's all right for me to risk breaking my neck,' Will complained, although he knew he'd end up changing the light bulb. 'I do have my own life, you know.'

The twinkle in Rowan's eyes was replaced with something more serious. 'Do you?' she asked doubtfully. 'I meant to ask, how did your final session with Roland go? Is that why you've suddenly acquired a dog? Is it a therapy dog?'

'Of course she's not,' Will snapped, stung at the suggestion. He'd finished his therapy because he didn't need it anymore, and to imply that he'd fostered a dog as a substitute for Roland was very wrong and also a little offensive. Will stepped through the open door of the shop to be met by the sight of the dog in question sitting like a queen on a throne, or more prosaically an old basket-weave chair that they sometimes incorporated into a shop display, her bottom cushioned from any stray bits of wicker by an old picnic blanket. Kneeling in front of her in subjugation was Will's half-sister, eighteen-year-old Sage.

'Oh my God, we love Blossom!' she said by way of a greeting, not even bothering to turn her head. 'Look! She does tricks!' Sage held up a palm. 'High five, Blossom.'

Blossom didn't need to be told twice. She raised a paw and was rewarded with something from a blood-smeared plastic bag.

'Ugh! What is that?' Rowan exclaimed.

'I popped to the butcher's to get some liver,' Mary said, poking her head out of the back room. 'You can see every one of her ribs, the poor little thing.'

'Blossom is the perfect name for a florist's dog,' Sage said, as she fed Blossom more disgusting raw liver. 'She can be our official shop dog.'

'She's not going to be the official shop dog. She's on short-term foster . . .'

'Dad said that she didn't seem to like you very much, right, Mum?' Sage titled her head in Mary's direction, but Mary could sense that there was a confrontation brewing and withdrew. Sage, on the other hand, 'was a messy bitch who lives for drama' according to her Instagram bio. 'She should just come and live with us, because we have a back garden.'

It sounded ideal. Mary, Ian and Sage lived in the big house that Bernie's parents had bought just before the Second World War. Ian had had his own flat when they got married, but Mary was happiest in her childhood home and Mary's happiness was Ian's number one priority, so he'd willingly agreed to move in with his in-laws.

When he'd come back from New York, Will had moved into the family home too, for three months. He'd had to put up with Mary cosseting and fussing over him, Sage alternating between sheer brattishness and A-level angst and Ian jawing on about inner tubes and aluminium clinchers. Will had almost cried tears of gratitude when the flat above the shop became vacant and he could move in there while he considered his next move.

He was still working on that, but his plans certainly didn't involve handing Blossom over to Sage who wasn't housetrained herself.

'Make the most of her, because Blossom is going to her rightful owner on Monday and I am counting the hours,' Will said, and he swore that Blossom, who'd just performed another high five, gave him a reproachful look.

An hour later, with the shop closed and everyone finally gone, Will took Blossom back upstairs. He unclipped her lead and she shot into the living room, no doubt to sit under the table. Will followed her, a hand at the back of his neck where he had a particularly painful knot of tension, which his fingers prodded rather than soothed.

He refilled the cereal bowl, which was doing time as Blossom's water dish, and decided that even though according to the schedule it was now time for Blossom's dinner, she couldn't be hungry if she'd been scoffing raw liver all afternoon. Instead Will made himself a cup of tea and sunk down on the sofa.

The evening stretched out before him. He hadn't reconnected with anyone but family since he got back from NYC. Not that he was the type of person who'd kept in touch with acquaintances from school or university. Will had always tried to look forwards rather than backwards. But living in Muswell Hill was very different from living and working in downtown New York, where you could just hang out with people with no expectation that you were doing anything other than just hanging out. He'd joined a gym, but that was because working out was good for his physical and mental health, not because he was looking for buddies to spot him, then go out afterwards for burgers and bantz.

Will wasn't lonely – it was impossible to be lonely with his family – but this last year, he'd been alone for quite a lot of the time.

He heard the now familiar clatter of claws on the wooden floor. 'You can't possibly want to go out,' he said to Blossom as she emerged from under the table. 'You did everything you needed to do ten minutes ago.'

An awful thought occurred to him. 'I bet all that liver has upset your stomach, hasn't it?'

He lifted his head in time to see Blossom approach him. Carefully, so as not to alarm her, Will swung his legs round so he could get up, but as he did, Blossom jumped up on the sofa to claim the spot that Will had just vacated.

'You're not actually allowed on the sofa. I have this rule – no animals of any kind on the furniture,' Will explained gently, as he and Blossom shared an uncertain look. 'It's not personal. But you don't smell that great and this sofa was very expensive. Come on, off you get!'

So as not to startle her, Will made a very gentle shooing motion with his hand. Blossom stood up, but instead of jumping off the sofa, she turned round. Once, twice, three times, then settled herself. She ended up about as far away from Will as she possibly could while still enjoying all the comfort of a well-upholstered velvet sectional. Her little body curled into a tight ball, her ridiculously large head resting against the sofa arm. Blossom had obviously decided that if the nice people downstairs could tolerate Will, then she could too.

Will tensed up for a good five minutes before he brought his arm up and let his hand make the most fleeting of contact with her fur. Blossom didn't flinch. She didn't even shy away when he stroked the length of her spine with the flat of his hand, so Will continued with the rhythmic movements, until Blossom let out a massive yawn, tongue lolling out so he had a bird's-eye view of all those sharp teeth, then settled back down. Maybe even a little closer to him now, as she started a volley of snores that were loud enough to raise the dead.

Carefully, so as not to wake her, Will reached for his phone on the side table. He took a close-up of Blossom in repose – she had no bad angles – then opened WhatsApp so he could send the picture and a brief message to Margot.

She's fine.

7.

Margot

Margot had planned to pick Blossom up as soon after she landed on the Sunday afternoon as humanly possible, so she could be rescued from the clutches of Will, who might be handsome but had finally replied to her second text message with a mere two words.

Nothing good ever came from a terse texter.

Alas, her plans to liberate Blossom were scuppered by Belinda from the rescue centre, who insisted on an official handover on Monday at their premises, so Margot could fill out the last of the paperwork. She was pleased that they were being so thorough and didn't offload dogs willy nilly, but still, it had been marginally easier to buy her flat than to adopt a dog who so desperately needed a loving home.

Margot was still hungover from the last night in Portugal, where they'd celebrated wrapping up the lookbook shoot with too much Aperol and not enough chips. Fortunately, there was a car waiting at Stanstead Airport that would drop Derek off then deliver Margot home. Also waiting for her was a voice message from Will.

'It's from the man who's got my dog,' she told Derek, who blanched slightly as if he couldn't bear for Margot to hit him with the highlights one more time. 'Maybe he's got round to replying to the last message I sent him.'

'One of your mammoth text messages that has chapters and a subplot?' Derek closed his eyes and tilted his head back.

'When will I learn that at my advanced age, last night's drinking is never worth today's hangover?'

'You weren't saying that when you were dancing on the bar,' Margot reminded him. 'And, excuse me, but not all my text messages are massively wordy.'

Derek grunted in reply and Margot turned her attention back to her phone. Maybe there was another photo of Blossom looking absolutely adorable, though Margot had experienced a sharp pang at the sight of her curled up on Will's sofa. After some analysis of the pang, she'd decided that she was a little jealous. She'd wanted her sofa to be the first sofa that Blossom curled up on. Still, there'd be plenty of time for that.

We need to talk before the handover. Shall we meet in Highgate Woods, on the playing field right in front of the café? See you there at 10 tomorrow?

Will obviously wanted to give Margot the inside track on Blossom. Her likes and dislikes, any weird little habits or triggers. What other earthly reason could they have for a pre-handover chat? Though maybe he wanted to see Margot again because there had been that frisson at the rescue centre, even though his texting etiquette left a lot to be desired.

Still, it was hard to shake the feeling of unease that settled on Margot for the rest of the day as she unpacked, did her laundry and in honour of her own hangover, ordered a pizza *and* garlic bread.

The next morning, as she hurried down Southwood Lane on the ten-minute walk to Highgate Woods, Margot was still feeling uneasy. Maybe Blossom had mange or fleas or something far worse and incurable? Maybe she wasn't house-trained? Maybe she'd bitten someone?

Each maybe was worse than the last, and so when Margot finally arrived at their rendezvous, out of breath because she'd set out late as usual, she'd convinced herself that only catastrophe lay ahead.

So it was quite a surprise, a pleasant one, to see Will and Blossom waiting for her. As Margot speed-walked across the grass, Blossom saw her first. She pricked up her wonderfully soft, floppy ears. Margot's heart lifted and she waved at Blossom, which was ridiculous, but Will, who was sitting on a bench, raised his hand in greeting.

'Hello! Hello!' Margot called out, even though she'd promised herself that she'd keep her cool no matter what the news was. Who was she kidding? She'd spent her entire life devoid of all cool. 'Hello, my precious, have you missed me?'

'Somehow, I've managed to survive,' Will said, and Margot could not work out if he was flirting with her or mocking her. He was very hard to read, so she simply repeated her affirmations in her head ('I am happy. I am positive. I draw happy, positive people towards me') and sat down. Immediately Blossom lifted her paw onto Margot's knee.

Blossom looked much better than the last time Margot had seen her. She was bright-eyed and alert, though still painfully thin and covered in bald patches.

'Oh my goodness, you're looking *so* beautiful.' Margot turned an accusing gaze onto Will. 'You might have properly replied to my messages.'

'Replying to your messages properly would have been a full-time job and I do have to work for a living, you know.' He didn't even have the grace to look embarrassed. On the contrary, if Margot never had any cool to keep, then it seemed as if Will was one of those people who hung onto his cool and never let go.

Not the kind of cool which was knowing the hot, new places to eat or reading all the novels on the Booker longlist before the longlist had even been announced, or getting his clothes in an exclusive shop off Savile Row which had been opened by an ex-*GQ* editor. No, it was the kind of cool that gave the impression that Will was up there, Margot glanced at the clouds puffing slowly across a clear, blue sky, and Margot was down there with the mud that was churning up the grass after last night's rainfall.

He wasn't remotely interested in putting her at ease or even saying hello. He just sat there, eyes fixed on the middle distance where a group of frolicking dogs and their non-frolicking owners were congregated.

Whatever. Margot wasn't here for Will. She was here for Blossom.

'I missed you so much,' she told the dog, who stared at Margot with those deep, soulful eyes as if she understood. 'We are going to have so much fun together.' Now that important message had been relayed, she turned to Will, who she could have sworn had scoffed faintly at her promise to the dog. 'So what was it that you wanted to talk about?'

He'd been sitting cross-armed and cross-legged but now he unfolded himself, leaned forward and put a proprietorial hand under Blossom's chin so she immediately gave him her full and undivided attention.

'There's no easy way to say this, so I'll just be blunt.' Margot was pretty sure that he was never anything else. 'Blossom and I have bonded while you were away, and I want to keep her.'

Margot had his number. Will's MO was obvious. He must have known that it was going to come as a shock, which was why he'd ripped off the plaster so quickly. He'd probably imagined that Margot would cry. Call him a few choice names. Declare that it was never going to happen. Then she'd come round to Will's way of thinking. It followed the pattern of several dumpings she'd experienced in the past. But that was before Margot had grown a much thicker skin. Besides, she might have let someone steal her cat but no way, *no way in hell*, was she letting someone steal her dog too.

So Margot didn't cry. Although she couldn't help that her mouth dropped open, giving her the appearance of a slack-jawed simpleton. Then she straightened up, set back her shoulders and tilted her head so Will could see her steady, absolutely not tearful, gaze. 'No,' she said firmly. 'She's my dog.'

'You haven't thought this through,' Will said, which made Margot flare her nostrils like a dragon about to breathe fire. 'You obviously have to go away for work.'

'Only twice a year, and when I go away again in spring, I'll have sorted out a dog-sitter,' Margot said immediately, because she'd had a whole week to think about how to adapt her life around Blossom.

'I can take Blossom to work with me every day,' Will pointed out 'And if I have to go out—'

Margot had to stop him right there. 'You're a florist, right? That's what you said at the rescue centre, so I bet you have to do loads of early morning starts going to Columbia Road flower market . . .'

'Trade doesn't go to Columbia Road, only Instagrammers . . .'

'Then on weekends, I expect you have to do wedding flow-ers, set up the church or registry office or what have you,' Margot went on, cutting through his sentences like they were made of butter.

'I'm not a florist. I manage my family's floristry business. It's a big difference,' Will bit out, as if Margot had accused him of running his own meth lab.

Margot didn't really care what that difference was. 'Well, you sound far too busy to look after a dog, and if you do want a dog, then no one's stopping you. Go and source your own.' Then she patted the bench and Blossom, the little darling, jumped up and sat down next to Margot, on the far side from Will.

'I could say the same of you,' Will said, his tone slightly more conciliatory. 'Like looking for houses, isn't it? You might get gazumped on your dream home, but then you find another dream home further down the line. I'm sure you'll find another dog that you'll like even more.'

'Blossom is not a house. She's a sentient being who I connected with the moment I saw her.' Margot didn't even attempt to sound conciliatory. There was no reason why she should. She wasn't the one in the wrong here.

'And then you went away and left her with me, and she's settled now. Plus, as I was trying to explain when you kept interrupting me—'

'I'm sure that I didn't interrupt you,' Margo interjected furiously, because how dare he?

'You've just done it again.' Will raised a self-righteous eyebrow.

There was nothing Margot could do but subside with an aggrieved huff.

'I live above the business,' Will explained. 'If I have to go to a meeting, Blossom hangs out in the shop because this is a dog that cannot be left alone. What are you going to do with her when you're at work?'

'I'm sorting out day care.' Margot could feel herself flushing. Sorting out doggy day care was another item on the long doggy to-do list.

'And what about when you go out in the evening?'

'She can come with . . .' Margot said weakly. Oh God, she hadn't thought any of this through.

'With me, Blossom always has someone there,' Will pressed his point home, though Blossom was leaning against Margot's side and hadn't looked at him in quite a while. Any fool could see that she much preferred Margot. 'I've spent a week earning Blossom's trust and now you want to uproot her just as she's started to relax. Besides, my mother and my little sister adore her and would be happy to dog-sit any time.'

'So she's going to be passed from pillar to post like a parcel,' Margot summed up triumphantly. 'Whereas I will devote myself to Blossom so she has continuity of care. Like, I've already arranged to have this week off as pawrental leave.' Had she just actually said 'pawrental leave' with a straight face like it was an actual thing that people said out loud?

'She really would be better off with me,' Will said, and he managed to make it sound definite, absolute. A statement of fact that couldn't be denied.

'But she would be more loved with me,' Margot countered with the same conviction. 'That's the most important thing. That she's loved and that she knows that she's loved.' There was a fraught interlude as Margot and Will glared at each other. 'She's a lucky dog, isn't she?' Margot relented slightly, and coaxed Blossom over her legs with little regard for Blossom's muddy paws and her expensive, blue and red check woollen coat, so that she settled between them.

She saw Will look down at Blossom's anxious face, the prominent ribs, the bald patches.

'Lucky, how?'

'A week ago, she was an abandoned, unwanted dog and now she has two people fighting over her.' Margot leaned down to kiss Blossom right on her snout and for the first time, Blossom wagged her tail. Well, it twitched once, which had to count for something. Will must have seen it too because he tried to get in on the act by scritching Blossom beneath her chin with a finger.

'We could share her,' he suddenly said. 'That would be a solution, wouldn't it? Split the responsibility and the expense and the pleasure of her company.'

Margot looked down at Blossom who was now leaning towards Will, her eyes closed in ecstasy as he continued the chin scritching.

Share her? It was ridiculous!

But then . . . Margot had been wondering, worrying, what to do with Blossom if she couldn't find a suitable day care. Also, who would look after her when Margot was on one of her many dates? Margot felt quite lightheaded as she mentally estimated day-care fees, insurance, dog food, vet's bills, and the start-up costs of beds and leads and squeaky toys.

But then . . . Will's plan also made Margot feel unbearably sad. Or maybe it was because, when he was caressing Blossom under her chin with two long fingers, Blossom had shut her eyes, and in that moment she stopped being a scared animal and simply revelled in the pleasure of a gentle touch.

Was it too much to ask that just once, Margot should be allowed to love someone and not have that someone snatched away? Or, in this case, have to share her love? Though, perfidious Percy had been very low-maintenance, especially as he spent most of his time in other people's houses – Blossom was going to demand much more of her attention and time.

'I suppose it's not the worst idea in the world,' she said at last.

8

Will

'Are you sure you wouldn't like a dog each?' Belinda asked when they'd presented her with their plan to dog-share.

'We've both fallen in love with Blossom,' Margot told Belinda, although Will hadn't mentioned the L word at all. 'I know that if we both got a dog, we'd be saving two lives, but the heart wants what the heart wants, right?'

'It's a very practical arrangement. I'm surprised more people don't do it,' Will said, as he filled in the second adoption form. But of course it wasn't just about practical arrangements.

Do you love her?

Will wouldn't say that he loved Blossom. But when Blossom had climbed up on his sofa and felt safe enough to go to sleep, a warm Ready-Brek glow had infused Will's entire being. Blossom trusted him, which meant that he was good enough. It had been a long time since Will had felt anything close to good enough.

This little dog (who was so alarmed at being back at kennels that she put an imploring paw on Margot's knee and stared at Will with worried eyes) had managed to get under his skin and halfway to his heart like nobody else ever had.

But he hadn't enjoyed the constant worrying about Blossom; a low-level static hum that had soundtracked Will's waking hours. And that last wee walk at 10.30 p.m., even though it was only five minutes, was an absolute killer. Then there was the hand-feeding and trying to find something that Princess Blossom would eat because she was having nothing to do with the half bag of dry food that she'd arrived with.

He'd done it for a week, with help. But it was so much responsibility. And full-time? That was a big ask. So, while Will had been happy, on reflection, to foster Blossom, he'd also been counting the hours until he handed her over to Margot where she'd spend the rest of her life being smothered and smooched.

But then there had been half an hour on Saturday evening, when Blossom had draped a paw over Will's knee and rested her head on his leg. The Ready-Brek glow upgraded to a full-on forest fire. This was more than a wary kind of trust. Blossom was actively seeking Will's company and comfort. This was actual snuggling! Even though Will absolutely and categorically wasn't the snuggling kind, he couldn't bear this whole experience to be a fleeting thing, a treasured memory. The comfort went both ways. When he ran his hand down the length of Blossom's spine and stroked her fur, it was Will who felt soothed, all his spiky edges filed down, the nagging doubts silenced.

And though he'd decided in that moment that he wanted to keep Blossom, sharing seemed like a viable solution. Even if it was sharing Blossom with Margot, who had far too much emotional bandwidth for Will's liking.

It didn't take long. Belinda changed the details on Blossom's microchip then asked them who was paying the adoption fee.

'I'll pay it!' they both said.

'Really, I'll pay it,' Margot repeated firmly, like if she paid the adoption fee it would be proof that she had a legal claim on Blossom.

'How about we both pay?' Will suggested, because he'd spent his entire working life strategising and compromising to achieve optimal results and there was no way he was letting Margot have the upper hand. 'We are both getting a dog from you, after all.'

'She was spayed a couple of weeks ago so Blossom's good to go.' Belinda came out from behind her desk. 'Are you ready for your freedom walk, young lady?'

First there were photos for the rescue centre's social media. Blossom decided that she was absolutely not being picked up, so Margot and Will crouched down on either side of her and posed for the pictures, even though part of Will was dying inside. This was not who he was. Yet, here he was, smiling tightly for the camera.

Then there was the freedom walk. All the volunteers lined up and clapped Blossom out of rescue and into the rest of her life.

'I'm not crying,' Margot said, her voice thick with tears, as Will opened the door for her. 'Shut up.'

'Never said that you were,' Will replied, because he didn't need to – it was that obvious. He'd rarely met someone who was so in touch with their feelings. It must be exhausting. 'Do you want a lift home?'

'Yes, please; and also, we need to talk about how we're going to do this,' Margot said as she followed him to his car. Or rather the ancient Volvo estate, emblazoned with a Bloom & Family logo, that Bernie had bought thirty years ago. 'Like, are we sticking to a weekly basis? What about registering with a vet and whose details are going on her collar tag? Also, I was going to go and get dog stuff now. A bed, blankets, that sort of thing.'

'I curated a very detailed shopping list. I'll ping it over to you.' Will took out his phone. He thought they'd be done handing over an hour ago. He'd also thought that he'd be Blossom's sole custodian and having to make the necessary mental pivot was hard. 'I was planning to stop off at the big pet superstore in Friern Barnet anyway. It's on the way home.'

Margot sucked in a breath when she opened the email Will had just sent her and saw the list. 'Two whole pages! How much does one dog need?' she asked, because clearly, unlike Will, she'd done barely any R&D into what owning a dog entailed.

'Quite a lot, actually,' Will said. 'And I'm sure that once she's registered with a vet there'll be add-ons like supplements, not to mention worming tablets and flea treatments.'

'She's not having fleas on my watch. Well, I guess she's going to need two of everything that's on this *massive* list,' Margot decreed with that stubborn tilt to her chin, which was so at odds with how soft she looked. Even her voice, carrying the same faint trace of a London accent as his did, was soft, even when it was issuing orders. 'So she doesn't get confused going back and forth. And this list is great, but she is my dog, too, so I should have some input into what she needs.'

When she put it like that, Will couldn't really argue when Margot selected two dog beds that were almost as expensive as his own bed. Apparently they were made from special orthopaedic memory foam and the faux fur cover was washable, so they were worth every penny.

He did argue when Margot selected six pink fleecy blankets. 'Pink? Do they *all* have to be pink? I mean, I'm secure enough in my masculinity' (he could have sworn Margot arched one of her perfectly winged eyebrows), 'but that is a lot of pink.'

Margot surveyed the quite staggering number of items spread between their two trolleys, then looked down at Blossom who was happy enough to trot between them and didn't seem to have an opinion on what her favourite colours were. 'I suppose they don't *all* have to be pink.'

'Also, why does everything have paw prints or bones on them?' Will wondered aloud as Margot picked up a big studded leather harness with a doubtful expression on her face. Will plucked it from her hands and put it back on its rail. 'I hate it when people put Staffies in those things. They look like bondage harnesses.'

'True.'

Finally they agreed to compromise on a red and white spotted collar and lead apiece, and a red harness.

Then it was on to toys and finally they reached the food aisles. 'I know it says on your list that a raw food diet would be best, but I don't have the freezer space,' Margot said, as Will looked bemused at the shelves upon shelves of dried food and tins of wet food and chiller cabinets of fresh food. He should have invested some funds into the pet-food market. 'I was going to sign up to a fresh, organic delivery service, if that's all right with you,' Margot continued.

It was obvious that there was going to be a problem if that wasn't all right with Will, and again, he found himself acquiescing. It was the best thing for Blossom, after all. God knows what kind of crap she'd been fed in the past.

Margot was banging on about treats now and how often Blossom should have them, though Will wasn't really listening but gazing at his trolley, which was piled high.

This was real. This was really happening. He'd signed up for a half-share in a dog and the mountain of stuff that that dog needed for everyday living. Committed himself to constant contact with this woman who was now looking at a packet of bully sticks and exclaiming, 'Urgh! These are made from bulls' penises! Gross; she's not kissing me after dinner. Oh! You forgot to add toothbrush and toothpaste to your massive list . . .'

9

Margot

They were both over three hundred pounds lighter by the time they emerged from the pet superstore. Will looked shell-shocked, as if cartoon birds should be flying around his head, and Margot was silently seething.

Will was determined to rob her of all the milestone moments of dog ownership. Margot had wanted to purchase Blossom's bedding and her collar and lead from a lovely doggy boutique in Highgate Village. She'd been looking forward to it, but instead she'd been strong-armed into accompanying Will to a big chain pet supermarket just off the North Circular Road. He'd already claimed half owner-ship of *her* dog so Margot would have been well within her rights to insist that they'd driven straight to Highgate to purchase two dog beds lined with a William Morris print fabric then peruse the boutique's exclusive range of acces-sories that could be colour matched to your dog

Now Will was trying to fit everything into his car: Margot's stuff on the back seat, his stuff in the boot. 'I have a system,' he said shortly when Margot offered to help, so she opened the passenger door and coaxed Blossom into the footwell before she got in herself.

Will's system didn't seem very efficient. It also seemed to involve a lot of swearing under his breath, then quickly slam-ming the door shut before anything could escape.

'Shall we drop my gear off first as it's on the way?' he suggested.

Margot desperately wanted to get home and begin what she'd unashamedly called her puppymoon in the 'Ovaries Before Brovaries' group chat with Tracy and her two other best friends. Then again, she was quite curious to see where Will lived and, more importantly, where Blossom would be spending every other week.

Will parked the car in a mews behind an Edwardian shopping parade in Muswell Hill. Blossom obviously knew the way because as soon as she exited the car, she tugged gently on her lead and looked expectantly at Margot and then at the entrance to the mews. Meanwhile Will had opened the boot and, despite his so-called infallible system, was looking a lot like a man who had no idea where to begin.

'May I make a suggestion?' Margot ventured cautiously because men always hated to be told what to do. Man-mansplaining, her work husband, Jacques, called it.

'Knock yourself out,' Will said with little enthusiasm.

'If you put things *in* the dog bed and then carry that, we can probably do this in one trip,' Margot said, as she tried to keep her tone neutral rather than impatient. 'Feel free to load me up like a little pack mule.'

'I suppose we could try it your way,' Will said, like Margot's way was ridiculous. They achieved their goal in one back-breaking, arm-aching trip, not helped by Margot having Blossom's lead wrapped around her wrist with Blossom at the other end of it and Will hustling both of them past the florist shop and through his front door with indecent haste.

Didn't he want his family to meet Blossom's other owner? Or perhaps all that talk about how his family had fallen in love with Blossom was just a ruse, though to what end, Margot didn't know. She stumbled up the stairs, Blossom leading the way, the new slow-feeding mat clenched between Margot's teeth, as Will brought up the rear. Eventually, after climbing two short flights of stairs, they reached a small landing.

'Permission to unload?' Margot asked, and even that didn't crack a smile out of Will as he stepped past her so he could unlock the door.

'Permission granted,' he said, and Margot gratefully let loose the jute bags and totes that Will had brought with him to the store. (At least she knew he cared about two things: Blossom and the environment.) 'I can take it from here if you want to . . .'

'See where Blossom is going to spend the time that she isn't with me? Don't mind if I do,' Margot said with a fixed smile, because he wasn't getting rid of her that easily. And if he was running some horrific dog-fighting ring and wanted Blossom as a bait dog, then now was the moment to find that out.

But if Will was running a dog-fighting ring then he wasn't doing it from the beautiful flat above the florist. From the small entrance hall, Margot walked into a huge open-plan room, with four large picture windows letting in every possible drop of autumn sunshine.

There wasn't much in the space: a huge white sectional sofa, a glass coffee table with sharp edges and a large TV suspended on the wall above the period fireplace. It was all very modern, very un-dog-friendly. It was just as well that Blossom didn't have much fur and that some of it was white because there was going to be dog hairs all over that sofa *and* the coffee table was the perfect height for her to walk into and cut her precious little face on. Margot would leave it a week or two and then 'suggest' that Will might want to stick foam corners on it or replace it with something a little less angular.

Through a wide arch was the kitchen and dining area. The kitchen had glossy white units with jutting-out handles, though they were positioned too high to inflict any damage on Blossom but the slippery floor tiles could prove to be very dangerous indeed. In the dining area was a table big enough to seat four, and under it, curled up on a pile of towels and blankets, was Blossom.

'That's where she sleeps?' Margot didn't even attempt to keep the scathing judgement out of her voice. 'Under the table?'

'Yes, her choice,' Will said, coming into the room with Blossom's new dog bed. 'It's where she felt safest and I wasn't going to drag her out of there.'

'No, but . . .'

'Once she settled in, she spent a lot of time on the sofa, but now she has her dog bed and numerous fleecy blankets—'

'Three blankets hardly qualifies as numerous,' Margot interrupted.

'. . . she'll be perfectly happy here.' Will looked around the room then at the dog bed in his arms.

'If I can make another suggestion . . .'

'But for now, the dog bed is going under the table so she knows that she has a safe space,' Will continued very firmly, as if he was fed up with Margot's suggestions.

She held her hands up in surrender. 'Do you need any help with unpacking?'

Will shook his head. 'I do have quite a lot of work to get through this afternoon.'

It was already two and considering that Margot only had a week with Blossom before she handed her back, half a day was already gone.

'If I order an Uber now, it will be here by the time we unpack my stuff from your car,' Margot said, digging her phone out from her coat pocket. The sooner she left, the sooner she and Blossom could start their puppymoon.

'Obviously I'm going to give you a lift,' Will said in a tight voice, as if something was pressing against his windpipe. 'Shall we go?'

10

Will

Will managed to get Margot out of the door and round the corner into the mews without anyone from the shop seeing them, thank God. Ian was still insisting that Blossom was a he. His mother had been absolutely bereft this morning when she realised there'd be no Blossom hanging out under the flower arranging table and Sage had already offered to speak to Margot on his behalf and 'tell her to go and get her own dog'.

'How are you going to manage with Blossom if you don't have your own car?' Will asked Margot as they left the mews.

'There's this thing, I don't know if you've heard of it: walking,' Margot said tartly, which was fair enough. 'Also, buses and tubes, though you have to carry dogs on escalators and Blossom doesn't seem to like being picked up. There are pet-friendly taxis too but I'm ready to lose my five-star Uber rating and argue with any driver who won't take Blossom.'

Will already pitied those poor Uber drivers, but for now Blossom looked quite content curled up in the footwell. She had such a soft nature that she'd be no match for Margot's unique blend of suggestion and complete lack of compromise, Will thought as they reached Highgate Village with its quaint high street full of independent shops: greengrocer, butcher, pharmacy, bakery, but also a Tesco Metro and the numerous coffee chains and estate agents that proliferated on every London high street.

'It's just round the corner on the Square,' Margot said, indicating right with one hand. 'The parking's not great, I'm afraid.'

The Square, just a whisker away from the famous Flask pub, was quite the address. Such a Highgate affectation to name it *the* Square like it was a cut above any other squares that London might have to offer. The houses on the north side of the Square where Margot lived weren't as large as the grand Victorian villas on the other side, and looked quite ramshackle by comparison, but still came with a hefty price tag.

Will was surprised that Margot had decided that the dog for her was a rescue Staffy and not some pampered Pekinese or Pomeranian with a pedigree.

He found a parking spot not too far from the 'poor end' of the Square and hadn't even switched off the engine before Margot had the door open and was scrambling out. 'Just pile everything up on the pavement and I'll do the rest. *I* only have four steps down to my front door,' she added, and Will stiffened with annoyance.

'Don't be ridiculous,' he snapped. 'I'll help you. And anyway, I want to see where Blossom is going to spend her time when she isn't with me.'

Margot was hoist with her own petard. 'Fine,' she said thinly, and Will proceeded to purposely ignore her system of putting everything they could in the dog bed, so it took several trips to ferry everything from the car and down the four steps that led to her basement flat.

'My garden flat,' Margot said as she unlocked her front door, which was painted a fashionable sage green. 'Welcome to your new home, Blossom.' She unclipped Blossom's lead and left her free to explore while she and Will brought everything in. 'I'll just quickly unpack so you can have your bags back,' she called over her shoulder as Will followed her into a tiny hall.

'No rush,' he said vaguely as he looked around. 'You could give them back when we hand over.'

The hall walls were painted teal, the doors off it a dark, smoky grey colour. Two of them were ajar. 'Sitting room and next door is my office. We can put everything in there for now and I'll sort it out later,' Margot said, then nodded her head at the door at the end of the hall. 'Kitchen, which leads through to the garden. Actually, I should probably let Blossom out.'

The kitchen was so small that Will stayed in the doorway as Margot took the three steps to the back door. 'Blossom!' she called. Blossom trotted in immediately. Blossom didn't come when Will called her, because she obviously didn't respect his authority. But Margot's wish was Blossom's command. She came to where Margot stood by the open back door and gazed out.

There wasn't much to gaze at. The garden was more of a backyard, mostly paved over, though a climbing rose was doing its best to trail up the back wall. There was a small wrought-iron table and two chairs and a number of planter pots, but it was the beginning of October and whatever had flowered in them was now long gone.

'Do you want to do a wee, Blossom? Preferably not on my plant pots,' Margot said, but Blossom stayed where she was. Will hated to be the bearer of bad news, but in this case, he allowed himself a small moment of blissful *Schadenfreude*.

'Blossom will only go on grass,' he explained. 'For, um, both things.' So, it served Margot right for being so smug about her 'garden'.

Margot turned to look at him. For a split second the clouds shifted so she was sunlit with nowhere to hide, and her cheery expression seemed more like a mask than a representation of how she really felt. Then she shrugged, almost as if she was physically shaking off the sadness, and smiled her bright, chipper smile.

'That's a bit annoying,' she decided. 'I was hoping to fudge the last walk by just sticking her outside, but I guess I'm going to have to get used to nipping into the Square in my pyjamas and a thick coat.'

'That five-minute walk at ten thirty is the worst of all the walks. You're all settled in for the night and then you have to force yourself out,' Will confessed, because he hadn't had anyone else to share these aspects of dog ownership with.

'So, how many times a day have you been walking her?' Blossom had backed away from the door now, so Margot shut it, locked it and turned back to him.

'Three times a day. Depends on my schedule but—'

'Do you want a cup of tea?'

Why couldn't she just let him finish a sentence?

'Sorry,' she said immediately, as if Will had said the words out loud. 'It's my worst habit. Cutting people off. As soon as I think things, they come spilling out of my mouth. But do you want a cup of something? I know you have to go back to work but we need to talk about walks and feeding times and how we're going to manage the handover.'

'That makes sense,' Will said, slightly mollified, though wary that she was about to issue him with a whole new raft of edicts masked as suggestions. 'I was going to ping you over my spreadsheet, but tea would be great.'

Margot looked up at one of the shelves above the hob, where there were various blue-and-white striped Cornishware china caddies.

'I can do you herbal. Camomile, peppermint, chai, green . . .'

'Just ordinary tea,' Will said. He should have known that even tea would be more complicated that it needed to be.

'Earl Grey or Lapsang . . .?'

'Builder's if you've got it.'

Margot reached for one of the jars. 'Head into the sitting room. I'll bring it through.'

He retraced his steps back to the hall then into the sitting room. Although the flat seemed tiny, the ceilings were high enough that Will, who was six foot in his socks, could stand at full height, but he still felt like he had to duck his head. Maybe it was because Margot had colonised every spare centimetre of space that she had.

The walls in here were painted a rich, French navy though one was completely obscured by a gallery wall; a collection of pictures in different sized frames, ranging from saucy vintage postcards to retro fashion illustrations and an old-fashioned embroidery sampler with the words 'Nevertheless, she persisted' cross-stitched on it. On the mantelpiece above the fireplace were all kinds of *bits*: candles in various stages of use, a nun in a snowstorm dome, a collection of china owls ranging in size from big to absolutely minuscule. There was also a photograph in a silver frame of a tiny girl who, judging from her mop of dark curls and the determined look on her face, had to be Margot. She was sitting on the lap of an older woman while her chubby hands clutched the fingers of an older man who was gazing at the two of them with a tender expression. Probably grandparents. Above the mantelpiece was a large painting of a woman reading that looked as if it were from the 1930s, though Will couldn't be sure because he knew very little about art or the 1930s. There were built-in cupboards on either side of the fire, a small TV resting on top of one of them and above that were shelves, crammed with books.

There was a sofa, its colour unknown as it was heaped with cushions (how many cushions did one woman need?) and a throw *and* a knitted blanket that reminded Will of an ancient poncho Rowan had worn when she was in her boho phase as a teenager.

There was just enough room for an armchair covered in egg-yolk yellow velvet, again piled high with cushions, so that when Will gingerly sat down, he had to dislodge most of them. He barely had time to view the room from a seated angle before Margot came in with a tea tray and Blossom at her heels.

'She hasn't left my side,' Margot informed Will cheerfully, as she placed the tray on a low table in front of the sofa. 'Wasn't sure of the sugar situation with your tea.'

'Just milk is great,' Will assured her, reaching out to take a mug, which was brewed to just the right colour and consistency.

'Do you want a biscuit? I have some very posh ones,' Margot said, proffering a plate. 'Pistachio nut and clotted cream shortbreads from Fortnum & Mason. I got sent a hamper from the people who stole my cat.'

'What?' Will refused the biscuits with a wave of his hand. 'You have a cat?'

'Not anymore I don't,' Margot said, taking a biscuit and biting into it with satisfaction. Will decided that it was probably best not to ask for clarification.

He felt very uncomfortable sitting there. It was such a feminine space. But it wasn't just that. Being in Margot's sitting room, her flat, felt like an intensely personal experience – as if her possessions weren't just chosen for functionality, but were imbued with meaning and significance. This was more than just a place where Margot lived. More than a home. Like Blossom's spot under his table, this was Margot's safe space and Will felt like an intruder.

Also, if he were to make any sudden movements, he'd send several of her belongings crashing to the floor, its weathered floorboards covered with an ancient Persian rug.

Blossom had been doing a perimeter sweep of the room, as much as she could given the circumstances, but when that was done, she paused in the centre of the room. She looked once to Will, then to Margot who was eating her posh biscuit like it was the greatest thing she'd ever tasted, then jumped on to the sofa next to her.

It wasn't so much a jump as an ungainly scramble and then she sat there looking longingly at Margot. Or rather, it seemed, the biscuit, because she reached out with her right paw, that she always used to such devastating effect, and placed it on Margot's arm.

'Oh! What do you think?' Margot asked as if she were genuinely soliciting Will's opinion and wasn't just going to do what the hell she wanted.

Still, Will would give it the old college try. 'Best not to. Human food can contain ingredients that are toxic to dogs.'

'Really? Like what?' Margot sounded sceptical as if this was just another way for Will to one up her.

'Chocolate; very poisonous. She'd have to have her stomach pumped if she got into a packet of chocolate buttons.'

'Not chocolate!' Margot gasped, taking Blossom's paw and stroking it. 'Oh, Blossom, a life without chocolate is like a day without sunshine.'

'Also grapes, raisins, onions, I'll add an addendum to the spreadsheet.' Will was painfully aware that he was coming across like a stuffy buzzkill intent on depriving Blossom of all manner of culinary delights. 'She can have dog treats though, but only as very specific training rewards. And those chews to keep her teeth clean.'

'You were going to tell me about the walk schedule,' Margot prompted, as she gently pushed Blossom's paw down. 'No, darling, you can't have the posh biscuits. Only dog biscuits and only when it's feeding time.'

Will had already said that he'd send her the spreadsheet he'd painstakingly compiled so that Blossom could optimise her best life, but he still explained the walk schedule. Out in the morning, out in the afternoon, one of these walks being at least an hour, and then the infamous five-minute late night wee walk. 'I haven't let her off the lead at all. I didn't dare. Especially as I was only fostering.'

'Should we let her off the lead?' Margot wondered. 'She certainly comes when I call her.'

That was because Blossom thought that Margot was the best thing ever and Will was merely OK for a man.

'Her recall isn't brilliant,' Will insisted. 'And she's still getting to know us – neither of us have bonded with her yet – so maybe we should wait a bit.'

'Perhaps we should see a trainer. Do you want to be trained?' she asked Blossom who was now recumbent on the sofa, her head in Margot's lap. 'Oh, you just want to sleep, don't you? Because you're such a tired girl.'

When Margot spoke to Blossom it was with a cutesy growl that had the same effect on Will's nerves as someone running their nails down a blackboard.

'Talking of which, she's to sleep in her bed,' he said firmly, because Blossom was a dog, even if she was a particularly forlorn, cute one, and they really needed to establish some boundaries.

'Really?' Margot looked crestfallen. 'But she's too cuddly to sleep on her own, aren't you, my precious, precious girlie?'

Yes. Boundaries needed to be established early on, otherwise who knows what horrors Margot would visit on Blossom? Will would turn up for the handover next week only to find that Margot had dressed Blossom up in something pink and frilly and was pushing her around in a pram.

'Your precious, precious girlie snores so loudly that I really thought we were having an earthquake,' Will said, and this time Margot looked absolutely outraged at his slanderous remarks. 'That's nothing compared to the smells that come out of her other end.'

'I don't believe that.' But Margot wasn't looking quite so delighted to have Blossom in such close proximity. 'Although that is good information to have. This rule-setting has been fairly painless.'

Will nodded. It was. He didn't mind rules, as long as he felt that he had some control over them. 'So, shall we circle back when we handover? I was thinking Sunday mornings in Highgate Woods. It's a good halfway point between us.'

'It is,' Margot agreed. She had the tip of Blossom's ear between finger and thumb and was softly rubbing it as the dog made contented, snuffly noises. 'Not too early. About eleven thirty and then we can still have our lie-in, can't we, Blossom?'

When she said that, Will was certain that despite establishing all these sensible rules, Margot was going to do exactly what she liked and spoil Blossom so much that she'd be absolutely ruined.

'Right, well, I'll be going then,' Will said, draining his last drop of tea, but he wasn't sure that Margot had even heard him, because she'd lowered her head so she could kiss Margot's snout again.

'You're so stinky. I think you're going to have to have a bath with the special lavender shampoo we've just bought and then I'll shower you in love,' she cooed.

Will was done with being the third wheel. He stood up. Margot managed to tear her besotted gaze away from Blossom for just one second. 'Don't worry, I'll let myself out,' Will said kindly. 'I can see that you two want to be alone.'

I I

Margot

It was a glorious week for a puppymoon. That delicious slide into autumn; the days still warm but with a crispness to them, the evenings chilly enough that Margot had transitioned from her summer-weight duvet to her mid-season one.

Nature was showing off its best colours. The Square now had a carpet of vivid red and gold leaves. There were vibrant orange pumpkins stacked up outside the greengrocer and rich glossy brown conkers lining Margot's path each time she stepped outside. Margot had taken her pawrental leave as three days' holiday and two days working from home on the colour palette and themes for next year's autumn/winter collection. Instead of visiting museums and art galleries or closeting herself indoors with vintage fashion magazines and fabric swatches, Margot found herself inspired by the world around her. She was turning into one of those outdoorsy people.

In the mornings, she and Blossom would head for Hampstead Heath, an ancient expanse of lush, open fields, rich woodland and countless ponds, that was the glossy green jewel in North London's crown. Margot had grown up in Gospel Oak, a brisk twenty-minute walk from where she lived now. The Heath had been an extension of her back garden. She'd spent long summer days at Parliament Hill Lido. On Sunday afternoons, the three of them, her mother, father and Margot, would go for a post-lunch stroll. One of Margot's happiest, most vivid childhood memories was being carried on her father's shoulders, high enough that she could see for miles, and never doubting that he would keep her from falling. For special treats, she'd loved going to the café for sausage, chips and beans, and ice cream for afters. When she was older, she'd hung out with her friends at the bandstand and sneaked off to snog boys. But all that had been a long time ago. A lifetime ago. Margot could hardly recognise the child, or the teenager, she'd been.

Now that she was grown up, the Heath was reserved strictly for the summer months. For short walks, picnics and for the annual trip to swim in the Ladies Pond with Tracy, after which Margot would declare on her social media that she'd been 'wild swimming', when really she'd been doing no such thing.

During that first week together, she and Blossom would begin at the Highgate end, walking as far as Kenwood House, then plunging into the innermost parts of the Heath along lesser trodden paths, dense with trees, where all Margot could hear was birdsong so it was hard to believe she was still in a bustling city. There had been a time when Margot knew every inch of the Heath, but she was out of practice. She could only hope that eventually they'd crest the top of Parliament Hill then shortly come out at the bottom of Highgate West Hill. Though three times Margot had got lost and they'd only walked up the hill back to Highgate Village once, and once was enough to convince Margot that she was having a heart attack. It was so steep and she was so unfit.

Blossom was happy plodding along at Margot's side and was so submissive that as soon as another dog approached, she'd immediately roll onto her back. 'Honestly, Blossom, you're a strong, independent woman, have some dignity,' Margot would say.

These dogs had owners who tended to travel in a pack. Mostly women of a certain age who all wore fleeces and sensible walking shoes and carried their dog treats in ancient Ziploc bags. Word quickly got out that there was a new kid on the block.

Blossom would hide behind Margot's legs as Margot went through her sad origin story ('She's about three. I've only just adopted her. No. Not an owner surrender. She was picked up as a stray in Neasden. I'm not sure if she'd been abused but she's certainly been neglected. No, they're not burn marks. The rescue centre said it was alopecia and I'm rubbing coconut oil on them. No, I haven't tried CBD oil, but I will, thank you. Yes, she is very placid for a Staffy.')

Then Margot was introduced to their dogs: an inordinate number of Cockapoos, quite a lot of miniature schnauzers, pugs and French bulldogs. Every breed was represented on Hampstead Heath. From sleek russet Vizslas and grey Weimaraners, to scruffy Lurchers, cherished Chihuahuas who all wore little jumpers, and even a couple of Staffies, whose owners would nod at Margot as if she'd been inducted into some secret club.

People who didn't live in London were always insistent that London was a brutal, fast-paced, unfriendly place full of harsh-faced strangers, but when you lived there, it wasn't like that at all. Margot knew most of her neighbours to say hello to (even Kate Moss!) and Daphne and Geoff who lived in the house above her were practically surrogate grandparents to her. They had spare keys to her flat and never minded when Margot went on an eBay spree and they had to take in her parcels while she was at work. She knew the baristas at her favourite independent coffee place and the staff at the newsagent and the two bookshops and the little Italian where they did a penne arrabbiata that was just the right side of spicy.

But in one week of walking Blossom, the people that Margot was on 'hello' terms with doubled, maybe even tripled, which made up for the fact that her legs ached worse than the time she'd been persuaded to do a lunchtime spin class.

Still, she could rest her aching legs on the sofa after walking, and Blossom would jump up too so Margot could spend hours marvelling at her dog; her soft, floppy ears and the groove down the middle of her skull (a Staffy trait apparently); her absolutely huge block head, roughly the size and weight of a regulation football, that was balanced out by her delicate face; those kohl-rimmed brown eyes and the little snout that Margot loved to pepper with kisses.

Then there was her completely hairless belly, which felt a lot like velveteen as Margot stroked it for hours, much to Blossom's delight. She didn't even mind when Margot smeared coconut oil on her bald patches, though she did try to lick it off.

Unlike the men that Margot had tried to love even when it became abundantly clear that they didn't love her back, she could pour devotion over Blossom and Blossom returned it tenfold. Blossom didn't even resent Margot for refusing to give her human food or forbidding her from climbing on the bed on their first night together.

'We don't know each other very well but I already love you,' Margot confessed after she'd coaxed Blossom into her own, very expensive, orthopaedic memory-foam bed and tucked her up with a fleecy blanket. 'But Will was right. You snore like thunder and your farts are the worst things my nose has ever experienced. No way are you sharing a bed with me.'

Blossom hadn't taken it personally. When Margot had woken her up the next morning, her tail had wagged simply at the sight of Margot's puffy, sleep encrusted face.

'It's just absolute unconditional love,' she told her friends on Saturday afternoon, when they surprised her with an impromptu 'doggy shower'. Margot was napping on the sofa with Blossom, big spoon to Blossom's little spoon, when there was a beep of a WhatsApp message: *Surprise! Open your door!*

Tracy, Jess and Sarah were congregated on Margot's doorstep with presents, a cake box and a pink 'It's a girl!' helium balloon.

Sarah, Margot's oldest friend, was leading the charge. She was one of the few people that remembered Margot as a child, her parents, the idyllic days of her early years. Margot and Sarah had gone to nursery and primary school together, in and out of each other's houses, until Sarah's family had moved to Hong Kong before the start of secondary school. Sarah had come back to London in her early twenties. Facebook had reunited them, and they'd never been parted since.

Tracy had shared a flat with Jess all the way through fashion college, which had led to Margot, in turn, sharing many bottles of white wine with Jess.

Over the years, the four of them had commiserated over bad jobs, bad boyfriends and bad landlords, had had several holidays together, many, many nights out and many, many hangover-soaked brunches the morning after.

Even marriage (Tracy) and marriage *and* kids (Jess and Sarah) hadn't withered their friendship, unlike the other friends that Margot had known over the years who had found partners and had inevitably left London. Sometimes before having children, sometimes just after, because with its pollution and its sub-standard housing and sky-high rents, London could literally kill you and any children that you might have.

Margot knew that there'd probably be a time when Tracy and Sarah left for sunnier climes, probably Margate or Hastings. Tracy was already sending the others links to properties in Margate often captioned, *You couldn't get a one-bedroom flat in Leyton for the price of this house*, and Sarah was adamant that she didn't want three-year-old Maisie and baby Bertie growing up with black snot up their nostrils and knife crime on their doorstep. It was likely only Jess would stay, because she was a born and bred Londoner and had never felt the pull of anywhere else.

But for now, the three of them were still in London and waiting for Margot to step aside and grant them admittance.

'Hello! Such a surprise! Oooh, cake!'

They crammed into Margot's hall to divest themselves of coats and shoes, and already her little flat felt full of chatter, the competing scents of three different perfumes and love.

'Where is she?' Jess asked, handing Margot the cake box.

'In there.' Margot nodded her head in the direction of the sitting room. 'She's a bit shy with strangers.'

'I hope she's not going to bite,' Sarah said. 'I was worried when you said you were getting a Staffy. I still think you're more of a Golden Retriever girl.'

Despite owning a miniature Dachshund, Sarah was a Golden Retriever kind of girl herself. When they'd been children, Margot, with her frizzy hair, sturdy build and argumentative nature, had longed to wake up one morning and discover that she'd become Sarah, because Sarah was leggy, blonde and had a wild, wilful optimism and playful nature that Margot usually found endearing. But not when Sarah cast aspersions on her dog. 'She's not going to bite. She doesn't even bark. And it's a complete myth that Staffies are aggressive . . .'

'Yes, and also did you know that they used to be known as the Nanny Dog?' Tracy sing-songed a verbatim account of Margot's many defensive WhatsApp messages after she'd broken the news that rather than getting a cute fluffy small dog in a neutral colour, she'd got a traumatised Staffy with bald patches.

'I hate all of you.' Margot tucked her arm into Tracy's as they sidestepped into the sitting room where Blossom was standing in the middle of the room, ears pricked, tail wagging. Not in the happy way that Margot was getting used to. This was a more frantic, rhythmic kind of wagging. She backed herself away until she was in the furthest corner of the room and able to hide behind the armchair. 'Give her some time to settle. I'll put the kettle on, shall I?'

'We brought some fizz as it's a special occasion,' said Jess, pulling out a bottle of Crémant from one of her bags. 'Couldn't afford champagne so we went for the next option.'

Margot popped open the bottle in the garden as she wasn't sure how Blossom would cope with the loud noise. It wasn't until everyone had a glass and a slice of lemon raspberry ripple cake from the Hummingbird Bakery that Blossom poked her head out from round the side of the armchair.

Her nostrils twitched and she inched forward, watchful, intent. She padded over to Jess who was wedged at one end of Margot's sofa with her plate on her lap (it was a bit of a squeeze for three people) and sat down in front of her. Then Blossom's right paw came up to land heavily on Jess's knee.

Blossom might be shy with strangers but she knew how to sniff out a mark. Jess was easily the softest of them all. Never a week went by without someone, usually her boss, taking advantage of her good nature. Maybe it was because she was so small; she barely came to Margot's shoulder, her baby face framed with the same blunt brown bob that apparently she'd had since primary school. It was her life's work to find nice shoes that would fit her size-one feet.

'Oh no,' Jess said helplessly. 'It's like I have no will of my own and I *have* to give your dog a piece of cake.'

'No!' Margot yelped so shrilly that Blossom broke off her street-urchin begging routine to give her a startled look. Then her huge manga eyes fixed back on Jess and the paw landed on Jess's knee again. 'She's not allowed to have human food. We agreed. Especially not refined sugar.'

Blossom didn't get any cake but she got a lot of presents. A new collar and lead in leopard print with diamanté accents. Several stuffed toys, a pink doggie hoodie that said 'Classy Bitch' and a bulbous, thick rubber thing called a Kong that looked like some kind of horrific sex toy. 'It's not! The man in the pet shop said that you fill the hole in the middle with treats and plug the top with peanut butter,' Tracy informed Margot in outraged tones. 'Although they had several other things in that shop, studded rubber sticks, that absolutely looked like dildos.'

'Blossom's definitely not having any of them,' Margot said aghast. 'She's got quite enough stuff already. This is all so kind of you. I'm glad I get to experience this because, God knows, it's looking unlikely that I'll ever have a baby shower. If George and I hadn't broken up, if he hadn't strung me along, I could be pregnant now. I could even have had a baby.' If George had been willing, then in the space of the year just gone, Margot's small, safe life would have become something larger and more wonderful. She'd have had her own family. Husband. Child. The rites of passage that everyone else seemed to take for granted, to find so easy to achieve, and yet they continued to elude her.

Margot couldn't help but sigh and willed herself to ignore the first tears welling up, the sob rising in her throat. She was sick of grieving for something that had never existed.

'George was all wrong for you,' Tracy insisted. 'You're glorious, Margs, and George was, well, he was—'

'Not glorious,' Sarah said crisply. 'Why you settled for George and his permanently smug, self-satisfied face, I don't know. You don't need to settle.'

'There comes a time when you have to settle,' Margot said, as she'd said every time one of her friends questioned her choice of George, who actually had been very nice and not that self-satisfied in their first months of dating. 'Otherwise you're holding out for some romantic ideal that's probably not going to happen and wondering if it's time to freeze your eggs.'

'Dude, are you still thinking about doing that?' Jess asked, and Margot nodded glumly in reply.

'But you have a fur baby now,' Sarah said from the armchair, where Blossom was leaning against her shins while having a shoulder massage. 'Honestly, Margot, having a traumatised rescue dog is much less work than a baby. I bet Blossom lets you sleep straight through.'

Blossom, like Margot, was not a great fan of getting up. In fact, she was not a morning dog at all, and after a week of late starts, Margot was dreading having to get up at eight again for work.

'It's still quite a lot of work,' she said trying to ignore the little prickle of hurt when Jess and Sarah shared that look that mothers shared when someone who didn't have children was trying to claim that their life was anything less than a walk in the park. 'But it's going to be very hard to hand her over tomorrow.'

Now all three of her friends sat forward. 'Yes! Next item on the itinerary: this man that you're sharing a dog with,' Jess breathed, she tapped Margot's knee in a peremptory fashion. 'Details, please.'

Margot knew that she wasn't perfect – she had a long way to go until she reached any kind of enlightenment – but she did try to see the best in everyone, as she'd like them to see the best in her. Still, it was very hard to discuss Will with any degree of enthusiasm.

'Well, Blossom seems to like him,' she said after a torturously long pause. 'So I suppose that has to count for something.'

'Does Margot not like him then?' Sarah asked. 'Have we found the one man in London that you don't think has any redeeming features?'

It was fair comment. Margot had dated the churlish, the unwashed, the uninformed and once, someone who'd done ten years for attempted murder although she hadn't known that when she'd agreed to meet for a quick coffee.

Even an absolute horror could turn into a prince, although none of them actually had. Neither would Will. He wasn't a prince in disguise. He was the man who'd fostered her dog and then refused to give her back.

Tracy begged to differ though. 'At the kennels, Blossom was so scared that he had to come down to her level. He was on his hands and knees,' she recalled lasciviously. 'Who doesn't love a man on his hands and knees? Although he did have a freeze-dried duck heart in his hand, which slightly killed the mood.'

'Then he had to get down even lower so he was laying on the floor,' Margot said, as Jess and Sarah, eyes wide, hung on her every word. 'I have to admit there was something quite attractive about seeing a man allowing himself to be so vulnerable, even though there was every chance that Blossom might reject him.'

'Attractive? It was incredibly hot is what it was.' Tracy fanned herself with one hand. 'And what Margot isn't telling you, is that he's also almost unbearably good-looking.'

'Yeah, but he's also unbearably arrogant,' Margot said. 'He's really stand-offish and he makes no effort to make other people feel comfortable around him. That's just basic good manners, isn't it?'

'Absolutely,' Tracy agreed. 'But come on, you have to admit that he is very, very attractive.'

The three of them leaned forward again. Margot glanced over at the armchair where Sarah was sitting, Blossom still leaning in to be stroked, and she remembered Will sitting there, his long legs sprawled out in front of him, a faint air of incredulity as he looked around her sitting room. As if all the things in the room – and each one had been lovingly curated by Margot – were frivolous and fanciful. His face, that exquisitely etched bone structure, his blue eyes, were made for so much more than the closed-off expression it usually wore.

'He might be good-looking but he's also one of those "ping" guys,' she said, to shocked gasps that Margot was daring to trash-talk an eligible man. 'He doesn't send emails, he "pings" them over. He can't just say that we'll catch up, no, we have to "circle back". Then there are the spreadsheets and annotated lists he sends me like Blossom isn't a beloved pet but last quarter's profit and loss accounts. He's a jargon-spewing machine with a superiority complex, but for some bizarre reason, Blossom seems to like him.'

Blossom might have warm feelings towards Will, but Margot woke up the next morning with a leaden, heavy sensation in her stomach, like she was booked in for an invasive medical procedure. Walking down Southwood Lane, Blossom at her side, towards Highgate Woods felt like walking the green mile.

Blossom half-heartedly wagged her tail when she saw Will waiting for them on the playing fields in front of the café. Margot was pleased to note that during the past week she'd merited a full wag of Blossom's tail.

'You're here,' Will said, pointing out the obvious and holding out his hand to take control of Blossom's lead, to assert his ownership. 'Any problems I should know about?'

He didn't even bend down to say hello to Blossom or stroke her behind her ears and Margot immediately wanted to snatch back the lead.

'No problems,' she reported. In the interests of fairness, she should probably have told Will that Blossom had acquired some new toys and a hoodie because they'd agreed that she'd have exactly the same things at both her homes. But, and Margot wasn't proud of this, she didn't tell Will because she wanted Blossom to have a much better life with her careful lady owner who cuddled her all the time and had a great selection of toys, than she did with the hard-faced man who was – oh!

Blossom had jumped up, something she hadn't done with Margot, her front paws pressed against Will's thighs and he was tickling her under her chin. 'So, I'll see you next Sunday then,' Will said, dismissing Margot though she wasn't going anywhere until she was good and ready. 'Enjoy the rest of your weekend.'

On that second dismissive note, Margot had no choice but to leave. 'Bye, Blossom, be good,' she said, but Blossom only had eyes for Will, and it was quite hard for Margot not to start bawling as she walked away but somehow she managed it.

12

Will

Margot walked away without even a backward glance at Blossom, who immediately returned all four paws to the ground and strained at the lead to go after her. Then the first noise emerged: a plaintive whimper, followed by another and another and another.

'Hey, Blossom! Give a man a break,' Will said softly, crouching down to stroke the quivering, unhappy little dog. 'You'll see her next week.'

But Blossom didn't understand the concept of time. The only thing that placated her was a bag of treats Will produced, even though he and Margot had both agreed that they were only to be used for training purposes.

As soon as they began to walk across the playing field, Blossom started pulling on the lead again. She'd been so well-behaved before. Obviously Margot had been spoiling her rotten.

There was more pulling when Will turned left and Blossom thought they should be turning right, but they weren't going back to the flat, but to the big house on one of Muswell Hill's lake roads where it was family tradition to go for Sunday lunch unless you had a good excuse. Like Ian and Alex, Will's brother-in-law, who were on their way to see Arsenal play Watford.

Will had barely got his key in the lock when the door was wrenched open by Sage. 'You took your time,' she said, which was no way to speak to her much older brother. 'Blossom! How we've missed you!'

'I'm docking your wages,' Will said, shoving past her.

'You're not the boss of me,' Sage insisted, because the hierarchical structure at Bloom & Family was very complicated and nuanced. Then she blocked Will's passage through the hall simply by sitting down. 'High five, Blossom!'

Blossom immediately sat down too and raised her very busy right paw, then looked at Sage for the treat that wasn't forthcoming.

'She's not a performing seal,' Will said, shooing the pair of them towards the kitchen where his mother was cooking Sunday lunch, aided by Rowan and the twins, Sam and Harry.

The tantalising aroma of lamb and garlic and herbs indicated that they might eat soon, but lunch prep was quickly abandoned so that Mary, Will's sisters and nephews could gather in a semicircle around Blossom, who held up her paw to 'shake hands' with Sam.

Will had his 'she needs time and space, let her come to you' speech all ready but it was clearly now redundant as Blossom was revelling in the attention. Especially when Mary cupped Blossom's face in her hands and stroked her behind her ears. 'Nanny's going to make you up a delicious plate of food because you need fattening up, don't you?'

It didn't set Will's nerves jangling in the same way that Margot's cutesy growl did, but it came close.

'She's not allowed human food, Margot and I agreed,' he said evenly. 'She gets organic, fresh dog food twice a day and that's plenty.'

Mary stopped gazing down at Blossom adoringly so she could glare at her only son. 'Nonsense. A little bit of lamb and some veggies aren't going to hurt her. I don't even know who this Margot is, but if I owned Blossom I wouldn't let her out of my sight for a week at a time. Maybe I should have a word with her.'

'Maybe you should,' Sage said, because she was a stirrer from way back. Rowan poured herself another glass of wine from the bottle of red that was sitting on the kitchen island and raised her eyebrows at Will; unlike Sage, they remembered a time when Mary wasn't so defiant. For the majority of their childhood, she'd never offered a contrary opinion and had kept her head down, stayed in the shadows. But a lot had changed since then.

'Oh no, I've completely forgotten how to arrange flowers,' Mary had protested when she, Will and Rowan returned to London when Will was twelve.

Shortly followed by, 'I suppose I could serve in the shop. But all those people . . .'

Before too long, there was a slow and steady transformation. 'I'm sure I could get the hang of using a computer. How hard can it be?'

Until the classic, 'Ian from the hardware shop is nice . . . I'll probably go out for a drink with him, but I'm not ready for anything more than friendship.'

'Such a pretty girl. I don't know whose dog you were before Will rescued you, but they didn't deserve you,' Mary was now saying to Blossom, who had jumped up, her paws on Mary's aproned middle, as she got more pets.

Mary still disliked change and she took a while to warm to new people, yet Blossom had been accepted with the most token of protests, and if his mother wanted to give her some lamb and a couple of roast potatoes then Will knew there was no point in arguing. He would just have to make the necessary adjustments to her food intake and exercise regimen for the next forty-eight hours, to allow for the extra calories consumed. Also what Margot didn't know wouldn't kill her.

Just like that, he felt his phone in the back pocket of his jeans vibrate and before he even pulled it, he knew that it would be a message from Margot.

How's Blossom doing after the handover? Has she settled down or is she missing me?

Honestly, that woman really needed to learn some emotional boundaries. Will tucked his phone away.

'Message from one of your women?' Sage asked with a smirk.

'Haven't you heard? He's taken a vow of chastity,' Rowan added with a matching smirk, which transformed into a frown as Sam and Harry, bored now that the adults were talking, began to kick a ball around the kitchen. 'Take that outside and take the dog with you.'

'Her name's Blossom!'

'Should they be unsupervised with her?' Mary and Will asked collectively, but the boys had already piled out through the back door, Blossom hot on their heels.

Will walked over to the window in time to see Harry and Sam hurtling down the length of the long garden with the ball, Blossom following them close behind. She didn't seem very ball-focused, but the previous week Will had pinged Margot a link to a long article warning of the dangers of giving dogs balls too often because it encouraged bad behaviour, and she'd messaged back *tl;dr* (Google had helped him decipher that as 'too long; didn't read').

After dinner, when Rowan and Mary were a bottle of red wine down, Sage was in a relatively quiet food coma and the boys and Blossom were back in the garden, they had their weekly meeting.

It would have been nice to just have a family lunch and not talk shop, but talking shop always seemed easier with full bellies and a drink for anyone who needed it.

Will clutched his glass of ginger ale and waited for Mary to start things off as head of the family firm but she nodded at her son. 'After you, Will. How's it all going with the new accountants?'

Will gave them a rundown on the new software they were going to use, an app to be installed on all of their phones so they could scan invoices and receipts as soon as they got them. Once they'd paid off the fine for late filing of last year's taxes, cash flow was looking quite healthy.

'The events side is really busy, isn't it, Rowan, even though wedding season is winding down?' he said, pulling his sister into the conversation.

'There's a big influencer event this week with all these *children* from Instagram,' Rowan said, as Sage bristled because she was one of those children from Instagram. 'As well as doing the flowers, four big arrangements and fifty table settings so guests can take their flowers home, they want us to set up and run a flower-crown station. How do we do that?'

'I can do that!' Sage piped up. 'I would be *fantastic* at doing that. I made flower crowns for my prom last summer, didn't I? And I could ask Catriona and Anjali to help. They're desperate to pick up some casual work.'

'Great,' Will said, because he had no knowledge of flower crowns, but he would be working out the going rate for a flower-crown station. 'Good to know that you'll be gainfully employed while you're on your gap year.'

Will hadn't meant to sound so pompous and big brotherly and he probably deserved Sage's snort of derision, but he didn't want Sage to idle away the year between school and university and then decide that she preferred the idling to getting a degree.

'Exactly, this is just a gap year. You're still going to university next October,' Mary said resolutely, so Will didn't feel quite so bad. 'My little Sage doing a law degree. I can't wait to see you in one of those funny barristers' wigs.'

'It will be years before my swag is ruined by a barristers' wig and anyway, next October is a whole year away,' Sage said and she shot an imploring look at Will, much like the imploring looks he got from Blossom when it was near to feeding time. They'd talked about Sage's future a lot when he'd been giving her driving lessons the past summer. Sage, after accepting a deferred place at University College, London, was having serious second thoughts, but Will had been adamant that she should get her law degree done and dusted and then she could worry about what she wanted to be when she finally grew up. 'That way, you'll have the foundation stones for a great career.'

'So, anyway, our Bouquet of the Week promotion seems to be going well?' Will said to change the subject, which segued into a discussion about what kind of discount they could get for buying in bulk from their preferred supplier.

'I'll talk to them,' Will promised, making a note on his iPad.

'And I love that we're posting videos on the website and Instagram to show the punters how to arrange their flowers,' Rowan added, because as well as looking after the events side of the business, she was also a skilled Sage whisperer. 'Even if it does mean having to look at Sage's ugly mug.'

'Your mug is uglier,' Sage said, although it wasn't. They looked like sisters, had inherited Mary's complexion and her delicate features, but while Rowan positively glowed with Alpine-like goodness, Sage looked a little sharper, a little more ready to take on the world with the expectation that the world would give her exactly what she wanted. Less Heidi and more Hildebrand, a bossy German exchange student. Also, Sage currently had hair the colour of candyfloss.

Then it was Mary's turn to talk, though her interests were more micro – the Shaws wanted something lovely for their granddaughter's christening. 'Can't believe they've got a grandkid. I remember helping Mum and Dad with their wedding flowers,' she said. 'We've also got three funerals. They're dropping like flies. One "nanna" and one "dad" in white chrysanths, then for the third one, they want us to make a packet of Silk Cut out of flowers.'

Mary was pink-cheeked from the cooking and two glasses of red wine, which usually relaxed her enough that she'd let Rowan and Sage clear away after lunch, but now she was looking rather haunted. 'Christ, I don't even know where to start with that one.'

'You'll be fine. There's bound to be something on YouTube.' With all the arrogance of the digital native that she was, Sage believed that there was a tutorial on the internet for everything, though Will would be very surprised if there was a whole subsection of YouTube devoted to making replicas of a box of cigarettes using carnations and binding wire.

It was a relief to escape. Blossom pulled all the way home, as if she couldn't wait to be back on familiar territory. As soon as Will got the front door open, she bustled past him instead of hanging back as she had done the week before.

When Will walked into the living room, he expected to find Blossom in her usual spot under the table, but why would she be under the table in her expensive memory-foam bed when she could be on the sofa, in the spot where he usually sat?

He'd never noticed it before but Blossom, seated, looked like a little drunk old man. She didn't sit on her haunches but right on her bottom, with her bowed back legs splayed out in front of her. He was tempted to take picture and send it to Margot, but it would only give her notions.

'Off the sofa,' he ordered with a jerk of his hand. 'You really are slipping into bad habits.'

Blossom didn't get off the sofa. Instead she doubled down: stretching out her front legs and staring up at Will with that woebegone expression that she did so well.

'I don't know why you're looking so sorrowful,' he told her. 'You've had a roast lamb dinner and apple crumble, against my better judgement. You've chased a ball around the garden and you've had at least one pair of hands on you at all times. Now, budge!'

In reply, Blossom rolled over and presented Will with her belly. Not in the submissive way that she did when approached by other dogs. Then, her whole body seemed to cringe, and her tail would wag in a frantic, metronomic way that, according to a long piece entitled 'Decoding Your Dog's Body Language', which he'd also pinged over to Margot, signalled distress.

There was nothing distressed about Blossom right now. She was spread across a huge section of couch for such a small dog, her belly displayed proudly, her limbs relaxed and supine. And because Will was being so slow on the uptake, finally she waggled her front paws and rolled ever so slightly nearer to him.

'I've created a monster,' Will muttered as he reached down to stroke Blossom's tummy. 'One quick belly rub then you have to get off the sofa.'

But it was a very big sofa and there were only two of them. Will preferred the right-hand end so he could stretch out his legs on the L-shaped section, but he could just as easily sit on the other side and still see the TV.

As soon as he sat down Blossom scooched closer to him and before she even realised what he was doing, Will picked her up and plopped her down on his other side.

There was a quick battle for the coveted right-hand end, which Will won, even though Blossom's main form of attack was to pin him to the spot and lick his face. Then they were settled for the evening, Will with his legs stretched out and Blossom next to him, on her back, so she could have belly rubs on tap.

When it came to bedtime, Blossom decided that she wasn't going to sleep in her bed under the table either. She gave Will a hurt look when he suggested it, so after he'd finished in the bathroom, he retrieved the bed and took it into his own bedroom.

Like everywhere else in the flat, Will's bedroom was functional. 'Spartan,' Mary said. But all he needed was a bed and a bedside table. His clothes went into the fitted cupboards on either side of the fireplace. He didn't need *stuff*. The latest phone, the designer clothes, the high-performance sports car didn't do anything to fill the gaping chasm inside of people. Inside of Will. He'd learned that the hard way.

But hearing Blossom's claws clatter against the wooden floorboards did give Will pause. Maybe he should get a couple of rugs so she'd be more comfortable. Also, at the handover, he should probably inform Margot that they needed to get Blossom's nails trimmed.

For now, he put Blossom's bed near the radiator and straightened her fleecy blanket. 'Night night,' he said, and he wondered if there would ever come a time when it felt normal to talk to a dog. Blossom was sitting on the floor, her head tilted as she surveyed him and her bed. 'Come on! Time for bed.'

It took much cajoling and coaxing, until finally Will picked her up, her legs stiff and unresisting, and *put* Blossom in her bed, where she stood, gazing at him, eyes unblinking. It was quite unsettling.

Will got into bed, aware of the staring canine on the other side of the room, and picked up the book he was reading.

He'd used to only read books on management technique and personal development. Now that he'd left New York and the world of banking behind, Will was secretly delighted that he never had to read another book about harnessing his potential or the smart habits that smart people use to get ahead.

He was currently making his way through Agatha Christie's backlist. Or, he was trying to read *Sparkling Cyanide* but it was quite hard to concentrate with Blossom still standing up in her bed, staring at him unhappily.

Margot had obviously been fussing and clucking over her during the previous week and now Blossom wouldn't settle unless she was tucked in and had lullabies sung to her. In which case, she was going to be disappointed because Will had his limits.

He didn't even say 'goodnight' when he turned out the light, as he didn't want to encourage her. But instead of settling down to sleep, turning his pillow over to the cool side, Will was tense and alert to any noise coming from the corner.

But all was silent. He let out a shaky breath and forced himself to relax.

That was when Blossom began to cry. Not cry. Dogs didn't cry, did they? She was whimpering, which was heart-wrenching, but you had to let them cry it out, Will knew that much.

After a few, long minutes, he'd had enough. He couldn't bear to listen to the desperate, pained little cries.

Will sat up and snapped on his bedside lamp to see Blossom still standing up in her bed. He pulled back the duvet and, with, a sigh, got out of his own bed.

'You're being very silly,' he said softly, padding over to her. 'You've got a lovely, comfy bed and a soft blanket. Let's get you all tucked up.'

Blossom was not for tucking. She refused to lie down and put her paw on Will's arm to stop his attempts to drape any kind of covering over her. Then she licked his hand and when he sat down on the floor next to her bed, she promptly crawled into his lap so she could lick at his face with desperate motions.

'Blossom, you have to sleep and I have to sleep in our own respective beds,' Will said, but Blossom was just a dog who had, obviously, spent seven nights tucked up in Margot's bed because as soon as Will stood up, Blossom scrambled after him and attempted to jump up on his bed.

She couldn't quite manage to get purchase on the wooden floor with her back legs – he really would have to get a couple of rugs – so Will gave her a hand.

'On the bed, not *in* the bed,' he said but she was already disappearing under the quilt head-first. 'Great. Just bloody great.' Will got back into bed, his feet encountering Blossom who was doing a U-turn so she could finally emerge from under the duvet and snuggle into Will. She burrowed against him, front paws pedalling until Will put an arm around and began to stroke the top of her head with slow, steady movements.

She fell asleep in an instant.

13

Margot

Margot had no idea, though she had quite a lot of theories, what Will had done to Blossom during his week, but the sweet, submissive dog who rolled onto her back whenever another dog came into sight had disappeared. Never to return.

In her place was a wilful little madam, who now tugged at the lead. The Heath was full of squirrels and Blossom wanted to chase after every one. And, because she and Blossom were attached by one hundred and thirty-eight centimetres of red and white polka-dot webbing, Margot was an unwilling participant.

Blossom now barked at other dogs and lunged for them when they got too close. Had very strong opinions about whether they should go right or left and seemed to think that treats were an entitlement and not a privilege.

She'd even jumped on Margot's bed the first night that they were reunited and had promptly disappeared under the covers. 'Not going to happen,' Margot had told her in a firm voice and hefted a protesting Blossom into her own dog bed. Margot had sat it out, cross-legged on the floor, until Blossom had given a grumbling sort of sigh and lay down.

'The thing you need to know about me, Bloss, is that I might appear to be soft and I might appear to be indulgent but I'm not a pushover,' Margot had told her as she tucked Blossom up and stroked her head. 'Many people have made the same mistake and lived to regret it.'

Blossom had huffed again, her sighing sounded weirdly and unsettlingly human, but Margot had no more bed-hopping nonsense from her.

Why is Blossom acting like a toddler going through her terrible twos? she'd messaged Will, but there was no reply. Margot didn't even know why she bothered. It was all right for him to bombard (no, sorry, 'ping') her with his spreadsheets and lists and boring, wordy peer-reviewed articles from experts in veterinarian science, but he was very resistant when it came to Margot weighing in on how best to raise Blossom. He'd been terse again, to the point of truculence, at the handover.

'How do you think it went?' he'd replied cryptically when Margot had enquired how their week had gone. Then he'd told her that Blossom needed to get her claws cut and he'd left. Not even a backward glance at Blossom, who pulled hard at the lead, as if she wanted to follow him.

'He's not worth it, Bloss,' Margot had said, and she couldn't help but hope that Will was tiring of Blossom. Her unruliness was clearly a direct result of his inept attempts to care for her and soon he'd want to give her up entirely.

Margot looked forward to that day, but she had more pressing matters to worry about on Monday morning. Pawrental leave was over and getting your dog into a reputable day care in North London was slightly harder than getting your children into a good prep school. Also, just as expensive.

Most places were already completely full, and of those that weren't, most said that they didn't take Staffies. One woman had even put the phone down on Margot as she was furiously explaining for the nth time that 'actually, I think you'll find that Staffies are one of only three breeds that the Kennel Club recommend to families with children'.

The only viable doggy day care was in Primrose Hill, just round the corner from the offices of Ivy+Pearl. The owner, a tiny, energetic woman with a tanned, creased face, no doubt from walking dogs in all weathers, had said that she loved Staffies.

'Not like the spoilt bastard little dogs you get round here,' she'd said, pulling a dog biscuit out of the pocket of her fleece for Blossom. 'You know where you are with a Staff.'

However, when Margot had googled her, she discovered that the woman only had a two-star Google rating and swore at any punters who left her bad reviews. There had also been an incident when one of her dogs had run away, been hit by a car and had to have a back leg amputated.

So Margot was left with no other option.

'You absolutely have to be on your best behaviour,' Margot told Blossom as she entered the security code to gain access to the corporate offices of the Ivy+Pearl clothing company. The offices were above the very first boutique that Derek and Tansy had opened when they'd made the move from punk clothing to streamlined women's separates. 'I hope your legs are up to this.'

It was a long climb up a narrow staircase to the first floor where she hurried Blossom past Audrey on reception (Aud on the board, as they called her), then up an even narrower spiral staircase, which led to the second floor where the creative team worked. Blossom wasn't keen on the slatted spiral staircase, so she took some persuading and finally, Margot was ready to face the music.

She looked around the large open-plan space, dominated by a huge table that multitasked as a conference table, cutting table and where they put out the Colin the Caterpillar cake, drinks and nibbles whenever it was someone's birthday or they'd had a good week of sales. Surrounding the space were a series of glass-walled offices, the biggest one belonging to Derek and Tansy who were nowhere to be seen.

In fact, given that it was Monday morning, there was no one around, which was very odd, but also very fortuitous because it meant Margot could sneak Blossom into her office without anyone ever finding out that—

'Dog in the office! Repeat, dog in the office!' cried a foghorn voice from behind Margot, which belonged to Jacques, her fellow designer, and suddenly she and Blossom were besieged on all sides.

Or rather, the four people who'd been camped out in the office kitchen having a gossip, emerged.

'She's very shy with strangers,' Margot hissed, pulling Blossom towards her, so that she, very obligingly, sat down on Margot's feet. 'You have to let her come to you.'

'Oh, hello! Hello, little doggy! Are you the goodest boy? Oh! Look at those little chicken-drumstick legs. I want to eat them!' Margot knew that her own crazy dog lady voice was creepy but Cora, Derek and Tansy's PA, had her beaten. Cora's age was a closely guarded secret, but she'd known Derek and Tansy for decades, back when they were punks and during the subsequent years, she hadn't changed her gothic look in the slightest. She was always decked out in long, flowing black dresses, her bird's-nest greying hair tied up with black lace ribbons, and she left the lingering smell of patchouli oil everywhere she went. Margot loved her dearly, but she really needed Cora to turn down the dial this morning.

Amina, the accessories designer, and Joe, their design trainee, were equally effusive though thankfully less creepy. Only Jacques hung back.

'I'm allergic,' he said, contorting his usually quite handsome face into a grimace and tugging at his beard.

'Can't you take an antihistamine?' Margot asked, as she waited for Derek and Tansy to appear. Maybe they were on the first floor with the sales and marketing team. 'It's only for today. Possibly longer. It's hard to say – oh no, don't put your hand out like that, Cor, it can be quite threatening to a dog . . . or, apparently not.'

Blossom had got over her initial shyness in favour of rolling onto her back and wiggling her paws until Cora stroked her belly. 'Do you like that? You do like that, don't you? Also, I see that you're not a boy. Sorry about that.'

'Antihistamines won't help when I go into anaphylactic shock,' Jacques said, but he was a terrible hypochondriac. He'd once called an ambulance because he thought he was having a heart attack, when really he'd been sleeping on his right arm, which was why it had gone numb. 'Ugh! It's trying to lick me.'

'She's nowhere near you,' Margot said calmly, though she didn't feel calm, but she didn't want her stress to affect Blossom. 'Where's Derek and Tansy? Are they downstairs?'

'They're off-site all day,' Cora said, between coos. 'Gone to Borehamwood.'

Both their factory and their warehouse were in Borehamwood, which meant that Margot had bought herself and Blossom a day's grace. In deference to Jacques's allergy, which he'd never ever mentioned before, though Margot had often been forced to listen to him regale her with tales of his many other ailments, she arranged one of Blossom's blankets under the table in the main room. Not that Blossom stayed there. She settled down under Cora's desk, only coming out at lunchtime when Margot took her to Primrose Hill for a walk.

The well-heeled denizens of Primrose Hill scooped up their Chihuahuas and their teacup Yorkies and their miniature Pomeranians as they saw Margot and Blossom approach. Though, to be fair, Blossom was straining at the lead, tongue hanging out, and lunging at any other dog that dared to look at her, so she was doing nothing to dispel the myth that Staffies were a vicious, aggressive breed.

On the plus side, it was good to get out at lunchtime for fresh air and exercise, instead of stuffing her face and depleting her bank balance in one of Primrose Hill's many lovely but prohibitively expensive cafés. And the next morning, Margot was prepared for the early start and even gave herself enough time to make a packed lunch.

She arrived at Ivy+Pearl at nine o'clock, though the official start time was nine thirty and the unofficial start time after everyone then popped out again to get breakfast and coffee was ten o'clock.

Blossom seemed most put out that her adoring public were nowhere to be seen. She sat at the door of Margot's office and refused to budge until Margot lured her over the threshold with a piece of chicken jerky. For one moment, Margot wished that she'd gone with her original plan to get a small, portable dog that could be hidden away in a dog carrier that masqueraded as a chic holdall. The only bag Blossom would fit in was a big blue IKEA bag.

'You have to be the best girl, Bloss,' she hissed, dropping to her knees to arrange Blossom's blanket under her desk. 'I want you to stay here all day, quietly, and if you behave yourself, then we'll have extra sofa snuggles this evening.'

Blossom happily sniffed under Margot's desk, executed a couple of circles, then dropped onto her blanket with a contented sigh.

She was so good and so quiet that even Jacques didn't notice that she was there. Jacques, who didn't so much as sneeze or pop out in hives. Instead, as he wolfed down his bircher muesli with fermented boysenberries, he told Margot that his wife, Solange, had been promoted to Head of Vibe at the digital advertising agency where she worked in Hoxton.

It always amused Margot that Jacques wasn't actually French ('my parents were just massively, massively pretentious') but his wife was. 'What on earth is Head of Vibe?' she wanted to know, as she sorted through button samples for the pyjamas she was working on for next year's autumn/winter range. 'Is there a Deputy Head of Vibe?'

'Might be Vice Head of Vibe. Nice bit of alliteration,' Jacques decided. 'But she's got a pay rise, Soho House membership and an electric scooter as part of her promotion package, though I made her promise to wear a crash helmet if she was going to use it.'

'I bet that went down well.' Solange was a big fan of things that were likely to cause her untimely death, whether it was cycling to work every day despite the fact that she could be knocked off her Pashley into the path of a heavy goods vehicle, or being heavily into parkour and jumping off high buildings for laughs. 'But I wouldn't say no to Soho House membership. Remember that your work wife would quite like a weekend away at Soho Farmhouse— oh, Blossom, no!'

Blossom had suddenly awoken from her slumber, and was out of the door as Jacques shrieked in genuine alarm.

'Margot! You *know* I'm allergic.'

Jacques still wasn't showing any signs of anaphylactic shock so Margot paid him absolutely no attention and leapt to her feet to head Blossom off, but it was too late.

Derek and Tansy were in the building. Not more than two metres away. Tansy was talking to Joe. Derek was perched on one corner of the big table with a bacon sandwich from the greasy spoon on Chalk Farm Road (no bircher museli and fermented super berries for him) and Blossom had decided that he was her new best friend because she was thundering towards him.

'What is that? What is it doing in the office?' Tansy demanded, taking a hasty step back. 'Margot! We said no.'

'Several times,' Derek added, as he looked down at Blossom who was now sitting in front of him, a slobbery trail of drool descending from each side of her mouth, when Margot really needed her to look cute and winsome.

'I couldn't find a doggy day care. There was one place, but it would have been too traumatising for her.' Margot put a hand on her heart and furrowed her brow at Derek, who was a much, much softer touch than Tansy. 'She was very distressed in the rescue kennels and I don't want to make her relive the experience. This will only be until I've sorted out a dog-sitter. Though they are very expensive. Very, very expensive.'

Derek didn't seem to appreciate Margot's predicament, but he did break off the corner of his sandwich for Blossom, who took it as delicately as if he were feeding her caviar.

'Don't try and soft soap him,' Tansy snapped. She was wearing her most severely cut black jumpsuit, which never boded well. 'Soft soap won't work on me. This beast will get fur all over the fabrics and you never said that you were getting a Staffy. They're vicious.'

Margot bit back her speech about the Kennel Club and families with children with some effort. Tansy didn't like back-chat about as much as she didn't like soft soap. Also, Derek could always bring her round.

'Not so vicious, Tan,' he said mildly. 'My grandparents had a Staff when we were kids. Sid. He was a great dog. Wouldn't hurt a fly. My nan would let him out in the morning and he'd come home in time for his tea, then on Saturday's my grand-dad would go and settle up with the butcher cause Sid popped into his shop every day regular as clockwork for a marrow bone.' He slid off the table and held out his hand to Blossom.

Margot had bit her tongue over Derek feeding Blossom

bacon and toast but now she couldn't be silent. 'Actually, Derek, she's not great with men,' she warned, although she was still yet to see Blossom being not so great with a man, apart from Will. She wasn't going to see it this morning either.

Blossom, sensing the need to be on her best behaviour and also because Derek still had the delicious aroma of bacon sandwiches on him, tilted her head in the most adorable away. Then she lifted her paw to shake Derek's hand.

'What a heartbreaker,' Derek said with a smitten expression on his face.

Tansy was less impressed. 'Dog hair! On the fabric!' she exclaimed again, before flouncing into the office that she shared with Derek and flinging herself down on the sofa.

Nothing more was said about Blossom's presence in the office for the rest of the week. Except Jacques, who kept huffing antihistamine nose drops, but as Margot pointed out, that could be due to autumnal leaf mould. Apart from still being no closer to a day-care solution and having a permanently wrenched shoulder from their lunchtime excursions to Primrose Hill, life at Ivy+Pearl carried on as normal.

Margot even caught Tansy absent-mindedly stopping to pet Blossom on her way to the fabrics cupboard and when Margot and Blossom got back from their lunchtime tug of war on the Friday, things had resolved themselves.

Under Margot's desk was a very chic, houndstooth dog bed. In the kitchen was a ceramic water bowl with Blossom's name on it and on the company Instagram there was a picture of Blossom and a brief introduction to 'Ivy+Pearl's Chief Puperating Officer'.

14

Will

Will had been hoping to make the handover as brief as possible to minimise Blossom's distress and also because he and Blossom were expected for Sunday lunch.

Margot, however, had other ideas. She'd arrived first and was waiting for Will on what was their usual bench, with a petulant expression on her face. It was a close cousin to a scowl; her delicate eyebrows pulled together, her generous mouth, small and pouty. Which was a pity because usually she looked so pretty, and also because it meant that Will had obviously displeased her in some way.

'Please stop pinging me all those really long articles that imply I don't know how to look after Blossom,' was her opening salvo, which was hardly fair.

'You message me too, with bullet points,' Will said in his defence. 'I don't need a play by play of Blossom's bowel movements.'

'If you were a committed dog owner, you would,' Margot countered. 'You didn't even care when I sent you a picture of the fluff that's growing on her bald patches.'

'I said that I couldn't see any fluff, but if you were concerned, you should take her to the vet's.' Will squatted down to say hello to Blossom, who was much more pleased to see him. Not only was her tail wagging this time, properly wagging, but her whole bottom was wiggling in delight. Will had rarely made anyone's bottom wiggle with delight. 'Hello, gorgeous girl.'

'Me or Blossom?' Margot asked drily, which was a surprise, as Will had been convinced she didn't have a sense of humour. 'Anyway, look at her bald patches now!'

Will looked. Then he looked again. Turned Blossom round just to make sure. Where there had been long strips of dark skin on both of her sides, they were now only a faint outline surrounding her newly grown fur. 'Wow.' He let out a low whistle. 'That happened in a week?'

'More like overnight.' Margot smiled far too smugly for Will's liking. 'She's obviously very happy with me. And talking of overnight, have you been letting her sleep on your bed?'

He hoped that Margot would think he was choking in outrage rather than panic. 'Of course not!' Will insisted, because when in doubt, deny, deny, deny. Besides, he wasn't lying. Blossom didn't sleep *on* his bed. She slept *in* his bed, tucked under his duvet, her head on her own pillow. 'Really? Do you really think I would let her do that? Didn't I send you that paper published by Washington State University about pack behaviours and how the hierarchical structure—'

'Stop! Please, stop.' Margot clapped her hands over her ears to make her point. 'Enough with all those boring articles. What Blossoms needs is love, not the findings of a load of boffins in a laboratory that have probably never even *seen* a dog.'

Blossom batted her gigantic head against his knee and looked up at him, and Will thought that there wasn't much he wouldn't do for her, but that wasn't love. Dogs by their very nature were co-dependent. What did Margot have to offer her? Apart from all this so-called love? A walk in the morning, some scant attention in the evening, then day care for the rest of the time. It was hardly worth her having Blossom at all.

'Did you sort out day care for her, because I'm not sure that . . .'

'No day care. She comes to work with me,' Margot said. 'She's been busy winning hearts and minds, haven't you, Blossom?'

Instantly, Blossom transferred her affections to Margot, even though officially it was now Will's week.

'I'm not sure I like the idea of her having to commute . . .' he began, but Margot held her hand up in protest.

'It's twenty minutes on the bus. It's hardly arduous,' she said. 'Anyway, she's started pulling on the lead. It's murder on my shoulder and—'

Will had heard enough. 'She doesn't pull with me,' he bit out, 'and this is now officially my week that you're cutting into so . . .'

Margot stood up, cheeks flushed in a way that had nothing to do with the wind that tore across the playing field and lifted her hair this way and that. She really was very pretty.

'Oh my God,' she sniped. 'So sorry for stealing ten minutes of your precious time.' Unfortunately, pretty only got a woman so far and then she had to rely on her personality, and Margot's personality left a lot to be desired.

Finally, she was going, stopping for one last tweak of Blossom's ears and Will and Blossom were alone at last.

Not that Blossom seemed to appreciate that she was back with her main man. She strained at her harness; her body a quivering arrow pointed in the distance to where Margot was now disappearing further and further from view, until she slipped between the trees and was gone.

It took all Will's powers of persuasion, half a bag of fish skins and a really firm hold of her lead before Blossom agreed to start walking across the field and through the woods and home to where his mother, who was now referring to Blossom as her 'grandfurchild', was peeling two extra potatoes just for her.

Blossom slotted back into Will's life and routine as if she'd never been away. Whenever possible she was glued to his side, and when it wasn't possible she was happy to hang out in the back of the shop with Mary.

It rained for most of the week and it quickly became apparent that Blossom was not a big fan of rain. She was, however, a big fan of digging her paws in and refusing to walk any further once she'd done the necessary. She spent most of the week much preferring Mary's company to Will's. Probably because Mary had now taken to carrying a bag of dog treats in the pocket of her apron.

Just as it was hard to refuse Blossom when she was taking up space on his sofa, in his bed and even demanding the food from his plate, so it was hard for Will to deny Mary anything she wanted. Whatever made his mother happy was fine with Will.

So, on Thursday morning when he'd finished doing the deliveries and popped back to Blooms', he found the shop quiet and Mary in the back room.

'Do you think I can persuade Blossom out now that it's only drizzling?'

Will glanced over at Mary, expecting her to crack a joke about Blossom who was snoring away under the workbench, but she was silent, her profile rigid, fingers clutched around a pair of secateurs.

'Are you all right?' Will asked in genuine concern. 'Has Ian done something to upset you because if he has then . . .'

'I miss them, Will. I miss Mum and Dad,' Mary choked out, the first tears trickling down her cheeks. 'I'm lost without them. I'm not cut out to be in charge.'

Will cringed, inwardly and outwardly. He was not the person for this job.

Mary's shoulders were heaving now with the strain of tamping down the sobs and Will placed a tentative hand on her back. 'I'm sorry,' he said helplessly. 'You're doing a great job. Everyone thinks so.'

'It's their wedding anniversary today. They'd have been married sixty-two years . . .'

'I'm sorry.'

'Dad would always order in golden roses for the number of years they'd been together.' Mary's voice wobbled so that even Blossom was roused to stick a concerned head out from the under the table. 'Mum had golden roses in her wedding bouquet.'

'We could do something nice tonight, go out for dinner maybe?' Will suggested even though he knew that wasn't the answer. That a meal at the family's favourite Italian on Southampton Row wouldn't heal the hurt, especially as that was where they'd always gone to celebrate birthdays, anniversaries and good news. They'd been going there for so long that the entire staff, most of them ancient, would line up to shake their hands in greeting. 'I'm sorry.'

'No need to keep saying sorry, Will. It's not your fault.' Mary took out a tissue that she had tucked up her sleeve and blew her nose loudly. 'I'm being silly.'

'You're not,' Will said, glancing down to see that Blossom, not surprisingly, now had her head resting against Mary's knee. 'Don't say that.'

They stood there in silence for a moment, then Mary sniffed and straightened her shoulders. 'Well, I should get on. None of these flowers are going to arrange themselves.'

Later that day, when there was a brief break in the weather, Will took Blossom to Alexandra Park. He was still castigating himself for not being more of a rock for Mary. For never, ever knowing the right words to say to someone. No wonder he'd barely managed sixty-two days with the same woman, never mind sixty-two years.

'Blossom, please stop pulling,' he said out loud, as the rain had scared everyone away apart from the one other dog-walker Will could see in the distance, their head down.

It wasn't that he was cold and unfeeling, Will reasoned as he returned to his previous train of thought. As he'd discovered in therapy, he hadn't allowed himself to feel and God knows he had his reasons for that.

Maybe that was why he'd connected with Blossom so quickly. She expected nothing from him (except a never-ending supply of treats) and passed no judgement on him. Even better, she never wanted to ask him about his feelings or tell him that he wasn't good enough. And now that she'd settled down, Will could show her affection without fear of rejection.

Blossom lived in the moment, and at this very moment, she was pulling so hard at her harness that Will was amazed that it didn't break under the pressure. Her entire being was focused solely on the squirrel that was darting from one flower bed to the next.

Will looked around again. The place really was deserted. The other dogwalker and dog had disappeared from view.

What harm would it do to let her off the lead? Roland had said that he was risk-averse, like that was a bad thing, but Will could take a calculated risk, now and again. There were no distractions and surely he'd established enough clear-cut boundaries that Blossom would come back as soon as he called her.

'OK, OK,' Will muttered, his mind made up. He bent down to release the hound. 'This will be our secret. Margot must never know. I'm trusting you to do the right thing, Blossom.'

But Blossom was already gone, chasing a squirrel from one flower bed to the next, then up the slope, behind which was bisected by steep, curved paths.

'That's enough now, Blossom!' Will called, because beyond those paths was a steeper grass verge, then the road that ran through the palace grounds. 'Come back! There's a good girl!'

The wind had picked up so Will wasn't sure that she'd heard him. Then she turned and stared right at him, head tilted, ears cocked.

'Come on! I have treats!' Will pulled the bag out of his jacket pocket and rustled them enticingly. He wasn't going to get stressed. She was going to come back . . .

The squirrel darted again, and Blossom turned away so she could dart after it; beetling up the verge, so for one agonising, heart-stopping second, Will couldn't see her. He scrambled after her, his heart racing, waiting for the squeal of brakes, the sound of a car horn, or, oh God, a bloody bus.

The grass was wet and Will fell to his knees, barely noticing that his hands were muddy as he pushed himself back up and staggered the remaining distance until he was standing on the pavement. Just across the road was Alexandra Palace, rising up over North London in all her Victorian splendour but Blossom was nowhere to be seen.

She hadn't been run over. That was something. Had she turned right, back in the direction they'd come? Or had she turned left, in the direction of Wood Green?

What was he meant to do? Head for home and hope that Blossom would be there? Even though to get home she had to cross several main roads. Or was she still chasing the squirrel through the park, maybe down to the boating lake? Will didn't even know if she could swim.

He was paralysed with fear, gripped in the clutch of inertia, her lead hanging limply in his hand. He was useless, spineless . . .

Then there was the toot of a horn and his entire chest clenched. But the road was clear, and a car was slowing down so that a woman on the passenger side could open her window. 'Have you lost a dog?'

'Y-y-yeah . . .'

'There's a dog just back there, running along the bank,' she said, then the car behind sounded its horn, so with an apologetic smile, they drove off.

Will ran along the pavement. There was another steep grass verge between the road and the palace, which was why most people took the designated steps. But not Blossom. She was running up and down the bank, still in hot pursuit of the squirrel.

He just stopped himself from shouting her name; actually choking on the first syllable when he realised she might bound across the road again to reach him. Thankfully, the road was still clear. He hurried across so he could shout.

'Blossom! Get back here, RIGHT THE HELL NOW!'

Blossom didn't pay Will any attention, but continued to run around in circles, though the squirrel was long gone.

'BAD DOG! BAD GIRL! YOU COME HERE NOW!'

But why on earth would she come to the man who was shouting at her? Will made a grab for her, falling to his knees again, but Blossom evaded him and took off, this time in the direction of the car park, because obviously she had a death wish and being mown down was preferable to being with Will.

After a good thirty minutes, two car park attendants managed to corner Blossom between two parked cars and Will was able to snap on her lead.

At the touch of Will's hand, Blossom cowered as if she was expecting an almighty walloping. Will had been furious because she wouldn't come when she was called and she could have been killed, but instantly his anger melted away. He wasn't that guy. He didn't want Blossom to ever think that he was that guy.

Will felt his chest clench again, as if all the breath had been knocked out of him. His heart and head were pounding and the sense of impending doom, as if the end of the world was well and truly nigh, was crashing down on him.

'Breathe,' he whispered out loud. 'Breathe. Breathe. Breathe.'

As Roland had advised him, he said the word again and again, like a mantra, a way to force the air back into his lungs.

It was just a panic attack. Just! Even though Will now knew that they were panic attacks didn't rob them of their power to immobilise and terrify him.

'I'm all right,' he said, and it was true. Somehow, he'd managed to keep hold of Blossom's harness and she was huddled into him, licking his chin. 'You're all right too.'

He stayed sat on the ground, the rain pouring down (because of course it had started raining again), until both he and Blossom had stopped shaking. Will pressed his forehead against hers, her fur clinging damply to his skin.

'I will never hurt you. And I promise I will never shout at you again. You don't need to be frightened anymore because you are safe. You will always be safe with me.'

He wasn't sure that Blossom believed him but as he walked her home, she walked docilely by his side, her tail very firmly between her legs.

Will was covered in mud. He wiped his trembling hands off on his jacket and pulled out his phone.

Margot answered on the second ring. 'Oh my God, why are *you* ringing me? Has something happened to Blossom? Is she all right? Do you need me to leave work and come over?'

If Margot ever found out what had happened during the last hour, Will didn't doubt that she'd go to court to sue for full custody. For one brief moment, he even wondered if that would be best for Blossom.

His family would never forgive him. And he wouldn't forgive himself that he couldn't make this one relationship work. Not to mention how much he'd miss the comforting solid weight of Blossom leaning into him, the way she'd grab his arm with her paw when he stopped with the belly rubs. The thorough tongue bath she gave his face every morning. Blossom wouldn't do those things if she were unhappy to be with him, would she?

'Will? Are you still there? Have you accidentally bum-dialled me? I hate it when that happens.'

'Just touching base,' he said, hiding behind the business jargon of his former life. 'I think we need to take Blossom to a trainer.'

'She's been pulling on the lead, hasn't she? I told you!' Will had to allow Margot her smugness but only because he'd had an unpleasant shock and was off his game.

'We're both novice dog owners,' he said. 'Training will help us establish boundaries and ensure that Blossom is living her most optimal life.'

'I've already established lots of boundaries with Blossom.' Margot refused to see the severity of the situation. Then she sighed. 'But the pulling is a problem and I would like to be able to let her off the lead . . .'

'No! She's never being let off the lead. Never!' Will could hear the phantom squeal of brakes again.

'Ha! You were the one who sent me an article quoting some-one from the RSPCA who said that all dogs should have a certain amount of time off-lead exercise every day, depending on size and breed,' Margot parroted. Then maybe she realised that she was plumbing new depths of being annoying because she stopped. 'Let's get her all trained up and see where we are. But positive reinforcement training, Will. I'm not paying someone to pin her to the ground to establish their domi-nance over her.'

Will was appalled. 'I would never let anyone to do that to Blossom.'

'Good, so why don't I do some googling—'

'I'll do it,' Will interrupted. 'You already sorted out the vet and insurance.'

It was true. He'd been sharing peer-reviewed papers on pet ownership 24/7 but he'd let Margot do the grunt work.

'Once I've found someone, I'll text you the details,' he added.

'That would be great,' Margot said eagerly. 'Are you sure nothing's happened; this is very out of character? You actually *asked* me how I felt about training, instead of telling me we were getting a trainer.'

'There was an incident with a squirrel,' Will admitted because he didn't want to keep lying to her. Also, he hadn't realised how controlling he'd been. It was shaping up to be a day of very unpleasant revelations. 'Not sure either of us will ever recover.'

'Did she nearly pull your shoulder out of its socket?' Margot's tone grew sympathetic. 'I know what that feels like. You text me the training details and I'll text you a link to these really great tiger balm patches. Deal?'

'Deal.'

15

Margot

Margot followed several dog trainers on Instagram who were always posting pictures of the dogs under their guidance and showering them with praise in the captions. 'Ziggy is only twelve weeks old and already toileting outside like the superstar he is.' 'Bagel has a well-earned rest after absolutely nailing her recall.' Also, a lot of these sessions took place indoors. Margot was a big fan of doing things indoors when it was the end of October; it had been raining all week and she'd had to purchase a padded, waterproof anorak, which she was trying to style out, but thus far, it had defeated her.

Still, it was warm and had lots of pockets for all the essential items that hadn't been essential a few weeks ago: poo bags, dog treats; anti-bacterial hand gel (those poo bags were awfully thin), a flashing LED light to clip onto Blossom's collar when they walked home on the dark nights. And Margot's new dog-walking anorak was perfect for their first training session on a Sunday morning in the middle of a North London park.

'You didn't think about one-on-one training, maybe, like, inside?' she asked Will, trying hard to keep her voice light and not at all accusatory. Sunday mornings, if Margot managed to surface before noon, used to be about bottomless brunches with her friends and flicking through the Sunday supplements.

Will obviously hadn't felt the need to buy a Dog-walking Anorak of Doom. He was wearing a navy pea coat, though it had capacious pockets, a grey woollen scarf tucked around the collar. His face was pinched and scrubbed pink in the scouring wind that whistled across the open space, but it just made his cheekbones even more pronounced.

'At least it's not raining,' he said. 'Note to self: next time I decide to take on a half-share in a dog, make sure that it's during warmer weather.'

This was a different Will. It had been fifteen minutes since they'd met at the park entrance and found their way to a cordoned-off area next to the cricket pitch where dogs learned to be well-behaved. Fifteen minutes, and not once had Will made a sarcastic remark, or been terse to the point of rudeness. On the contrary, he'd made every effort to engage Margot in conversation, not that engaging her in conversation was ever difficult. As more than one of her exes had commented dourly, 'You do love to talk, don't you?'

Blossom was a little subdued now they'd arrived at their destination. She'd been far from subdued getting there though, yanking them this way and that every time she saw a squirrel. Margot had never realised how bountiful squirrels were in autumn, as they stored up food for winter and tormented dogs. One squirrel had even trolled Blossom by throwing a couple of mouldy acorns at her as they'd passed underneath a tree. Blossom, predictably, had then done a good impersonation of a demented hell beast.

She was hell-beasting now; snapping and snarling at any other dog that veered too close to them.

'Did you find this place on Google?' Margot asked Will. ''Cause, after you sent me the details, I couldn't find it when I looked it up.'

'If it's not on Google, does it even exist?' Will asked, but he was smiling; a nice smile, not the usual supercilious curl of his top lip. Margot smiled back. The memory of that brief frisson they'd shared when they'd first met sent a tendril of warmth snaking its way along her spine. Though that could have been the bio-warming technology of her high-performance outer-wear. 'It's a word-of-mouth kind of place. I phoned up the rescue centre and they recommended it. Talking of which, isn't that . . . um, er, Dreadlocks?'

A woman with an even more utilitarian anorak than Margot's, her dyed orange dreadlocks twisted into a topknot, was waving at them. 'Sophie from the rescue centre? Yes, it is.'

Sophie came bounding over. 'Hello, hello! And hello, Blossom! She's looking so well. Her fur grew back in, then?'

'Literally overnight,' Margot said as Blossom nosed the hand that Sophie was proffering. 'She's put some weight on, too.'

'Despite the fact that she's decided to be picky. Only the finest organic, fresh food for Blossom,' Will added, and again, he wasn't even being sarcastic but speaking the truth.

'Right,' Margot agreed. 'For a stray who no one wanted, she's become very bougie.'

Margot would have been quite happy to stand there and regale Sophie with fascinating facts about Blossom, but Sophie, who helped out with the training, said they were about to start and all too soon they were standing in a shivering line along with the other new members of the class.

Three dogs and their assorted owners were sent off to the puppy socialisation area, which left the rest of them eyeing each other up. Particularly Blossom, who took great objection to the Schnauzer next to them.

They were banished to the end of the line so Blossom could have her space. 'Please, sit down, Bloss,' Margot begged, but Blossom's blood was up and she wasn't going to listen to reason.

'Go on, sit!' Will made a gesture with his hand last seen when Barbara Woodhouse was still on television. Blossom ignored the command and jumped at Margot, who tried to push her gently away.

Margot and Will did their best to pay attention as they were instructed on current borough regulations. 'An on-the-spot fine of eighty pounds if you're caught not picking up your dog's business. Who's got their poo bags with them?'

Will flinched as Margot pulled out a clutch of green, biode-gradable poo bags and waved them enthusiastically. 'Might as well get credit where we can.'

'Like getting a mark for writing your name correctly at the top of your exam sheet?' Will pulled out his own collection of poo bags. 'We're certainly not going to get credit for anything else. Blossom, sit!'

They were shown how to examine their dogs; opening their mouths to check their teeth, then moving along their bodies with firm hands and finally lifting their tails. Blossom abso-lutely did not want her tail lifted and her business end scruti-nised, not that Margot could blame her.

Then they moved on to calling their dogs to check that they recognised their own names. Something that Blossom failed at miserably because she'd clocked another squirrel and was on her hind legs, front paws on the railings, and if Will hadn't had such a firm hand on her harness, they wouldn't have seen her for dust.

Sit, as had already been established, was a miserable failure. Blossom was determined to behave as if she'd been recently possessed.

Jim, a grizzled old man in a dark green fleece almost obscured by patches from dog shows he'd attended, who'd apparently been running the dog-training classes for decades, bore down on them.

'We're about to be expelled before the end of the first lesson,' Will muttered.

'Why don't we take a walk?' Jim suggested. 'Maybe try putting her lead on her collar and not her harness?'

'We can't do that,' Will said firmly.

'She pulls so hard that she starts choking,' Margot explained. 'I know it doesn't seem like it, but she's actually much better behaved on her harness.'

They walked along a quieter path and Margot gave up a silent prayer as Blossom at last calmed down and, miracle of miracles, sat down when she was asked so Jim could examine her collar.

'I see you've got both your phone numbers on here, but by law, you need your surnames and your postcodes, too,' he said. There were so many tedious things you had to do to qualify as a responsible dog owner.

'Maybe we should swap tags each week?' Will suggested.

Margot nodded 'And we should put her name on the tag too, right?'

Jim took out a treat. 'It's up to you.' He placed the treat almost at ground level and Blossom promptly lay down. 'Good down, Blossom.'

Margot and Will looked sourly at the furry, four-legged love of their lives who was proving to be an appalling suck-up. 'We should definitely put her name on the tag,' Margot said.

'Absolutely not,' Will said in that superior tone of voice that always made Margot's entire being bristle. 'That's just asking for someone to call her name then walk off with her.'

'But we're not going to let her off-lead, and what if we were out walking and I got run over or you had a fit and died . . .'

'Are you going somewhere with this?' Will asked. 'Preferably in the next half hour.'

Margot had known the nice guy act couldn't last forever. At least now it was perfectly all right to glare at him. 'If something happened to one of us while we were out and she was left on her own, then at least people would know what her name was. That would be some comfort. Blossom, don't jump up!'

Blossom was no longer doing a 'good down' but pawing at Margot, and Will was doing that hand gesture again and a firm 'Sit!' which Blossom ignored.

Then she saw another squirrel and set off, pulling Margot through a turned over flower bed so she was scratched by the thorns of a dormant rose bush.

It took Jim and his soft but authoritative 'Blossom, come! Good come!' to get Blossom back and then, because she knew she'd tried every last one of Margot's nerves, she decided to roll on her back to see if there was any chance of a belly rub.

'Not bloody likely,' Will said.

Margot was in complete agreement. 'No belly rubs ever again.'

'OK, I've seen enough,' Jim said. He gestured in the direction of the little prefab hut by the cricket pitch where all the cones, plastic fencing and other dog-training paraphernalia were kept. 'Let's step into my office.'

Was he going to take Blossom away from them? Did he have that kind of power? Margot pulled a face at Will, who shook his head and shrugged.

Instead of phoning the dog warden to have Blossom impounded, Jim pulled out two white plastic chairs so Margot and Will could sit down.

'She's not always like this,' Margot said, because she was determined to get a fair hearing. 'When we first got her, she was very timid and scared.'

'She would get on her back if another dog approached her, not lunge at them with her teeth bared,' Will explained. 'She's become a different dog over the last two weeks or so.'

'Oh my God, is it because we're sharing her and she's not getting the continuity of care that she needs?' This was what Margot had been dreading, their own version of *Sophie's Choice*, not that it had been Margot's choice, and if anyone was having Blossom full-time then it would be her. Though to be perfectly honest, she didn't particularly want sole custody of Blossom in her present incarnation. 'She only started behaving badly after Will's second week.'

'This isn't my fault,' Will snapped. 'She was fine until after *your* second week.'

'It's nobody's fault,' Jim said kindly. Margot was sure he was saying that just to make them both feel better. And if it was someone's fault, then it was more likely to be Will's because he was stand-offish, chilly and incapable of giving Blossom the love she needed. 'She was a stray and was picked up showing signs of neglect?'

'Maybe abuse too. She was very nervous around men,' Margot said pointedly and gave Will a sharp look. Not that Blossom was nervous around men anymore. Currently, she was nosing Jim's hand in the hope of more treats.

'So, she's had a tough time and lots of new experiences in the last few weeks, but she's got the message that she's now in a safe, loving space. She knows that she's got somewhere warm to sleep, she doesn't have to worry about being hungry or thirsty.' He stroked Blossom's muzzle with his knuckle. 'Which is why she's testing her boundaries. Getting to have a second puppyhood.'

'Aww ...' Margot could feel herself melting and, sensing weakness, Blossom abandoned Jim in favour of sitting down in front of Margot and prodding her with her paw until she got a treat. 'Um, good sit, Blossom,' Margot added weakly, because she'd absolutely let Blossom take advantage of her forgiving nature.

'She's going to be a lovely dog once she's dialled this back . . .'

'She's already a lovely dog,' Will insisted. It was his turn to get the paw and have to produce a treat. He couldn't praise Blossom for sitting down because she'd already been sitting down when she swivelled in his direction, so he went with a feeble, 'Good paw, Blossom.'

Jim leaned forward, his elbows resting on his knees. 'She's going to be a lovely dog, but right now she's taking the piss out of the pair of you.'

16

Will

After telling them off for spoiling Blossom and sending her mixed messages with their inconsistent behaviour, Jim was clear about what Will and Margot had to do. As well as the 'good sits' and the 'good downs' and turning in the opposite direction every time Blossom pulled, they needed to spend more time together.

He and Blossom . . . and Margot. This was not what Will had signed up for. It was hard right now to remember why he'd wanted a dog in the first place. Why he'd wanted Blossom and why he'd agreed to joint custody of her. Not just agreed, but instigated the arrangement.

'It's going to take *forever* just to get out of here,' Margot groaned as she came to a halt, Blossom still in forward motion, and turned around. 'This doesn't seem to be working.'

'Shall I have a go?'

'Thank you.' Margot relinquished the lead, and because Blossom was completely taking the piss out of them, she took the opportunity to snatch Will's glove out of his pocket (the treat pocket, needless to say) and send it flying into the middle of a muddy puddle with a toss of her head.

It was as if she'd done it on purpose. But surely that couldn't be the case, and anyway, hadn't Jim just given them both a lecture on how wrong it was to anthropomorphise their dog?

Margot went to retrieve his glove and narrowly avoided face-planting into the puddle herself. 'Sundays never used to feature mud quite so highly.'

'I miss my former mud-free life,' Will said bitterly. 'Now I spend all my time brushing it off of Blossom then vacuuming dried mud out of every corner of my flat.'

Margot smiled. Not her smug smile but something a lot more sympathetic. 'Regretting buying that white sofa now, are you?'

'You have no idea.' Blossom yet again began her infernal tugging at the lead, and Will quickly did a U-turn and started walking in the direction they'd just come from. 'How are we ever meant to get out of this park, if we have to keep turning around?'

It took them a good hour. By then, Blossom's bottom half was black with mud. Will had always thought of mud as brown, but his new exposure to it, and because Blossom's favourite sniffing points were always perilously close to mini-bogs, meant that Will now knew that mud was black and viscous. Also, it didn't smell good.

'I'll have to give her a bath.' Margot sounded as if she might cry without too much provocation. 'Not sure that they'll even let us on the bus.'

'If I had the van then I'd give you a lift, but I came on the bus too.' It was so much better when they weren't sniping at each other. Jim had said that that was another thing they had to stop, arguing in front of Blossom.

'You can argue all you like when she's not around,' he'd told them. 'But all this nonsense about what the other is doing and not doing is getting you nowhere fast. You're not in competition. You both love her, that's enough.'

Will had rather thought that they were in competition. In a constant tug of war for Blossom's affections, but she seemed to like them both. (Will would have preferred to think that her tail wags were more effusive when she saw him, that her snuggles were deeper, but it was simply not true. Or at least, it was hard to quantify.)

'It's all right,' Margot said with one of her hearty sighs. 'I can manage.'

'I could get the bus with you and lend a hand with bath time?' It wasn't the most enthusiastic offer he'd ever made. Mary would be cross that he was a no-show for Sunday lunch and would spend most of Monday morning sighing in a passive aggressive manner while insisting that, 'I'm fine. No, really, I'm fine.'

'Well, I suppose, if you don't mind.' Margot's acceptance of his grudging offer was far from heartfelt either.

Will had forgotten how small Margot's flat was; how colourful and cluttered.

The bathroom was no exception. Decorated with cream subway tiles and accents of black and mint green. There were bottles and jars and pots of lotions and unguents crammed into a full to bursting cabinet and a set of recessed shelves, as well as lined up on the tiled bath surround. Plants and scented candles jostled for space on the windowsill and while he detached the shower head from the wall, Margot opened another heavily stocked cupboard, which housed a grumbling boiler, to retrieve some towels.

All they needed to do now was retrieve Blossom, who'd slunk into the bedroom as soon as her lead had been unclipped and her harness removed. 'As if she instinctively knows she has to have a bath,' Margot marvelled. 'Though I haven't actually bathed her yet, just dabbed with doggy wet wipes.'

'She might like having a bath,' Will said without much hope, as Margot put a towel down in the tub so that Blossom wouldn't damage the enamel or slip. Will had to concede that she was very thoughtful like that; always ready with a gesture that would minimise someone else's discomfort.

They'd got off the bus at the same time as an old lady with her shopping trolley, and Margot had lifted the trolley down without even being asked, though she'd winced as it put a strain on her infamous wrenched shoulder. Even walking the fifty metres from the bus stop to her front door had involved saying hello to five different people.

Will had been back in Muswell Hill for over a year but he barely knew any of his neighbours. If it were impossible to avoid a regular customer or someone with a dog (unfortunately dog owners were a very chatty breed) then he'd reluctantly offer them a tight smile.

Much like he was doing now as Margot asked him to get Blossom while she started running a shallow bath. 'We have that moisturising lavender doggy shampoo from the pet superstore,' she said as Will advanced towards her bedroom – the flat was so small that she didn't even have to raise her voice to make herself heard. 'So, she'll smell nice as well as being freshly laundered.'

Blossom seemed quite happy to continue smelling like sewage. As soon as Will entered the bedroom, she disappeared under Margot's bed. Margot couldn't make do with a duvet and a couple of pillows like any sane person. She was what Sage would call 'extra', and so were the folded grey satin throw edged with pale pink pom-poms, the duvet cover reminiscent of a spring meadow, and approximately twenty pillows and cushions featuring everything from candy stripes to embroidered parrots.

The rest of the room, what Will could see of it amid the shelves inset on either side of the fireplace full of neatly folded clothes and neatly paired shoes at the bottom, two clothes rails, a shelf of books above the bed and a bedside table featuring yet more books, was painted pale pink. It was as if Will had stepped inside a seashell. It was clearly and solely Margot's domain. Not the kind of room that was set for seduction or even had a regular male visitor (the other bedside table was notable for the vase of deep pink cactus dahlias that sat on top). There could be a boyfriend for all Will knew, but Margot hadn't mentioned one, and if there had been a significant other in her life, then surely he would have come up in conversation? Anyway, a boyfriend would have taken a very dim view of his beloved sharing a dog with another man and texting that man with the frequency that Margot texted Will.

He tried to imagine what kind of man Margot would be attracted to. He'd have to be very good-looking to come up to her exacting standards, and someone who knew his own mind so he wouldn't let Margot ride roughshod over him. Although maybe Margot's hypothetical boyfriends enjoyed it when she rode roughshod over them. She'd be very forthright in bed, very firm . . .

'Has Blossom made a run for it? What's taking so long?' Margot shouted, pulling Will away from such dangerous thoughts and back to retrieving Blossom from under the bed.

Her potato-shaped bottom, tail at half mast, was poking out, but Blossom was obviously counting on the fact that if she couldn't see Will, then he couldn't see her.

'We have a bit of a situation,' he called out as he heard a muffled exclamation, then Margot was at the doorway.

'Should we tug her out?' she wondered. 'I don't want to damage her back legs. They always look so delicate.'

'Or traumatise her.'

They both stared at Blossom's generous rear end, then back at each other.

'We could google it . . .' Margot said doubtfully, but Will was all out of any other ideas, so he pulled his phone out of the back pocket of his jeans.

'Have you got any peanut butter?' he asked Margot after a quick and productive Google search.

'That's the most rhetorical question since records began,' Margot said, and she headed for the kitchen.

In the end, they'd had no choice but to pull Blossom out from under the bed so Will could carry her, face like thunder, paws pedalling furiously, to the bathroom and put her in ten centimetres of lavender-scented water. She sat there, shoulders hunched, huge head hanging down, body averted from the flannel in Margot's hand, until Will brought out their big gun.

He opened the family sized tub of peanut butter, spooned out a generous dollop and smeared it on the tiled wall nearest to Blossom's miserable face.

Her nostrils twitched and though she clearly didn't want to give in to such a blatant attempt at bribery, she really was *highly* food motivated.

As she licked the peanut butter off the tiles, Margot scrubbed her and Will rinsed her down with a gentle cascade of warm water from the shower head.

The whole operation only took seven minutes and a minimal amount of splashing before Blossom was deposited on the bathmat and wrapped in a towel. She tolerated Margot's brisk rub down then sat there, staring at Will and Margot both sitting on the edge of the tub.

It wasn't the forlorn, desperate expression of the very damaged dog from a few weeks ago. Oh no. This was the pissed-off face of a dog who'd been done an egregious wrong. Will had never seen such spectacular side-eye before.

'You are ridiculous,' he said to Blossom. 'But you smell much better than you did.'

'Absolutely ridiculous,' Margot echoed. 'I'd forgotten that she had white bits rather than grey bits.'

Margot stood up and stretched, and even though she was wearing a loose-fitting sweatshirt, which proclaimed Woman

Up, Will had to avert his eyes. Margot wasn't a woman, not in that way. She was Blossom's other owner. They were, as Margot was far too fond of saying, co-pawrents. So there was no point in Will appreciating that Margot *was* a woman and that she had some very admirable qualities, like the pale strip of soft-looking, intriguing flesh that had momentarily been revealed.

It would only lead to complications and sharing Blossom was already complicated enough. Time that he made his excuses and—

'I don't know about you, but I am ready for a large glass of wine,' Margot said with great feeling. 'Red or white?' She left the bathroom as if she was expecting Will to not just stay, but to follow her into the kitchen. So he did.

'Not for me, thanks,' he said as Margot turned to him with a bottle in each hand.

'Oh, I have beer instead?'

Will shook his head. 'No, really . . .'

'Well, what about a gin and tonic?' She smiled brightly. 'Bar's in the other room. Who doesn't love a gin and tonic?'

'I don't,' Will said baldly, because in his experience it was better to just come out with it. He followed her into the living room. 'I don't drink alcohol.'

He hadn't even noticed the little vintage sideboard in the living room, but Margot had already slid its door open to reveal an impressive collection of bottles. She shut it quickly and Will prepared himself for one of her usual onslaughts or interrogations about why he didn't drink. Was he on antibiotics? Was he an alcoholic and how many days had he been sober?

He'd heard them all, numerous times.

'In that case, I bet you're in need of a cuppa,' she said, her expression as neutral as a can of magnolia paint. 'Builders, isn't it?'

He really should have been long gone, but instead he sat down in the armchair while Margot made tea and something to eat ('You must be hungry. I got a sourdough loaf yesterday, which I need to use up. Do you want a posh cheese toastie?') and watched as Blossom, still indignant and still with the stink-eye, rubbed every inch of her newly clean body against the sofa.

There was something cosy and comforting about sitting in Margot's wonderfully capacious armchair while his part-time dog now repeatedly dug her snout into an embroidered velvet cushion. From the kitchen, he could hear the kettle coming to a boil, a drawer opening then the sound of cutlery against crockery and the wonderful, Sunday afternoon-ish aroma of toast and cheese under the grill.

He really should be going but he didn't want to move, so Will stayed exactly where he was.

17

Margot

To celebrate their new *entente cordiale* and to show Blossom that both Mummy and Daddy loved her equally, Will turned up at Ivy+Pearl on Tuesday lunchtime so they could walk Blossom together.

'There's a man here for Margot. Apparently she's expecting him,' Audrey announced over the intercom, which was only ever used in an emergency. Evidently a man turning up for Margot was an emergency.

'You're dating?' Jacques swivelled around in his chair so Margot got the full benefit of his martyred expression. 'You didn't think to run this past me first?'

'Not a date. Blossom's other ... um ...' Despite the long lecture from Jim on Sunday, Margot still didn't like to think of him as Blossom's other owner. In fact, she didn't like to think that she was Blossom's owner either. Blossom wasn't a thing, a possession. She was a living being with her own likes and dislikes who had allowed Margot to share her life. 'Can I say co-pawrent?'

'Not out loud and never again!' Jacques said, clapping his hands over his ears as, through the glass, Margot saw Will arrive at the second floor. 'He's quite good-looking. Just your type.'

'I don't have a type,' Margot said crossly, because she didn't. Having a type implied that she was close-minded and ...

'He's breathing, so he's your type isn't he?' Jacques had just had his autumn/winter looks signed off and the success had gone to his head.

Audrey's announcement had brought everyone to the doors of their offices so they could get a good gawp at the man for Margot. Even Tansy – Margot would have expected better from her.

But the person most pleased to discover that Margot might actually have found a man who was committed enough to come and see her at work wasn't even a person. It was Blossom, who had been slumbering and farting and snoring under Margot's desk, but the blaring intercom announcement had woken her up.

She shot out of her bed, her claws tap-tap-tapping on the wooden floor as she hurled herself at Will, who'd been standing there with a discomfited look. As Blossom jumped up at him, though Margot had told her a million times not to do that, the aloof expression was wiped off his face to be replaced with a smile of pure delight.

'Maybe Audrey should have said that there was a man here to see Blossom,' Jacques drawled, then yelped as Margot dug him in the shoulder on her way out of their office.

Instead of telling Blossom to get down, or, as Jim suggested, gently walking into her so she had no choice but to put all four paws back on the ground, Will picked her up, one arm securely under her bottom, so she could put her paws on his shoulder and lick his face.

'You shouldn't let her do that!' would have been Margot's opening salvo, to mask the bitter pang of jealousy that Blossom would never let Margot pick her up, but mindful that they were meant to be presenting a united front, she settled for a non-confrontational, 'Hello, I'll just get my coat.'

When Margot returned with her coat, most of the Ivy+Pearl

workforce had found a reason to loiter by the big table so they could get a proper look at Will, who now had Blossom sitting so she could give him a high five.

'There's something about seeing a man so obviously adored by his dog that's making my fanny throb,' Cora muttered to Margot's horror; she hoped that Will hadn't heard her. But no, he was too busy being fawned over by Amina.

'Yes, she's about three, picked up as a stray in Neasden,' he was saying as if Margot hadn't already told them about Blossom's ignominious start in life. 'But she's fully embracing middle-class life now.'

'Well, we all love her,' Amina said in a breathy voice, even though she was a newlywed and shouldn't have been eyeing Will up and down like she was wondering if she had room for him in her flat in Dalston. The flat she shared with *her husband*.

'OK, let's go,' Margot said cheerily, though she felt little cheer and more like having strong words with her colleagues, but especially Audrey, who usually made all visitors wait in reception.

'This is a nice place to work,' Will remarked once they were out on the street and away from prying eyes and nosy beaks. 'Very convenient to have Primrose Hill so close by. She's still pulling then,' he added.

'I don't think she's ever going to stop pulling,' Margot said sadly. 'I know that I'm meant to stop and start walking her in the other direction, but I only get an hour for lunch.'

'I won't tell Jim if you won't.' Will held up a brown paper bag that Margot hadn't noticed he was holding. She hoped it contained some kind of food because she was starving. 'I have a secret weapon in here.'

'What kind of secret weapon? It's not a no-pull harness is it, because Jim was very against them and I think they're quite cruel . . .'

'But Jim was very pro long lines,' Will said pulling out a long, long, long, long red lead. 'Shall we try it out once we get into the park?'

The long line would give Blossom freedom to roam and explore and sniff other dog's wee-mails, but give Margot and Will control over her if she started any argy bargy with another dog.

As soon as they were through the gates and on the lower slopes of Primrose Hill, Will unclipped Blossom's lead from her harness and attached the long line.

For the first few seconds Blossom was far more interested in eating a particularly tufty clump of grass. Sometimes it was like walking a miniature cow.

'So far, so good,' Margot decided, but she'd spoken too soon, because when Blossom realised that she was no longer tethered to a measly 138 centimetres, she took off at a gallop.

The long line slithered after her, stretching out in all its ten-metre glory until Blossom reached the end of the line and the almighty tug reverberated down the length of rope and jolted every bone in Margot's body. 'Sweet mother of God, I've dislocated my shoulder!' she squeaked. 'Your turn.'

Will didn't have much better luck. It turned out that rather than appreciating the greater freedom that the long line gave her, it made Blossom furious that said freedom was just a cruel illusion.

Margot had also never realised what malicious gits other dogs could be. They'd approach Blossom and when she went berserk, diving after them and snapping her teeth as Will tried to reel her in like a prize marlin, the other dogs would tease her. They'd come closer then dart away, making Blossom even more frantic.

'They're just being friendly,' owner after owner shouted gaily as their dickhead dogs tormented Blossom.

'We could get her a yellow lead and a yellow coat, which signifies she's a nervous dog,' Margot told Will, who looked unimpressed.

'Most people wouldn't know what a yellow lead signified,' he pointed out, as he succeeded in getting Blossom close enough to grab. 'And I'm not sure yellow is her colour. Sit!'

It was a very firm, very authoritative sit, that made even Margot want to drop her bottom to the ground. Instead she settled for a shiver. The good kind of shiver. There was something to be said for a man who could take charge in a crisis. But she didn't want to get the good kind of shiver from Will. No good would ever come of *that*. It was time for a pivot. 'You can also get a coat that says "I need my space, I'm a bit of a twat",' she revealed.

Will clipped Blossom back on the shorter lead. 'Do they do them for humans too?' Yup, the good shiver was gone, but before Margot could insist in the strongest possible terms that she wasn't a twat, he added, 'It would save me from getting stuck in these long conversation with other dog walkers. They really like a chat, don't they?'

'I *love* talking to people about their dogs,' Margot gasped. 'It's one of my favourite things about having a dog.'

'Really? It's one of my worst.'

She still couldn't tell when he was joking. His face, unless he was gazing at Blossom when she was being particularly delightful, really was stuck like that. Grim, forbidding, detached – much like his general demeanour.

But surely that was *because* Margot didn't know him well enough. They shared a dog and she'd been to his flat and she knew that he was a florist. Correction: he worked in the floristry business. She also knew that he had a family; and she presumed that he was single. Although Will could be married with two kids or divorced with five kids or out with a different woman every night for all Margot knew. It was hard to imagine Will in flirt mode, though she was sure if he put his mind to it he could be quite devastating. Sometimes, when he was cooing at Blossom, lavishing her with endearments in a husky voice, Margot had felt a very slight quiver. Much like she was feeling now as she pictured Will leaning in to flirt with some random woman . . .

Margot was forced to take stock. So far, in their short acquaintance, Will had made Margot feel many things: teeth-grinding, fist-clenching irritation, a quick white-hot flash of anger every now and then, and also a near-constant seething resentment. But he'd also been responsible for a couple of frissons, a good shiver and a very slight quiver.

What was wrong with her? Was she so starved of male company, so despairing of likely candidates to build a future with, that she was even considering – No! Not even going there!

It was simply because outside of work, Will was the only man that she saw on a regular basis. God, she really needed to find some new dating apps to install because she was fed up with swiping left on the same sorry faces again and again.

By now they'd lapsed into silence broken only when Will veered off path.

'One of my other least favourite things about dog ownership is having to deal with this,' he said bending down, face squinched up to avoid any fumes.

Margot waited until Will was gingerly carrying a full poo bag between thumb and forefingers, then did a quick inventory of her internal organs to make sure that there were no quiver, shivers or frissons. There weren't and, quite frankly, she'd have been alarmed if there had been given what she'd just witnessed Will doing.

But, by the same token, she wasn't grinding her teeth or clenching her fists in irritation either. They'd somehow achieved a state of benign neutrality, if not harmony, which had to be a good thing for Blossom's sake. This was all about Blossom, after all.

'Hang on! About turn!'

'What?' They'd been walking, but now they stopped and did a swift one-eighty, though why they were bothering when it didn't seem to have the least effect on Blossom's lead-tugging, she didn't know. Margot tutted in pure frustration but when she glanced at Will he was staring down at Blossom, his austere features softened, the tiniest of smiles hovering on his lips. 'You really care about Blossom, don't you?'

'I do,' Will sighed, as if the caring was against his better judgement. 'Even when she's making actual "nom nom" noises as she's eating her dinner; if a person did that, I'd never speak to them again.' Which was reasonable enough as far as Margot was concerned, even though she was a person who said 'pawrent' out loud.

'I also like the way that when we're cuddled up in be—'

Margot tutted as they stopped. Again. Had Will been about to say 'bed?'

'I knew it! She is sleeping in your bed, isn't she?'

'Of course she's not,' Will said stoutly. 'Cuddled up on the sofa, I was about to say, and how I like it when she headbutts my arm until I lift it up and put it round her.'

'That is cute,' Margot agreed. She wanted to pursue the thorny topic of where exactly Blossom slept when she was at Will's but, in the interests of diplomacy and not arguing in front of their charge, she decided to let it go.

Face screwed up again, Will dropped the poo bag in the correct bin. 'Should we start heading back?'

'We should,' Margot said without much enthusiasm, as this afternoon she was going to troubleshoot a problem with a pattern for a jersey jumpsuit with a wrap-style bodice. Basically, a onesie for women who wouldn't be seen dead in a onesie.

'And I suppose another reason why I care so much about Blossom is that my mother adores her. Anything that makes my mother happy is all right with me.' The tiny smile upgraded to a full grin. Will had dimples. Who even knew?

Margot was instantly full of questions. So many questions. What did Will's mother think about the whole co-pawrenting thing? How did his father get on with Blossom? Was his father still around, because Will had never mentioned him? But Margot stopped herself because if Will wanted to tell her then he would. The trick was to stay quiet (something Margot always struggled with), then the other person would speak to fill up the space. It was a technique she used to great effect on dates – it would bring even the quietest man out of his shell because who didn't love talking about themselves?

In the six or so months since she and George had parted ways, and long before George had come into her life, Margot had been on more dates than she could remember. They'd all merged into a blur of men's faces, glasses of white wine spritzer because she didn't want to get drunk with all the dangers that could pose and hands relaxed in her lap while she jiggled her toes or rotated her ankle and generally fidgeted under the table, while a man talked about himself and didn't ask Margot a single question.

'You're not getting off that lightly,' Will said, interrupting Margot's unwelcome reminiscences of first dates past. 'What's your favourite thing about Blossom?'

18

Will

'Just one thing? It's impossible to narrow it down,' Margot complained. She gestured with one hand at Blossom who was tugging Will down the steep path towards the gate. 'I love her Beyoncé strut. I love the way she leans into my legs when we're on the bus or she's sitting under my desk. There's something so satisfying about the weight of her. She's like a proper dog,' Margot mused. 'To think I was planning on getting something small and fluffy.'

'I couldn't see you with something small and fluffy,' Will said, because despite her addiction to soft furnishings and the cutesy growl whenever she addressed Blossom, there was something fundamentally no-nonsense about Margot.

'It was the portability that I was drawn to. Nothing portable about Blossom.' Hearing her name, Blossom looked up at Margot, who instantly reached into her pocket for a treat as per Jim's instructions for whenever she made eye contact. 'Good look, Blossom.'

'So, that's what you love most about Blossom?' Will prompted. 'That she's a chonk?'

Margot nudged Will with her elbow. The first time he'd seen her at the rescue kennel, he'd thought she was soft. Too soft. Now, the power of her nudge nearly winded him. 'Did you just say chonk?'

He had. Out loud. 'You have no witnesses and I'll deny it in court,' he said firmly and Margot rolled her eyes.

'I can't believe you just called Blossom a chonk when she isn't, she's just big-boned. Like me.'

There was something different about Margot today. At first Will had wondered if it was because they were doing their best to not fall into the familiar pattern of bickering in front of Blossom. But it wasn't just that Margot in relaxed mode was different – Will realised that she looked different.

Usually, she was in jeans, wellies and a top with a feminist message. More recently in a voluminous padded anorak that could be repurposed as a tent. Her curly hair pulled back in a ponytail, face set in a querulous expression.

He'd only ever seen Dog Walking Margot, and today he was with Work Margot, who was wearing a dress: something black with flowers on it that swished when she walked, with green tights and black ankle boots. No muddy trekking through the woods or across the Heath today but sticking firmly to the tarmac paths.

Her hair was still pulled back but her eyes seemed larger, her skin rosier, her lips ... her lips looked very ... *nice*. Will had been around enough women to finally twig that today Margot was wearing make-up. She looked perfectly fine without make-up, but with it, she looked *really* fine. And if she were big-boned, then being big-boned was really working for her too.

'You look all right to me,' Will muttered, then wished he'd kept quiet, because it wasn't like Margot had asked for his opinion on what she looked like, so there was no need for him to offer it. Also Will had lived on the earth long enough to know that when a woman did want your opinion on how she looked, ninety-nine times out of a hundred it was a trap and your answer was going to get you into a world of trouble.

'Then why are you staring at me like that?' Margot demanded, elbow poised again, but she took pity on Will and his ribs and decided not to deploy it for a second time.

'Anyway, this needs some serious thought. I have so many favourite things about Blossom that I don't want to reel off the first one that comes to mind, then realise later that I've missed out on something vitally important. But for the record, I love that she smells like warm corn snacks,' Margot said dreamily. 'Especially when she's been curled up and sleeping. Sometimes I sniff her belly, is that weird?'

There was no point in dissembling. 'So weird.'

'Nothing wrong with a little bit of weird,' Margot said, with a fond look at Blossom, who'd stopped pulling in favour of walking with her nose on the ground. 'Oh, Jim says that she's not meant to do that either.'

'I think we've had enough excitement and correction for one walk.'

'You've got that right,' Margot agreed, as they continued to amble downhill towards the park exit.

'You could always message me when you've narrowed down your favourite things about Blossom,' Will suggested. The devil on his shoulder made him add: 'With bullet points.'

Margot put a hand to her heart as if he'd struck her a killer blow. 'So mean,' she complained, but it was without a scowl or a darkening flash of her blue eyes. Instead, it was like they were playing a volley, lobbing balls back and forth. Not to score points or catch the other one out, but for the sheer pleasure of keeping the ball in the air. 'One of those messages you never, ever reply to?'

'I'd feel guilty about that, but then you only reply to about twenty-five per cent of my messages.' Will knew that they both had to do so much better when it came to their electronic communication. 'It's just as well that we've decided to spend more time together. For Blossom's sake.'

'Yes, we're only doing it for Blossom,' Margot agreed, a little too eagerly for Will's liking. He wasn't *that* awful to be around. 'And talking of which, I also love the way that she's always so pleased to see me, even if I've only nipped out to get a pint of milk from across the road.' Margot gave a small, sad huff. 'Although sometimes I wonder if it's just relief that she hasn't been abandoned again.'

'It's hard to know what she remembers and what she doesn't. When we get the broom out to sweep up in the shop at the end of the day, she runs and hides,' Will admitted guiltily, though it was no reflection on him.

'Yeah, and when we see the bin men throwing rubbish sacks into a dustcart, she goes absolutely crazy,' Margot shared. 'Much worse than when she's seen a squirrel. Poor Blossom . . . I know they say that dogs live in the moment, but they obviously have some memories of their past.'

'But we're helping her build new memories every day,' Will said firmly, because it did no good to keep reliving the past again and again. It didn't change anything. The past had still happened; shaped you, or rather, pulled you into a shape that was twisted and bent, and then you were left to try and right yourself. But if the past left its marks, then he had to believe that so did everything that came after, especially if it was good stuff. 'We're almost back at your place.'

They'd left Primrose Hill and were now walking back along Regent's Park Road, the smudgy grey building where Margot did her fashion stuff in view.

It was time for Will to hand over the lead. 'Well, this hasn't been too painful,' he said, and Margot's face fell. 'Not that I expected it to be painful.'

'In that case, shall we do a walk together on Saturday, if you're not going to be too busy in the shop?' Margot suggested.

She *still* seemed to think that Will worked *in* the shop. That the business was just one flower shop and Will only worked there, taking money and wrapping bunches of mixed blooms and advising customers of what was in season, as he had done when he worked school holidays and weekends when he was a teenager. And yes, true, he did all of that, but he did so much more.

Probably wasn't the time to get into that now. He still got that feeling, like his insides were plummeting to the ground, like a lift that had snapped its cables, when he thought about the circumstances that had led him backwards rather than onwards to further glory.

'We're not actually that busy on Saturdays,' was what he did say. 'Fridays, yes, everyone wants flowers for the weekend, but Saturday, they can spare me for the afternoon. Shall I come to yours for twelve?'

'Perfect,' Margot said. They'd reached Ivy+Pearl now and she tapped a code into the security pad on the wall. There was a buzz and she pushed the door open, so she was half in, half out.

There was one brief moment of exquisite awkwardness as they both considered the appropriate way to say goodbye.

Will bent down to pat Blossom's side. 'Bye, Blossom,' he said, then straightened up. 'See you Saturday.' He held up his hand in a brief salute and Margot smiled and waggled the fingers of one hand, until Blossom had had enough of both of them and dragged Margot through the door.

19

Margot

All too soon, it was suddenly December and very definitely winter. The mornings were dark, and in the afternoons the light was gone by four. All the leaves had fallen from the trees, bare branches silhouetted against barren grey winter skies, and turned to mulch underfoot.

But London looked quite splendid when she glittered with frost and shone with twinkling lights. In Highgate, the local residents' association had even considered adorning the public conveniences opposite Margot's flat (though as public conveniences went, they were very picturesque and had the look of a small country cottage) with fairy lights, but decided that was going too far.

Margot was pleased that the cold weather meant less mud. She was also pleased to be busy at work on spring/summer of the year after next, because if there was one antidote to the cold, icy weather, it was thinking about what kind of bikinis women would want to wear eighteen months from now.

But as the month flew past on steroids and Christmas grew ever closer, Margot felt the usual despondence take hold. Each year was dotted with difficult dates: birthdays, anniversaries, and solemn occasions that she marked by lighting a candle, but these dates were personal only to Margot and the losses she'd suffered, the ache that never really went away. Christmas was more of an all-encompassing hurt. Every advert on telly, every conversation at work or with friends

about plans for Christmas were really about family, together-
ness, belonging, all the things so desperately lacking in
Margot's life. Still, December also brought endless Christmas
party invites and she attended every single one.

One party and one conversation with one stranger could
alter the trajectory of Margot's life. All she needed was one
age-appropriate, financially solvent man who didn't describe
all his exes as 'crazy' and didn't think that settling down
equated to Margot trying to trap him. Otherwise Margot was
looking at forty, then fifty, then sixty still with no family of her
own but at least six rescue dogs. 'I call it the manypaws,'
hooted one of her new dog-walking friends, who was sixty-
five, happily divorced and besotted with her three ex-racing
greyhounds who were all equally besotted with her.

What was it about Christmas that shone a bright light
into the nooks and crevices of Margot's life and found it
wanting? Margot had a lovely flat, a fulfilling job, tons and
tons of friends and Blossom. And of course, Margot had her
logical family, but this Christmas, for better or worse, they
were all headed off to spend the holidays with their biological families.

'At the dreaded in-laws this year,' Tracy said at their annual
Christmas brunch. Back in the day, this annual event used to
start at eleven and finish when someone either threw up or
snogged someone they shouldn't. 'Wish me luck.'

This year Christmas brunch was at a dog-friendly gastro-
pub in Islington so Blossom could come, and Sarah could
catch up on her Christmas shopping afterwards. Sarah had
brought eleven-month-old Bertie along, who was immediately relinquished to Margot's tender care so she could wrap
her arms around his chunky, wriggly body and inhale great
whiffs off the top of his head, while Blossom looked on in
dismay.

Margot smiled and drank freely of the bottomless Prosecco, which she tried to mop up with buttermilk pancakes, so in the end she felt both tipsy and a little nauseous. She hugged Bertie to her, gently prising his fat fingers away from her curls and listened to her three friends moan about having to leave London to stay with parents, and on Boxing Day, travel once again to stay with in-laws. She commiserated with Tracy about her mother-in-law's dry turkey. She nodded in understanding when Sarah confessed that instead of buying ethically sourced wooden, educational toys for her children, she was going to buy the plastic, flashing tat that all their friends had. Margot was also very sympathetic about Jess's impending ordeal of being in the same house at the same time as all five of her sisters.

'World War Three will break out before midnight mass,' Jess grinned. 'But then we'll get home and Santa will have been, even though we know that it's really my dad who's drunk the sherry and eaten the mince pie. He won't go to church because he doesn't believe in organised religion.'

Margot may not be able to join in with her scant memories of family Christmases past, but she could still take pleasure in hearing about other people's Christmases, of photos in terrible matching festive jumpers, and how Sarah's family had once been evacuated after setting not just the Christmas pudding alight but her mother's velvet curtains too.

It wasn't until they were waiting for the bill, a mere two hours after they'd arrived, that Jess put a hand on Margot's arm. 'Margot, we've been banging on about our Christmases the entire time,' she said softly. 'Please tell me you're doing something nice on Christmas Day?'

Usually, Margot spent Christmas with Geoff and Daphne from upstairs, but this year they had booked to go away with friends. Margot's plan B of Jacques and Solange had been foiled when Solange had had the temerity to want to spend Christmas with her family in Rennes.

Margot could give the appearance of being happy and fulfilled and single all year, except for the 25 December, when she felt like the loneliest person in the world. As if she could sense Margot's distress from under the table, where she'd been sitting quietly, Blossom nudged Margot's leg with her big head.

'Well, it's my first Christmas with Blossom so it's going to be pretty special,' Margot said. The thought was genuinely uplifting. 'We'll sleep in until a decadent nine thirty then head off to watch the Christmas swimmers at the Ponds . . . Probably pop into the Flask for a glass of something and a sausage roll on the way back and then, because I don't even like turkey that much, Christmas dinner will be just the good bits: pigs in blankets, stuffing, roast potatoes, parsnips and carrots all done in goose fat.'

'Talk about doing Christmas right,' Tracy said. Margot could hear the relief in her voice that Margot wasn't going to be acting out scenes from both *Bridget Jones* and *A Christmas Carol*. The miserable scenes, not the scenes where Bridget snogged Mark Darcy or Tiny Tim's Christmas wishes all came true. 'Spare a thought for me as I'm forced to watch the *Morecambe and Wise* Christmas special with the volume turned up extra loud and the subtitles on.'

'And we'll be woken up at the arse crack of dawn by an over-excited toddler who'll spend the day hopped up on sugar,' Jess added. They'd now reached the part of Christmas brunch where her friends one-upped themselves to convince Margot that a singleton Christmas was infinitely preferable.

Margot took comfort from another Blossom headbutt until she did a swift calculation in her head. Then, although she was trying so hard to be upbeat and onboard the Single at Christmas train, Margot thought she might cry. Christmas fell during Will's week.

Suddenly, getting up at nine thirty and walking on the Heath and even popping into the Flask before heading home for a pared back, solitary Christmas dinner (no point in buying a turkey for just one person) didn't sound like fun. Without Blossom at her side, they were just the sad pastimes of a single woman desperately trying to fill the day.

Margot felt her phone vibrate and, glad of the distraction, retrieved it from her bag. It was a message from Will as if he too could sense her distress.

After training and handover tomorrow, can I tempt you over to Muswell Hill? Have a surprise. W

Margot couldn't imagine what the surprise was. Will wasn't the type to like or do surprises. But then she thought of how in the past few weeks, Will had become much better both at the giving and receiving of text messages, and despite her despondency, she felt a little better. Will was thinking about her. Planning a surprise for her. Like, they were becoming friends. Kind of.

Sarah and Jess were arguing over the bill as they always did. 'But I didn't have a cocktail, though I did have a coffee and you didn't . . .' Until Tracy chimed in with, 'For fuck's sake, just split it four ways like we usually do.'

Then it was a flurry of coats and kisses, and Jess had to rush off to pick up her daughter from a birthday party, and Sarah had Bertie back in his sling and a determined glint in her eye as she prepared to do battle in Tiger.

'You're all coming to me New Year's Eve, right?' Margot checked because even if Christmas plumbed the pits of despair, she always rocked New Year's Eve. She held an open house that started at eleven with a rolling, child-friendly brunch buffet and lasted until the last bottle of Prosecco had been drunk and the last firework had lit up the London sky.

'Wouldn't miss it,' Tracy said, brushing Margot's cheek with her lips. 'We'll come for the evening and stay to the bitter end.'

'You really don't mind if I bring my horrible kids?' Sarah checked, and Margot nodded and said that of course she didn't mind. She'd been wearing a smile for two hours now and it was making her face ache as much as her heart.

20

Will

Although the various women in his life, both family members and more fleeting female companions, always claimed that Will could be at best oblivious, and at worst insensitive, he could tell that there was something troubling Margot.

As they spent their Sunday morning training session walking with a stooge dog, Lady Violet, a very dignified basset hound, Margot was quiet. Normally, she'd be nattering away to Violet's owner, demanding to know Violet's antecedents, what she was fed and where she slept, but today she was monosyllabic. Even her curls seemed to have lost their usual bounce.

Will regretted having asked her back to Muswell Hill, which would involve at least a coffee before he could send her on her way. Then he remembered the surprise and couldn't help but smile.

'Blossom's appalling behaviour is nothing to laugh about,' Margot said primly. 'Neither is my wrenched shoulder. I'm booked to see an osteopath this week.'

'Well, let's swap then,' Will said, gesturing at Blossom who was tugging away on her lead and mouthing at the supremely unbothered Violet.

'No, it's all right.' Margot's tone was sharp, and on the way to Muswell Hill on the W7 bus, she sat and stared out of the window. It was left to Will to grimly keep the ball of conversation up in the air.

He told Margot about Sage's cunning plan to evade doing a law degree, which involved expanding the flower crown side of the business to include festivals and Women's Institute classes.

'She says it's the millennial version of flower arranging,' Will said as the bus chugged up the very steep hill that gave Muswell Hill its name. 'I think it has potential, but no ifs or buts, she's still doing a law degree.'

'We made flower crowns at the last hen weekend I went on,' Margot offered.

'Noted,' Will said, they hadn't even thought about the hen-do market.

'A twig got stuck in my hair and they had to cut it out,' Margot said glumly, and after that Will decided that maybe the five-minute walk to the surprise should be a time of quiet reflection.

For once, he wasn't riddled with self-doubt and uncertainty because this surprise was so, dare he even think it, adorable, that whatever was bothering Margot would drift away like the flimsy, striped convenience-store carrier bag that was being buffeted by the sharp breeze.

'Is the surprise in your flat?' Margot asked as they walked along the Broadway.

'Just across the road,' Will said, pausing as Blossom's pulling was increasing exponentially the closer they got to home. 'Shall we turn her round?'

'Let's not,' Margot sighed. 'We've been turning her round for *weeks* and it hasn't made the least bit of difference.'

She folded her arms – a difficult move in her bulky anorak – for the last two hundred metres until they came to a stop outside Woof! Will had spent more money in Woof! these last two months buying Blossom everything from organic food and treats to Staffy-proof chew toys (none of which turned out to be that Staffy-proof) than he'd spent on himself all year.

Margot didn't bother to hide her disappointment. 'Don't get me wrong, I love buying things for Blossom, but it's hardly a surprise.'

Will took a gentle hold of Margot's puffy sleeve so he could steer her a couple of crucial metres. He gestured clumsily at the window. '*This* is the surprise!'

Margot stared at the festive window display for a few seconds that were far too long for Will's liking.

'Oh! Oh, my!' She pursed her lips, blinked, then rooted in her pocket to pull out a pack of tissues.

'Is that the wind making your eyes water?' he asked hopefully; this was meant to be a good surprise.

'No, this window is making me cry,' Margot choked out. 'Blossom! I love your funny, furry face so much.'

Woof! had put out a call to find the 12 Dogs of Christmas to star in their festive window display. Mary had picked up the flyer, come up with the initial concept, and then Sage, well, Sage had really run with the idea.

They'd made Blossom a floral crown of holly ('But plastic holly, we don't want her precious head to get scratched') and mistletoe, then while Mary had thrown treats at her, Sage had snapped away with her camera. The result was a picture of Blossom making her finest derp face: crazy eyes going in different directions, and open mouth, pink tongue lolling out, while wearing the most festive of headpieces.

It was a foregone conclusion that Blossom would take centre stage in the window, with the eleven other dogs (their pictures much, much smaller) arranged around her full-length portrait.

Underneath each picture, was the question, 'Have you been a naughty or nice doggy?'

Blossom (or Sage, to be more accurate) had answered: 'Don't puppreciate you asking if I'm naughty. Am always the goodest of girls.'

'I love it,' Margot exclaimed, gloved hands clasped in rapture even though tears were still pouring down her cheeks. 'Can I get a copy of the picture?'

'It will be your Christmas present,' Will promised, though he hadn't been planning on getting Margot one. He didn't even do Christmas cards. 'Do you want to get a coffee?'

Margot's hands were twisting now. 'Coffee would be great.'

'There's a café across the road—'

'I know it's your week, but can I have Blossom for Christmas?' Margot burst out. 'It's a big ask but it would mean the world to me.'

'Let's get coffee.' Will could tell that Margot was in an agony of suspense, but this was a conversation that he didn't want to have standing in the middle of the street. He felt even crueller for making her wait while he bought coffee and bagels from the café. It wasn't until they were back at his flat and she was sitting on his sofa, still in her coat, that he could reply.

'I'm not saying this to be difficult or a dick,' he began, which pretty much promised that he was going to be difficult and a dick. Margot visibly deflated in her bulbous coat.

'I take it that's a no then,' she said dully.

'It's a no, but only because all my family are so excited about having Blossom with us for Christmas Day,' Will tried to explain, as Blossom wandered in from the kitchen where she'd been noisily drinking from her water bowl.

Now she burped then jumped up on the sofa to lean against Margot, who put her arm around her, but said nothing, simply stared down at her coffee, her face set and still.

Usually Margot wasn't one to hold back from expressing herself, so Will was left floundering. 'I thought you'd be spending Christmas with your family,' he said. 'You're a Londoner, right?'

'From Gospel Oak originally,' Margot revealed in a rusty voice, as if the tears weren't far off.

'Look, you don't want to be carting Blossom and a ton of presents across the Heath to Gospel Oak,' Will pointed out. 'I get that it's your first Christmas with her and you want it to be special but—'

'I'm not going to see my family for Christmas,' Margot said abruptly, the words all sticking together. 'It's just me.'

'I'm sorry.' Will meant it. He could understand, even empathise. Families were complicated and sometimes the best, the safest thing you could do for your own sanity was not to see them or speak of them or even know if they were alive or dead. 'How long have you been estranged?'

Margot raised her eyebrows and to Will's surprise she smiled. Not her usual grin, something more low-key. 'No! Not estranged.' She set down her coffee cup on the side table and finally unzipped her coat so she could shrug it off, as if she was settling in for a long explanation. Will braced himself. 'Dead, not estranged.'

Apparently the explanation wasn't going to be that long after all.

'I'm sorry,' he said again. 'Your parents, then? That must be tough not to have at least one of them around.'

'I've got used to it.' Margot wrapped both arms around Blossom so she could squeeze her and kiss the side of her face, which Blossom seemed to tolerate rather than actively enjoy. 'My parents were quite old when they had me. My mother was forty-five when I was born, my dad was fifty-four.'

Occasionally, Will wondered if he could bear to have children. He knew that he needed to come to a decision, make peace with the past sooner rather than later. So he'd still be young enough to be one of those engaged dads that played football and went camping and all the millions of other wholesome activities you'd do with your children, if you were a good, kind, generous father.

'Fifty-four is quite old,' he said carefully.

'Mick Jagger and Rod Stewart have had children much later, though I don't expect they're getting up to do night feeds or change nappies,' Margot said. 'I loved my dad, even though he was older than all my friends' dads. He took me swimming after school and to museums and there's no reason that he shouldn't have lived to a grand old age, but he was knocked down crossing the road when he was sixty-one.'

She'd been seven. When Will was seven, he wished that his dad was dead, but then he hadn't had the kind of father who took him swimming or to museums.

'That must have been hard,' Will offered awkwardly.

Margot nodded. 'If I'd had a much younger father, he might still have got knocked down and killed by a drunk driver. And then it was just me and my mum, and she was great too and I miss her so much . . .' Her voice became too thick for her to carry on. She turned her head away so Will couldn't see her face, but Blossom turned herself round in Margot's arms so she was able to put her paws on Margot's thighs and start licking her face.

Will got up, stood there for one helpless moment, then went to the kitchen to tear off a few sheets of kitchen roll. 'I'm a man living on my own. I don't have tissues,' he told Margot as he handed them to her, and she managed one hiccuppy laugh. Then she tried to manoeuvre Blossom into a more comfortable position by lifting Blossom's paws off her legs. 'Bloss, you weigh a ton.'

Blossom lay down so her front legs were now draped over Margot's thighs. Margot winced and tried to shift her again. 'She has the sharpest elbows.'

There was quite a lot of tussling until Blossom was persuaded to stop sitting on Margot and burrow against her instead, her head on Margot's lap, her eyes reproachful that Margot had dared to question her paw placement.

Will wished that they were done with the previous conversation, but he knew that they'd only taken a break. 'You were talking about your mum,' he prompted gently.

Margot shrugged. 'She died when I was eighteen. Cancer.'

'That really sucks,' Will said, because it did. He wasn't one for platitudes, but Margot seemed to appreciate the lack of clumsy condolences.

'It was the absolute worst. Beyond words. Not just because I loved her and we really were best friends, but Mum and Dad were both only children so there were no aunts and uncles, no cousins.' She smiled weakly. 'I'm the end of the line and I'm OK with that. Really OK. But at Christmas, I'm not as OK as I usually am.'

'I get that.' Will looked at Blossom who had now, inevitably, rolled onto her back and was prodding Margot with a paw until she got a belly rub.

'I might not have a "family" family.' The hand that wasn't rubbing a soft belly made quote marks in the air. 'But I've made myself a logical family. I have so many people in my life who love me, and I love them. Real ride or die people . . .'

'I'm glad.' Will had his "family" family who had to put up with him because they were bound together by blood and shared DNA and all the things that had happened to them, which meant that Will couldn't let anyone else get close enough to become logical family. 'You should have people like that in your life.'

'Usually I'd spend Christmas with friends, but this year they're all out of town.' Margot did that thing where she scrunched up her forehead, so her eyebrows almost touched in the middle. 'I wouldn't mind spending Christmas on my own if I had Blossom, because then I'm not really on my own . . . So do you think you might change your mind? Can I have her just for Christmas Day maybe?'

Despite what all his ex-girlfriends thought, Will wasn't made of stone. He had real feelings, real emotions, where possible he did try to do the right thing. So he did the only thing he could in the circumstances. 'You're not going to spend Christmas alone. Not on my watch,' he said forcefully. 'You will see Blossom on Christmas Day because you're going to spend Christmas with my family.'

And may God have mercy on your soul.

21

Margot

Margot would have been perfectly content to have only Blossom's company for Christmas Day rather than the company of Will and his family. Yet here she was, late on Christmas morning, barrelling down Southwood Lane while trying to keep the large box she was carrying steady. Will had been adamant that she should just bring herself, but Margot hadn't been raised by wolves – she'd been raised by a mother and father who'd loved her very much. And this morning, like every other Christmas morning, Margot had sat in the bath and cried because she missed them. Their absence was a blistering pain that would never really heal.

After they were married, Roger and Judy Millwood had bought a dilapidated house in Gospel Oak and planned to do it up and fill it with children. The doing-up had happened but the children never came, until fifteen years later when Judy Millwood was shocked to discover that rather than entering the menopause somewhat early, she was actually five months pregnant.

So, it had been just the three of them. 'We three, we happy free,' Roger had always said. He was an English teacher with a passion for nonsense verse. Every time that Margot took off her socks and shoes, he'd always quote with great relish from 'The Jackdaw of Rheims'. 'The cardinal drew off each plum-coloured shoe, and left his red stockings exposed to the view.'

Judy taught art, and each Christmas they'd hang up their hand-made decorations. The delicate paper chains that draped across the walls, the personalised Christmas tree baubles and the stocking with Margot's name cross-stitched on it that would hang above the fireplace.

They'd only had seven years as a happy three, but still Margot could remember those Christmases, though she worried that her memories were worn so thin that soon they might crumble to dust.

Yet Will still had his family close to hand and Margot couldn't help being curious about Blossom's other life. The people she spent time with when she wasn't being doted on by Margot but also being given firm and clear boundaries. From what Will had said ('You have to understand that my mother thinks of Blossom as her third grandchild . . .') Margot didn't think there was very much in the way of firm and clear boundaries during Will's weeks, which explained a hell of a lot, quite frankly.

Will had offered to meet Margot at their usual spot in Highgate Woods and walk with her the rest of the way. It was becoming evident that Margot had misjudged Will when they'd first met. Though to be fair, he had stolen her dog, but she was over that now and very grateful that today she didn't have to turn up on her own at the Bloom family home like an unwanted Christmas parcel.

Despite her misgivings, Margot was cheered at her first sight of Blossom and Will. Blossom had a pair of flashing antlers perched precariously on her head and as she saw Margot approach, her tail started wagging and she pulled so hard on the lead, that Will staggered to keep his balance.

'Happy Christmas,' Margot said, leaning in to give Will a kiss on the cheek because it felt like the appropriate thing to do. But Will was still trying to stop Blossom from jumping up at Margot so the moment was made about five times more awkward that it already was.

'Happy Christmas,' he replied, and his skin was cold against hers and, as ever, his scent reminded Margot of sea salt and fresh air, like a long, invigorating walk on a windy day. Margot was so used to doing two kisses that she tilted her face for the second, but Will had already stepped away. 'Sorry.'

'It's quite hard to know the correct etiquette, isn't it, when you share a dog with someone?' Margot wondered aloud.

'Someone should write a book,' Will said vaguely as he cast his eyes over Margot.

She'd put in some extra effort and tonged her hair, so her curls weren't as wild and untamed as usual. She'd even done her full half-hour make-up routine, which involved primers, highlighters and blending eye shadows and though it was hidden by her blue-and-red check coat, she was wearing her fanciest daytime dress; a fitted green midi dress sprigged with tiny red roses from Rixo.

Margot hoped that Will's family didn't spend Christmas Day in their pyjamas, considering Will was now frowning at her.

'What?' she asked defensively. 'What's wrong?'

He tapped the huge cake box she was holding. 'What happened to just bringing yourself?'

'There is no way I'm rocking up empty-handed to have dinner at someone's house.' They started walking. 'Not across the field, please. I have my nice boots on, not my dog-walking boots.'

It was Margot's favourite kind of winter day. There were blue skies and enough sun to create dappled shadows through the trees, but the air was sharp and crisp. It was sunglasses weather *and* hat, scarf and gloves weather – a boon to anyone who loved accessorising as much as she did.

Everyone they met was in good spirits and even Will managed to say 'Happy Christmas' to complete strangers with minimal unease. They even ran into Eric, a singular-looking Pugalier with a ferocious underbite and soulful brown eyes, the only dog in North London that Blossom didn't currently have beef with.

All too soon they were leaving the woods to walk along the last section of the Parkland Walk – a disused railway line turned nature reserve – pausing halfway to look out over a viaduct at London laid out in all her glory.

'Better view than the one at Ally Pally,' Will said, pointing out Parliament Hill, then further to the Shard and St Paul's and beyond. 'I think those distant hills might be Kent but don't quote me.'

They came out at the top of Muswell Hill. Will steered Margot and cake box to the right, then they took a left. Margot had a fizzing in her stomach as the nerves set in.

'You look as if you're walking towards your execution, rather than Christmas dinner with all the trimmings,' Will noted. 'Believe me, my mother is far more nervous about meeting you than you could ever be about meeting her. She's actually doing Brussels sprouts two ways just in case you judge her harshly for only doing one kind.'

Margot hated Brussels sprouts but now probably wasn't the time to mention it. She felt her palms go clammy in her woollen gloves as Will unlatched the gate of one of the grand Edwardian houses that Muswell Hill did so well. The garden path had tessellated black and white tiles, which led to a smart red brick house with glossy white window trim and decorative fretwork above the front door. Wisteria branches crawled along the outside of the house. In summer, it must have been a glorious sight.

Her heart was thundering as Will fumbled in his pocket for his keys before the door was flung open, revealing a pretty girl in her late teens with hair dyed the colour of wisteria in full bloom. 'You took your time,' she complained. 'You were only meant to be half an hour.'

'This is Sage, my little sister. She seems to have forgotten all her manners,' Will said, moving aside so that Margot could step in first. Blossom, however, had decided that she should have order of precedence and headbutted Margot's legs in her rush to get to Sage, who obligingly tweaked her ears. 'This is Margot.'

'Blossom's other human,' Sage said. She was much better at kissing someone hello than her older brother,, doing both cheeks too. 'I wish I could say that I feel that I know you, but I hardly know anything because Will never spills the good stuff.'

'There really isn't much to spill.' Margot hadn't taken two more steps, before a woman about her own age came down the rather grand staircase.

'Hello, hello,' she said, arms spread in greeting. 'I'm Rowan, Will's other sister.' Two small boys pushed past her, followed by a man with a laid-back cheery countenance and dark hair almost as curly as Margot's. 'These horrors are mine. Sam and Harry. Don't worry, I can't tell them apart either. And the tall one at the back is Alex, my husband. Say hello, darling.'

'Hello, darling,' Alex said with a wave, as he hurried past. 'I would stop but I'm on twin patrol.'

'He drew the short straw,' Rowan said, jumping down from the bottom step so she could take Margot's hands.

'Lovely to meet you,' Margot said, again gifted with two very expertly given kisses on the cheek, then Rowan was disappearing down the hall.

'Oooh! You brought cake,' Sage pointed at the cake box, which was drooping slightly now. 'Shall I grab that, while you take off your coat?'

'It's quite hard to know what to bring when you're going to the house of people who run a florist,' Margot said, as Will helped her take off her coat and woollies.

'Let me unleash the hound then I'll put them away for you,' Will said, bending down to unclip Blossom, who didn't even wait for her harness to come off before hurtling down the hall and through an open door.

'Oh, is that my darling girl? Nanna's saved all the giblets for you!'

'You know when you and Will decided that Blossom wasn't meant to have human food?' Sage rolled her eyes. 'Well, Mum ain't got *no* time for that.'

Margot had had her suspicions. The vet had been very surprised at how quickly Blossom had reached her target weight. 'Anything else I should know about?' she asked Will, who was hanging her coat on an old-fashioned coat stand by the front door.

Will's face was a perfect blank. 'Nothing that I can think of,' he said.

Sage snorted from behind Margot. 'You don't know half of it. Now come and meet Mum,' Sage said cheerfully, beetling down the hall so it was just Margot and Will left.

Margot smiled weakly. 'Your mother really doesn't mind me gate-crashing?'

'You're not gate-crashing. You're the guest of honour.' Will smiled and put a hand over his heart. He was wearing a thin black sweater over a grey T-shirt – the sweater soft enough and luxurious enough that Margot, who knew a thing or two about fabric, could tell it was cashmere. 'My mother is the least scary person you could ever meet, I promise you.'

He was a lot taller than his sisters, but they all had the same twinkle in their blue eyes. Margot had never seen Will's twinkle before, but maybe it was the combination of Christmas cheer and being on home turf that had completely obliterated his resting bitch face.

'OK, then,' Margot said bravely. 'Lead on.'

Will's hand settled gently at the small of Margot's back to steer her down the hall. Usually Margot would have something to say to a man who put his hand anywhere near her without her explicit permission. But Will wasn't just any man and the warm weight of his hand was a comfort until Margot realised that the nerves fizzing in her tummy were roughly 67 per cent terror at meeting the other woman in Blossom's life and 33 per cent frisson. Yes, definitely a frisson. Margot shivered and yes, it was the good kind of shiver, and she was so perturbed by both frisson and shiver that her nerves were entirely gone as they entered the kitchen. Margot hadn't really needed Will to lead her: she could have simply followed her nose. The unmistakable scent of Christmas: turkey roasting, potatoes sizzling in goose fat, cranberries simmering on the hob and even bacon frying.

The kitchen looked like it hadn't been updated since the eighties. No Shaker-style units in Farrow and Ball colours or a butler's sink and Smeg fridge in here. There were dark mahogany units, a gigantic range cooker and three women bustling about in a cooks' ballet.

Sage was scoring an ominously large pile of Brussels sprouts and Rowan was stirring a saucepan full of red cabbage. Margot didn't need an introduction to the third woman who was busy opening oven doors and prodding at the pigs in blankets under the grill and peering over Rowan's shoulder to check on the cabbage. If Christmas cooking was a ballet, then Mary Bloom was the prima ballerina *assoluta*.

If Margot had been in any doubt as to who she was, Blossom, who was sitting in front of the double oven, two slavering trails of drool hanging from her mouth, eyes fixed unwaveringly on Mary, would have given the game away.

'This is my mother, Mary,' Will said rather unnecessarily. 'This is Margot, she's brought a cake.'

Mary turned towards Margot. Margot forced herself to stand up straight, keep the smile on her face.

It was easy to see the family resemblance. Mary, Rowan and Sage all had the same colouring, the same china blue eyes, the same fine blond hair, though Sage's was currently lilac and Mary's was greying. But Mary's features were blurry and more careworn than her daughters. She was also very thin, the wiry kind of thin that Margot always associated with an intense sort of person, as if their nerves fuelled their metabolism.

'Thank you for having me,' Margot said uncertainly, because Mary Bloom was staring at her with Will's eyes, which was rather disconcerting. 'So kind of you to let me crash your Christmas dinner.'

Mary Bloom smiled then, so she didn't look blurry or careworn anymore, but as if Margot's presence in her house on Christmas Day was the most amazing thing that had ever happened to her. 'It's my absolute pleasure. I've been so looking forward to meeting you.'

22

Will

Will had been dreading this moment – the two main women in Blossom's life, and increasingly in his life, meeting.

Margot was smiling. She hadn't stopped smiling since they arrived, but it wasn't the kind of smile that lit up her whole face and made her eyes sparkle. It was more manic than that.

And his mother? She was giving Margot the full wattage beam of her best smile; the smile that was like coming home after years trying and failing to find yourself. It was a smile that bathed its recipient in a golden glow so that Margot's own shaky smile became the truest vision of itself.

'Shall we hug it out?' Margot asked. Will and his two sisters all winced. Mary was great at smiling but not so big on hugging. 'It's just I know how much you adore Blossom and take such good care of her, and I adore Blossom, too, so I feel like we're already on hugging terms.'

'Oh, yes. Well, I suppose that would be all right.'

If Will had thought that the cheek-kissing of earlier was awkward and excruciating, then compared to Mary and Margot hugging, it was a passionate embrace. Mary's shoulders touched her ears and her arms were like iron girders as they briefly encircled Margot, then released her with indecent haste.

Margot didn't appear to notice that Mary had very unwillingly had her defences breached. 'And again, thank you so much for having me here. I hope it's not an imposition.'

Mary was all smiles again now that she'd been released from the enforced bondage of Margot's arms. 'You're not to mention it again,' she said, wagging a finger. 'We're delighted to have you.'

When Will had told his mother that they'd be one more for Christmas dinner, and briefly explained Margot's unhappy circumstances, Mary had agreed instantly, as Will had known she would. Then, as he'd also suspected, the doubt and worry had set in.

'What will Margot think of the house? Everything is so old and out of date. I still think of it as Mum and Dad's house and it feels wrong to start ripping up carpets and getting rid of those nasty kitchen units that they chose together.'

'I'm a very plain cook, Will. I hope this Margot isn't expecting anything too fancy. Should we not have turkey? Should we have a goose instead? She's not vegetarian, is she? Oh God, is she a vegan?'

'What will we do if the twins kick off? Shall I tell Ian to tell Rowan not to give them any chocolate until after lunch? It will be better coming from him.'

And so it went, on and on and on until this morning when Mary had sent him off to meet Margot with a doleful, 'Well, it's too late to cancel now. She'll just have to take us as she finds us.'

Will didn't know why he'd been so worried because Margot and Mary seemed genuinely thrilled with each other. He stayed in the kitchen for a good ten minutes just to check that Sage was behaving herself and that Mary wasn't stuffing Blossom to the gills with human food, because he knew that Margot wouldn't be able to stop herself from saying something.

But all was calm. Margot was cheerfully tackling the mountain of washing-up from breakfast and Christmas dinner prep (she'd refused to take no for an answer) as she and a beaming Mary talked about their favourite subject in the entire world.

'Yes, we have the subtitles on all the time too. How can such a little dog snore so loudly?' Mary was asking as Will and Alex took Sam and Harry (who'd inevitably eaten every single chocolate coin they could find and were bouncing off the walls) into the garden with Blossom for a pre-dinner kickabout.

'Margot seems nice,' Alex said, as he and Will sat on the wall that separated the patio from the lawn. Sam and Harry's version of football, which involved preventing Blossom from getting hold of the ball long enough to puncture it with her incisors, wasn't for the faint-hearted.

'She is nice,' Will replied. Margot *was* nice. She was kind. She was thoughtful. She was the only woman he'd ever brought round to meet his family without fear that she'd judge him, or them, harshly. And Christmas Margot was the prettiest incarnation of Margot yet; her face luminous and her dress clinging to the curves that Will always pretended not to notice because it made life easier.

'Bit more than nice, perhaps?' Alex probed gently. 'Easy on the eye, likes dogs, can cope with the Blooms en masse. Rowan wouldn't let me meet you all until we'd done a year together and she knew it was serious.'

Will prodded his brother-in-law with an elbow. 'Rowan asked you to do some discreet digging, didn't she? Because she doesn't know the meaning of discreet.'

'Happy wife, happy life, mate.' Alex looked down the garden to where his two sons were now trying to climb the ancient apple tree, while Blossom circled anxiously below. 'Don't do that, lads! Nobody fancies a trip to A&E today.'

He'd barely raised his voice. Sam and Harry continued to ignore him. Will stood up so he could shout properly. 'Come down NOW! If you break that apple tree, Nanna will kill you before we can even take you to hospital. I'm not joking.' Will looked to Alex for support but he just waved his hand vaguely, as if Will was doing a splendid job in disciplining his beloved sons and he had nothing to offer. 'Also, Christmas presents will be going back!'

The boys only came down from the tree when Will physically removed them from it. He was carrying them back up the garden, one under each arm as they wriggled delightedly, when the back door opened and Rowan appeared clutching a jar of piccalilli. There were patches of red dotted along her cheekbones.

'It's all kicking off,' she hissed, and Will instantly dropped both boys so he could get to the kitchen where he just knew Margot would be schooling Mary in all aspects of dog ownership and care.

The kitchen was full of steam and hot air and shouting. Not from Margot, who was sitting at the kitchen table and steadfastly staring down at her phone as if she wasn't even aware of Sage at full volume and gesticulating wildly while Mary fluttered her hands.

'Honestly, I'm not a mind reader! How was I to know that you wanted your stupid decorative prawn ring as some kind of seafood centrepiece? You should have said and then I wouldn't have decimated it and put it in bowls. I was only being helpful!'

'You never think. It was meant to go on the table intact, as a focal point, and now it's ruined,' Mary insisted, her voice breaking. 'Christmas was meant to be perfect; now it's spoiled.' She pointed with a rigid finger at what was allegedly once a decorative prawn ring but was now prawns in some kind of mousse and sauce distributed evenly between nine small bowls.

'It was going to end up in the bowls eventually, Mum,' Rowan bravely intervened.

'The one part of the meal that I contributed to,' Sage continued, pacing up and down now. 'I was the one who bought the prawn ring and now you're saying that I've ruined Christmas. Thanks!'

'You've done lots of contributing,' Mary said in a whisper, a dishcloth in her hands which she held up as if it were a protective shield. 'You did one of the big shops with me and you helped me with the timings and you laid the table, but the decorative prawn ring was meant to be a *centrepiece*!'

'Oh my God, it's just prawns in gloop . . .'

'Sage,' Will said in a low voice. 'Come on, let's just not.'

'Why? Because it's Christmas and everything has to be perfect? Well, newsflash, Mum, just because I dared to break up the sodding decorative prawn ring doesn't mean—'

'Shut up!' Rowan hurled the jar of piccalilli on the floor, where it shattered so hard that Mary and Margot both jumped. 'Shut up! Mum's right. You are ruining Christmas!'

'What is all this racket?' said a voice from the back door. And there was Ian, clad from head to toe in Lycra. 'Oh, love, who's upset you?'

He clomped into the kitchen in his funny cycling shoes so he could take Mary in his arms, stiff and resisting as usual, and pat her hair. 'It will be all right.'

'Ruined,' came her muffled voice.

'Not ruined,' Rowan insisted, as she crouched down to start picking up the larger pieces of glass. 'Sage, can you find me some newspaper to put this in?'

'I didn't mean to shout,' Sage persisted. 'But you were totally overreacting. Christmas isn't ruined.'

'Except now we've got no piccalilli,' Will said, which was his own feeble attempt to defuse the situation.

There was a muffled little laugh. 'Don't be silly. There's another three jars in the pantry,' Mary said, and she gently pulled free of Ian's arms so she could put her hands to her reddened face.

Rowan and Sage worked between them to clear up the mess, Ian went upstairs to wrestle himself out of his cycling gear and have a shower before dinner. Then a timer beeped, which meant it was the appointed hour for Will to wrestle the seven kilo turkey out of the oven again.

Margot was still there, sitting at the kitchen table, her bottom lip caught between her teeth. Not even Margot's famous ability to instantly bond with strangers could ease the embarrassment, the hideousness of the situation. Mary shook her head, her eyes moist again. 'Margot . . . what must you think of us?' Her voice trembled. 'I'm absolutely mortified.'

It wasn't even as if Blossom could suddenly bustle in to alleviate the tension, she was still in the garden with Alex and the boys, who'd missed all the excitement, thank God.

'You shouldn't be.' Margot smiled briefly, clumsily. 'Usually I spend Christmas with friends, which is lovely. But it's not the same as having a family Christmas and a family Christmas isn't perfect until there's been an almighty argument, is it?'

'That's very kind of you to say, you're a very nice girl, but I'm devastated,' Mary said, and she was crying again.

The three of them, Will, Rowan and Sage, looked at each other in horrified despair. Normally Mary was all sunshine and sass, but when she got like this it could take hours, sometimes even days, before she found her happy place again.

'This won't do,' Margot said, scraping back her chair so she could hurry over to hug Mary who was now scrubbing at her face with the tea towel. 'I never knew my grandparents,' Margot continued, 'but the year that my grandmother got so incensed with my grandfather that she upended the bread sauce over his head went down in family legend, so, compared to that, a no-longer-intact prawn ring and a broken jar of piccalilli is nothing. Now, should we supervise Will with this turkey?'

'How do you always know the right thing to say?' Will asked Margot later, when he drove her home.

Margot had had far too many gin and tonics (Ian always made them too strong) to walk home on her own. Not that Will would have let her. She was also now the proud owner of a large, cumbersome, framed print of Blossom in her holly crown. In return she'd given Will a pair of bright blue socks with Blossom's face on them, which he was never going to wear but it was the thought that counted.

Christmas, rather than being ruined, had turned out all right. Really all right.

Will had expected an awkward atmosphere to hang over the table but it dissipated in the time it took to pull crackers and for Margot to insist that they all wore the paper crowns, though usually the Blooms didn't bother. Margot fitted in like she was family. Groaning over the jokes in the crackers, forcing down Brussels sprouts even though nobody (not even Mary) liked them, and playing charades.

They only left when Blossom fell asleep on Mary's lap wearing a baby-sized T-shirt that proudly proclaimed 'My grandma loves me', and Margot could slip away without a scene.

Now she yawned as she considered Will's question. 'I don't *always* say the right thing,' she decided. 'But I am a bit of a people pleaser. You kind of have to be when you're eighteen with no family to fall back on.'

'I don't think you're *that* much of a people pleaser,' Will dared to say, because it was the truth and there had been times when Margot had gone out of her way to displease him. The bullet-pointed, micro-managing texts at the beginning of their acquaintance sprang to mind.

'People pleasing is one thing, but I also don't let people walk all over me either.' Margot's words were more slurred than usual. 'But it's never a bad thing to be kind, is it? To put yourself in someone else's shoes and to think of what you'd like to hear if you were them.'

'You're a much better person than I am.' As usual, not a drop of alcohol had passed Will's lips, so he couldn't imagine why he was being so candid with a woman who wasn't a stranger anymore, yet walked the hinterlands between being an acquaintance and friend.

There was a pause as if Margot was quantifying exactly what sort of a person Will was. 'You're not *that* bad,' was the faintly damning verdict. 'In fact, I'd love you to come to my New Year's Eve open house. Unless you have plans.'

Will didn't have any plans. Although he'd quit therapy with the promise that he was going to forge emotional connections outside of his family, he hadn't so much as downloaded a dating app or flirted with the beautiful Sunita who lived in the flat next door and said a breathy hello to Will every time they bumped into each other – though maybe the breathiness was because she had asthma. Either way, his New Year's Eve was wide open, unless he went round to his mum's to give her and Ian a hand as they babysat the twins.

'I might be free,' he said, as he pulled up in the Square.

'I'll be open for callers from eleven a.m. so come round any time from then,' Margot explained, as she tried to extricate herself from the seat belt. 'Sorry, I'm all fingers and thumbs.'

'Let me,' Will said. Their hands collided in the dark. His fingers cool where hers were warm. They'd touched a hundred times in a hundred prosaic ways. Handing over dog leads, treat packets, both empty and full poo bags, but now Will felt a brushfire shock at the sensation of his skin against Margot's skin.

He didn't know if she'd felt it too, but he heard her sigh before she let her hand drop. It was his turn to fumble with the seat belt until finally she was free to go.

Margot wasn't going anywhere. 'And we're handing over on Sunday anyway.'

It was business as usual then. All about Blossom. 'At least we don't have to go to training. Even Jim respects the Christmas holidays.'

'Time off for good behaviour, except Blossom doesn't know the meaning of good behaviour,' Margot said. It was so cosy and cocooned in the car that Will wondered if they'd stay there for ever, eking out this camaraderie borne from spending a tumultuous Christmas Day together. 'Talking of which, I didn't want to say anything in front of Mary, but I can't believe the amount of food, *human* food, Blossom shovelled away.'

Margot managed to get the door open with a lot more skill than she had used with the seat belt and the cold night air rushed into the cosy cocoon, abruptly ending their companionable moment. It was done. Over.

'She only gives Blossom meat and vegetables,' Will said, as he climbed out of the car. 'It's not *so* bad.'

'She had *three* roast potatoes,' Margot pointed out. 'And I did have to say something about how chocolate and raisins are toxic to dogs.'

'You said it very diplomatically and I'm very grateful for that.' Will rolled his eyes as he retrieved Blossom's portrait from the backseat. Then he felt guilty about rolling his eyes. 'Thank you for today.'

Margot shook her head. 'I should be thanking you.'

'About what happened earlier with Mum ...' Will tailed off; it was easier than having to explain things that he'd only explained to his therapist.

'It's all right,' Margot said gently. 'Everything is good. I had a great Christmas. Definitely in my top ten of favourite Christmases.'

Will smiled because she was impossible but oh-so kind and the fairy lights strung between lamp posts were reflected in Margot's eyes and he was seeing stars. 'There you go, saying just the right thing again.'

Margot shrugged. 'It's my superpower.'

And this time, when she leaned forward to brush her lips against his cheek, it wasn't awkward at all.

23

Margot

Margot had never given birth, that she knew. But friends who had, more than once, told her that they'd repressed how truly awful giving birth was and so it came as a complete surprise the second, and even the third time round.

'It's nature's cruel trick, otherwise there'd be a hell of a lot of only children,' Sarah had said, four months after the birth of her little Bertie, when she was still unable to sit down without the aid of a donut cushion.

Margot felt much the same way about her New Year's Eve at-home. From 1 January to approximately 31 March, she swore that she'd never undertake such a Herculean endeavour ever again.

But from April to August, the horror began to recede so that only positive memories of happy faces and good times remained.

Then during the three-day heatwave that was the highpoint of the British summer, Margot would long for winter. As she got trapped underneath the armpit of someone who eschewed deodorant on a Central Line train, all she could think about was Jack Frost nipping at her nose. How much nicer autumn/ winter clothes were – Margot wanted to be buried in a long-sleeved midi dress with pockets and a pair of her beloved black opaque tights. How much yummier the food was – salad wasn't really dinner whereas shepherd's pie and crumble for afters definitely was. Then she'd bypass thoughts of Christmas, because Christmas was problematic, and skip right to New Year's Eve and how fantastic it would be to have an at-home once again.

'Blossom, next year if I decide to throw a New Year's Eve at-home, you're going to have to stage an intervention,' Margot told Blossom, who was sitting in the kitchen doorway, drooling. It was 8.30 a.m. on New Year's Eve. There were already sausage rolls baking in the oven and Margot was currently grating a huge block of cheddar for her cheese straws. 'Why do I have to make life so complicated?'

Blossom didn't answer at first. Then she whined, but it was less an answer to Margot's rhetorical question and more, 'You have cheese. I *love* cheese.'

'For a start, why do I have an at-home, like I'm some Victorian lady who receives visitors between the hours of three and five? I should just have a brunch or a tea party or an evening cocktail soirée, not some time-consuming, stressful combination of all three,' Margot said, waving a piece of cheese about for emphasis, which made Blossom whine even more.

'And why do I insist on baking from scratch when shops sell all these things for much less than the price it takes to make them and don't use up every utensil I possess and every last ounce of my energy? Don't even get me started on the tidying.'

Blossom wasn't going to go *there* but she did take a couple of delicate steps into the kitchen. Her bravery was rewarded when Margot said, 'Oh go on, then,' and she was allowed to hoover up the cheese crumbs that had drifted down to the kitchen floor like a fine powdering of snow.

The day before had been spent in a frenzy of cleaning. Steaming her rugs, washing every piece of glassware, crockery and cutlery she possessed until they gleamed. Moving all her bulky items into Geoff and Daphne's hall, as she did every year, while lamenting how small her flat was.

Now Margot was slaving over a hot stove and a hot oven and panicking because her Ocado delivery, with enough booze to sink a small flotilla, was running forty minutes late.

'And I had to pay nine pounds ninety-nine for a New Year's Eve delivery when normally it's free,' Margot complained, but Blossom had decided to retreat to her favourite spot on the living room sofa until the sausage rolls came out of the oven.

Margot had to stop wafting bad energy around the flat. 'I am positive. I am calm. I am baking food with love. I am going to throw a great New Year's Eve at-home.'

Three hours later, Margot was the consummate hostess; throwing open the doors and the windows (all that baking had turned the temperature up to tropical) of her little garden flat to her nearest and dearest.

The first wave of callers was mostly friends with kids, who'd had an enervating walk on the Heath first or a fractious drive across London. Margot was delighted to see all of her godchildren and assorted siblings, plus the children of friends who'd decided that they didn't want Margot to help their offspring reject evil and turn away from sin. She was the happy recipient of many sticky kisses and grubby hugs before most of her small visitors hung out with Blossom in the sitting room, *Mary Poppins* on the TV, home-baked treats to munch on.

The second wave was the in-between crowd. Friends who had several places to be that evening but wanted to start at Margot's where they knew there'd be food to line their stomachs and a gentle start to the proceedings.

By nine o'clock, it was the faithful. Those that were going to see in the New Year at Margot's and even though all her homemade treats were gone, she'd done a run to Tesco Express and her bathtub was still full of ice and alcohol.

The party had spilled out on all sides, as it always did, into Margot's courtyard garden and onto the Square, which was where Margot was with a gin and tonic in one hand and Blossom's lead (with Blossom attached) in the other, talking to Jacques and Solange, when Tracy and her husband, Den, arrived.

'There she is!' Den said, greeting Margot with a hug, though with her hands full, he didn't get much of one in return. 'We have six bottles of Prosecco. Shall I put them in the bath?'

'Yes, please.' Margot wondered if she should switch from gin to Prosecco, then decided that mixing spirits and wine might harsh her pleasant buzz.

'I'll take one of them,' Tracy said, pulling a bottle from the box and smiling at Jacques and Solange. 'So, here we all are again! How you doing, Margs?'

Margot raised her glass. 'Feeling no pain.'

They talked about Jacques and Solange's Christmas with her family in Rennes and how they'd all been thoroughly repulsed by the mince pies Jacques had brought. 'Even though they were the luxury ones with brandy in them!'

And then, because it was New Year's Eve, talk turned to New Year's resolutions.

Jacques was going on a digital detox. Solange was doing Dry January. Tracy was taking a crack at Veganuary, but Margot wasn't having any of it. 'January is depressing enough. All the parties are over, your credit card bill needs paying, it's dark and cold, why deprive yourself of Instagram, alcohol and the odd bacon sarnie?' she asked her friends, whose faces fell as they began to regret their parsimonious decisions. 'Sorry, to piss on your chips.'

'Don't mention it.' Solange sounded as if she really wished Margot hadn't mentioned it. She stared down at her empty glass. 'If I do decide to do Dry January, then I really need to drink while I still can.'

'And I can at least do no screen time after eight p.m., because then it interferes with my body's natural circadian rhythms,' Jacques said. 'You know how I feel about the health benefits of a good night's sleep. Though it is possible to have *too much* sleep, which can be as harmful as smoking.'

'I definitely need a drink now,' Solange said, and she and Jacques hurried back to the flat.

'Was I a bit too strident?' Margot asked Tracy, as she let Blossom drag her to the patch of grass that was her preferred wee spot.

'Of course you weren't,' Tracy said. 'Anyway, you don't really need New Year's resolutions because you do all your positive affirmations and whatnot every day. Do they really work?'

Margot let out a breath and watched as it curled in the air. 'I think so. I hope so. When you're in a positive mindset, then it opens you up to possibility.'

Tracy scuffed the ground with the toe of her boot. She seemed quieter than usual. 'Shall we sit on that wall?' she said, gesturing at the low wall near the public toilets.

'Lead the way,' Margot said, though as usual it was Blossom who led the way.

It was good to sit down, Margot had been on her feet all day, and she said as much to Tracy, who frowned.

'Is there something the matter?' Margot felt the first flutter of foreboding in her stomach. But Tracy had been enthusiastically chugging away at the bottle of Prosecco, so she couldn't be pregnant, and Margot didn't need to flutter. She'd be happy if Tracy was having a baby, more than happy, even though every time one of her friends got engaged or married or had a baby or left London, it was as if they were moving away from Margot either emotionally or geographically. Sometimes both.

'I have a feeling that this year coming is going to be a big year,' Tracy said, almost as if she'd heard Margot's silent despair.

'Planning to win the lotto, are you?' Margot teased with a lightness that she'd have to fake for a few minutes until she managed to reset herself back into a more positive frame of mind.

'I wish.' Tracy sighed. The flutters started again and upgraded to a full-on tremor when Tracy took the glass out of Margot's hand so she could curl her fingers around Margot's. 'I have to tell you something.'

'Do you? Really? Can't it wait?' Margot asked a little desperately, because that *something* always tested her. While she was hugging and congratulating her friends for their good news, it was hard to quiet that nagging, resentful voice in her head, demanding to know when was it her turn?

'It's not a bad thing,' Tracy insisted, but she wasn't looking very happy about it, whatever it was. 'But it's a change. A big change.'

'Change is good.' Margot knew then that it wasn't a good change. It wasn't a promotion or a house renovation; it was a change that would cause huge upheaval and make everything different.

'Me and Den, this isn't a decision that we've made lightly,' Tracy said, squeezing Margot's hand so that Margot wondered if it was something really, really awful, like the two of them were getting divorced. But no, Tracy would have said something before. 'We're moving.'

Margot bit down on her tongue to ward off a giggle that threatened to spill out of her. 'Is that all?' It would change things, but not in a really fundamental way. 'Please say that you're staying in London.'

Tracy shook her head.

'Kent coast, then? Margate? Or Hastings?' When Margot's friends left London those were the two most popular destinations. 'Though personally, I wouldn't move to Hastings. If you're going to live by the sea, then you might as well live somewhere that has a sandy beach.'

'It's not Margate or Hastings.' Tracy took a huge gulp of Prosecco. 'I'm moving home.'

It was Margot's turn to frown. 'But London is home. You've lived here for decades.'

Another almighty swig. 'Home home. Back to New Zealand.'

Margot heard a roaring in her head that turned out to be a group of revellers staggering through the Square on their way to the Flask.

'Happy New Year!' they shouted. Margot raised a hand in acknowledgment before swivelling back to Tracy, who looked as if she was waiting for the Grim Reaper. Like, he might give her an easier time.

'But why would you move to New Zealand?' Margot tried to keep the base note of betrayal out of her voice.

A ghost of a smile flickered across Tracy's face. 'Because I come from New Zealand, remember?'

'But you said that you couldn't wait to leave. That it was full of sheep and not much else. That no famous fashion designers had ever come from New Zealand and when you first came to London and saw that everyone on the Tube was reading a book, you cried happy tears,' Margot protested. Her other superpower was never forgetting anything anyone said if she could later rely on in it court, and use it as evidence against them.

Tracy wilted in the face of Margot's perfect recall. 'That was nearly twenty years ago and a lot has changed. New Zealand has changed. Jacinda is Prime Minister, they have a really strong fashion scene and I've been headhunted to take up the position of Dean of Fashion Studies at a university in Wellington. Also, my parents are getting older and I wish I were closer to them especially if . . . if . . . well, that's the other thing Den and I have been discussing. About starting a family and how we don't want to, can't afford to, bring up kids in London.'

'You couldn't compromise on Margate instead of going to the furthest possible point away from London?' Margot asked; she tried to sound light and teasing but it was hard when her heart was hurting.

'I'm sorry, Margs, but this . . . it just feels like the right time.' Tracy looked down at Margot's empty glass, then offered her the bottle of Prosecco. 'Do you want some?'

'God, yes!' Now Margot couldn't give a toss about mixing spirits and wine. She took the bottle and downed three long gulps.

Everyone but Margot was getting on with their lives. Hitting those big milestones that you hit when you found someone who wanted to share the rest of their life with you. Whereas Margot was stuck for the simple reason that there was no one who wanted to share the rest of his life with her.

They sat there in silence. All Margot's thoughts were variations on 'why is it never me?' until she realised that me didn't come into this. This wasn't about Margot. It was about Tracy.

'I am happy for you,' Margot said, even if she still didn't sound happy. 'These are really big life changes. Kids, emigrating – though is it emigrating if you're migrating back to where you were raised? But anyway, they're exciting changes too. This coming year is going to be your best year ever.'

'You're a good woman, Margs,' Tracy said quietly, taking back the Prosecco so she could have her turn. 'I'm sorry.'

'You have absolutely nothing to be sorry about,' Margot said firmly. 'I don't need to be factored into your big life decisions and you shouldn't have to apologise for them either.'

Tracy loped an arm around Margot's shoulder so she could land a sloppy kiss on her cheek, which Blossom took great offence to. She rose up so she could put her front legs on Margot's knees and headbutted Margot's free arm until she got the strokes that she wanted.

'That dog is never going to let you have another boyfriend,' Tracy noted.

'Not really an issue at the moment,' Margot sighed. 'I don't think there's a man in this world who could love me as unconditionally as Blossom does.'

There'd been absolutely no spark with any of the men Margot had been introduced to at the many Christmas parties she'd attended. And there'd been zero sparkage with the last guy she'd been on an actual date with a fortnight ago. When Margot had sent him a polite message to say that although they hadn't really clicked, she wished him luck in finding his one true love, he hadn't taken it very well. *I didn't even want to fuck you, you fat bitch. You're too old for me anyway. Tick tock tick tock.* Even though he wasn't worth it, Margot had spent the rest of the evening crying.

'I bet there is,' Tracy insisted. She took another gulp of Prosecco, as if she needed extra fortification for what she had to say. 'Look, Margs, you are an amazing person. You're a diamond in a world of cubic zirconia. You're the bee's knees. You're the captain's table . . .'

'Are you about to break into a chorus of "You're the Top"?'

Tracy glared at her diamond of a friend. 'I am not. I'm just trying to say that though I don't think anyone's life should be defined by the getting and keeping of a man, there is someone out there who is worthy of you.'

Margot leaned forward to rub her forehead against the top of Blossom's silky head. 'I wish he'd hurry up and get here.'

'This is absolutely going to be your year too,' Tracy promised. 'I can feel it.'

'Well, it could well be the year that I get my eggs frozen. That way I have a solid backup plan,' Margot mused, but Tracy shook her head.

'Those eggs are going to stay unfrozen because you're going to find the man of your dreams on a muddy dog walk. Your eyes will meet over a stinky poo-bag bin . . .'

'Just like in a Georgette Heyer novel . . .'

'I know, right? Or if that fails, there's bound to be at least one good 'un on the old dating apps,' Tracy suggested brightly. Margot didn't have the heart to tell her that good 'uns didn't send unsolicited dick pics. Anyway, Blossom took up all of her time and when she wasn't with Blossom, she was thinking about Will and how he bloody well better be taking good care of her. Maybe she needed to reprioritise her life choices.

'I barely grieved for what I had with George because I knew that I needed to get back out there as soon as possible. But maybe I have let things slide since I got Blossom. She's made me so happy and fulfilled that I haven't been as diligent with my dating as I used to be. It's time to get myself out there again,' Margot said, with absolutely zero enthusiasm for the Sisyphean task that was finding a vague approximation of The One. It just felt a lot like zero returns for maximum effort. 'I think I need to mix it up. Maybe I'll change my profile picture to one with me and Blossom.'

'Brilliant idea,' Tracy said, upending the Prosecco bottle to show that it was empty. Not one single trickle remained. 'If they don't like dogs, why would you want to date them? Although you do know a man who likes dogs. And he likes Blossom best of all out of the dogs.'

'Will is out of bounds. He's Blossom's co-pawrent,' Margot said. She didn't know how they'd got on to the topic of Will, who definitely wasn't in the running as a candidate for life partner. He'd be horrified at the thought.

Margot had simply meant that a picture of her and Blossom together would send out the message that there was no way that Margot could be too much. Not if her dog was her number one priority in life. Any man hoping to date her would have to work extra hard to take the second largest part of her heart. 'I am happy for you, Tracy. I really am.'

'I know you are,' Tracy said, getting to her feet and brushing small twigs and stones off her arse. 'You coming inside? Now that I'm no longer drinking, it's actually quite cold.'

'I'll be in in a minute,' Margot promised and she waited until Tracy had hurried across the Square, then she raised her hand in greeting at Will, who was standing on the other side of the road, outside the Italian restaurant, which was still doing a roaring trade.

24

Will

Will hadn't wanted to disturb Margot while she was so deep in conversation with her friend, so he'd stayed where he was and hoped he didn't look like a creepy stalker.

Though, really, was there any other kind of stalker?

Eventually, Margot's friend stumbled away, high heels skittering on the paving stones, and Margot waved as if she'd known that Will was there all along.

They both waited until the friend disappeared from view, then Margot stood up and tried to point Blossom in Will's direction. But Blossom was not for turning.

'Blossom!' he called out, crouching down and holding his arms wide. 'Blossom!'

For a dog who could hear Will *silently* munching on cheese two rooms away in the middle of a thunderstorm, Blossom was looking everywhere but at Will.

'It's just as well you're pretty, 'cause you're a bit stupid, Bloss,' Margot said.

Will tried again. 'Bloody hell, Blossom! Over here!'

Her ears finally pricked up, her nose twitched and her tail started rotating like a helicopter blade, then Blossom charged at him with such speed and velocity that when she reached her target, Will toppled to one side with an overjoyed Blossom on top of him, licking his hands, face, up his left nostril – any part of him that she could reach.

Will looked up to see Margot standing over him. From a

distance and from the slump of her shoulders, she'd looked sad, but now that she was close enough to offer a hand to help him up, she looked almost as pleased to see Will as Blossom had. Her smile, her eyes, her skin sparkled in the fairy-lit night.

'Nobody could ever accuse Blossom of playing hard to get,' Will said as he took Margot's hand, and she pulled him up with a strength that could only come from owning a Staffy who pulled on the lead.

'I'm glad you came.' Margot sounded like she genuinely meant it. 'Let's get back to the party so I can introduce you to everyone.'

They were words that struck terror in Will's heart. Margot's little flat was so full of people that it was straining at the seams and he was going to be introduced to all of them, then left by Margot to make awkward small talk. Spending the evening in his flat on his own was suddenly looking like a much more attractive option.

'I got in some of that fancy non-alcohol stuff that you can mix with tonics – I have several pregnant guests, several pre-pregnant guests and a couple of people that are in recovery,' Margot told him, as they squeezed through the throng taking up both sides of the tiny hall. 'Sorry, was that tactless?'

'Not at all.' Will had to raise his voice to be heard over the roar of conversation. 'I'm not in recovery.' Not from alcohol abuse, anyway. 'I'm just . . . Never touched a drop of the stuff or wanted to.'

They'd reached the kitchen, where the party had spilled out into the little patio garden. Margot opened the fridge to retrieve a bottle. 'Well, then I envy you never knowing what a hangover feels like. Though I suppose having to suffer through other people's hangovers might actually be worse.'

Wasn't that the truth, Will thought, as Margot gently moved a young woman wearing fairy wings to one side, so she could open a tiny dishwasher, which let out a cloud of steam into the already unbearably hot room. Then, with all the flair of a magician's assistant pulling a rabbit from a hat, she retrieved a clean glass.

'One glass, one bottle of non-alcoholic spirits and the mixers are chilling in ice in the bathtub.'

Will expected Margot to leave him to get on with things. She was the hostess of a very crowded party after all, but when Margot said that she was going to introduce him to everyone, she'd meant it. Fortunately, she had a way with an introduction that meant that Will and the person in front of him weren't left thinking desperately of something to say.

'This is Will, he lives in Muswell Hill, runs a floristry empire and he's Blossom's co-pawrent,' she said to an elegant woman with sallow skin, a glittering smile and a razor sharp, black bob. 'Will, this is Solange, real wife of Jacques my work husband. Solange is French and she's Head of Vibe at a Hoxton branding agency.'

'What the hell is Head of Vibe?' Will immediately asked, forgetting to be tactful, but Solange didn't mind and the ten minutes that followed weren't at all excruciating, apart from when it transpired that Solange was loosely acquainted with one of his former bosses in New York.

'He dated one of my old interns,' Solange informed him. 'And he used to be one of my favourite hate follows on Instagram, though lately all he seems to post are inspirational quotes from Tony Robbins and *The Art of War*, and those interminable stories where he's running daily half marathons.'

Will couldn't help but shudder. He, too, had run half marathons three times a week and had *The Art of War* committed to memory. 'When I worked with him, I had no choice but to lean hard into the bro company culture. We used to go to CrossFit as a team bonding exercise.'

'Madness! I take my team for sushi,' Solange said, then they moved on to talking about their favourite sushi until Jacques arrived with a packet of fancy crisps, because he couldn't remember if he was allergic to rapeseed oil.

Margot was waiting in the wings to introduce Will to someone else and an hour quickly sped by talking to Margot's osteopath, who was very concerned about Margot's wrenched shoulder and had the two of them considered a smaller breed of dog? Den, married to one of Margot's best friends, and Daphne from the house upstairs who used to go to Blooms' as a little girl with her mother, who'd bought fresh flowers every Friday.

Will was standing in the little patch of ground in front of Margot's flat talking to Daphne, people sitting on the steps that led up to the street, when he saw Margot through the open living-room window. She was trying to persuade Blossom to get off the armchair so an elderly man could sit down.

'Excuse me,' he said to Daphne, and knocked on the upper part of the window. 'Margot!'

She didn't hear him, but the people sitting nearest did and word quickly passed to Margot.

'Do you want me to take her for a quick walk?' Will called through the open window.

It took Will a good five minutes to negotiate getting back into the flat as he was stopped by so many people who were either big fans of Blossom and knew about his co-pawrent status or were regular and enthusiastic Blooms' customers. One couple, professional opera singers, were both.

Margot met him halfway, dragging a very reluctant Blossom with her. 'If you don't mind some company, I could do with a bit of fresh air,' she said. 'I'd forgotten that throwing a party is quite exhausting.'

Will had been hoping for ten minutes of quiet. He hadn't been so sociable since . . . Since . . . He couldn't even remember the last time. Probably one of those awful work functions he used to attend as part of his former life, where everyone spoke in jargon, and when they weren't jargonising, would say, 'I don't do small talk. I prefer to connect with people at a really granular level. What's your most traumatic childhood memory?'

'Where's your coat?' he asked, hoping to stall Margot. She shook her head.

'Between all these people and all the booze, I am *boiling*,' she said, her cheeks red and a hectic glitter to her eyes.

Somehow they managed to retrieve Blossom's lead and harness, then weaved their way through the people on the steps, and out onto the street.

'I'm all talked out,' Margot said, which Will was sceptical about, but she didn't say one single word as they walked across the square then along the tiny alley and up the steps that led onto Hampstead Lane.

Will didn't plan on heading to Hampstead Heath, which was treacherous underfoot even in daylight. Trying to navigate the meandering paths, full of dips and rogue tree roots, in the dark with a dog that pulled and a woman under the influence wasn't a good idea.

Instead, he manoeuvred Blossom and Margot around the corner onto Highgate West Hill until they reached the covered reservoir built in Victorian times, and which, to the untrained eye, resembled a huge grass mound surrounded by ornate railings.

'Where's the gate?' Will asked, as they circled around it.

'It's locked,' Margot said. 'Otherwise a whole load of pissed-up people might accidentally tamper with the water supply. Not that you're pissed up.'

'Are *you* pissed up?'

Margot did keep leaning into him and she'd only do that if she were hammered. 'I was pleasantly buzzed, but not having a coat on has sobered me up,' Margot decided, but she put a hand on Will's arm when he tried to turn them so they could head back to the tropical climes of her party. 'No, I'm all right. A bit of cold air never hurt anyone.'

'Unless they get pneumonia and die.' This was what Sage meant when she called him Mr Buzzkill. 'Although pneumonia is a virus, so you can't catch it from being cold. Sorry. I'm going to stop talking now. Do you want my coat?'

The whole time he'd been at the party, he hadn't had the opportunity to take it off. Now he tried to shrug out of it one-handed.

'You're all right,' Margot said, taking a step back. 'No point in you being cold too. Let's find somewhere to sit and then, if you promise not to get the wrong idea, I can huddle against you for warmth.'

'No wrong idea to get. We're just two people who share custody of a dog.'

'Co-pawrents, I think you meant to say.'

'Never,' Will said with an exaggerated shudder that made Margot laugh, but the message was loud and clear. Any attraction Will might have for Margot was one-sided, and even if it hadn't been, it would complicate things and Will didn't do complicated like he didn't do commitment or cornichons.

There was a bench not too far away. Will gestured to it as if he was ushering Margot to the finest table at the Ritz. She sat down with a flourish, the glittery silver skirt of her dress swishing behind like a curtain of stars, but before Will could sit down, Blossom jumped up and leaned into Margot as if she needed to huddle for warmth too.

Will sat down on Blossom's other side and instantly she pressed her stocky, solid weight against him.

It was a clear night, barely a cloud in the sky, so that what few stars there were could be seen twinkling clearly. It was darker where they sat, away from the street lights and fairy lights and Christmas lights of the village. Will marvelled that in a bustling capital city, it was possible to be so alone.

But he didn't feel alone. He glanced over first at Blossom, who had gone back to leaning into Margot. Her fur gleamed ghostly white and she was shivering a little. Will wanted to say that they should probably buy her a winter coat, but he didn't want to be the kind of man who walked a dog wearing clothes and, also, he didn't want to break the perfect silence.

His gaze moved on to Margot. She had her arm around Blossom, the back of her hand brushing against Will's arm. Her face was in exquisite profile, lips slightly parted, her hair a glorious mess of curls.

Something had been building up inside him ever since they sat down. A feeling that at first Will couldn't identify, but when he put his arm around Blossom too and she made an agreeable snuffling sound and Margot turned to smile at him, he realised what it was and why it had taken him so long to identify it.

Contentment.

People were far too fixated on happy, but happiness could be so fleeting, circumstantial. Whereas contentment, it felt more permanent. More sustainable. It was a warm glow of belonging, of rightness, compared to the elusive and ephemeral happiness.

Maybe it was best to stop thinking and just live in the moment. This night. This bench tucked away in a forgotten little corner. This dog. This woman.

He didn't even know how long they sat there, but suddenly the calm was shattered by the distant sound of tooting car horns, a faint cheer and the first firework climbing high in the sky and leaving a trail of pink sparks behind it.

Margot turned to him and smiled. 'Happy New Year.'

'It *will* be a happy new year,' Will vowed and it was perfectly natural, the proper thing to do, for both of them to lean back, past Blossom, so they could mark the occasion with a kiss. On the cheek. Nothing to see here.

But the angle was awkward and Blossom was in the way – that was Will's story and he'd swear to it on a whole stack of bibles – so he ended up brushing his lips against Margot's mouth, which she opened in a gasp, because he must have taken her by surprise. But then she kissed him back with a fierceness that took Will's breath away.

Her mouth moved under his, her hand creeping up to touch the side of his face with icy fingers. Will's hand was moving too, to catch a handful of her curls and gently tilt Margot's head back so he could kiss her deeply . . .

'Jesus!'

'Rude!'

The kiss stopped as suddenly as it started when Blossom, either furious at being squashed or furious that, for once, she wasn't the centre of their worlds, managed to headbutt both of them.

'One day she's going to break my nose,' Margot said, standing up and brushing down her dress. She was in shadow, so it was impossible to see her face, and if Will couldn't see her face, which never hid anything, then it was impossible to know what she was thinking about. 'We should get going,' she said briskly. 'Bad manners to duck out of my own party.'

And that seemed to be the end of that.

25

Margot

You could tell a lot about a man from the way he kissed. How kind he was, how generous he was, how caring he was. But there was a flipside to that: Margot could also tell how selfish someone was, how her pleasure, her comfort, her feelings were unimportant.

Will's kiss had been pretty close to perfect. He'd cupped her head as if Margot was made of something precious and fragile, and she'd never imagined that his mouth, which had said some very unkind things, could also be an instrument of pleasure.

But sometimes, a kiss was just a kiss. That was how people marked the end of one year and the beginning of the new one; they turned to the person nearest to them and embraced. It didn't mean anything. Will was deeply tangled and embedded in her life, but by default. He was Blossom's other person.

It was a complication that Margot didn't need. What she needed was to find someone to kiss that she didn't share a dog with.

No time like the present. 'Blossom, selfie!' Margot pulled out her phone, and Blossom, who was sitting next to Margot on the 134 bus, immediately rested her head on Margot's shoulder and found her light. Like mother, like fur daughter.

Blossom didn't take a bad picture. Unfortunately, Margot did, and it took several attempts before there was a picture where they both looked cute but like ladies who didn't take any nonsense. Then it was just a few swipes of a touchscreen to log into Hinge, Bumble and the dreaded Tinder, to change her profile picture and her tag line to 'Designer, Dreamer, Dog Mum'.

The next day, Margot woke to a winter wonderland of snow. She'd also woken up in one of the most advanced cities in the developed world that had ground to a halt because quite a lot of white stuff had fallen from the sky.

Getting a bus was out of the question, as no buses could manage the steep climb up Highgate Hill, so Margot had no choice but to walk down to Archway station.

'Blossom! Stop! Pulling!' was Margot's constant and terrified refrain as she tried to go slowly down a snow-covered hill as a strong, powerful dog kept yanking her forward. By the time they reached the turn-off for Whittington Hospital and gritted pavements, Margot had fallen over once, her shoulder was screaming and she now had to pick Blossom up to travel on the escalator.

Only Will was allowed to pick up Blossom. When Margot picked up Blossom, two arms clutched around her middle, Blossom twisted and wriggled and generally acted as if she was being dognapped. It was a wonder that neither of them plunged to their deaths, taking out several other commuters at the same time. Thank God their destination, Chalk Farm, had a lift.

All too soon it was time for Blossom's lunchtime walk. Margot had wondered if Will might join them, he often did on a Tuesday, but he'd gone back to his terse ways since New Year's Eve. Not that Margot needed Will. She could manage just fine. Although, since Christmas, Margot had been added to a #TeamBlossom WhatsApp Group and now Mary was inundating Margot with messages. Worried that Blossom might get salt or grit in her paws. Terrified that she would freeze to death because she had no fur on her belly. Also very perturbed that Margot's office might not have central heating. Margot was sure that even when she was a panic-stricken new dog owner, she'd never sent Will quite so many messages.

But right now, the only people she was messaging were her colleagues.

'I'll pay actual money for someone to take Blossom for her lunchtime walk,' she pleaded on the Teams chat, but there were no takers.

So, it was just Margot and Blossom skidding along Regent's Park Road to Primrose Hill. 'Blossom, why can't you behave just this once?' Margot begged as she clung to lamp posts and other pieces of street furniture, although Jim had said that she had to stop projecting her own fears and issues onto Blossom. 'Would it kill you to do a wee on the pavement? Come on!'

Blossom was more interested in chugging along like the little engine that could. When they finally got to Primrose Hill, Margot's fingers blue as they peeked out of the top of her finger-less gloves, her shoulder aching, her bottom sore from her fall earlier that morning, Blossom became incensed. When there were so many dogs frolicking in the snow, who could blame Blossom for rearing up on her hind legs and barking furiously? Margot only stayed upright by grabbing hold of a railing.

It wasn't a controlled environment. They weren't under the watchful eye of Jim. There was no Will to hold out his arms and call Blossom so she'd come running. There was also every possibility that Blossom might try to eat another dog, but if she stayed on the lead, there was also the very real possibility that Margot would fall over and break something.

Margot tried to slip and slide a little further along the path to where it was quieter, but they were moving uphill and she couldn't get any purchase.

'I am a positive person. I have an unbreakable bond with my dog who will come back instantly. My dog will not attack another dog and have to be put down,' Margot muttered under her breath as she unclipped Blossom's lead.

Blossom took off like a rocket, a blur of fawn and white hurtling across the snow-covered slopes.

'Blossom! Blossom, come!' Margot called, but Blossom was gone, over the brow of the hill, never to be seen again.

What had she done? What the *fuck* had she done?

Back over the hill came Blossom, paws barely making contact with the ground. Her back legs couldn't keep up with her momentum, so every now and again she'd do a hoppety little skip to get all four legs in alignment as she joyously galloped towards Margot, who crouched down, arms wide to receive her.

Blossom slightly adjusted her flight path so she didn't go crashing into Margot, which Margot very much appreciated. 'You are such a good girl! You are the best girl!' she gabbled, pulling out the treat bag. 'Good come, Blossom! Bloody good come!'

But Blossom didn't want treats. Rather than the taste of freeze-dried liver, she craved the sweet taste of freedom. Off she bounded again, tail wagging so hard Margot was amazed that she didn't take off as she watched Blossom complete a wide circle.

'Someone's got the zoomies,' said a fellow dog owner, like Margot completely swathed in hat, scarf and disreputable padded anorak. 'Love the snow, does he?'

'He's a she,' Margot said automatically, she didn't even get aerated about it anymore. Everyone was always misgendering Blossom. 'It's the first time I've ever let her off the lead. She's a rescue, you see.'

By now, Blossom had completed two loops and rather than attacking any other dog, she was at the head of a glorious, excited chain of canines, all of them barking and yapping, as they followed Blossom's hedonistic lead. From all corners of the park, more dogs appeared and joined in, like a snowy, lunchtime edition of the Twilight Bark. Margot realised that there was absolutely no point in attempting to recall Blossom right then. And why would she want to when she'd never seen Blossom look so happy?

With tears streaming down her face, Margot waited until Blossom finally ran out of steam. She flopped onto her back, gave several good wiggles, then trotted nonchalantly back to Margot, who plastered her snout with kisses then let her have the whole bag of liver treats.

Jim always said that when your dog came back, even if you'd been waiting in the pouring rain for half an hour, you had to act as if you were delighted to see them. You had to make the coming back, and yourself, much more fun than the not coming back. Now, wasn't that a metaphor for a successful relationship?

'You are the best girl there has ever been,' Margot told Blossom, and not one word was a lie because once Blossom was safely back on her lead, she trotted obediently at Margot's side, like a little show pony, and didn't pull once.

'But it will be our secret,' Margot decided as they carefully crunched over the compacted snow on Regent's Park Road. Margot didn't know when she'd become that person who had conversations with their dog in public, and actually, she didn't really care. 'Will must never know because he'd be very cross, and I can't deal with Will being cross with me again. So, feel free to tug on the lead when you're with him.'

However, Blossom's tugging days were over. It was as if when Margot had released her from the bondage of her red and white polka dot lead, a switch had been flipped. She tugged just a little the next day, but when Margot, with heart in her mouth and terror in her soul, let her run free again, free as the wind, Blossom was a perfect angel when it was time to leave Primrose Hill.

Ever since then, the pulling had stopped. Margot's shoulder was extremely grateful. Blossom had even stopped hurling herself at other dogs. Now, she was mostly non-reactive (Jim's Holy Grail of dog behaviour) either on- or off-lead and hadn't so much as growled at her sworn enemy, Popsy, the Cockapoo who lived on the other side of the Square and was often seen in Blossom's favourite wee spot.

Margot's little girl had become a woman.

26

Will

Nothing good was going to come from kissing a woman like Margot.

Margot shared his life in a way that Will hadn't been prepared for when he'd suggested that they share a dog. She'd been in his flat, she was in his calendar, and God knows she'd been in his family home on Christmas Day and witnessed his family at their worst. Not the very worst, but bad enough.

If he kept kissing Margot, not that Margot had seemed up for a rerun when they parted on New Year's Eve, then sooner or later, he would fuck things up the way he always did.

Fucking things up with Margot wouldn't just affect Will, it would affect his family and it would affect Blossom. So Will did what any grown man would do in the circumstances – he'd gone silent for a week. When they met at training on Sunday, he was going to play it cool. Friendly but disengaged, which was never a stretch for him.

But when Will saw Margot and Blossom some distance away as he waited outside Jim's hut, his heart did something strange. It seemed to beat just a little too fast for just a little too long while he watched Margot get closer in her cumbersome navy anorak. She had a red woolly hat on with an extravagant faux fur pom-pom which bounced as she walked, and when she got close enough to raise a hand, her smile was as tentative as his.

'Hi,' she said, looking everywhere but at him. 'It's really muddy today. Good job I wore my wellies.'

Will was relieved to have the excuse to look at her feet and not her face. Her wellies were red to match her hat and splattered with mud.

'All right?' he asked then wished he hadn't, because it was as if he was daring Margot to say that actually it wasn't all right, and where had he been all week, and by the way, how dare you kiss me on New Year's Eve?

She didn't say any of those things, but stared down at his feet, encased in equally mud-splattered hiking boots. 'Of course everything is all right. Why wouldn't it be?' She sounded almost defensive.

'I didn't say that . . .'

'What is going on here?' Jim demanded, his many keys jangling with every step as he hurried over to save Will from himself.

'We thought classes were starting again,' Will said. 'You sent out a text.'

'You did, Jim,' Margot added. 'Otherwise I'd still be in bed right now, believe me.'

Will didn't want to think about Margot in bed, neither did Jim. He had far more pressing matters to concern himself with.

'What have you done to Blossom?' He stared down at the dog, actual emotion creasing his face. 'Have you put her on Prozac?'

It was then Will realised what was wrong with this picture. Or rather, what was wrong with Blossom. She'd been wagging her tail the whole time that Margot had walked towards him but when they'd reached Will, Blossom hadn't jumped up once. Hadn't sullied his jeans with a single muddy paw. Hadn't turned into a hackle-risen harpy and tried to go for another dog.

Instead she was sitting at Margot's side and minding all her ps and qs. Margot smiled weakly.

'Yeah. About that. Promise you won't get mad.'

Will didn't know if she were talking to him or Jim. '*Is* she on Prozac?' he asked incredulously, because if Blossom was on mood-altering medication, then that went against everything they'd discussed about how they were going to raise Blossom. It also went against everything that Margot believed. All her banging on about a free-range, organic diet with absolutely no additives or chemicals, then she goes and puts Blossom on an antidepressant. 'She's not depressed. She's just had a hard start in life, Margot. God, I can't believe you'd put her on Prozac and not even talk to me first.'

'What happened to your positive reinforcement training?' Jim chimed in on the chorus as little patches of red broke out on Margot's guilty face. 'You could have persevered with the long line. I won't have a dog on Prozac in my class. It's a betrayal of my training methods and—'

'She's not on Prozac,' Margot snapped. 'I would *never* do that. But what I did do . . . I know that you said she wasn't ready, Jim, but it was snowing, it was slippery, she was going to pull me over. I had no choice.'

The suspense was killing Will. 'What *did* you do?'

Margot pulled an awful, cringing face, which transformed her prettiness into something grotesque. 'I let her off the lead, OK? I let her off in the middle of Primrose Hill and after half an hour of zoomies, she came back and, I don't know how to explain it, she's been amazing ever since. No pulling.'

Will shook his head. He couldn't have heard her right. 'No pulling?'

Margot nodded her head so vigorously that there was a good chance the pom-pom might become airborne. 'She hasn't so much as looked at another dog funny. There have even been a couple of times when she's sniffed another dog's bottom.' She pulled another ghastly face. 'I'm as confused as you are.'

'Well, I'm completely confused,' Will agreed. He couldn't help but smile despite his vow to be disengaged. 'Blossom, are you a good girl now?'

Blossom held up a paw. A very muddy paw, but Will shook it all the same.

'Well, it was obviously lead aggression,' Jim sniffed, which was the first that Will and Margot had heard of it. 'When they're on the lead, especially if they've had bad experiences in the past, they can become reactive when another dog approaches because they're not in control of the interaction; they can't get away if cornered. Didn't we cover this?'

Margot rolled her eyes. 'We really didn't, Jim.'

'Yeah, you might have thought to mention it,' Will added drily.

Jim shrugged. 'Just as well we did all that work on her recall,' he said a little too smugly for Will's liking. 'Anyway, not a normal class today. The examiner has turned up from the Kennel Club. I'm sure I put this in the text.'

'Again, you really didn't, Jim.' This time Margot gave Will the benefit of her extravagant eye roll, which made Will smile. He couldn't even pretend that it was a cool, disengaged smile.

'Great news about Blossom's improvement,' Jim ploughed on regardless. 'She's not ready to take her Good Citizen Bronze Award test today but why don't we put her in with the others and see what we still need to work on?'

'Can you even believe him?' Margot muttered to Will as they followed Jim to the cordoned-off area where Blossom would be put through her paces. 'You promise you're not even a little bit cross with me for letting her off the lead?'

How could he be cross with Margot when, if he hadn't let Blossom off-lead in the first place and almost got her run over, they wouldn't be here. Not just spending time training Blossom but spending time together?

'Well, I am a little bit cross,' he said, and pretended not to notice when Margot gave him the finger in a very un-Margot-like way.

27

Margot

All the instructors were at great pains to tell them that Blossom wasn't ready to take her Bronze Good Citizen certificate, but they hadn't experienced the new, improved Blossom. Blossom v 2.0, now with added obedience.

Also, they *did* get a point for having poo bags with them. Margot liked to think that she and Will absolutely smashed their questions on being responsible owners. Blossom did a fantastic sit and, for once, she didn't even object when Margot was asked to lift her tail, when usually she clamped it down like Noah shutting the doors of the ark.

Blossom also rocked her recall. Then it was time to show how she could walk on a loose lead and not lose her shit if another dog came too close.

'We're just seeing how far you've come,' Margot told her, as they watched the other dogs take their turns. 'There'll be no judgement if you have a hissy fit when that Husky gets all up in your space. Your awesomeness can't be quantified by a standardised test.'

Will loomed over them. 'Would it be cheating to conceal a treat in our hands, so her focus is on that and not on the other dogs?'

Margot stared up at him from her crouched position. It wasn't the most flattering angle, but Will still managed to look chiselled. His hair just the right amount of windswept, a healthy glow on his face, while Margot knew her hair was tangled, and the performance anxiety plus her Uniqlo thermals and padded anorak meant that she was bright red. She hoped there no heat-seeking missiles in the immediate vicinity.

'Her focus is *meant* to be on us,' she reminded Will, and if she sounded tetchy, it was because of the stress of the situation and the simple and unwelcome fact that she didn't know how to be around him anymore. 'It's cheating and we can't cheat. That woman from the Kennel Club sees everything.'

'Do you want to take her or shall I?' Will asked as the lady from the Kennel Club, yet another jolly-looking woman of a certain age who liked to wear sleeveless fleeces and seemed to prefer the company of dogs to humans, pointed at them. 'Actually, you go. You have the magic touch.'

As she walked Blossom to the starting point, Margot's face was red again because she was flushed with pleasure at Will's compliment. It was barely a compliment, but that was the effect kissing a man had on Margot. Reading too much into things.

'Lady in the red hat with the little Staffy, off you go!'

'Blossom, you are the best girl. You walk beautifully. You never pull,' Margot muttered as she and Blossom weaved through traffic cones. 'You are a positive dog who only has positive experiences with other dogs. Ignore the Husky and I'll let you eat more roast chicken then you've ever seen.'

Blossom looked up at Margot with trusting eyes as if she understood every word, especially the bit about the chicken. 'Lovely focus from the little Staffy,' Kennel Club lady called out rapturously, as they passed the Husky without incident and their lead remained in the 'smile' position.

Margot had never thought this day would come, not in her wildest dreams. But as they lined up with the other dogs and owners, it was inevitable that Kennel Club lady would go down the line and say, 'Pass,' when she came to Margot, Will and Blossom. 'You've got a cracking little dog there.'

'Did Blossom pull off the coup of the century?' Will asked incredulously.

'She did! She bloody did!'

'Blossom! I have never been prouder of anyone,' Will said in a gravelly voice and he scooped Blossom up so he could kiss her face, though he always told Margot not to do that because it was unhygienic. Although she always countered with the fact that dog's saliva contained a naturally occurring antiseptic and so it couldn't be that unhygienic.

He was certainly kissing Blossom now, who had her front paws on Will's shoulder so she could lick him back, and Margot wanted to get in on the kissing and the licking so she threw her arms around both of them.

'You really are my best girl,' she said to Blossom, who obligingly turned her head so she could lick Margot too.

Even though there was a wriggling Staffy between them, Margot was suddenly and painfully aware that she was pressed up against Will and he had an arm around her too. He was smiling, not just at Blossom, but at Margot, and when Blossom moved her head so she could lick Margot's neck, Will was able to press a kiss to Margot's cheek.

'She couldn't have done it without you,' he said. 'You deserve a Bronze Good Citizen certificate too.'

Margot really did but she couldn't take all the credit. 'Joint effort, I'd say.' And yes, kissing Will would lead to nothing but trouble, but she couldn't be in his arms and think of anything else but kissing him. He was so close, and yet, for her own sanity and so she didn't yank him closer still and force a kiss on him, Margot needed to remove herself from this situation. From this embrace. But God, he smelt *amazing* . . .

Luckily, as if he knew where Margot's thoughts were headed and wanted no part of them, Will stepped back so he could gently place Blossom back down on the ground. Then he stepped forward and Margot was in his arms again.

Or was he in her arms?

It was hard to say.

It was also impossible to tell who kissed whom first. But they were definitely kissing. Not even a brief victory peck but the kind of kissing that was too heated, too desperate, for a muddy dog-training area in January.

With no Blossom in the way, Margot was free to press herself against Will, who was hard and lean in all the right places, so for one glorious moment, Margot wished that he'd throw her down right there in the mud and really give Jim something to jangle his keys about . . .

'Oh!' Margot felt Will's hands on her arse and finally came to her senses. It was far too soon for *that* and completely inappropriate. She gave a little yelp and pulled her head back.

Will's hands were actually clasping her elbows and it was Blossom who was up on her hind legs with her paws on Margot's posterior, and some serious side-eye that said quite plainly, 'Why are you kissing? This is my special moment! Stop making it all about you, Margot.'

'Someone's feeling neglected,' Will murmured in Margot's ear, which made her shiver slightly. The good kind of shiver was back. He freed Margot so he could scoop Blossom up again.

They stayed for the certificate ceremony and a photo op with Will and Margot crouching on either side of Blossom, who looked proud and noble, as was only fitting. Then Margot sent the picture to the #TeamBlossom group.

Blossom is OFFICIALLY a good girl!

It was time to hand over Blossom, then not hear from Will for another week. She could hardly bear it. Margot waved goodbye to Jim, who'd insisted he knew Blossom would pass all along, and they began the trudge through the park.

'So, are we agreed that we're never coming here again?' Will asked, rubbing his hands together in glee at the prospect. 'Blossom's unlocked all the achievement levels that she needs to and there are better ways to spend Sunday mornings.'

'I suppose,' Margot agreed with less enthusiasm. Obviously, Will's Sunday mornings would be improved without Margot featuring in them, so why had he kissed her? Or had she stuck one on Will and he'd kissed her back to be polite? In which case, it was one of the most tragic kisses in Margot's portfolio.

'Are you hungry?' Will wanted to know as they circled the lake.

Always. 'I could eat,' Margot conceded.

'Do you want to get some lunch to celebrate? Your local, the Mitre, is dog-friendly, isn't it?'

It was, and if they were going to have A Talk, and they really needed to, then at least they were going to do it somewhere that served a very nice Malbec by the glass.

28

Will

Margot kept up a bright, constant chatter all the way back to Highgate. 'I knew the Husky wasn't going to pass. He always winds Blossom up. He's a bit of shit-stirrer, really.' So they didn't have to talk about any of the things that they really needed to talk about.

When they got to the Mitre, a former Georgian coaching inn, with a British heritage plaque, olde-worlde wooden beams and roaring log fire to prove it, Will went to the bar to order their drinks. When he came back with menus, Margot was deep in conversation with the family at the next table.

'. . . and if you are thinking of getting a dog then I would definitely adopt,' Margot was saying, though she momentarily paused to shoot a grateful smile at Will as he put a large glass of Malbec down in front of her.

Will sipped his lime and soda and watched Margot engrossed in her conversation, her hands gesturing wildly, until her knee lightly bumped his knee under the table by way of apology.

'So lovely to meet you but we must order lunch before we die from hunger,' Margot said with a charming smile. 'If you do get a dog, I'll be seeing you on the Heath in all weathers.'

'You're not doing Vegan January, are you?' Margot asked as she looked at the menu. 'Everyone at work is. I don't mind going meat-free a few days a week, but what even is life without cheese?'

'I'm doing Dry January,' Will pointed out, raising his glass. 'And Dry February, March, April and so on.'

'I did wonder why you don't drink, not that there's anything wrong with not drinking.' Margot looked down at her glass with a faintly guilty expression, which soon evaporated as she took an appreciative sip. 'You've *never* drunk?'

'Once. A very long time ago,' Will admitted hesitantly; the memory of it was enough to scrub away the warm, cosy pub, the homely smells of Sunday lunch, even the comforting weight of Blossom's head on his feet as she lay snoring on the floor. He remembered the cold, clammy feel of his skin, the hard bite of a hand on his arm, lifting a bottle to his lips again and again.

I'm raising a man. Not a limp-wristed sissy boy. C'mon, drink!

'And it was bad enough to have you swearing off booze for the rest of your life,' Margot decided. 'I was thirteen when Cerys across the road got married. I got absolutely paralytic on snowballs and threw up on my mother's hollyhocks as she tried to get me home. "You've learnt your lesson, Margot," she said. "You'll never abuse alcohol again." How wrong she was!'

'Poor hollyhocks,' Will murmured, and he wished that his own tale of first-time drunkenness had involved the same kind of parental caring. Not being forced to drink measure after measure of whisky until Will vomited all over himself, the carpet, the sofa, and still he'd been made to match his father sip for sip. Even now, the faintest scent of whisky made him retch. 'I was eleven. It was quite the salutary lesson and I've never touched a drop since.'

His voice was as cold as the memory, and Margot glanced up from the menu to Will's frozen face. She looked contemplative, as if she wanted him to explain further, add in the details, but he couldn't say another word.

'So much easier not to drink these days,' she said briskly. 'Have you noticed that when you get to your mid-thirties, all your friends have suddenly started running marathons, swerving alcohol and eating plant-based foods?'

Never had Will been so grateful for a change of subject; Margot's miraculous ability to read the room.

'Rowan decided that she was going to do the London Marathon to mark her thirty-fifth birthday,' he told Margot. 'It involved buying a lot of fancy kit from Sweaty Betty, two weeks of Couch to 5K, and that was the last we ever heard of Rowan's running ambitions.'

Margot was still laughing as she went off to order burgers for both of them, and when she came back she had another lime and soda for Will and a bottle of flavoured tonic water for herself. 'I should probably attempt to do a Dry-ish January,' she said. 'So, do you run? You look like you run.'

Had Margot been checking him out? If so, she'd been very subtle about it. Just as Will liked to think that when he noted how Margot was looking, he was discreet about it. What hadn't been discreet was his reaction earlier at the feel of her body pressed tight against his. The blood had roared around his veins and he'd been relieved when Blossom had killed the mood before Will had had time to embarrass himself.

Even the sense memory of Margot's curves made Will feel uncomfortably warm and take a long sip of his drink before he could reply to Margot's question. 'Used to run. When I lived in New York, I was very fitness orientated. We had these company CrossFit sessions before work where we all got very competitive over burpees and lunge pulls and lifting tyres.' *Jesus!* Were any of his memories happy ones?

'Sounds horrific,' Margot said as cheerfully as a person who'd never done a burpee could. 'I'm just grateful, thanks to Blossom, I can now walk all the way up Highgate West Hill without going into cardiac arrest. So, where were you working that enforced torture was company policy?'

That was the thing about sharing a personal anecdote. It led to more questions and answers that didn't just reveal an unhappy truth, but your unhappy soul, too. Will looked hopefully in the direction of the serving hatch but no food was coming to save him.

'I worked in finance. Banking,' he admitted, because people who weren't bankers didn't like bankers very much. 'In layman's terms, I was the man in charge of checks and balances, making sure that we didn't invest in anything dodgy or illegal and that our clients didn't try to launder huge amounts of money through us. You'd be amazed at how many times my colleagues didn't think that these things were an issue.'

'OK,' Margot said, reaching down to grab hold of Blossom's harness because someone had dropped a piece of bread on the floor a couple of tables down. 'I suppose that didn't make you popular with your workmates, if they were wanting to live out all of their *Wolf of Wall Street* fantasies. Is that why you were lifting tyres pre-breakfast? To try and bond with them?' Margot was so perceptive. Maybe too perceptive. It had taken Will months and Roland's gentle coaxing to make the same connection that had taken Margot less than five minutes. 'Are you the kind of person who thrives under that kind of pressure?'

'Obviously not, or else I wouldn't be back working at the family's floristry business and living above the shop,' Will said. No, he didn't say. He snapped.

Margot mimed zipping up her lips. 'All right, I got the message. I'm shutting up now.' Then she pulled a face like a dowager duchess who'd just seen a man wearing brown shoes to church.

'I'm sorry.' Will made sure to catch Margot's eye. 'It's a touchy subject and I'm a touchy bastard about it.'

'You don't have to explain things,' Margot assured him as she tried to persuade Blossom not to climb up on her lap. 'I tell people that I'm curious when actually I'm just very nosy.'

'I'm embarrassed by it now,' Will conceded. 'I was always very career-focused, goal-obsessed and strategy driven up until three years ago when I ended up working under Topper Livingston Mercer the Third .'

'I would never trust a man called Topper.'

'Then you're a very wise woman,' Will said. For fifteen years, his star had been in the ascendant. For all the risks involved in high finance, first in Paris, then in Berlin and finally in New York, Will had carved out a very successful career path by being calm and measured; his aversion to risk was seen as an asset after the financial crash of 2008. The women he dated were calm and measured too. They were just as ambitious as Will; more focused on the forward trajectory of their careers than their romantic relationships.

With that wonderful thing called hindsight, Will now realised that he should never have left a large corporate multinational investment bank, where he relished the rules and the bureaucracy, for a smaller, privately owned entity, with a Wild West attitude to high finance. But they'd offered him the role of Senior Vice President, a seven-figure salary, plus annual bonus, stock options and a whole raft of benefits, from courtside seats for Knicks games at Madison Square Gardens to access to the company yacht. Not that Will cared about basketball or catching the rays on a superyacht, but he had bought into the company culture of high-octane performance both in and out of the office.

'It became practically a spiritual quest to rise above my past, own my present and bench-press my bodyweight. I would kill it at the team-building weekends, where we'd confront our fears by abseiling down skyscrapers or go white-water rafting. I cringe to think about it now.'

'It all sounds fucking appalling,' Margot admitted, as their laden burgers arrived.

Will had very quickly discovered that his appointment had been opposed by Topper, the senior Board Director whose great-great-grandfather had founded the firm. Topper was a WASPy frat boy turned fifty-something finance bro, with a devil-may-care attitude, a third wife who'd been a Victoria's Secret model and a neon sign on his office wall that said 'Go Hard Or Go Home'.

He and Topper had somehow co-existed in a state of mutual loathing for two and a half years until Will had put the brakes on Topper's new fund, his 'magnum fucking opus' as he called it. Will had run due diligence and found several red flags, and the board, by the narrowest of margins, had agreed with him. That was when Topper had started freezing Will out. Trash-talking him around the bars and racquetball courts of Wall Street. Cultivating a relationship with the junior members of Will's team who, unlike the other places Will had worked, had no sense of loyalty. They'd have knifed their own grandmothers to get ahead.

But Will had faced down and survived worse bullies both in his career and in his personal life, so he continued to beat Topper at every endurance challenge the older man could dream up, and he continued to provide checks and balances so they never fell foul of the Securities and Exchange Commission.

Then Mo had died and Will didn't know how the world, his world, would carry on without her in it. Then the world had to manage without Bernie too.

'You need to decide if your personal life is more important than your career,' Topper had said coldly when Will had come back from the UK for Bernie's funeral, though he'd only just come back from taking time off for Mo's funeral.

Margot paused with the burger halfway to her mouth. 'Please tell me that eventually you came to your senses and told Topper to do one.'

'I suppose I did in a way.' Will picked up his own burger though he no longer had the appetite for it. 'We had yet another team-building day at some fancy hotel in the Bowery: workshopping and actualising our best selves, which would culminate in each of us walking on hot coals. You know, at the time, the idea of walking on hot coals as a metaphor for facing my fears and vanquishing my personal demons didn't sound that ridiculous.'

'Oh. My God.' Margot had given up on her burger and was staring at Will open-mouthed. 'You didn't?'

'I was planning to,' Will said. 'I was waiting in line and telling myself that I could do it, I was strong, I was powerful, nothing could hurt me, and then . . .'

Will couldn't believe that he was doing this: telling Margot, over burgers, about one of the most humiliating episodes of his life. He'd only told Rowan, because there were no secrets between them, and Roland, his therapist.

'And then?' Margot prompted, gripping the edge of the table.

'And then, I had terrible chest pains, couldn't breathe, and ended up in the emergency room with a suspected heart attack,' he said abruptly, as Margot's face softened and she tilted her head.

'Oh, Will.' Margot reached over to pat Will's arm. 'Panic attack?'

'How did you know?'

'It's the only appropriate response to being next in line to walk on hot coals. Also, you seem pretty fit for someone who had a heart attack a year ago.' She picked up a chip. 'Did Topper sack you for not walking on hot coals?'

'He didn't.' Will would have been able to sue him for all those Livingston Mercer millions. Topper had actually been very solicitous of Will's welfare when Will had turned up the next morning (he'd skipped CrossFit) with a bottle of beta-blockers and his mind reeling from the ER doctor's blunt assessment that he was a person suffering from anxiety. That he hadn't left his past behind, but rather internalised it until it had manifested the night before in the sharp, terrifying pain in his chest, like something or someone had squeezed all the air out of him. 'We had a chat about how people with positive mental attitudes can overcome everything.'

'Such bullshit,' Margot chimed in, chewing a chip furiously.

'It was bullshit.' Will could see that now, but at the time, before he'd ended up in the ER, he'd really wanted to believe that he could make himself anew, just from running a half marathon every other day, burpees and reading loads of personal development books. 'Then Topper reminded me that his ethos was to go hard or go home, and I heard myself say, "In that case, Topper, I think I'll go home."' Will spread his arms wide. 'And here I am.'

'What a bastard,' Margot managed to say around a mouthful of beef, bun and various relishes. 'I hope his trust fund goes bust and he ends up selling batteries out of a suitcase on Madison Avenue.'

It was highly unlikely, but a nice thought. 'I'll drink to that,' Will said and they clinked their glasses. 'And now I'm taking a year-long career sabbatical, but my year was up four months ago and I still don't know which direction I want to pivot in. Anyway, my burger is getting cold . . .'

You couldn't really talk when you were trying to get your mouth open wide enough to negotiate a burger, and Will was happy to have the time to regroup and also to admonish Blossom, who was now sitting upright and alert like a very stocky meerkat and drooling on Will's leg.

It wasn't until they were finishing the last of the chips, that they could talk again. Worse luck.

'Now I'm rethinking my whole daily affirmations thing,' Margot said at last. 'Maybe I'm just Topper in a dress.'

'But you're putting positive energy out into the universe, not sucking every last ounce of positivity out of everyone you meet.' Will couldn't believe that he was defending Margot's right to positively affirm, but today had been full of surprises.

'Thank you for that and thank you for sharing your story with me,' Margot said. 'It won't go any further.'

Will appreciated the thought even though they didn't have any mutual friends. Then he made a vow to himself that Margot was never to be left alone with his mother. Mary would only blame herself. 'Thanks,' he muttered.

'I know what you mean about feeling as if you don't fit in,' Margot said, as she drenched a chip in ketchup. 'At school, I was the girl whose dad had died, which made me stand out in a way that was just . . . It was unbearable.'

Will could understand. At school he'd stood out too, not because his dad had died, but because his dad was alive and was responsible for his pinched face, his hunched shoulders, why he and Rowan could never ask any friends back to their house. That had been unbearable too, but Will had already told Margot far too much about his past.

'I'm sorry, that must have been so hard, especially when you were missing him so much. But you seem to fit in now,' Will pointed out, practically giddy with relief that they'd changed the subject. 'You seem to know practically every person in North London.'

'It's that not-having-a-family thing,' Margot said, admitting defeat and pushing away the last of the chips in their trendy enamel mug. 'I've compensated by having a lot of people in my life, but there's no one who remembers what I was like as a baby, or what my first word was and why I was absolutely terrified of balloons.'

'Sand,' Will offered with a rueful smile. 'I had to be carried on to the beach.'

'It's a weird, untethered sort of feeling to know that you can never go home, because home is just me in my flat.' Margot turned her head so she was in profile, and for a moment, Will thought she might be crying. Her bottom lip trembled, her nostrils flared, but then, with superhuman control, she smoothed her features down. 'So many people tell me that I'm lucky that I own a flat in Highgate, but I'd much, much rather that both my parents were still alive so I'd never had an inheritance to spend.'

'I know it's a cliché and I'd never want to diminish what you've been through, but a lot of people have really awful families that they can't wait to escape,' Will said carefully. He felt as if he was picking his way through a field strewn with landmines, and the last thing he wanted to do was negate Margot's grief. 'Being able to make authentic connections with people is a real talent. It's not one that I'm very good at. Can I give Blossom the last chip?'

'Go on, then,' Margot said with weary resignation, either because of the losing battle over Blossom versus human food or because of the unhappy direction the conversation had taken. 'I have friends. My logical family. But lately I feel so distanced from them.'

Will felt as if the collar of shirt was too tight. That would explain the strange tingling sensation at the back of his neck. He wanted to tell Margot that she'd be better off talking to

someone who was naturally inclined towards listening sympathetically then giving advice. Will had a sneaking suspicion
that, despite all the therapy, even Blossom was more emotionally intelligent than he was.

'Oh right,' he said, in a strangulated voice. 'Why's that
then?'

'They're all getting married, having babies and moving
away. Not always in that order.' Margot's smile was a badly
rendered copy of itself. 'I haven't managed to do any of those
things.'

Will put a finger between his collar and his neck. 'Um, do
you want to do any of those things?'

'God, yes! Of course I do!' Margot pushed away her glass
as if it suddenly disgusted her. 'I've spent the last eighteen
years mourning not just my mum, and my dad, but being part
of a family. Meanwhile, all my friends have managed to find
someone and start their own families like it's the easiest thing
in the world. I haven't. I'm left behind and that's why I feel as
if I don't fit in.'

'Well, I'm sure it will happen.' Now that Will thought about
it, it did seem strange that Margot was single when, apart
from the micromanaging, she was the kind of woman that
men would want to settle down with. Topper and his posse of
finance bros had always been adamant that there were women
you fucked and women you married, 'wifeys' they called them,
rather predictably, but Margot was definitely a long-haul kind
of girl.

She was pretty, smart, creative, independent. That would
be more than enough, but she was also kind and always
knew the right thing to say. Not the sort of woman that
you'd let slip away. Margot was soft kisses, soft curves, the
kind of softness you could get lost in. Will tugged at his
collar again.

'I want it too much, that's the problem,' Margot was saying. 'I give off that deadly whiff of desperation. One sign of interest from a man and I become really needy. Even more needy than Blossom.'

'I'm sure you're not.' Will was suddenly aware that he was doing nothing but mouthing platitudes, which he would have hated if the positions were reversed. 'Blossom's neediness is limitless.'

Another tenth generation copy of a smile. 'You're not looking to settle down and start a family, are you?' she asked idly. Will felt that tingle at the back of his neck again.

'No,' he said flatly, because there was no other way to say it. He was still trying to find the emotional reserves just to start dating again. 'Not in my immediate future.'

'Which is why we have to stop with the kissing,' Margot said in a rush. 'Because it's weird . . .'

'My kisses are weird,' Will echoed, which wasn't the point at all, but it was where he'd got stuck.

'Your kisses aren't weird, and if I were still in my twenties, then I'd love nothing more than to be kissing a really handsome man with no thought of where the kisses might take us. And don't look like that, Will. You must have at least one mirror in your flat, so you have to know that all your features are very pleasing to the eye.'

Will felt his face heat up. Not just at the unexpected compliment, because the only person who currently told him that he was 'a gorgeous boy' was Mary and she was contractually obligated to do so, but because Margot was much braver than he was, even though she'd never abseiled down a skyscraper. She'd initiated this awkward but necessary conversation with all of her usual grace, and she was even managing to maintain eye contact, though Will longed to stare at his feet, at the burger debris on his plate, even at Blossom who was enthusiastically nibbling at one of her paws. Anywhere but Margot's steady gaze and equally flushed face.

'You're very pleasing to the eye too,' Will said, and Margot raised her almost empty glass in gratitude for his clumsy flattery. There had been a time when women thought Will was quite suave because that was the image he'd desperately tried to project. But a lot had happened since those evenings in foreign cities, where it was easy to spout meaningless patter at women who knew the rules of the game they were both playing. No strings, no regrets, no hard feelings.

Will didn't want that anymore, but then he didn't know what he did want. Only that Margot wanted something completely different.

'I'm thirty-six and, lovely as it's been, I can't waste time kissing people just for the sake of it,' she said a little sadly, her features drooping, which slightly soothed the sting of rejection. 'I need to be really single-minded and focused on starting a family as soon as possible'.

Will nodded. It all made sense. He wasn't sure he'd ever be ready for what Margot was craving. 'Shall we just agree that a New Year's kiss was the right thing to do, and so was a celebratory kiss because Blossom passed her Bronze Good Citizen Certificate?' he asked casually – he'd spent years making himself say things casually instead of letting his emotions run rampant. 'We can't help it that we're both extraordinarily good-looking.'

Margot smiled as if she didn't want to smile but couldn't help herself. 'But we're still friends?'

'It's not even a question,' Will said. 'Of course we're still friends.' For someone who had no talent when it came to friendship, Will had somehow managed to make a friend when and where he least expected to. A friend who he liked. Really liked. 'Co-pawrents too, don't forget.'

'My greatest achievement in life is that you now say co-pawrents without any visible wincing.' Somehow, again without Will knowing how, Margot had managed to cut through the awkward atmosphere that had engulfed them.

'On the inside I'm wincing,' Will said, and having Margot laugh and nudge him with her elbow wasn't as good as kissing her but it would have to do.

29

Margot

Name: Dale
  Age: 41
  Status: Divorced, looking for dates and long-term relationship.
  Likes: Long walks, intelligent conversation, good food and wine, and snuggling up on the sofa.
  Dislikes: Smokers, moaners and cheaters.

'Dale, forty-one, is obviously bitter about his divorce,' Jacques said, reading over Margot's shoulder as she perused her likely online matches during her lunch hour the next day.

It was excessively cold out, with a piercing wind that penetrated right through to the marrow, so Margot was relieved it was a non-Blossom week. She missed her dreadfully, not least because Blossom doubled up as a hot water bottle, but Margot wasn't missing the icy hour standing about on Primrose Hill while Blossom frolicked.

It was also excessively hard to think about throwing herself back into dating when Margot couldn't stop thinking about Will. Since their kiss on New Year's Eve, she'd constantly replayed the memory of his lips on hers, his hands on her, his body against hers. But instead of adding their last and final kiss to the rotation, Margot knew that she had to try and pretend that it hadn't happened. It certainly wouldn't be happening again.

Being sensible and grown-up wasn't very much fun. When

Margot was a kid, she'd thought that being an adult meant that she'd never have to eat her greens or go to bed at a reasonable hour. But life wasn't all chocolate for breakfast and staying up all night; it was having to do the right thing even when the right thing felt like the wrong thing.

As well as the kissing, the really stellar kissing that made her cheeks heat up, which she absolutely wasn't thinking about, she was still processing what Will had told her about his last three years in New York. He'd been honest with her in a way that she'd never expected from that closed-off stranger she'd met four months before.

He'd shared so much of himself, but Margot still had so many questions left unanswered. There were still more layers to carefully peel back before she could get to the heart of this complex, contrary man. Margot knew all about the layers that kept you safe and the rest of the world at bay. People assumed that sometimes she was sad because her parents were dead. Those were the facts, the headlines, and no one really delved any deeper than that. But underneath the loss were emotions that were harder to talk about. Loneliness of course, and, even after all these years, a grief, which still had the power to hurt if Margot took it out of its box and held it up to the light. When Margot thought of her mother's last year, there was also guilt, a corrosive shame that washed over her like acid. There was panic too; you could never know how life might turn out, how long you had left, which was all the more reason not to kiss handsome, conflicted men and to take a chance on Dale, forty-one.

'He has a kind face,' Margot said, squinting at her phone. 'Don't you think he has a kind face?'

'A kind face for someone whose moaning, smoking wife cheated on him,' Jacques agreed, but the pickings on the dating apps were slim (even though January was meant to be the month where traditionally everyone dumped their old loves and started looking for new ones) and Margot couldn't afford to be that picky.

Hi Dale,

Congratulations! We're a match! I'm Margot, a clothing designer who also loves long walks and snuggling on the sofa – so does my dog, Blossom. (She's the pretty one in my profile picture.) I also like good food and wine, but I can't always guarantee good conversation.

I see you're North London based. Fancy a walk with me and Blossom?

Experience had taught Margot that there was no point in fannying about with endless messages. It was better to meet up with potential matches as soon as possible. Rather than being a many splendoured thing, love was a numbers game. The more men you met, the more chances you had of finding The One. Or more accurately, The One That Will Do. Lord knows, Margot had put the work in and was due her happy ever after as suitable recompense.

Done, Margot thought, pressing send on the message without even trace amounts of anticipation. It had barely gone into the ether when her phone chimed and her stomach clenched as she saw it was a message from Will. Not on the #TeamBlossom group chat either.

'Oh God, now *what*?' she muttered under her breath as she opened the app.

Should have probably consulted with you first, but Mum was adamant that Blossom was freezing so we went to Woof! and bought her a coat. I don't think she likes it. W

There was also a video attached. A video of Blossom taking two steps in her new coat and then sitting down with a baleful glare at the phone, or rather at Will who was holding the phone and laughing.

'Come on, Blossom, off we go!' he said in a very jaunty manner. Blossom wasn't having any of it.

Not that Margot could blame her. Blossom was wearing a padded black garment that was far too big and cumbersome for her and was secured at the waist with a Velcro belt so that the ends of the coat flapped behind her.

It was the dog equivalent of your mum buying a school coat two sizes too big 'because you'll grow into it'.

Why though? She messaged Will back. *Of all the coats?*

It was the only one large enough to get over her big, fat (but also completely loveable) head.

Send me her measurements. Neck, shoulders, fattest part of her ribcage, then lengthways from neck to tail.

A couple of years back, Derek and Tansy had considered doing a range of baby clothes, but focus groups had ixnayed the whole idea. Margot still had some prototype babygro designs on her hard disk and was pretty sure that they still had some of the fleece-lined jersey they'd used for last winter's onesies.

She'd been looking for a project to work on during her off-weeks when she wasn't attempting to throw herself back into dating with renewed enthusiasm and vigour.

And Margot had to concede that she did feel a tiny bit enthusiastic as she prepared for her first date with Dale, forty-one, a few days later.

Dale was still maintaining the story that he loved long walks (*My ambition is to do the West Highland Way one summer*) so on Margot's work-from-home Wednesday, they'd planned a stroll on Hampstead Heath. (*And of course, bring Blossom. I love dogs.*)

It turned out that a daytime-date-cum-dog-walk had a completely different vibe to meeting-for-a-drink-after-work-and-hoping-that-it-might-lead-to-dinner-and-then-who-knows?

There was no frantic wrangling of an outfit that would take Margot from day to evening, make her look sexy but not slutty, that she could also sit down in.

It was January. It was cold. 'Too cold to snow,' people said, though surely it was colder in places like Norway and Sweden, yet it still managed to snow there. Margot was wearing jeans and a jumper, which proclaimed This Is What a Feminist Looks Like. Margot had thought that she might wear her Veja trainers, but it was too cold, too wet and too slippery underfoot for anything other than her sheepskin-lined hiking boots. Besides, Margot thought it unlikely any man was likely to fall in love with her at first sight just because she was wearing a pair of fashionable and over-priced trainers. Something that twenty-something Margot would never have believed.

But even scouring winds blowing in from Siberia weren't enough to convince Margot to wear the Dog-Walking Anorak Of Doom. She wore her thick wool blue-and-red check coat and matched her hat, scarf and a dash of scarlet lipstick to it. She was ready to go.

She didn't have any of the first date nerves that usually kicked in. Though, there was a brief moment of panic, but that was only because Margot thought that she'd forgotten to stash some poo bags in her coat's capacious pockets. She was more preoccupied with how splendid Blossom looked in her new pink snowflake onesie, getting admiring glances from people hurrying past.

'Cute dog,' Dale, forty-one, said when Margot arrived at Whitestone Pond. 'Also, hi!'

He waved woolly gloved fingers at Margot and she smiled while they both gave each other a fleeting once over. Dale was bundled up against the elements in a North Face anorak with fur-trimmed hood, face half-obscured by a grey scarf. He was wearing jeans and sensible walking boots and he was about half a head taller than Margot. So far, so good.

'Shall we set off, then?' Margot asked, gesturing across the road to Hampstead Heath, glittering with frost

'Let's do it,' Dale agreed. 'I thought about bringing my Nordic poles, but I was worried you'd think I was a total wanker.'

'I probably would until I realised that they were doing a great job of keeping you upright,' Margot said as they crossed the road.

Daytime-dating-cum-dog-walking was a complete revelation. There was no stilted conversation as they both sipped at a glass of something alcoholic and hoped desperately that it would lubricate the situation. There was no awkward meeting of eyes, or, even worse, not knowing where to look. And there was absolutely no question – not even the implication – that there was going to be any kind of hooking up afterwards.

Instead, they clomped slowly across the Heath, pausing to admire nature and all its frozen delights, from a crystallised spider's web, the delicate splintering ice on the ponds and the crunching sound their feet made on the solid, spiky grass. They both complained about how cold it was and, when they'd exhausted that topic, Blossom could always be relied upon to do something hilarious. In this instance, she hunkered down to do a wee and went sliding across the path.

Dale talked about his dog, Bucky, a Labradoodle, who mostly lived with his ex-wife and their two kids. But he didn't seem at all bitter about the divorce.

'We married really young. Had kids really young and by the time that both of us had figured out who we were, we also realised that we weren't in love with the people that either of us used to be,' he said, and though the line sounded rehearsed, Margot didn't mind.

When you were dating, seriously dating, you got used to repackaging some of the most awful and defining moments of your life into neat sound bites.

The two kids were twenty-one and nineteen, both at university, but because it was only the first date, Margot couldn't ask Dale how he would feel about having a second batch of children when he was barely done raising the first.

Still, as they thawed out with coffee at Kenwood House, she was pleased when Dale asked if she'd be up for another date.

'But somewhere warmer,' he suggested hopefully. 'Maybe for dinner if you don't mind leaving Blossom at home.'

Margot hadn't explained about the dog sharing. It was too complicated. Also, she didn't want to think about Will while she was on a date.

'Next week, then,' she said with a smile, because Dale had pushed down his scarf so he could drink his coffee and he *did* have a kind face, though she still wasn't sure what the hair situation was like. Margot wasn't shallow enough that a little male pattern baldness would put her off. Unless Dale had hair plugs. Hair plugs were a definite deal-breaker.

It turned out, a week later, when they met at the last little Italian trattoria left in Soho which hadn't been flattened to make way for the Crossrail, that Dale was one of those men who had realised his hair was trying to say goodbye and had shaved the whole lot off.

Dale also looked relieved when Margot took off her coat to reveal one of her trusty midi dresses – this one in a black-and-white check – and her hat to reveal that she did have a full head of hair.

Because they'd already had one date, it was much easier to

pick up the threads after they'd ordered warming bowls of pasta and a bottle of red wine.

Dale was a TV script editor and had several amusing anecdotes about egotistical actors and even more egotistical directors. He wouldn't name names, he wasn't a bragger, and he didn't only talk about himself, which a lot of men *still* did, even though they must have all received the memo by now stating very clearly that that sort of thing just wasn't acceptable.

He listened attentively as Margot told him about having to shoot winter fashion in the middle of a heatwave. As dates went, this one was perfectly OK, but all Margot could think about was getting the Tube home.

In an ideal world, Blossom would be waiting for her, to hover impatiently around her feet while Margot made a cup of tea, then when Margot sat down on the sofa, Blossom would tuck in tight next to her and Margot would put her chunky wool throw around them both.

But Blossom was tucked in tight with Will and it was time for Margot to get down to business.

'This has been lovely,' she said after their plates had been cleared and they'd asked for a brief respite before they thought about pudding.

'It has been lovely. Best two dates I've had,' Dale said, smiling with his kind face. 'Though I feel like a but is coming. Is it?'

Margot spread her hands out on the table, took one calming breath, then made sure to look Dale in the eye. 'I'm looking for a long-term serious relationship,' she said. 'I want children.'

Dale swallowed hard. 'It has only been two dates. I'd really love to see where this goes.'

It had been two good dates, but Margot also knew that she'd have no regrets if there wasn't a third date. Like, when she'd watched two episodes of something on Netflix and decided that she'd much rather watch *Schitt's Creek* again. There just wasn't that spark. That connection.

Not that she could tell Dale that. 'I'm thirty-six. I don't have time to see where this is going to go,' she explained softly, because that was also the truth and a lot more palatable to Dale than, sorry, but I'm just not that into you.

They decided not to have coffee but split the bill and said their hurried goodbyes in the restaurant doorway.

Margot watched Dale, and what could have been her uncertain future, hurry away, then adjusted her scarf and mentally prepared herself for the frostbitten walk to the Tube station. On the plus side, it wasn't even eight thirty and within an hour, she'd be home, toasty warm . . .

'Hey! Hi, Margs! I thought it was you,' came a piercing cry from the other side of the tiny street and Margot looked up to see Sage standing there holding two buckets.

Weird. Random. But mostly weird.

'What are you doing here?' Margot asked, crossing the deserted street. 'Why are you holding two buckets?'

'I've just shown a bunch of influencers how to artfully arrange some seasonal flowers into photogenic posies at a PR event,' Sage explained. She shivered, probably because she wasn't wearing a coat and her fashionable high-waisted jeans finished some way above her ankles. 'Give me two minutes to load up and I'll give you a lift home.'

Sage had done the workshop with two friends who had promptly abandoned her once she'd paid them. It took fifteen minutes for Sage and Margot to clear up the flower debris then load Sage's unused supplies into the Blooms' van. Still, it beat bussing and Tubing it home.

'Are you missing Blossom?' Sage wanted to know as she navigated through the narrow Soho streets.

'Always,' Margot said. 'I love snuggling her on a cold night. What did you think of the snowflake onesie I made her?'

'We need a new word to describe how fucking adorable she looks in it because none of the current ones will do,' Sage decreed. 'OK, I need to shut up and focus on my driving until we're out of Soho.'

Margot obligingly shut up until they were stuck behind a bus on Tottenham Court Road. It was that fallow period when all the Christmas decorations had been taken down and it was cold and wet and felt like nothing nice would ever happen again. Then the Valentine's Day displays would go up and Margot would feel resentful and bitter because there was no one to buy her a bunch of red roses with the price jacked up.

Sage overtook a bus and just managed to slide through the lights before they turned amber. She sighed in a self-satisfied sort of way.

'You're a very good driver,' Margot noted, which made Sage preen. 'I can't drive, never even had a lesson, and yet here you are, bossing it through Central London like an old pro.'

'I only passed my test a few months ago,' Sage explained. 'When Will came back from the States, he'd take me to practise in the big Tesco car park when it was really quiet, to build up my confidence before we went out on the roads.'

'Will did?' All evening, Margot had been pushing thoughts of Will away. Now she gave in to the inevitable and thought about him. How, even though it was awkward, and it was frequently awkward, she missed spending time with him.

'Yeah. Have you any idea how expensive driving lessons are?' Sage let out a long, low whistle. 'I'd already gone through three driving instructors and even Dad, Captain Calm, said I was a menace on the roads. So, thank God for Will. It's funny, 'cause although he's my brother, my whole life he'd been living somewhere else and always seemed kind of distant. So those evenings we spent driving around empty supermarket car parks were when we really got to know each other. Nothing like having a meltdown over reversing to really bond two people.'

'Did he get very cross with you?' Margot asked, remembering how cross Will had got with her in the early days of their co-pawrenting.

Sage grinned. 'Mostly not cross, even when I freaked out on Apex Corner roundabout and did seven complete loops. He was white knuckling the dashboard, but he didn't even raise his voice, just kept telling me to get in the far-side lane and remember to use the indicator.'

Margot felt she had been a little uncharitable. 'He was quite patient with Blossom, especially when we had to sit in the park in close proximity to the squirrels so she could build up her tolerance.' She shook her head as she remembered the futile exercise Jim had insisted they do. 'I was ready to throw in the towel after ten minutes, but Will insisted we could do the full hour.'

'Yeah, he's good at all that Jedi mind-shit,' Sage said. 'He's even persuaded Mum to start walking Blossom. Normally the only walking she does is around the big Tesco. It's amazing that her leg muscles haven't atrophied.'

'Not all of us like to exercise,' Margot murmured. 'Especially if there might be sweat involved.'

'I hope you didn't get the wrong idea about us when you came round for Christmas,' Sage continued regardless. 'All families are weird. Sometimes, I think mine are weirder than most, then I go round to a friend's house and I'm like, no, you're all totally weird too.'

'It wasn't weird on Christmas Day,' Margot insisted, though it had been weird and uncomfortable and she'd sat at that kitchen table embarrassed to be there and embarrassed on behalf of the Blooms who couldn't have wanted her to be there either.

'It was *so* weird.' Sage glanced across to meet Margot's eyes and for one moment, she wasn't a teenage girl who went out without a proper coat on, but wise beyond her years. 'I love my mum. She's been through some stuff, some really serious shit, long before I arrived, which has left its mark on her. Like, she wants everything to be perfect and when it's not, she freaks out for a bit. But it is always for a bit then she's fine. Like, she's funny and I love hanging out with her and nobody can be perfect all the time. I bet you're not.'

'Oh God, I'm *never* perfect,' Margot exclaimed. 'I've given up even trying.' She reached out to brush Sage's arm with her hand. 'You and your mum are lucky to have each other. All of you are lucky to have each other.'

'Yeah, I know,' Sage said, hissing as a taxi pulled out in front of her with no warning. Then she smiled slyly. 'Mum thinks you *are* perfect, by the way.'

Margot found that hard to believe. They'd WhatsApped a storm, but she'd only met Mary once and the other woman had spent most of that time fretting about dinner. 'She does?'

'She's constantly worrying that we're not looking after Blossom as well as you do. Then there was the whole speech about how it couldn't be good for Blossom to be shuttled back and forth and that it would be wonderful if you and Will got together. For Blossom's sake.'

Margot didn't know Sage well enough to tell if she was winding her up. What she did know though, was that whatever her reaction was, it would be reported back to the assorted Blooms at great length and in great detail. As it was, she was in agony to know what Will had thought about this declaration. Also what he'd said about it and how he'd looked while he was saying it.

Margot attempted a carefree chuckle. 'Blossom is very happy to be shuttled back and forth between the two of us. She gets double the love.'

'Yeah, but . . .'

'I wouldn't go via Kentish Town if I were you,' Margot said in her most officious voice. 'Take the left fork towards Parliament Hill and then we can scoot down Highgate West Hill. All right?'

'You're the boss,' Sage said lightly, then she was silent.

Margot stared fixedly out of the window, but she could tell that Sage kept looking over at her and grinning.

30

Will

January became February became March. The bleached white winter skies became blue once more and the stark branches of the trees were budded with leaf shoots.

It was still muddy underfoot, but there was the promise of spring. Of no longer needing to have Blossom's onesies (she had six at the last count – three for Will, three for Margot, or as Mary said 'one on, one off and one in the wash') drying on radiators.

Sage was full of the joys of spring when she came barrelling into the shop one Saturday morning in late March. As usual, she was five minutes late and, as usual, she sent the front door crashing back on its hinges.

'If that door breaks, it's coming out of your wages,' Ian said, as he always did. He was perched behind the till, on his first mug of tea, slightly sweaty because he'd already cycled to Regent's Park to do laps with his bike club, the Muswell Hill MAMILs.

'You should be happy that I'm so enthusiastic about coming into work,' Sage said, disappearing into the back room to hang up her coat.

'She is enthusiastic,' Ian remarked. He adjusted his glasses, which were slipping down his nose. 'Not that enthusiastic about going to university though. Still, it's her life, she has to make her own decisions, right?'

Will looked around to make sure that no one was listening. 'She's nineteen. She goes out without a coat even when it's snowing and she's incapable of entering or leaving a room without damaging the door. I would say that maybe she needs some gentle guidance when it comes to huge life-altering decisions.'

'If Sage needs some advice, she knows where I am,' was Ian's inevitable reply. Sometimes Will thought that his stepfather's parenting skills bordered on benign neglect, but if that were the case then Sage was thriving. And benign neglect was preferable to how Will and Rowan had been raised.

'But don't you think Sage would make a good barrister?' Will persisted. 'She's so argumentative and determined to have the last word. She'd be sure to have all the capital's criminals banged to rights.'

'With no hope of parole,' Ian added, then pretended to be studying the order book with great attention as Mary appeared in her new navy fleece and her special Skechers walking shoes.

For the last few alternate Saturday mornings, Mary took Blossom out for a brief walk to Alexandra Park around a grassy area known as the Grove, mostly to hang out with her dog-owning friends and gossip. Now she spent several minutes checking that she had dog treats, poo bags, coin purse and phone in her new cross-body bag, then left with a cheery wave and a, 'If I'm not back in half an hour then me and the girls are having a coffee.'

Ninety minutes later and Mary and Blossom still weren't back. Long enough for even Ian to wonder what was keeping her and for Sage to start catastrophising. 'What if she's been run over at the top of Dukes Avenue? They should have a zebra crossing there! Or what if Blossom has seen a squirrel and pulled Mum over and she's lying in a ditch somewhere? And what if . . .'

They were saved from anymore 'what if's by Will's phone chiming.

With the girls in the Grove café. Penny ran off and I had to stay there to update everyone. Blossom hasn't had much of a walk, can you come and get her?

Will wasn't sure who Penny was, but he shrugged on his jacket – it was warm enough now to forgo his heavy winter coat – and set off for the park.

He'd never say anything to Mary, but Blossom never got much of a walk with her. She hated letting her off the lead and when she did, Mary would continuously call Blossom back. Now, when Will or Margot walked Blossom, she'd frequently stop, look back at them and refuse to move until she got a 'Good girl!'. Worse, Mary refused to believe that treats were rewards for good behaviour and not something to be doled out willy nilly.

Lately, Blossom had decided to sit down mid-walk until she got a treat. No wonder that last time he and Margot had taken Blossom to the vet, they'd been told sternly that Blossom had gained all the weight she needed and was fast heading in the other direction.

'She's not fat!' Mary had protested at the news. 'She has a very large ribcage.'

Will decided that he'd talk to Margot about it when they met later and come up with a plan of action. It was a habit that he'd got into lately: storing away anecdotes and amusing things that had happened. Polishing them, refining them, working on his jokes so he'd tease that radiant smile out of her or, even better, make her laugh. When he made Margot laugh, she'd usually finish up by gently shoving him.

It came to something when a gentle shove from from Margot, even just simply thinking about the possibility of it, could completely derail Will's thought processes: he'd taken the right-hand path into the park and not the left. Now he had to cut across the green, the grass springy and wet with hidden patches of squelchy mud, to get to the café. He could see Mary's gang congregated outside, all of them in fleeces.

Will grinned as Blossom looked at him, then looked back at the busy tables to see if there might be any food in her near future. She decided that there wasn't and came running to meet Will with her purposeful, bustling waddle.

'Hello, madam.' Will stepped back so she couldn't jump on him with muddy paws. 'No, don't sit down. You need to stop snacking between meals.'

Blossom looked at him with sorrowful eyes, but she was given away by the joyous beat of her tail as they walked to the café where Mary and her friends were now regaling some new arrivals with the latest update.

'. . . she got chased by those two German Shepherds . . .'

'. . . everyone's told him to keep them on a lead if he can't control them . . .'

'. . . of course, he says they're just being friendly, but Nancy's Pug got pinned down by one of them . . .'

'. . . anyway, Penny took off and she was gone for fifteen minutes . . .'

'No, it was half an hour at least and Jayne was frantic . . .'

Will felt compelled to interrupt. 'Penny's a dog, right?'

'Oh, Will! Penny is Jayne's Juggle,' Mary said in exasperation as if Will should know who Penny and Jayne were.

'And a Juggle is . . .?' he couldn't help asking, despite the condemning stares from Mary's friends, who pretty much ruled the park, and God help you if you didn't pick up your dog's poo quick enough.

'It's a Jack Russell cross Pug cross Beagle,' he was told crossly. Will stuck around long enough to hear that Jayne's husband had opened the front door to find Penny sitting on the step.

'We couldn't get rid of you if we tried,' he told Blossom, as he clipped on her lead to cross the road that snaked through the palace grounds, the same road she'd taken a mad dash across in pursuit of a squirrel all those months ago.

She was a different dog now. Walking calmly across the road then sitting down and waiting for Will to unclip her again so they could take their usual route. Now Blossom was free to sniff and explore, her true personality had emerged, and her true personality was a sassy, salty little madam, who liked to think that she was in charge of the open spaces of North London, but especially Ally Pally park.

During the week, the park was quiet in the mornings. Usually the only people Will saw were his fellow dog walkers. He didn't even bother to try and get out of saying hello now. In fact, sometimes he found himself walking *with* one of them so they could both discuss their dog's likes, dislikes and weird foibles.

But on Saturdays, the park was full of people getting their exercise on. At the Grove, they'd already passed a small, all-ages group doing gentle exercise and running to various markers. On the South Slope in front of the palace, there was a large gaggle of twenty-somethings being shouted at by two burly men in camouflage gear – the military boot-camp gang.

At the bottom of the South Slope, were a steady stream of runners, joggers and stragglers doing the weekly park run. On every bench, people in tight Lycra were stretching and patting Blossom's head as she trotted along to supervise all this strenuous activity.

It didn't make Will nostalgic for his days of half marathons and burpees, but he could start running again now it was warmer. Maybe he could join a running club . . .

Blossom had gone on ahead now, towards two young guys sparring: one of them throwing punches, the other deflecting his blows with a pair of focus pads strapped to his hands. Blossom stopped to look at them then. And kept on stopping. God, she was lazy.

'Good girl, Blossom!' Will called out, but still Blossom didn't move. The two boys stopped boxing and looked at Blossom. Will increased his pace.

'She's very friendly,' he called out as he got nearer. 'She won't hurt you.'

'Think there's something wrong with your dog, bruv.'

Will broke into a run. Had she stepped on broken glass? Or landed awkwardly on one of her impossibly delicate back legs?

Blossom was standing there, panting hard, tongue out so she could frantically lick her lips; a sure sign that she was in pain or stressed.

'Didn't even touch her, innit,' one of the lads said, taking a step towards Blossom, who cowered away from him. 'Not even doing nothing.'

'Sorry, she's a rescue,' Will murmured, all his focus on Blossom. He squatted down so he could run his hands over her, check her paws, but at his first touch on her flank, she snapped at him, then collapsed on her belly so she could crawl away.

'She even your dog, though? She ain't acting like she's your dog.'

Will couldn't blame them for doubting his ownership, because every time he spoke to Blossom, or reached out a hand, she slunk further and further away from him, until she was hiding behind a wooden bench, still panting furiously.

He hadn't seen Blossom this afraid since the day that he'd first met her and he'd had to bribe her with freeze-dried duck innards to come to his side.

'Blossom,' Will said, his voice as low and as soft as he could make it. 'You know that I would never hurt you. You're safe with me.'

The bench backed onto a hedge, its leaves prickly and sharp, which didn't stop Blossom from burying herself in the foliage. Everything Will could think of to do, which wasn't much, only scared her more. The last thing he wanted to do was send her into such a blind panic that she ran across the road again.

He didn't know whether to sit down or stand and loom over her. He didn't know what to do.

Inevitably, predictably, Will could feel his chest getting tight, his skin growing cold and clammy, the fear rising up in him.

No.

Breathe.

Not now.

Breathe.

This was just a panic attack.

Breathe.

A physical manifestation of his inner turmoil.

Breathe.

Will's inner turmoil was meant to be better now.

Cured.

Fixed.

Breathe.

Though obviously it wasn't.

Breathe.

Except now he had someone to call. Someone who always knew the right thing to say. He had a person.

31

Margot

On her non-Blossom weeks, Margot was *still* up to her neck in the dating pool, which also meant that was *still* despairing of ever finding a single man who was kind, funny, not completely hideous to look at, financially solvent and ready for some serious commitment.

'It would be easier to find a fucking unicorn,' she'd told Tracy, as she'd helped her with a massive declutter so she and Den could then pack up what was left of their possessions and move halfway across the world. Margot wasn't exactly sure why she was enabling this hare-brained scheme, as she held up various possessions and asked Tracy if they were sparking joy.

What with all the bad dates, not one of them worth committing to even a second date, Tracy clearly still intent on emigrating to New Zealand, and heated debates at Ivy+Pearl about whether rose gold was still a thing and how did everyone feel about copper and gunmetal, Blossom was the only thing that kept Margot sane.

Blossom . . . and Will.

They pretended that they were hanging out together because it was better for Blossom – that even though she had two homes and two different routines, she had two owners who could put their differences aside, and present her with a united front. Not just the endless messaging back and forth, but meeting up each week for a Wednesday lunchtime walk and then again on Saturdays.

So, it was only natural that Margot would compare the men she met with Will. Compare them and always find them wanting.

Will would laugh at that joke.

Will would never pinch one of my chips without asking first.

Will would never, ever address all his remarks to my boobs.

Will would offer to walk me to the Tube station even if it was totally out of his way.

But what Will would and wouldn't do was immaterial. Margot and Will wanted different things in life, so a couple of snatched kisses was all that she was ever going to get.

Still, as Margot put herself through a very low-impact yoga routine in her living room one Saturday morning in late March, she was finding it hard to stay in warrior pose and engage her core when her core was being battered by anticipatory flutters at the thought of seeing Will in a couple of hours for their usual walk.

She was just coming up from a very inept downward dog when her phone started to ring, which she ignored. Instead she concentrated on her breathing and tree pose as the phone rang out then, after a brief pause, beeped as the caller left her a voicemail. Then it rang again. Beeped. On the third cycle, she gave up tree pose and picked up her phone from the coffee table to see Will's name flashing up.

'Hello? Are we still meeting later? You could have just messaged instead—'

'I need you,' Will said urgently. 'There's something wrong with Blossom.'

'What's happened? Is she hurt? Are you at the vet?'

'I'm at Ally Pally. Can you come now? I'll pay for the Uber.'

'Oh God, don't worry about that,' Margot said, already grabbing socks and trainers. 'You're freaking me out, Will.'

'I'm kind of freaked out myself,' he muttered, then gave Margot directions and made her promise that she'd come immediately.

It only took five minutes for the car to arrive. The driver wanted to talk, assumed that Margot was off to do some kind of physical activity as she was still in her yoga clothes, but she was so rattled that she didn't even fret about losing her five-star Uber rating for cutting the poor man off before he could even finish a sentence.

'Can you stop at the traffic lights in front of the palace?' she demanded as they came into view.

'Can't do that, it's a main road and there's a bus behind us,' the driver said laconically.

'I will give you a hundred per cent tip,' Margot promised, and he immediately came to a screeching halt, so she could scramble out of the car, cross over the road in the face of oncoming traffic, then race down the steps.

Will was standing with arms crossed, just a little distance away. There was no sign of Blossom; her lead dangled from Will's hand.

'Where is she?' Margot shouted, but Will shook his head and put a finger to his lips, so Margot had no choice but to hurry over. Some people might even have said it was a run, though Margot did not run. Not ever.

'She's here,' Will whispered as soon as Margot was in earshot. 'She's hiding in the bush behind that bench. There were two lads boxing, and I think it must have triggered a memory because she froze on the spot and when I tried to touch her, she snapped her teeth at me. Even the sound of my voice . . . I would *never* hurt her. I'm not like that.'

'Well, of course you're not,' Margot said quickly with a glance up at Will. He was ashen, as if someone had reduced all his filters. 'Have you got any treats?'

'I've tried treats, but every time I go near she backs even further into the bush.' Will shoved his hand into his hair. 'I don't know what to do. Do you know what to do? You usually do.'

Margot had absolutely no idea what to do. She got down on her hands and knees and peered through the slats of the bench to catch a glimpse of white fur, a heaving belly.

'Blossom,' she said softly. 'Hey, little girl. Mummy's here.'

Will didn't even snort in derision at the dreaded M word, which he always said was much worse than co-pawrent.

'Do you want to come out and say hello to me? Do you want cuddles?'

Asking Blossom if she wanted cuddles was always her cue to race into the living room and jump on the sofa for a snuggle session, but now it didn't even warrant a reaction.

Margot looked helplessly at Will who shrugged and grimaced. 'She's been there for an hour now,' he said. 'I don't want to drag her out and make things a million times worse.'

'She has to come out in her own time,' Margot agreed. Grimacing, she lowered herself until her bottom made contact with the cold, hard ground and crossed her legs. 'Could you go to the café and get some bacon?'

From the way Blossom was shaking and panting, Margot doubted that even bacon would lure her out. In fact, she was just as worried about Will. His face was putty-coloured, he was breathing hard and he kept putting his hand to his chest. Then there was the pacing and the pulling at his hair.

He obviously needed to do something to ward off what looked like an incoming panic attack. 'It's worth a try, maybe?' he asked hopefully. 'Will you be all right?'

Margot's buttocks were already on fire. 'I'll be fine,' she assured him. 'If there's any new developments, I'll call you.'

There weren't any new developments in the twenty-five minutes that Will was gone, apart from a brief stand-off with a muscle-bound man in tight shorts and singlet who wanted to use the bench to stretch on, and was told by Margot, in no uncertain terms, to do one.

She continued to talk to Blossom in a soft, calm voice. 'It's OK to be frightened, Blossom. There are times, lots of times, when I feel like crawling into a bush too. But then I remember that there are people who love me . . . OK, it's only friend love, but you have to take what you can get.'

'Um, I have freshly cooked bacon.' Margot swivelled round to see Will standing there with a discomfited expression and a Styrofoam container. 'I got you some water too. Any change?'

'She's not panting quite so much. Shall we see if her greed overcomes her fear?'

'I'm crossing everything.' Will sat down next to Margot and handed her the takeaway box.

Even Margot's mouth watered at the scent of freshly fried bacon. She held a piece as near to Blossom as she could. 'Come on, Blossom, you love bacon.'

There was a rustle of leaves as Blossom's snout came forward, but when Margot tried to touch her, she retreated.

'Why don't you put the bacon on the ground next to her?' Will suggested. After a heart-stopping few minutes – Margot even contemplated phoning Jim for help – Blossom emerged from the bush just enough that she could quickly gobble up the bacon. Then she sat there behind the bench, still panting.

If only there was a way to let her know that she was safe, Margot thought. Then she had an idea. 'Don't judge me for what I'm about do,' she said to Will. 'Because let's not forget that you now refer to yourself as co-pawrent without any shame.'

'We've been through this before. I'm ashamed on the inside,' Will said with barely any trace of his usual snark. 'What *are* you about to do?'

What Margot did every night when she put Blossom to bed. She'd tuck a fleece blanket around the dog, stroke down her back with a slow, steady hand, then sing a lullaby to the tune of 'Little Donkey'; Blossom was usually asleep before Margot had got through one verse. Obviously, she was going to have to modify the lyrics a little bit, which were already cloyingly sentimental but the circumstances were truly exceptional.

'Little Blossom, Little Blossom, time to come out now
    Mummy loves you, so does Daddy, you're their precious girl.'

No one, not even the most besotted of lovers, could ever say that Margot had a good voice, but she could carry a tune, mostly, and anyway, it wasn't as if Blossom was Simon Cowell. But Blossom also knew that when Margot sang to her, it meant that she was safe, she was loved, she could go to sleep thinking only happy thoughts.

Now when Margot sang to her, it must have summoned up the same feelings of protection, of being loved, because she inched herself out of her little nook and crawled into Margot's lap.

'There she is,' Margot breathed, her arms wrapping around the still shaking dog. 'There's my girl.'

She kissed the top of Blossom's head, and when Blossom didn't flinch, Margot smothered her face with kisses.

'She has scratches on her belly from the bush,' Will said in a strangulated voice. 'I'll move away so I don't freak her out again.'

Blossom's shakes had begun to subside, and she was just as much Will's girl as she was Margot's.

'You're not going to freak her out,' Margot said firmly. 'Just stroke the top of her head with your fingers and see what she does.'

Will looked like Margot had just asked him to dip his hand in hydrochloric acid, but he brought the tips of his fingers towards Blossom and made contact with her moleskin softness as he traced along her head.

Blossom tried to lick him.

Will's sigh was as loud as the March wind that had picked up since they'd been sitting there. Margot had thought that her legs were numb, but when Blossom decided that she'd much prefer to sit on Will's lap and trod on Margot's thighs to get there, she realised they were still capable of feeling pain.

'We're friends again, then?'

It was a rhetorical question because Blossom was licking every bit of Will's face that she could reach; normal service had resumed.

32

Will

Blossom ate all the bacon and drank half a bottle of water from Will's cupped hands but was too weak to walk home.

Every time they took a few steps, she'd sit down and hang her head sadly.

'I know how she feels,' Margot said, rubbing her own legs. 'My arse is never going to be the same after an hour sitting on cold tarmac.'

Usually when Will saw Margot she was bundled up in what she called the Dog-Walking Anorak Of Doom or wearing one of the many dresses she owned that covered her from neck to mid-calf. But today, she was wearing workout clothes. Tight leggings with mesh panels so he was tormented with glimpses of Margot's skin. On top, she was wearing a vest that insisted 'On Wednesdays We Smash The Patriarchy', which was loose enough and low cut enough that Will was also tormented by glimpses of a sturdy sports bra. He'd never appreciated what an erotic garment it could be.

'You should zip up your hoodie,' he said, taking hold of the bottom of the grey marl hoodie that wasn't doing a very good job of what it was meant to be doing; covering up all of Margot that had been hidden up until now. With hands that weren't working very well, he managed to do the zip up himself. 'You'll catch a cold.'

'Yes, Dad,' Margot said smartly. Will really hoped that wasn't the way she saw him. 'Come on, Blossom. Quicker you move, quicker you'll be home.'

Blossom got to her feet, staggered a few more paces, then collapsed again.

'She's been through a lot. No wonder she's exhausted.' Will was exhausted himself. He gave an anticipatory sigh, then bent down to pick Blossom up. 'If I end the day without a hernia, it will be a miracle.'

'I would say that we should take turns to carry her, but I have no upper-body strength,' Margot said cheerfully. She rubbed her thighs again, though Will wished that she wouldn't because he couldn't help but follow the motion of her hands with his eyes. 'No lower-body strength, either. I'm a very puny being.'

'Hardly puny,' Will said, though he still worked out regularly and yet he was struggling with eighteen kilograms of dead weight in his arms. 'Haven't you got a sweatshirt that says you're a member of the Strong Girls Club?'

Margot grinned. 'False advertising.'

Now that all the Sturm und Drang was over, Will had time to replay what had happened, to take stock and focus on the tangential. 'You were saying to Blossom about friend love . . . about how it was better than nothing.'

There was a moment of exquisite silence. Then Margot shrugged. 'Was I? I don't remember.'

Will felt compelled to persist in the face of zero encouragement. 'The internet dating isn't going well, then? You're still looking for love?'

Margot sighed. She opened her mouth then shut it. Sighed again, as if she was regretting this conversation almost as much as Will. 'I'm not looking for love,' she said, which was a bit of a curveball. What was she looking for then? 'I'm looking for a nice man, who can handle his drink, isn't bankrupt – he doesn't even have to have all his own teeth – who's ready to settle down and start a family.'

The bar seemed very low. So low that it was touching the ground. 'That doesn't seem so hard to find.'

'Are you fucking kidding me?' Margot snorted and came to a halt, her hands on her hips. Will shifted Blossom in his arms so her face wasn't buried in his neck and she was no longer able to enthusiastically lick him, and stopped too. 'Needle meet haystack.'

Will had always had a type when it came to women and that was women who weren't looking for anything serious either. He'd had several long-term relationships; three years with Sofie in Berlin, eighteen months with Charlotte in Paris, two years with Naomi in New York. Nothing serious didn't preclude staying the night or weekend breaks, but it also didn't include having to meet each other's families or long, torturous conversations about where things were heading. He'd been happy with that. Or the man he'd been then had been happy with that. The man he was now still wasn't ready – no, wasn't *able* – to commit emotionally, but Margot could. Would. Should.

'You've destroyed my belief system. I had you down as a hopeless romantic,' he said, which earned him another snort, this time with added eyeroll.

'Hopeless is right,' Margot muttered and started to walk again. 'I'm not a romantic, not anymore. What I am is pragmatic. And also thirty-six. When you're past thirty-five, if you want to settle down, then you have to settle. So, love is all very well, Will, but if I have to factor *that* in too, I'll still be single and heading straight towards my seventies.'

If someone like Margot had given up on love, then what did that say about the world? 'Any man would be lucky to have you,' Will said, his face reddening. He couldn't blame it on the morning's exertions. He was blushing because it was probably the most emotionally intimate thing he'd ever said to a woman, but it was important that Margot knew that she was deserving of love and she didn't need to settle for anything less. 'There's someone out there who is going to fall head over heels in love with you.'

Margot shook her head, the movement so small that it was almost imperceptible. 'Doubtful,' she decided. 'And if he is out there, then he's taking his own sweet time.'

By now they'd reached the Grove and the avenue of trees that took them to the top of Muswell Hill.

From a distance, it looked like a gentle slope, but Will knew from bitter experience that there was nothing gentle about the incline. It was harder and more strenuous to walk up than to tackle some of the steepest hills that North London had to offer. And Will knew about hills. In his former life, he'd run the notoriously hilly Blue Ridge Marathon in Roanoke, Virginia. He would have liked to challenge Margot further, though he couldn't bear to hear about the recent dates that she'd been on, but he needed every breath in his body for the ordeal ahead. As it was, he was already panting like he'd just reached mile twenty.

'Maybe you should put her down,' Margot said, eyeing Will and his canine cargo. 'Do you always carry her like that?'

Usually Will hoisted Blossom up so he could wedge an arm under her rear and she would wrap her front paws round his neck and rest her chin on his shoulder, but today he was cradling her in his arms like a baby. 'No, this is a first.' He peered down at Blossom. 'Am I jiggling her? Is she in pain?'

Margot shot Blossom a suspicious glance. 'She's looking kind of smug,' she said. 'Like she's absolutely milking it.'

Will gratefully came to another stop so he could get a good look at Blossom. She did seem to have a roguish glint in her eye. 'Are you faking it, Bloss?'

She waggled her front paws by way of a reply.

'Totally faking it,' Margot confirmed.

'So disappointed in you, Blossom,' Will said, as he lowered her to the ground. 'No telly privileges for the rest of the week.'

Blossom sat down and held up a paw in protest.

'You've been rumbled,' Margot told her, bending down to tickle her ribs. 'Go on, off you go!'

Blossom shot off as if she'd been scalded. As usually happened when she got told off, her ears were pinned back, her bottom going in one direction, her tail going in the other, as she indulged in an almighty flounce that said very plainly, 'You're not my real parents and you can't tell me what to do!'

Then, flounce over, she did two complete circuits around the fence that encircled a veteran oak tree then zigzagged from one side of the path to the other.

'Why couldn't we have got a normal dog?' Will asked Margot as they went off-road onto the grass where Blossom was sprawled on her back with her legs in the air.

'If she's rolling in fox poo then you're cleaning it up. She's not officially mine for another twenty-four hours,' Margot said. Will grinned at her and it would have been the easiest thing, the most natural thing in the world, to take her hand and walk home like that.

But there was nothing easy about them. Especially not their dog, who came trotting over to lay down again. Her meaning was unmistakable: 'You seem to be cross about something. Maybe stroking my belly would make you feel better. Got to be worth a try, right?'

Margot obligingly bent down, groaning as her muscles protested, to rub a hand along Blossom's taut tummy, which was made from the softest substance in the world.

But Will got there first. Their hands collided for one blissful moment, then they separated. Will taking the top, Margot taking the bottom, as Blossom got the best belly rub of her life, so that she was panting and wriggling and unsure of whether to make them stop because it was too much, or to carry on because it wasn't enough.

'Is she . . . is she laughing?' Margot wondered aloud, anthropomorphising Blossom yet again. Though to be fair Blossom was the most human dog Will had ever met.

'It's because she's panting,' Will said, crushing Margot's dreams. He must stop doing that. 'Panting because having your belly rubbed is very strenuous, isn't it, Blossom?' and he redoubled his effort with the belly rubbing until Blossom really did push them away.

They started for home again. Blossom back on all four paws, walking between Margot and Will as they trudged up the avenue of lime trees. But every time one of them looked down at her, Blossom would look up, her eyes adoring, her mouth wide open in an unmistakable, irrepressible grin.

By the time they reached the Broadway, Margot said she was ready to drop. 'Just to be clear, we're not doing our usual Heath walk today, are we?' she clarified. 'My legs are screaming at the thought of any more walking.'

'Oh God, please no. I never ever want to walk anywhere ever again,' Will confirmed. 'Also, just to be clear, my mother doesn't need to know what happened with Blossom, right? She'd be beside herself.'

'I'll take it to my grave.' They came to a stop outside the florist, there was a small queue winding through the buckets of flowers on display as Sage served customers and Ian took their money. Margot tore her eyes away from a galvanised steel bucket full of brightly coloured tulips so she could look at Will. 'So . . . I guess I'll see you . . .'

'We should have tea.' Will was nowhere near ready to say goodbye and not see Margot until their handover tomorrow. 'Would you like a cup of tea?'

Margot nodded. 'Thought you'd never ask.'

'Might even be able to throw in a sausage sandwich,' Will said, guiding Margot by the elbow and Blossom by the lead, into the shop. 'Let's drop Blossom off first.'

33

Margot

Will stepped through into the back room where Mary was making up a bouquet. Her movements were quick and efficient as she entwined roses with laurel and eucalyptus, but her hands stilled as soon as she saw them.

'I expected you back ages ago,' she scolded. 'And now here's Margot all ready for your afternoon walk. You *always* walk on the Heath on Saturdays, don't you?'

Margot felt Will tense up. 'Change of plans, Mary,' she said easily. 'We met at Ally Pally and already had our big Saturday walk. We're shattered.'

'Blossom hasn't even had her breakfast yet,' Mary said in shocked tones. But for the first time ever, Blossom rejected food in favour of climbing into the elevated dog bed (a purchase that Mary had been very conscientious about clearing with Margot first) heaped with fleecy blankets, curling herself into a small ball, and promptly falling asleep.

'You've worn her out,' Mary lamented as Will and Margot left the shop. 'Poor thing's exhausted.'

'She's not the only one.' Margot slumped against the wall as Will unlocked the door that led up to his flat. 'I've experienced all the emotions this morning. Every single one of them.'

'I'd offer to carry you up the stairs, but I'm exhausted too,' Will said with a ghost of a smile. He held out his arms. 'Happy to give it the old college try.'

'You really would have a hernia,' Margot said, shaking her head as Will gestured at the stairs. She was all about the body positivity, but now all the drama had abated she was painfully aware that she was in her yoga pants, which she never ever wore out of the house. Sweaty Betty might claim that they were bum sculpting, but they were also bum exposing, and no way was she going to subject Will to the sight of that as she climbed up to his flat. 'Gentlemen first.'

Actually, it worked out rather well, because Will's long legs and firm arse were very pleasing to her eyes. Which wasn't the reason why Margot was bright red by the time they reached the top. No, that was because she'd done a yoga workout, endured two very stressful, upsetting hours in Ally Pally park, and then had to climb stairs.

'Shall I hang up your jacket?' Will asked, but Margot burrowed into her hoodie. Now she was also remembering what was underneath it: a vest with gaping armholes, gaping neckline and underneath that a sports bra that did sterling work when it came to supporting but was quite possibly the most unattractive item of clothing Margot had ever possessed.

'I'm all right,' Margot insisted as Will hung his own jacket up on a hook in the hall, put his keys down on a narrow side-board then gave Margot a brief but assessing glance, which made her toes curl up in her trainers.

'You look hot,' he said, and Margot savoured those three words for approximately three seconds. 'I mean temperature hot.' And she was done savouring. 'I have normal tea, or I might be able to dig around and find a chamomile teabag in a drawer.'

'You make the chamomile sound so appetising, but I'll have regular tea with a splash, and I mean just a splash, of milk, please,' Margot said, stepping into the large open-plan living space. 'Wow, looks quite different in here.'

The minimalist décor was minimalist no more. There was a large Persian rug in the seating area, its red hues picked up in the cushions and the throws (three throws!) on the once pristine L-shaped white sofa. Like her own flat, there was dog-related debris all over the place. From a half-chewed pig ear taking pride of place in the centre of the room, to assorted tennis balls in varying stages of destruction and several deflated corpses of stuffed toys.

There were few things Blossom enjoyed more than murdering a small stuffed animal from the pound shop. She'd rip its seams and scatter its synthetic filling to the four corners of the room to get to its squeaker and destroy it. Then she'd indignantly resist any attempts to dispose of her kill trophies. As Margot stepped over the remains of a small purple elephant, she could see that Will had similar issues.

'Having a dog and a pared back aesthetic really wasn't working,' Will admitted as he filled up the kettle. 'Are you hungry?'

Margot contemplated her thighs. 'Starving. You said something about a sausage sandwich.'

Will smiled as he rubbed the back of his neck. 'I did. Sit down, make yourself at home.'

There was nothing Margot would have liked more than to collapse on the sofa, a red velvet cushion under her head, but instead she walked over to where Will was surveying the contents of his fridge and hauled herself up on one of the stools arranged around an island, which separated the kitchen area from the rest of the space.

She watched Will cut slices from a granary loaf and pop them in the toaster, crack eggs into a cup, then prod the sausages now sizzling in a pan on the hob.

Margot had rarely seen Will so comfortable in his own skin. There was always something restless, almost nervous about him, so that she often worried that she was the one making him restless and nervous. It was quite the revelation that he had this other side to him.

'Ketchup or brown sauce?' he asked, as he expertly slid a fried egg, its yolk golden and just the right side of runny, onto the sausages lined up on a piece of toast.

'Neither.'

Will brandished his spatula at her, an incredulous expression on his face. 'You don't do condiments? What kind of a monster are you?'

'Condiments would only interfere with the integrity of the egg yolk.'

Will shook his head as he placed the second piece of toast on the side of the plate and handed it to Margot.

Making her a sausage and egg sandwich was the nicest thing anyone had done for Margot in ages. Will plonked down a packet of butter and took the stool next to her, so his leg brushed against hers as he picked up his own sandwich. This low-level flirting was lovely. 'I suppose I should have a butter dish but needing a butter dish isn't something that's ever come up before.'

'I don't have a butter dish either,' Margot said, as she carefully manoeuvred the sandwich to her mouth so that the sausages didn't make a bid for freedom, and bit into it.

They ate mostly in silence apart from a few appreciative murmurs. It felt very intimate, despite Margot's greasy fingers and the egg yolk that dribbled down her chin.

'You missed a bit,' Will said, as she dabbed it with a piece of kitchen roll, and touched his own greasy finger to the spot. Her thighs quivered from that inconsequential, incidental touch. Though, truthfully, parts of her had been quivering ever since Will had declared that any man would be lucky to have her.

But all too soon it was over: the world's best sausage sand-wich, the flirtatious mood. Will abruptly scraped his stool back to remove their empty plates.

'Do you want another cup of tea?' he asked over his shoulder as he opened the dishwasher.

Margot really should be going. She had so much to do today. Laundry, cleaning, taking her fancy boots in to the cobblers . . . 'I'd love one, thanks.'

When Will returned with another mug of tea, he took the stool next to hers again, closer this time and facing her, so Margot's leg was trapped between his knees.

She didn't know if it was deliberate. At this moment, she felt like she knew nothing. All her senses were locked on this man sitting next to her. How he smelt of the outside; of fresh air and wet grass. That he was speaking though Margot couldn't even hear what he was saying, but the timbre of his voice vibrated through her.

All she could do was stare at Will as he sipped his tea, scratched his temple, then drummed his fingers across the countertop.

Eventually he became aware of the weight of her gaze, how Margot's attention was all on him, and he put down his tea. So he could take her hand, thread his fingers through hers.

It was the first time that he'd deliberately, purposely, touched her since the kisses that they never talked about, that they weren't going to do again.

'Margot,' Will said. He made those two syllables sound like a caress; she could feel their gossamer touch on her skin.

'Will,' she said, and he was so close that all she had to do was lean forward slightly and then her mouth was on his.

Oh! He pulled back ever so slightly, not enough for Margot to stop, because then his arms closed around her and he was kissing her urgently.

It was a messy kiss with no finesse, all clashing teeth and mouthing at each other. It was exactly what Margot needed. She clutched at Will's hair so she could pull his head down, get the purchase she needed so she could dip her tongue into his mouth. But still, it wasn't enough.

Then his hands were on her hips, smoothing down her arse to lift her up. Margot flung her arms around Will's neck at the same time that she wound her legs around his hips so she was on his lap, pressed as close to him as she could get. And still, it wasn't enough.

Because his kisses were already making her fall apart. His tongue in her mouth now, darting lazily, in a promise of what was to come.

'Take it off,' she muttered, working one hand free to tug at her now hated hoodie. She leaned back, safe in the knowledge that Will wouldn't let her fall.

'You want me to take this off?' he clarified, one hand leaving her hips so he could take the zip pull between finger and thumb. 'All the way off?'

'All the way.'

Never had Margot known anything as erotic, as charged, as the way Will slowly, ever so slowly, pulled down the zip on her M&S hoodie, his blue eyes blazing and never once looking away from her heated face.

He got to the bottom, pulled the two ends apart, and for one gasping moment, pressed the flat of his hand at the tender spot just below her bikini line.

'Off,' he drawled in her ear, teeth biting down on the plumpness of her earlobe, his hands back on her hips so Margot could tear off the hoodie and while she was at it, she pulled her vest over her head.

She didn't care that she was left in her prosaic grey and royal blue sports bra, which resembled rigging more than it resembled underwear. She didn't even care that her belly was spilling over the waistband of her yoga pants because Will couldn't take his eyes off her and he kept running his tongue over his bottom lip again and again.

'You're so hot,' he said, and he didn't mean temperature hot this time, though Margot did feel as if she was about to come to the boil. 'So overdressed.'

'Hardly,' Margot whispered, clutching a handful of his plaid shirt. 'You're wearing more clothes than I am.'

'Ah, but you're much sexier out of your clothes than I am,' Will said, biting down on her earlobe again and smiling when Margot shuddered. 'Did you like that?'

'Yes, God, yes.' Margot was busy with the buttons on his shirt. She'd never imagined that Will, with all his offishness, his unease, would be this commanding, this sure of himself. It was unbearably sexy.

'I'm only getting started,' he said, coaxing Margot off his lap, so for a second she was uncertain and standing on her own two wobbly feet, then he patted the worktop and raised his eyebrows.

Margot wasn't sure why, but Will seemed to know what he was doing, so she hoisted herself up on to the island. And that was much better, because Will took hold of her knees and, eyes fixed on her face again, slowly and deliberately pulled her legs apart.

One step put him *there*, where she was already aching, and when they kissed, Will's mouth on hers, his hard cock pressed into her, Margot was bumping and grinding as if she was about to drop it like it was hot.

Will pulled his head back, took his mouth away, so that the only place they were touching was where his groin was digging into hers. Then he slipped a finger under the strap of her bra.

'Would you take this off?' he asked gently. Margot shook her head. She didn't want to kill the mood, stop where she hoped this was heading, but she'd sweated at various times during the course of the morning. She'd have to struggle out of her damp bra and sitting down did her breasts no favours, and there were always deep red marks on her skin when she took it off. 'Do you want to stop?'

'I absolutely don't want to stop,' she said, wrapping one leg around his hip and shimmying. 'If you're really good, maybe you can see them later.'

'I'm going to be very good,' Will promised with a little half smile, a dark glint in his eyes, which she'd never seen before today. 'I hope you won't have any complaints.'

Margot didn't have any complaints. She could hardly speak, her mouth buried in Will's shoulder as the heel of his hand rubbed against her clit, his fingers thrusting inside her as her own hand worked the length of him, revelled in the feeling of him hot and hard.

The angles were awkward, her yoga pants and knickers in the way, Will's jeans unbuttoned but still on, but they made it work. She lifted herself off the counter to grind against his hand as she came, his fingers keeping her at the summit of an exquisite peak, until Margot couldn't take it any more and had to twist away.

Then it only took a second to take Will's hand, sticky with her own come, and guide it to his cock, put her hand over his so they could work him off together. 'Just like that,' she whispered in his ear as he bucked against her. 'I want to see you come.'

Will came on Margot's stomach as she sat on his kitchen worktop, his eyes fixed on her face, neither of them able to look away. She hadn't even taken her bra off and yet it was still some of the best sex she'd ever had.

'Today is just one surprise after another,' Margot said, and this should have been one of the most excruciatingly embarrassing moments of her life. Sitting there with her leggings and knickers half yanked down, her skin damp and sweat stains on her bra, but Will was still looking at her like she was some kind of goddess.

'It's not even noon,' he said, as he buttoned his jeans back up. 'Who knows what else the day will bring?'

34

Will

Will could tell Margot was a little embarrassed. Not by what had happened, because when she slid down from the counter-top, she put her arms around him for one too-brief moment and brushed her lips against his cheek.

But then she grabbed her hoodie to hold it in front of her. 'I look an absolute state.'

'You don't, you look beautiful,' Will said and it wasn't a line. She was flushed and glowing, a Venus in athleisure wear. 'Do you want me to drive you home?'

What he really wanted was for Margot to stay and it should have been the simplest thing to say that out loud. But now that their clothes were back on and they were heading towards something deeper and more meaningful than getting each other off, Will found that he was stumbling in the dark.

'I have to have a shower,' Margot said firmly, arms crossed over her hoodie. 'But if you have something I could borrow, I mean, if you wanted me to stay.'

Margot made everything simpler. 'Yeah, I do want you to stay,' he said.

Will sorted out clean towels and a little pile of clothes then waited outside the bathroom door until he heard the shower turn on and Margot swear as she waited for the water to go from needle sharp cold to warm.

It felt like the longest fifteen minutes of Will's life until Margot emerged, freshly scrubbed and pink-cheeked in a pair of his tracksuit bottoms and an old Ramones T-shirt from his university days. She'd obviously decided that she couldn't face putting her bra back on, and though Will didn't want to be caught staring, he could see the shape of her breasts under the faded black cotton and he was already half hard again.

'I don't know why I bothered having a shower,' she said shrugging, which made even more delectable shapes under the black cotton.

'Why's that?' Will's voice sounded like it belonged to a man who smoked forty Marlboros a day.

'Because you're going to get me all hot and sweaty again, aren't you?' Her eyes drifted down to where he was hard again.

He fleetingly touched the bulge in his jeans, embarrassed that he was like a teenage boy with no control, but when he did Margot let out a shaky breath, then her hand reached up to cup the heavy weight of her breast.

'I've never wanted anyone as much as I want you,' he told Margot, and she smiled goofily, which was much more Margot than when she was playing seductress. Or maybe they were both Margot. There was still so much that he didn't know about her. 'In bed, this time?'

'Yes, please,' she said, already turning to head down the hall towards his bedroom. 'My back couldn't take another go on your kitchen island.'

By the time Will stumbled after her, Margot was already in his bedroom, face obscured as she pulled his T-shirt over her head. Will had had a vague plan that he'd undress her slowly, kiss every centimetre of skin that emerged, but he revised that in favour of finally closing his hands around the unbelievable softness of her breasts and tumbling her down on his bed.

It was much better second time around on a firm mattress, Margot naked and spread out before him like a feast. There was no awkwardness, no worry that he was doing something wrong, that he was wrong, because this was Margot. Who liked to micromanage every situation. In exacting detail. Which was far more of a turn-on in bed than it was when she was sending Will bullet-pointed text messages.

'Gently at first, then you can do it harder.'

'You can use your teeth and another finger. Yeah, like that.'

Then, 'Just shift a little higher. Little bit more. Oh, *there*! Yes, just there. Don't even *think* of stopping.'

Afterwards, when they were both flat on their backs, panting slightly, his duvet tangled around their feet, Will rubbed his thumb against her still hard nipple. 'God, you're bossy.'

'Not bossy,' Margot said, without any heat. 'I just know what I want.'

'Bossy.' With superhuman effort, Will managed to roll over so he could raise himself up on one elbow and look at Margot all over again; she was all soft peaks and valleys. 'It's not a criticism. Far from it.'

Then Margot shivered, which did amazing things to her breasts, but Will wasn't sorry when she pulled the duvet around them, and nestled into his side, so he could wind his fingers through her curls.

'I hope you weren't expected downstairs in the shop,' she said.

Will groaned. 'If they needed me, they'd have let me know.' Then he thought of his phone still in the kitchen and how it could have been chiming and buzzing all this time. 'If it was really urgent, my mum has got a spare key.'

'That would have killed the mood.' Margot shook with muted laughter.

'Let's not even think about it,' Will decided. 'And Sage knows to pop Blossom out mid-afternoon.'

Margot sighed, her breath ghosting against his shoulder. 'Poor Blossom. She was so terrified.'

You can do this, Will thought to himself. Because we're not friends. And we're not kissing. We're beyond both of these things. So, you should tell her. You have to tell her. You want to tell her.

And he did. For the first time, he wanted to tell someone. Not someone. He wanted to tell Margot, because he didn't want to shut her out. He was so tired of keeping secrets, the weight of them always wearing him down.

'Before you came, she snapped at me,' Will said, and he thought that maybe the trick was to keep his voice flat, emotionless. Not get too carried away.

'Only because she was scared, Will,' Margot said softly.

'I know. She'd been triggered back to a place where some-one was unkind, cruel . . .' Will looked at the ceiling, at the recessed lights, the spot where he'd thrown his shoe at a fly and it had chipped the paintwork. He always meant to do something about it. 'I know that place too.'

Margot's hand curved over Will's heart. 'Your dad,' she said simply, because she always made the impossible seem possible.

'My father,' Will corrected her. 'Dad sounds like he played football with me, took me fishing, gave me a pound to get sweets. That's what dads do.'

Peter Hamilton hadn't done any of those things, but if you spoke to his friends, the blokes down the pub, they'd have told you that Pete was the 'salt of the earth'. 'He'd give you the shirt off his back.' 'Hasn't got a bad bone in his body.'

Good old Pete. Always the first to get his round in and the last to leave a party.

But eventually he would leave the Old Red Lion or the bar at the British Royal Legion and come back to the little terraced house and his family, and resume his reign of terror.

Because Peter Hamilton was a man corroded by disappointments, big and small. By potential and promise never realised. And the fact that he was a functioning alcoholic and a mean drunk.

All he needed was the love of a good woman. Who'd believe him when Peter promised that he wasn't going to drink any more, that he was going to do better, be the man she deserved. So, Amaryllis Bloom said yes when he proposed, because she was a good woman with a good heart who always rooted for the underdog.

'But he didn't change,' Will said heavily, still staring at the chip on the ceiling. 'Why should he when he had someone to take out all his anger on, to blame for his own failings? He never laid a finger on Mum, but he didn't have to. He beat her down with his words, with his constant belittlement, made her believe that she was worthless, and he did the same to Rowan and me.'

Will couldn't remember a time when his father was anything other than a source of fear. The sound of his car on the drive, his key in the lock, his muttered curse as he dropped his keys in the bowl on the hall table were the opening chords of a grand opera, and by the end of the evening, its dramatic climax would be his sister sobbing quietly in her bed, his mother sitting rigid on a hardback chair in the living room because she wasn't allowed to sit on the sofa anymore 'like a fat, lazy cow', while Will took the brunt of his father's anger, his seething resentment, because nothing made Peter Hamilton more bitter than having a son.

'If I got top marks at school or did well at sports, he was furious. Jealous. Felt like he'd been emasculated,' Will said.

He'd understood this long before he started therapy with Roland and began to unpick the tangled knots that had kept him tied up for so long. 'But if I did badly at anything, it was because I wasn't good enough. I would never be good enough. I'd never be successful at anything. Never be a real man, but a snivelling little sissy.'

'Oh, Will . . .' Margot's hand was still cupped protectively over his heart and she didn't say anything more than that, didn't interrupt his flow, the stagnant stream of memories.

'He had so many rules. We weren't allowed to watch telly, weren't allowed out in the garden, weren't allowed to have friends round or go over to theirs, and anyway, we were all too useless, too ugly, too dumb to have friends. All we had was him and he was disgusted by us.' Will took a couple of deep, centring breaths, though he didn't feel centred, he felt dangerously adrift. 'I get it. That he felt he had no control over his life, so he controlled us. He wasn't capable of looking inwards, of taking responsibility so he blamed us. I get that, but just because I understand it doesn't mean I'm able to move past it.'

'So, what happened? He's not around anymore . . .' Margot gently prompted.

'There was one night, nothing special about it, but he was going in on Mum; I'd just turned twelve and realised I was as big as him now and I'd simply had enough.' It had taken him three sessions to spit these words out with Roland. The first session, he hadn't been able to speak at all, but saying something once made it easier to say it the second time. Especially where there was someone keeping guard over your heart. 'I got between him and Mum and I said to him . . . I said, "Don't talk to my mum like that. She doesn't deserve it."'

Margot curled even tighter into him. 'What did he do, then? 'Cause you said that he never laid a finger on you.'

'He didn't lay a finger on Mum, but he knocked me across the room.' Which had been a good thing because it had finally woken Mary up from the deep, dark spell that Peter had cast on her. But before the good thing, there'd been a very bad thing. 'We had a dog. Muttley. Actually, I think he was the only thing in the house that my dad really loved, no judgement with dogs, right? It always made him mad that Muttley preferred me, and when he hit me, Muttley went for him. He was only a little thing, but my dad took him by the scruff of his neck, slammed him hard into the wall, then stormed out, shouting that we'd never see him again. We waited until we were sure that he'd gone but it was too late . . . Muttley, he was . . . We buried him in the back garden.'

'Oh God!' It was gone three now, though the morning felt as if it had happened to someone else centuries ago. The mid-afternoon sun streamed in through the windows, though it seemed as if the day should be overcast and cloudy, not glorious with the promise of warmer days ahead. Margot lifted her head so she could wipe her eyes with the edge of the duvet. 'I'm so, so sorry. What a shitty childhood.'

'It did get better,' Will said, sitting up and groping behind him so he could prop himself up on the pillows, Margot following suit, duvet tucked under her arms. 'Because before he came back, we'd gone. Mum phoned Bernie and Mo, my grandparents, she'd barely spoken to them in years. Too ashamed, too convinced that she was a disappointment to them too. Anyway, Rowan and I came home from school the next day and there they were, all our stuff packed in the Blooms' van and we left, and that was that.'

It wasn't quite that. Peter had turned up in Muswell Hill a couple of weeks later but Mo, redoubtable Mo, all four feet and eleven inches of her, had seen him off. Although with hindsight, Will and Rowan had decided that Bernie and Mo had probably paid Peter to get out of their lives for good. There'd been another Blooms' in Winchmore Hill, with two flats above the shop. It had been sold, not long after they arrived back in London.

'Thank you for telling me,' Margot said, and she took Will's hand and entwined their fingers, then brought his hand up to her mouth so she could kiss it. 'Some of it I'd already worked out. After Christmas Day ... but I didn't want to pry. I thought that if and when you wanted to tell me, then you would.'

'Now I have.' Will wasn't done. Sometimes he felt as if he'd never be done. Never be finished with it. 'You're only the second person I've told. I told my therapist.'

'Well, that's understandable,' Margot said, squeezing his hand tight.

'My father would say real men don't need therapy,' he said, glancing sideways to gauge Margot's reaction, which was an extravagant rolling of her eyes.

'Yeah, well, your father is an absolute bastard and nothing he says should carry any weight.' She crossed her arms.

'So, you don't think there's anything wrong with seeing a therapist?' Apart from Rowan, who'd had post-natal depression after the birth of the twins, Will didn't know anyone else who'd been in therapy. Apart from when he lived in New York and then everyone was in therapy. But not in London, not in the small world that he now lived in.

'Look, if I feel sick, I see a doctor. When I wrenched my shoulder, I went to an osteopath and when my soul is hurting, I go and see Olivia, my therapist, so I can get my groove back. Or find a new groove.' She tried out a little smile.

'I'm not in therapy anymore,' Will assured her. He'd been right to quit when he did – if *this* wasn't forging an emotional connection with another person then he didn't know what was. But he was surprised that Margot was in therapy. Or rather, that she treated therapy as ongoing, rather than getting fixed then moving on with her life. 'You see your therapist on the regular?'

'Not regularly. There have been gaps, large gaps.' Margot blew out a long breath that ruffled the curls that were falling in her face. 'After my mother died, I was so lost. I felt so alone. It wasn't just grief . . . there was a lot of other stuff mixed in with it and I didn't know how to navigate all the big, scary feelings that were blocking my way.'

Despite everything that he'd gone through, Will had always had Mary and Rowan. He'd never suffered entirely on his own. 'I can't even imagine what that would feel like.'

'Yeah, it's not fun,' Margot said. 'So I saw Olivia when I was in my early twenties and then when I hit thirty, I had another huge emotional crisis, stuff that I hadn't really addressed when my mum died . . .'

'What kind of stuff?' Will asked as delicately as he could.

Margot sat up so she could turn her face away from Will. The tense line of her shoulders was a section break. A boundary that wasn't to be crossed – for now. He had so many boundaries of his own that Will knew to be respectful of other people's. 'Stuff that I'm ashamed about and also all the stuff that comes when you're a single woman who's always been looking to replace the family that she lost, and then you hit thirty and realise that you're not getting any younger . . .'

With a quiet sort of jolt, Will remembered their conversation in the pub a few weeks ago. How Margot had said that she didn't have time to be kissing men just for the sake of it.

And now they'd done more than just kissed. A hell of a lot more. But Will was sick of regrets. Though usually it was regret for all the things he hadn't done, rather than for something he had.

'I can't be sorry that this has happened,' he said softly, running his hand down the length of Margot's spine. 'But I'm aware that we both want different things, so I understand if you want to go back to just being two people who own a dog.'

Even as he said it, Will realised that there was no going back. At least, not for him. But he didn't know what going forwards would mean when Margot so desperately wanted to settle down and Will still couldn't work out what it was that he actually wanted.

'Oh God, I'm naked in your bed and you're already trying to get rid of me!' Margot turned round so she could elbow Will in the ribs. 'Was it *that* bad?'

Will was pretty sure she was teasing him, but not one hundred per cent sure. 'You know it wasn't. Definitely in my top five. Maybe even top three.' He wound one of her wild curls around his finger like he'd been dying to do ever since they'd first kissed. 'Are we okay?'

Margot didn't answer at first. She was still sitting up, still half turned away, her face in profile so he could see her furrowed forehead. 'Yeah, we're okay,' she said after a very long pause. 'I still want what I want and that's not going to change, but this could be . . .' She shrugged. 'One last hurrah? I mean, we're both adults so there's no reason why we can't be adult about this.'

It wasn't that easy. There were so many moving parts. So many opposing forces. Margot's needs. Will's issues. But it was hard to think about all that when Margot was naked in his bed and she was laying back down again as if she had no immediate plans to leave. Also, she was smiling. 'Anyway, now that we've cleared that up, I'd love another cuppa.'

After the tea, they must have fallen asleep because Will was woken by a knocking on the door.

Not the bedroom door, thank God, but the front door. Margot's head emerged from under the duvet as he pulled on his jeans, and called out, 'I'm coming! Hang on!'

'Wasn't that what I said an hour ago?' Margot asked. Her hair was going in all directions, her face was sleep-creased and puffy but still beautiful. Will hurried to the door; he could already hear a key in the lock.

He wrenched it open to see Mary standing there with Blossom. 'About bloody time,' she snapped. But Will was more alarmed by the way Mary's eyes were fixed on a point over his shoulder as she tried to see past him. 'Is Margot still here? I never saw her leave.'

Will decided it was best not to inform Mary of the latest developments on the Margot front. 'I must have switched my phone off. Sorry you got lumbered with Blossom. Shall I take her?'

'Not lumbered, I *love* looking after her,' Mary said as she handed over the lead and Blossom stepped through the door then sat down on Will's bare foot and held up her paw. 'She has already eaten despite what she's telling you and she won't need another walk until just before bedtime. I would have taken her tonight but I'm going out with Wendy and Kate. To that new Italian that's opened in East Finchley.'

'Who are Wendy and Kate when they're at home?' Mary expected him to know every single one of the friends she'd made in the twenty years he'd been away, plus Sage's friends, and all their customers. Then Will paused. Did he sound over-bearing? Controlling? He took a deep breath. 'Sorry, I just don't think you've mentioned them before.'

'I'm sure I have,' Mary said, standing her ground, because she wasn't the Mary from all those years ago. 'Wendy has a Red Setter called Oriel and Kate has two Miniature Schnauzers called Sonny and Cher.'

Mary, and Margot for that matter, also seemed to think that Will knew every dog within a three-mile radius. He shook his head. 'No, not ringing any bells.'

'I was at school with them!'

'You were at school with two Miniature Schnauzers called Sonny and Cher? Wow!'

He deserved the slap on his arm that Mary gave him. 'You know perfectly well what I mean. I was at school with Wendy and Kate and we've reconnected. It's amazing who you bump into when you have a dog to walk.'

'Well, have a nice time. Are you going to be drinking? I'll come and pick you up, if you like.'

Mary hitched her handbag higher up her shoulder. 'Ian's already said that he'll come and get me, but I'll be fine. The 102 goes door to door, or I can get a cab. Sage put the Uber app on my phone.' Mary was already turning to go. 'Stop fussing. I'm a sixty-year-old woman, not a child. And tell Margot I said hello.'

Mary was already clattering down the stairs as Will looked down at Blossom who was still gazing at him mournfully, like she didn't know where her next meal was coming from. 'Don't look at me like that. You could live off your stored fat for a good three weeks,' he said, bending down to unclip her lead. 'Now, don't go— Shit!'

Blossom was already charging down the hall and into the bedroom. Will was just in time to see her jump on the bed, then wriggle under the covers, as Margot squeaked and squirmed.

Blossom appeared from under the duvet, settled her head on Will's pillow and nudged Margot with her paw. All highly suggestive of the fact that Will's bed was not forbidden territory. Not even a little bit.

No wonder Margot was sitting up with an aggrieved expression, as she looked at an unused object in the corner of the room. 'I would ask why Blossom's bed looks like it's never been slept in, but I think I already know the answer.'

35

Margot

Margot and Will had already known each other for six months. Will had seen the best and the worst of Margot. Not just Margot on New Year's Eve when she was dressed up in her glittery finest or rosy-cheeked from leaf-crunching walks on the Heath. He'd seen her in the Dog-Walking Anorak Of Doom and the time she'd had to clean up Blossom's diarrhoea with a pocket pack of tissues, a clutch of poo bags and some hand sanitiser.

When you added up all of that, it meant that they'd gone straight from nought to sixty. Scratch that. Nought to a thousand. They could cut out all the boring stuff. The dating. The 'are we exclusive?' And just get on with whatever the hell it was that they were getting on with.

Mostly they were getting on with getting it on. Usually laying in Margot's bed (because Margot had a much better mattress and they didn't have to run the gauntlet of various inquisitive Blooms), basking in the afterglow, a furious Blossom consigned to the living room.

Two weeks since that fateful Saturday, and apart from one night when Margot had had to get up very early to visit the Ivy+Pearl factory in Borehamwood, they hadn't spent a night apart. Thirteen nights when it felt like Will had kissed every inch of her, held her down, held her open, took Margot over the edge. In the mornings, too, though it meant a very early start in order to fit in an orgasm before Blossom's first constitutional of the day.

Will in a relationship, or whatever the hell *this* was, was a revelation. He was kind, caring, though Margot already knew that, but all his ambivalence and aloofness were gone now the two of them were together.

But with Will living above the shop and being so entrenched in the family business, the Blooms quickly discovered that he and Margot were more than just friends.

As well as a man who liked her as much as she liked him, Margot suddenly acquired the one thing that she'd always longed for: a family.

But first, Rowan and Sage took her out for drinks to a Muswell Hill bar, which only served organic wine and made their own pickles. It had been billed as a girls' night out, but it soon became clear that they wanted to make sure that Margot's intentions towards their big brother were honourable.

'They couldn't be more honourable,' Margot assured them over a bottle of Sancerre, because she couldn't tell them that this was one last victory lap before she went on to find that kind-faced man who was probably not going to be as great in bed as Will was.

'Whenever we visited him in New York, he could be a bit weird when he was seeing someone. Never wanted us to meet them,' Rowan said lightly, as if she wasn't quite sure if Margot knew what the reasons behind that weirdness were. 'You just have to ride it out.'

'And don't break his heart, because then we're going to have a problem,' Sage said so darkly that Margot quaked in her Veja trainers, even though she was *almost* old enough to be Sage's mother. 'We'll have you blackballed by every florist within the M25. You'll never be able to buy a bunch of mixed blooms again. Right, Ro?'

'Damn right, but you're not going to break Will's heart.' Rowan raised her glass of organic Sancerre, which didn't taste any different to non-organic Sancerre. 'I have such a good feeling about this.'

'I hope so,' Margot said, trying to quell the optimism that had dared to raise its head. She'd never been one of those women who'd envisaged what she'd look like in her wedding dress (blush pink, duchesse satin with fitted bodice, three-quarter length sleeves, a mid-length ballerina skirt and pockets, thanks for asking) but now she skipped right ahead to three years in the future.

A noisy, chaotic kitchen, something bubbling on the stove, Blossom snoozing on the sofa (in Margot's most fevered fantasies, she and Will could afford a house big enough to accommodate an eat-in kitchen, which in turn was big enough to accommodate a sofa) and a chubby-cheeked little boy of two in the IKEA high chair that all of Margot's friends had, Will smiling indulgently as his son spooned pasta everywhere but his mouth. And Margot was taking a cake out of the oven while she herself had a bun in the oven. A little girl this time. Although the Blooms were all about nominative determination – it turned out that Will was named after the flower, the sweet william – Margot would call her Judy, after her own mother.

But she tried to keep this to herself, was actually horrified at where her thoughts kept wandering, because it was never going to happen. Will didn't want any of that. And Margot was ever mindful of Judy Millwood's own advice: 'It's best to always keep a little bit back, Margot.'

When times were good was when Margot missed her mother most. There had been many occasions when she'd longed to be able to cry in her mother's arms, but the happy times were rarer, and she wanted to share them with the person who'd loved her best.

Maybe it was missing her own mother so keenly which allowed Margot to form such a fast bond with Mary Bloom.

Five weeks in and they'd set up a regular date for a long walk on Margot's work-from-home Wednesdays. As Margot had suspected, how a person behaved on Christmas Day was absolutely no indication of what they were like the other three hundred and sixty-four much saner days of the year.

The Mary who she walked around Highgate Woods with, stopping for a coffee and a flaky pastry at the café halfway through their circuit, certainly wasn't the same woman who'd been in floods of tears over a decorative prawn ring. She was very panicky about Blossom being off-lead but was as enchanted as Margot with pretty much everything that Blossom did.

'She bustles about like she's doing inventory,' Margot remarked on their second walk, as Blossom wiggled her back-end officiously and checked every tree and supervised every other dog's behaviour.

'She really needs a hard hat, a hi-vis jacket and a clipboard.' Mary smiled proudly. 'I'm afraid that if Blossom was human, she'd be the most appalling jobsworth.'

'Yes! She would be the ultimate Linda from Accounts, always pinning notices up on the staff message board about people not respecting the tea-making rota,' Margot added.

It was funny how you could go from taking the piss out of your own dog to suddenly going deep, but over the course of a few weeks, Margot found herself confiding in Mary. How sad she was that Tracy's departure to New Zealand was imminent. How much she missed her own mother more, not less, as time went on.

Both of them skirted around the topic of the man who'd brought them together, though Margot longed to pump Mary for information. Had she met any of Will's previous girl-friends? What had Will said about her? Had he told Mary that they were just taking things day by day?

In turn, Mary talked a lot about her own mother, 'mighty Mo', and her beloved dad, Bernie, and how their passing had ripped the heart out of their family.

'I suppose I should step up, become the matriarch, but it's very hard to stop being one thing and become another,' she said obliquely to Margot, who nodded, but would never betray Will's confidence about the family's unhappy past. 'That's why I was so happy when Will decided to come home. Although I'd lost Mum and Dad, I'd got my son back. He said it was only for a while, but he's put down roots now, with Blossom . . . and you.'

'He has,' Margot agreed, though she could hardly squeeze the words out past the lump in her throat. She was meant to be a pragmatist, and here she was getting notions. Hopeless, romantic notions.

'I know he has to get back to his career at some point, that's he probably missing the hustle and the bustle, but there are banks in London, aren't there?'

She and Will were seven weeks in by then, halfway through a glorious May when the woods were studded with bluebells. The two women walked under a canopy of green leaves, pierced with shafts of sunlight.

'Maybe Will likes the change of pace,' Margot murmured, as she daringly removed her cardigan because the morning was warm with the promise of summer.

'But he's always been so driven. Always on to the next thing,' Mary insisted. But then she'd changed the subject to how she was thinking of branching out from a flaky pastry and having a scone instead, and the moment was over and the little flame of hope that Margot had dared to light was abruptly extinguished.

Week eight and it was time for Will to meet Margot's friends en masse. He'd already spoken to Tracy and Den on New Year's Eve but that had been fleeting. And he'd met Sarah and her family: husband Paolo, three-year-old Maisie, baby Bertie and mini-dachshund, Dorothy, when they'd gate-crashed a monthly dachshund walk and gone for Sunday lunch afterwards. At one point, when Sarah was in the loo and Paolo had gone to the bar, Will was left holding Bertie, who grabbed huge handfuls of his hair and tugged hard. It would have been a perfect opportunity to ask Will if his boundaries had shifted. Specifically, if he ever found himself even idly thinking about having children with Margot, but Will's pained expression had said more than words ever could.

But Will hadn't met Jess at all, and now it was also time for the very last of the last goodbyes: Tracy and Den's leaving party in their almost empty flat in Walthamstow because the international movers had come the day before.

'I will cry,' Margot warned Will as they drove through Finsbury Park. Having regular sex with someone who didn't drink meant that she was no longer reliant on public transport or an Uber if she was feeling very drunk or very flush. 'I feel like crying now and we're not even there yet.'

'You're allowed to cry,' Will said, putting his hand on Margot's knee. It was warm enough for bare legs now, but instead of sliding his hand up a few thrilling centimetres, he patted her skin lightly. 'Though I'd give it an hour before you properly unleash.'

'If Den's dad has written a speech, that will be it for me and my mascara,' Margot said. 'At their wedding, even the vicar was sobbing.'

'Just as well I decided not to wear mascara tonight.' Will caught her eye. This was perfect. So far, Will hadn't put a foot wrong. But soon he would, and that would make things better. It was easier to think about expiration dates and exit strategies when someone started acting like a dick.

*　　*　　*

'It's still very early days,' she said later, when it was just the four of them. Margot, Jess, Sarah and Tracy, the old gang back together for one last time, huddling on the patio even though late May was still a bit too cold to be out of doors, without tights, after eight p.m. 'Who knows what the future has in store for us? But, oh my God, we are having so much sex.'

'Yes, you might have mentioned that once or twice,' Jess said a little bitterly, because *she'd* mentioned once or twice that after having her daughter, Alice, her pelvic floor had been absolutely destroyed, and she never wanted to have sex again.

'It's always the quiet ones,' Margot sighed, staring through the French doors where Will was in the kitchen talking to Den's sister and her wife. 'Beneath that slightly gruff exterior is an absolute beast. I still can't look at his kitchen island without blushing.'

'Note to self: never go round to Will's for a home-cooked meal.' Sarah pretended she was making a note on her phone. 'I do miss the heady, early days of a relationship, and all you can think about is how long before you're naked again.'

Margot rubbed her arms. They really were going to have to go in soon. But she couldn't bring herself to suggest it. Not yet. Not when she didn't know when the four of them would be together again. Maybe never. But that didn't mean she could let Sarah's last remark go unchallenged. 'Oh, we're not in a relationship,' she insisted. 'We're just seeing each other. I told you, head not heart. My last fling before I settle down.'

The three of them seemed to sigh in unison. 'Margs, there is nothing about this that feels like one last fling,' Tracy pointed out gently.

'Yes, I know that we've known each other for *months*, but that doesn't automatically make it a relationship. It just means that we're friends with some pretty amazing benefits and we'll go back to being just friends when this is over.' Tracy and Jess were nearest, so Margot grabbed each of their hands. 'Don't burst my bubble, please.'

'You've spent the last six years saying you were prioritising having children over anything else,' Sarah muttered. 'That your ovaries were calling the shots.'

'I've asked my ovaries to stand down for a while so I can have a little bit of fun with a really lovely, really handsome man.'

'He seems like a sound bloke, and it makes leaving a little bit easier knowing you're happy, but I know you, Margs. You're always all in, right from the start,' Tracy said, hanging onto Margot's hand so she couldn't pull free. 'You don't know the meaning of chill.'

'I am *so* chill.' Or rather, Margot was trying to be chill and it was bloody killing her.

'So, you haven't asked him what the two of you'll be doing for Christmas even though it's only May?' Jess asked sceptically.

Margot shook her head. 'I haven't. I wouldn't do that because we're not *in* a relationship.'

Technically it was the truth. At no time had Margot questioned Will as to what his Christmas plans were, because she already knew that he'd spend Christmas with his family. And of course, Margot would probably spend Christmas with them too. She'd shared their last Christmas and that was before she and Will were anything.

'You're only thirty-six,' Tracy reminded her. 'We've always told you that you've got loads of time before you need to start worrying about having kids.'

That was easy to say when you'd already found your One and had been together long enough to make plans about having a family. It was easy enough to nod in agreement like Jess and Sarah, but they'd already found their Ones too. They already had children, had put down roots, had a permanence to their lives that they took for granted.

They didn't know what it was like to be thirty-six, nearly thirty-seven, and still feel as if your life was somehow transient. They'd never had dark, sleepless nights, agonising about whether to freeze their eggs because time was marching on, their reproductive systems were no longer shiny and new, and there was still no sign of a half-decent man on the horizon.

So, Margot was giving it as much time as she could for a woman who was in a race with her own biological clock. Who had waited so long to be someone's person, their family. And now, she was doing her best to convince herself that it was a relief not to have that constant pressure weighing down on her.

Margot glanced through the window again at Will, who raised his head from his contemplation of something on his phone. He looked directly at Margot, smiled and mouthed something that she hoped was, 'I'm missing you'.

Will wasn't a half-decent man. He wasn't a make-do. The last one standing in the last chance saloon. He was so much more than that, even if he didn't realise it himself.

'Exactly,' Margot said. 'A few months of fun with Will isn't going to hurt me.'

36

Will

Will had known that getting together with Margot wasn't going to be some fly-by-night, flash-in-the-pan thing. But the actual reality was terrifying, like being on a rollercoaster and Will always threw up when on rollercoasters, which is why he didn't go on them anymore.

But it was also not terrifying, because this was Margot. Kind, funny Margot, who always knew exactly what to say. Sexy Margot, who pursued her passions in the same way she pursued life – with focus, determination and a hell of a lot of text messages.

If Will had known that Margot would be completely insatiable – not a complaint – then maybe he'd have done something about the two of them sooner. But this wasn't just about sex. It wasn't just about the two of them either.

It was Will and Margot (and Blossom, of course) and a cast of thousands. Not an exaggeration, Margot easily had a thousand friends, and in the space of a few weeks, Will was sure he'd met all of them several times over.

Then there was his family. There was a reason, several very good reasons, why Will had never introduced his women to his family. Apart from his sixth-form girlfriend, Emily, whose grandmother was pally with Mo, and Dovinda, who he'd dated in New York. (Dovinda had gate-crashed a family brunch with Bernie, Mo, Mary and Ian who were in town, turning up at the restaurant unannounced after looking at

Will's phone when he was in the shower. Dovinda had big trust issues, which had met Will's intimacy issues head on. It was amazing that they'd lasted as long as they had. Four months.)

But Margot had already met his family, and as soon as they found out that there was something to find out, they'd all but adopted her. There were the Wednesday-morning walks with Mary that filled Will's heart with dread, because he'd told Margot a story, which wasn't completely his to tell.

Mind you, the Wednesday-morning dread was nothing compared to the taste in Will's mouth, like he'd been licking batteries, when Margot was invited on a girls' night out with Rowan and Sage.

Of course, it had been fine. Rowan insisted that she 'already liked Margs because she makes you happy,' and even Sage, who had the brutality of youth, had given Margot a seal of approval. 'She's all right,' Sage had said. 'Just don't fuck it up like you usually do.'

'I don't usually fuck up things.'

'Well, you must have fucked up all the relationships you had when you were abroad or else we would have met them,' Sage pointed out, because she was nineteen and absolutely bloody relentless.

But none of those relationships that he'd had when he was abroad had left a vast array of beauty products in his bathroom. Nor met his family. Or had any idea about the man he really was, as opposed to the man he pretended to be.

It was still hard to believe that he had felt safe enough to unburden his soul to Margot, and it wasn't a quid-pro-quo deal, but still Will had often glimpsed a sadness in Margot. A bone-deep sorrow that was to do with losing her parents, especially her mother, but despite his gentle prodding, she'd shied away from telling him what lay beneath the 'big, scary feelings' she'd mentioned.

Not that Will could blame Margot for holding back. They both knew that this wouldn't and couldn't last forever. So, although Rowan and Sage had declared their love for Margot, they were only eight weeks in. It was far too soon to be thinking about love, let alone talking about it, when there were so many words still unspoken between them. It played on Will's mind as he stood in the kitchen talking to Den about his impending emigration to New Zealand, and watching Margot through the window.

She was in a group with Tracy and her two other best friends (Will still wasn't sure how many best friends one person could have). Huddling together because, now night had fallen, it was cold, but also huddling together because the conversation seemed intense, and at one point Margot ran a careful finger under one eye as if she were brushing away a tear.

Immediately, Will felt guilty. As if he was responsible for that tear, for the intensity of the conversation. 'He's scared of commitment like I'm scared of spiders,' he could imagine Margot saying.

'Tracy is really going to miss Margs. Keeps threatening to smuggle her into our hand luggage,' Den said, and Will realised that he'd been standing there, saying nothing, slack-jawed as he gazed at Margot.

'Margot feels the same way,' he replied. 'But please don't smuggle her into your hand luggage, because I'd miss her.'

It was the truth. But Will didn't have to miss Margot because she wasn't going anywhere. She was staying right there with him for however long this lasted. Will had always liked a plan. A strategy. A roadmap for where his life, his career, was heading. These past sixteen months, he'd been drifting, and that couldn't last forever either, but the drifting had brought

Blossom and then Margot into his life, so there was something to be said for not always having a plan.

Will's phone chimed. When Mary Blossom-sat, she liked to provide her son with updates every half an hour.

She's farting and snoring. The stench and the volume is like nothing else but I don't have the heart to wake her and kick her off the sofa.

Will smiled and looked up to catch Margot's eye through the rather smeared window. 'I miss you,' Will mouthed and she smiled. Will couldn't help smiling back. There were so many reasons why Margot shouldn't be with him, but he was bloody glad that she was.

The huddle broke up and its four members dispersed. He expected Margot to reach him first, but it was actually Jess, who looked about twelve but wagged her finger at Will in a way that was alarmingly similar to how Mo used to tell him off.

'You'd better not be a wrong 'un,' she warned Will. 'Our Margot doesn't deserve a wrong 'un.'

'I'm absolutely not a wrong 'un,' Will said to Jess's back as she rummaged in the fridge for another bottle of wine, though she'd clearly had enough to drink.

'That's what a wrong 'un would say,' she told him sorrowfully, so he couldn't win either way and decided that he'd be better off looking for Margot.

He'd only got as far as the kitchen doorway when he was hemmed in by Sarah, a blond-haired Valkyrie who looked as if she should be riding a chariot into battle. Especially as she greeted Will with the words, 'If you do anything to hurt Margot, then I will hunt you down and hurt you back, like, tenfold. All right, mate?'

'I'm not going to hurt Margot,' Will insisted, though he had a horrible feeling that if Margot got so much as a paper cut on Will's watch then Sarah would be exacting retribution.

He finally found Margot in the lean-to with Tracy, making plans to go to the airport with her and Den. 'There's no way that you're going to leave the country without me waving you off.'

'You'll cry, Margs. You know you will.'

'I'll try really hard not to,' Margot said, but her fingers were crossed behind her back when Will touched her arm.

'Been looking for you everywhere,' he said. Margot turned to him with a relieved smile, like he'd come to rescue her.

'Now you've found me,' she said with some satisfaction, curving into him as Will put his arm around her waist.

Tracy looked at both of them and frowned. She opened her mouth then closed it again with an audible huff. Will held up his hand.

'If I may?'

Tracy nodded. 'Go on then.'

'I'm not a wrong 'un. I'm not going to hurt Margot. Margot is absolutely the best woman I've met in a long, long time . . .'

'Apart from Blossom,' Margot murmured.

'The best *human* woman I've met, and we're good, and you don't need to worry about her or me or us. Right, Margot?'

'Damn right!' Margot snuggled a little closer to Will as Tracy nodded.

'OK, then,' she said. Tracy didn't sound exactly OK, but that was on her.

Will had managed to articulate his emotions in a way that had made Margot happy and didn't leave him feeling as if he was being swept into deeper waters than he could safely navigate on his own.

If Roland could only see him now!

Relief and optimism made Will pick Margot up and twirl her when they got home, after stopping en route to pick up Blossom from Mary's. She hit him and said that she'd give him a hernia, as she always did, and Blossom jumped up at both of them, excited at this new game and wanting to be a part of it.

'You're very smiley,' Margot noted, once she'd managed to free herself from Will's arms. 'What's got into you?'

'I'm always very smiley,' Will insisted, as he wound his arms round her again and kissed her neck in a way guaranteed to make Margot squirm.

'You're not, actually, but the whole moody thing really works for me.'

'Nothing's got into me, but I'm about to get into you.' His hands were already lifting the hem of her dress.

'Can we take a rain check until you've given Blossom her last walk?' Margot managed to say before Will kissed any more words right out of her mouth.

Blossom didn't get her last walk until nearly midnight and Will slept better than he'd done in days, only waking when he heard the sound of the shower. He listened to Margot's morning noises. The ancient shower head above the bath gurgled happily, over which he could hear Margot singing a snatch of 'Good Morning' from *Singin' in the Rain*. She'd never met a show tune that she didn't like. Then the hum of the electric toothbrush.

Will rolled over to see Blossom sitting by his side of the bed, unblinking. Margot had been quite adamant that Blossom was not sleeping in *her* bed, despite Will's own flagrant disregard for the rules they'd drawn up together. Blossom was having a hard time understanding it.

'I still let you sleep in my bed,' he murmured, scratching her under her chin and reaching for his phone on the bedside table.

There was a WhatsApp from Mary telling them that she was making chicken for lunch and not even asking if Margot was coming too, because Margot's attendance at Sunday lunch was now mandatory.

There was an email from the organiser of a running club replying to Will's enquiry about dates and times, and the usual 20 per cent off offers and 'Summer Sale Starting Now!' emails from companies that Will had never given his address to.

He certainly hadn't given his email address to someone called Josh from a company called Blue Sky Solutions, who thought that it was perfectly acceptable to send Will a business email at seven thirty on a Sunday morning. Then Will had to check himself, because there had been a time when he'd been that person who sent out business emails well before seven thirty on a Sunday morning.

> *Hi Will,*
>
> *I wanted to reach out and touch base with you.*
>
> *I'm Senior Partnership Manager at a boutique recruitment agency, which represents many blue chip, forward-facing clients.*
>
> *Your name has come up in discussions about how we can move the needle on a project for a company that should be smashing it in the financial tech world but are experiencing high levels of churn. Would love to run a few ideas up your flagpole.*
>
> *If you feel that you currently have the bandwidth to pivot to a more consultative role, let's take this offline ASAP and set up a face-to-face. Would be useful to know if we're all looking at the same blips on the radar screen.*
>
> *Why don't we circle back on this in 48 hours? Ping me if you have any immediate questions.*
>
> *All best,*
>
> *Josh*

Immediately, Will felt a gnawing anxiety chomping away in the pit of his stomach. Instead of trying to push it away and think of happy thoughts like the sound of Margot now halfway through a rousing version of 'I Have Confidence' from *The Sound of Music,* he did what Roland had taught him to do. He sat with the feeling, explored it and tried to break down what it was about it that had tied his internal organs into knots.

He decided that it was probably the glimpse back into the corporate world. Once again, Will was forced to look at the man who he'd tried so hard to be for twenty years: a successful over-achiever, both in the boardroom and the ranking charts of whatever extreme sporting event he'd signed up for. Not an automaton, not exactly, but someone who had tight control over their emotions.

Now his life was busier, fuller, but in different ways, because it seemed to Will as if he had no control over his emotions anymore. His heart was wide open and Blossom, his family, and yes, Margot, had stepped right in and made themselves at home.

He couldn't stay at Blooms' forever. Any person with a half-decent grasp of numbers would be able to replace Will and then he could go back to the world of finance. The gnawing feeling in his gut downgraded to a light chewing. His life now *was* fuller, and he didn't want to live to work in a job in an industry that was all-consuming. So, actually, how had Josh put it? Pivoting to a more consultative role might be a good compromise. Will could pick and choose his projects, work on a part-time basis, so he wouldn't be abandoning either Blossom or Blooms'.

The chewing in his stomach was now the lightest of nibbles and that was only because Will was remembering how he too had once excelled in all that bullshit business speak. But he wasn't that person anymore. He was still a work in progress, though he had to admit he was starting to like the man he was becoming.

The noises from the bathroom had stopped. Then Will heard the clatter of a lid on the porcelain sink, which meant that Margot was about to apply various lotions and potions to her skin, which also meant that it was time for her daily affirmations.

Right on cue. 'I am happy. I am kind. I am hopeful. I am strong. I am an exemplary dog owner. I am a very chill friend with benefits or whatever.' There was a pause, another clatter then an unhappy little sigh. 'I just want to be loved.'

Will waited for the inevitable stab in the gut as fear took hold of him, but it never came.

37

Margot

Even though on Sundays they usually had a long dog walk before heading over to the Blooms for lunch, yesterday Margot had cried off.

'You don't mind, do you?' she'd asked Will in a distracted manner. 'Just I've been neglecting all sorts of life admin and I have to get up ridiculously early to go to the airport tomorrow morning.'

'I'm already coming second to your tax return.' Will had put a hand to his heart and fake-staggered like Margot had dealt him a mortal blow as he and Blossom had left.

They didn't need to spend every hour that they weren't working together, especially when Margot was feeling things that she had no right to feel.

Besides, Margot really had had bills to pay, an oven to clean and felt quite sick when she'd had to set her alarm for four thirty so she could see Tracy and Den off to New Zealand.

Margot was not a morning person. Getting up early always left her woolly headed and faintly nauseous, so it was hard to remember why she'd thought this was such a good idea.

'Remember that we had a deal,' Tracy reminded Margot as they waited at check-in. 'You could only come if you promised not to cry.'

'Far too grumpy and hungry to even think about crying,' Margot snapped. Beyond the terminal doors, the sun was now high in the sky, which felt all wrong. On days when something

terrible was happening, the weather should have the decency
to be cloudy with a chance of rain. 'And I told you not to wear
jeans if you wanted to get upgraded.'

Neither Den or Tracy got upgraded, but they still decided
to celebrate with Prosecco and a fry-up. 'Because in airports,
the normal rules don't apply,' Den insisted, as they clinked
glasses.

Every time Margot had flown with Tracy – hen weekends
in Ibiza, a Christmas shopping mini-break to New York in the
halcyon days of a strong pound, two weeks in Mykonos –
they'd always start their trip with Prosecco and a fry-up.
Although the Prosecco slid down far too easily, this time
Margot could only manage to nibble forlornly at a rasher of
bacon.

'Don't drink too much and cry,' Tracy warned, as if she
wasn't worried about clearing security or getting to her gate in
time, or even making a new life for herself in a country where
she hadn't lived for twenty years. The only thing she was
worried about was Margot weeping all over her.

'I'm not going to cry,' Margot croaked. Den, sensing that
there was a very real possibility that Margot would cry, said he
needed to stretch his legs. The minute he left the table, Margot
turned to Tracy who was also picking her way round her plate
with little enthusiasm. 'I'm going to say the same thing I said
to you on the morning of your wedding.'

'What? Wear comfortable pants because you don't want to
spend the whole of your most special day picking your thong
out of your arse?' Tracy asked with a defiant tilt to her chin.

'That's good advice for life, not just for your wedding day.'
Margot put down her knife and fork and pushed her plate
away. She couldn't even finish one measly piece of toast.
'Look, I'm sure you'll be happy, I want you to be happy, but if
you're not, you don't have to go through with this.'

Tracy pushed away her own plate. 'Margs.' It was equal parts warning and endearment.

'If you get there and you realise that it still is sheep and not much else, I won't think any of the less of you if you decide to come home.' Margot knew she was being off-message and a little bit selfish, but she couldn't let Tracy go without a token protest.

'Don't do this,' Tracy whispered. 'Don't tell me that I have a get-out clause. Tell me it's going to be all right.'

'It's going to be all right,' Margot said obediently, as the first inevitable wave of tears streamed down her face.

'Margs . . . oh, Margs,' Tracy sighed, reaching across the table. 'I'm worried about you.'

Margot managed a watery smile. 'I'm probably going to spend the rest of the day in tears, but somehow, some way, I will manage without you. Not going to lie though, I wish you—'

'You'll barely manage without me!' Tracy brushed away Margot's declaration of friendship with an impatient hand. 'Which is why I'm worried about you and that Will.'

'Why are you saying his name like that?' Margot straightened up from her slumped position because Tracy had tucked her hair behind her ears, so she obviously meant business. 'And, while I appreciate your concern, there's nothing to be worried about. Things are going well. Really well. Surprisingly well.'

'You're in love with him,' Tracy said flatly, as if this alleged love was a statement of fact, but also something that was a terrible idea.

'I'm not in love with him,' Margot said automatically, and she was just about to launch into her speech about how it was nothing serious, just one last glorious affair before she settled for the next man who swiped right or picked a sperm donor out from a glossy brochure. If that was her future, then didn't Margot deserve to have a bit of fun first with a man who was witty and handsome and gave her an orgasm every time? A man who she was halfway to falling in love with . . . 'I'm *not* in love with him. I'm not!'

'Do you want to say that once more and try to make in convincing?' Tracy had folded her arms now, like Margot was one of her students begging for another essay extension. 'All you've talked about, been fixated on, since you turned thirty, is having children, having a family. That love isn't even an option anymore. And yet here you are in love with this Will . . .'

'Yes, OK, I *could* love him,' Margot whispered, her eyes stinging with tears that she was holding back through sheer granite determination. 'There's a lot to love about him.'

Tracy sighed. 'And could he love you?'

Margot couldn't speak. So she shrugged instead.

'Does he want to have children, have a family with you?'

'Don't,' Margot begged, the tears rallying for an encore performance. 'Don't do this to me.'

'George hurt you and you weren't even in love with him – No, Margot, you weren't,' Tracy said, as Margot held up her hand to protest, though it was true, she hadn't loved George. Had only stuck it out for two years because of all George's vague promises, hints, the hope that he'd stop prevaricating and give her all the things she wanted. Margot had resigned herself to having George's faintly irritating presence in her life because she'd be compensated by the family that they'd have.

But Will hadn't made any promises or dropped any hints. He'd stated quite unequivocally for the record that commitment, deep emotional commitment, wasn't for him. He didn't want the things that Margot wanted. He'd been honest with her and, knowing that, she'd still ended up in this place where—

'You're going to get hurt and I won't be here for you,' Tracy said. She was crying now and Tracy hardly ever cried so it made Margot start to sob. 'You have to get out now, Margs, while you'll only be a little bit hurt.'

'It will still hurt a lot,' Margot choked out. 'It will hurt like hell.'

'I would love nothing more than to be proved wrong, but if he can't make you happy and give you all the things, all the love, you deserve, will you promise me that you'll call a halt?' Tracy reached over the table to take Margot's hand, squeeze her fingers. 'It's not going to end well, but it will be worse the longer you leave it.'

'I know. I know,' Margot said, properly crying now. She was still crying half an hour later as she waved Den and a weeping Tracy through security.

Why was it that everyone she loved left her? They moved on and Margot was still stuck in the same place. Even when she made changes to her life, getting a dog that she adored, getting involved with someone who she could probably adore too if he didn't have more boundaries than an Ordnance Survey map, she was still no nearer to her goal. A man, a baby, ideally another baby after that, a family.

But irrespective of all that, her best friend of twenty years had left the country and Margot didn't know when she'd see her again. Her phone chimed just before Margot reached the Tube. Hope sprang ever eternal. Maybe Tracy had decided not to get on the plane after all.

Hope the getting up early and the send-off wasn't too traumatic. Do you need Blossom cuddles tonight? Will try and prise her from Mum's clutches. W x

Just when Margot was sure that this thing with Will was unsustainable, he always found a way to pull her back in.

* * *

Five minutes after Margot got home from what had felt like the longest day at work ever, she was opening the door to Will and Blossom.

She could hardly bring herself to look at him; as it was, she'd spent most of the day either in tears or fighting back tears, so it was easier to kneel down and bury her face in Blossom's neck, which always smelt like biscuits. Albeit sometimes really stinky biscuits.

'How are you?' Will asked, his voice soft with concern. He closed the door behind him and stepped past Margot and Blossom. 'Can I get you anything? Cup of tea? Chocolate?'

She just wanted to be left alone with Blossom whose love was always limitless and unconditional, but when Margot reluctantly raised her head, she saw that Will was standing in the kitchen doorway, removing his jacket.

'Are you staying?' Margot asked, and in her emotionally fraught state, even that simple enquiry about Will's immediate plans felt like a loaded question.

'For a bit,' Will said. He smiled. 'I've thought of something that might make you feel better.'

Even *that* wasn't going to make her better, she thought, as Will headed, predictably, for her bedroom. She busied herself with taking off Blossom's lead and harness, making sure she had fresh water, then washed her hands before confronting Will. She couldn't live like this. Half on edge, half in hope. Tracy was right. It was better to rip off that plaster as quickly as possible, even if it did take several layers of skin with it.

Will was perched on the edge of the bed as he took off his shoes. He was wearing one of his fancy slim-cut suits. He must have had meetings in town. More usually he wore jeans and expensive trainers. Margot leant against the door, which was difficult as she had so many handbags hanging from the

hook, and was trying to think of a way to start this awful reck-
oning that they had to have, when Blossom trotted in.

What Margot wouldn't give for a cuddle session with
Blossom on the sofa.

'It's late,' Margot pointed out.

'It is,' Will agreed, straightening up. He patted the bed. 'Will
you come over here?'

'Will . . . I'm not really in the mood.'

'Neither am I, but although I'm not an expert in these
matters, you really look like you could use a cuddle,' he said,
and although they often snuggled after sex, to hear the C word
come out of Will's mouth and see the awkward, pursed shape
of his lips immediately after he said it, was enough to almost
make Margot smile. Almost.

She allowed Will to gently pull her down on the bed and
she rolled onto her side so Will could curve his body into
hers; she was always the little spoon. They lay like that for
several moments, but it felt stilted and unnatural. Margot
was hyper aware of the sound of their breathing, ragged and
out of sync, the tense arrangement of their limbs, and she
was about to tactfully call a halt to it when a furry face
appeared, and Blossom rested her chin on the edge of the
bed, her brows furrowed, her expression both sorrowful and
hopeful.

'No,' Margot said firmly. 'You know you're not allowed on
this bed.'

Will shifted so he could see over Margot's shoulder. 'Go on,
let her up. Just this once.'

'But it won't be just this once, will it? She'll expect to get on
this bed for ever more. Just like when you gave her a handful
of Cheerios before her last walk that one time, though I still
don't understand why . . .'

'It was the only way to get her off the sofa . . .'

'And now she expects a handful of Cheerios every blooming night at the same time.'

Will leaned over Margot, his weight pressing her into the mattress, so he could just graze the end of Blossom's snout with the tips of his fingers. 'Look at her! She feels left out.'

And to think that when they'd first become co-pawrents, it had been generally assumed that Margot was a soft touch, when actually Margot established clear and direct boundaries and mostly stuck to them. Mostly.

'Margot. You're making Blossom sad.'

Margot flopped onto her back. 'Oh, go on, then,' she capitulated with a weary sigh, patting the bed. 'You can come up, you monster.'

Blossom didn't need to be told twice. She was up on her hind legs instantly, paws scrabbling but not able to find purchase on Margot's pink satin bedspread and probably catching it with her claws, which was one of the many reasons why Margot didn't want her on the bed.

With a frustrated groan, Margot scooched over so she could grab Blossom under her front legs and heft her onto the bed. That would be Blossom's cue to do what she always did when they were at Will's: commando crawl along the bed and insinuate herself between Margot and Will, not caring who got hurt on the way.

But not this time. She stood at the end of the bed, uncertain of her victory, then circled three times before settling next to Margot with a contented little sigh, so that Margot was both big spoon and little spoon.

It was perfect.

Will murmured words, nonsense really, one arm wrapped tight around Margot, the other hand stroking her hair back from her hot face still swollen from all the crying. And she in turn had her arm wrapped round Blossom, her hand stroking the vellum softness of her belly and the dog's happy grunts rumbled and reverberated through her.

Margot remembered the last time she'd felt this safe, this protected, this cherished.

We three. We happy three.

It wasn't a memory so much as a vague, shadowy recollection of a sensation that Margot had felt before. Once. Many, many years ago. And it was coming back into focus now, growing brighter, gaining more depth.

A nightmare. A storm raging outside and she'd been frightened, tearful enough that she was allowed into her parent's bed. Tucked in between her mum and dad, held tight so nothing could get at her, enveloped by their arms, their love.

And Margot couldn't believe that she'd ever forgotten, because she realised now that she'd spent her entire life attempting to recreate that moment, this feeling. She'd coalesced it into one thought, one concept: family.

The Welsh had another word for it. *Hiraeth.* A word that could hardly be translated but signified a bittersweet memory of missing something or someone, while being grateful of their existence.

She started to cry again, very quietly, because this moment too wouldn't last. Margot had thought she could make do with a kind-faced man. A companion. But she'd been a fool. She couldn't make do without love.

Now here she was, feeling the way she did because she loved this dog and, God help her, she loved this man who was kissing the back of her neck, making soothing sounds as he did so. And it was not just implausible, but impossible, that he could love her back. Not when he didn't want the things that she wanted. He would leave her at some point in the near future. Or was it the distant future? It hardly mattered. What mattered was that he wouldn't be there.

38

Will

The next morning as Margot was in the bathroom, for once not singing show tunes, Will planned out a speech. A speech felt like the right way to go. He'd never been so intimate with another human being as he had when he'd held Margot as she'd cried. So he wanted to lightly touch on his fears around commitment, then firmly state for the record that he was in this with Margot, whatever this was, and they could figure that out together.

But he didn't even have a chance to get 'Look, about last night' past his lips, because when Margot came out of the bathroom, she was already dressed and had a rigid look on her face.

'I've just remembered that I have to be in work super early,' she said, but she wouldn't look him in the eye. 'I have to leave now.'

'How about I give you a lift?' Will asked, because he really did want to make sure that Margot was all right after all the drama of yesterday. Make sure that they were all right too.

'That would take ages . . . rush hour,' she mumbled vaguely, still refusing to make eye contact. 'I'll get the Tube. You can take Blossom if you want. It is your week after all.'

Blossom had been snoring away under the duvet and barely stirred at the mention of her name. Since he and Margot had been doing whatever it was that they were doing, Blossom's designated weeks had stopped in favour of a more organic system. This talk of it being Will's week was deeply troubling. In a tight voice he asked, 'Is something wrong? With us?'

'Look, I haven't got time to get into something. I really have to go,' Margot said, almost braining herself on the collection of handbags hanging from the hook on her bedroom door, such was her haste to leave the room.

'So, there is something wrong?' Will called after her, flinging back the duvet, but he reached the hall just in time to hear the slam of the front door behind Margot.

Rather than being authentic and deep and intimate (all things that normally Will shied away from) had he crossed a line last night that he shouldn't have? He was the one that brought barriers and boundaries with him wherever he went, never really appreciating that other people put up walls too.

He sleepwalked through the morning deliveries, got a parking ticket because he didn't see a 'no loading' sign and had no appetite for lunch. The shop was quiet, so he wandered round the corner to the mews, where Rowan had a huge team prepping for a midweek wedding in a back garden the size of a field in Highbury. The whole affair was going to 'look like a fairy grotto by the time we're done,' Rowan promised grimly, as she expertly strung together vertical garlands of soft lilac and delicate pink flowers, which would form a flowerwall for the guests' own photos.

'Can I help?' Will asked. 'Nothing too tricky, though.'

'I was going to ask you arrange the bride's bouquet.' Rowan shook her head at the very thought of it. 'Actually, can you assume scary banker mode and tell the bride's mother to stop putting sides of salmon in the fridge where she said I could put the table centrepieces? Then tell the bride's youngest brother that wearing a white rose buttonhole isn't going to turn him gay.'

'I don't mind dealing with a fractious mother of the bride, but I'll ask if she'll have a word with her homophobic, flower-hating son,' Will said. After he'd made a very diplomatic call to the mother of the bride, he drew up a stool and lent a hand with conditioning the buckets and buckets of flowers, so they'd reach perfection on the day of the wedding and not a moment sooner. There was something soothing about the repetitive motion of cutting stems on hundreds of white roses then handing them to the next person in line who carefully placed them in buckets of nutrient-enriched water.

'I know that you're far too highfalutin to have spent an afternoon conditioning wedding flowers, but thank you,' Rowan said hours later when they were locking up for the night. 'Bit of a waste of your fancy business degrees.'

'Never hurts to mix with the proletariat,' Will muttered, but he felt too heavy-hearted for a spot of light banter. 'You fancy a quick drink?'

He wasn't one for confiding in his family. He'd come back and slotted into a slightly uncomfortable role as the troubleshooting prodigal son. There to be leant on, to sort out problems, to provide a buffer, but he and Rowan had always had a different relationship. They'd never lost the closeness they'd had as children.

Maybe it was the only happy legacy of their childhood. Six years ago, after Rowan had had the twins and was struggling with post-natal depression, she'd call Will in the small hours – early evening in New York – when she was doing the night feeds. They worked their way through a complete re-watch of *The West Wing* together, but sometimes Rowan had just wanted to talk, to whisper her deepest fears down a transatlantic phoneline. That cycles of abuse tended to be repeated and what if it turned out that she was a terrible mother?

Rowan wasn't and never would be a terrible mother. She'd also married a man who was the polar opposite of their father.

He might be so laidback that he was in permanent danger of falling over, but Alex had been rock-like during that difficult year. Will had been there too, because he and Rowan understood each other in a way that only came from sharing a parent like Peter Hamilton. More than anyone, Rowan would understand what Will was going through now. She was the one who'd insisted that he start therapy when he'd come back to London, half-broken.

But now Rowan shrugged helplessly. 'I would love to, but I promised I'd be home in time for dinner, then to do bath time and stories. They hardly see me on the weekends at the moment.'

'Of course.' Will watched as she bolted and locked the studio doors. 'We should catch up properly. When wedding season isn't too weddingy.'

'I'll book you in for some time in October,' Rowan said, putting the keys in her bag. She glanced at Will, then glanced again. 'Are you all right?'

'I'm fine,' Will said with a determination that made Rowan frown.

'You say fine in exactly the same way that mum says fine when things are absolutely not fine,' she said folding her arms and leaning back against the door. 'I can give you five minutes of prime quality time. What's up?'

'Nothing . . .'

'I can and will smack you . . .'

'OK, OK.' Will held his hands up to show that he was defenceless. 'When you started seeing Alex, how long before you knew that you . . . That he was . . .'

'That I loved him? That I wanted to spend the rest of my life with him?' Rowan supplied. 'Is this about Margot?'

'She wants a family. She's always been very upfront about that, even before this . . . *this* . . . It was meant to be very casual between us, Ro, but is it fair to her when she wants someone who's going to be in it for the long haul?'

'Wow. This is a lot to pack into five minutes of quality time,' Rowan said with a sigh, but her expression was thoughtful. 'So, you definitely don't see things working out with Margot, especially not having a family?'

This was a very strange, intense conversation to be having outside some lock-ups. 'It's not the "with Margot" part that's the problem. Margot would be a great mother, a bit helicop-tery, but only because she cares. She's conscientious. She wants everyone to be living their best lives,' Will said, because that's what she'd wanted for Blossom, and no one could say that Blossom wasn't living her best life. Apart from Blossom herself, who'd say that there should be a lot more sausages and belly rubs on tap.

Rowan hmmed in agreement. 'So, million-dollar question, how do *you* feel about having children of your own?'

'Do you remember after you had the twins and you said that there were many ways to fuck up when you have kids?' Will traced a half circle with his foot. 'Would having kids be the thing that makes me turn into Peter? Or would I realise that I'm not able to commit to being a father? That, just like he told me, I'm useless. That I'll never amount to anything.'

'You are as far from useless as it's possible to get,' Rowan said hotly, because she was Will's sister and contractually obliged to say that. 'Look, why don't you come back with me and have some dinner?' she suggested just as Will's phone, which had been silent all afternoon, because absolutely no one needed him, chimed three times in quick succession.

It was Sage.

Where are you?

You were meant to be coming round for dinner half an hour ago. Mum said that she told you this morning.

There's an emergency. Get your arse here immediately.

'Actually, can we take a rain check?' he asked Rowan. 'Sage is having some kind of existential crisis and my presence is required.'

Rowan shuddered. 'Rather you than me.' They started walking up the mews. 'I expect a full debrief tomorrow.'

Ten minutes later, he found Sage in the kitchen with Mary and Ian, who was sat at the kitchen table with bike parts spread out on an old newspaper and a perplexed expression on his face. The back door was open, Blossom was lying in a patch of sun in the garden, all four legs in the air like a tipped cow, and a spirited discussion was taking place about whether they should eat outside.

Suddenly Will was ravenous. 'What's for dinner?'

'Soy and honey-glazed salmon with new potatoes and a salad,' Mary said, taking a vegetable knife out of the drawer. 'You can start chopping up the tomatoes and cucumbers if you want to make yourself useful.'

Sage was staring at her phone; whatever the emergency that had required Will's attention, it seemed to have been forgotten. 'It's so annoying,' she said. 'When I take a pic of me in a flower crown, I get several hundred likes, I even get a couple of booking enquiries. But when I take a picture of me and Blossom in matching flowers crowns, that shit goes viral. Look!'

The picture of Blossom wearing a headpiece of cream and pink sweet peas and peonies was so cute Will was surprised that it hadn't broken the internet. Even so . . .

'I hope you're not exploiting Blossom for likes,' he said to Sage sternly, but Sage just waved a languid hand in his face.

'She should earn her keep somehow,' she said before launching into a spiel about how she'd spent the day working with a designer on the Bloom & Family new-look packaging. 'We like the logo. That whole art deco thirties thing is so on-trend, but it also needs updating a little, don't you think, Mum?'

'As long as the new logo incorporates a drawing of Blossom in a flower crown, then I'm happy,' Mary said. 'And it needs to look good on the 'Gram.'

'Well, that goes without saying.'

Will paused from taking the salad stuff out of the fridge to look pointedly at his youngest sister and his mother. Since when did Mary start referring to Instagram as 'the 'Gram', and why were they now having a very loud, very showy chat about social media and influencers, and creating bespoke experiences for people through the medium of floristry? Sage had just uttered the sentence, 'Making memories with marigolds,' and was pointedly ignoring Will who was now rolling his eyes.

'So, anyway, Mum, I was thinking we could be doing amazing things with the shop Instagram.'

'We've got the Facebook page,' Ian pointed out.

It was Sage's turn to roll her eyes. 'Nobody uses Facebook anymore, Dad, only old people. No disrespect.'

'Yet I feel disrespected,' Ian said, bopping Sage gently over the head with the oily rag he was using to clean his bike innards.

'The thing is,' Mary said, 'we really need to exploit our social media channels. We have less than seven hundred followers, but Sage has . . . How many followers do you have, Sage?'

'She has loads,' Will said, because he now knew what this emergency was about. 'Over ten thousand.' He put down the cucumber and knife and turned around. 'I take it this isn't about our social media channels but about Sage not wanting to do a degree anymore.'

'Very interesting you should say that, Will.' Mary looked up from where she was scrubbing the new potatoes. 'Now that you bring it up, did you know how many extra hits we got when Sage hosted that flower-crown workshop for influencers? Maybe you could do one of your spreadsheets to see how much extra revenue she's bringing in as she captures the millennial market.'

'Sage is getting a degree. End of,' Will said firmly and, he hoped, definitively.

'It's not end of,' Sage said just as firmly, because she'd never had to spend her formative years walking on eggshells, which also meant that she never shied away from an argument. 'You can't actually physically force me to go to university if I don't want to. But I'd much rather that you were cool with me choosing a different path, than not being cool with it.'

Will shook his head. 'You were dead set on being a lawyer.'

'I was sixteen! I watched a lot of *Suits* the summer after my GCSEs and I shouldn't be making career decisions based on that.' Now Sage threw an imploring look at Ian, who shrugged helplessly. He was a man torn between the three great loves of his life: his wife, his daughter and the bike parts in front of him, which needed his immediate intention.

'Well, ultimately it has to be Sage's decision, doesn't it?' Ian didn't even look up from his bike innards.

'And also, I'll be saving nine grand a year in tuition, not to mention living expenses,' Sage pointed out. She now had her hands on her hips and was bobbing her head from side to side in a way that all her family and friends dreaded.

'That is true,' Ian now chimed in. 'Going to university is *so* expensive and we don't want Sage to be saddled with debt for years.'

Will had had enough. 'Obviously, I'm going to pay for your tuition and your living expenses,' he said tightly, an orange pepper clutched so hard in his hand that it was almost pulp. 'I set up a trust for you on the day you were born.'

'You didn't have to do that, Will . . .' Mary said, her face flushed.

'I did it because I have . . . had a good job,' Will continued, putting down the knife before he ended up chopping off one of his fingers. 'And after you've done your degree, you'll be able to get a really good job too, you'll earn lots of money. And do you know what that means?'

Sage wilted in the face of Will's righteousness. 'Um. No. What does it mean?'

'It means that you'll be financially independent,' Will told her in a choked voice, because he didn't feel that far from tears. 'You won't be reliant on anyone else for money. You'll never be forced to stay with someone who makes you unhappy or, worse, hurts you, simply because you can't afford to leave. And *that* is why you're going to university.'

'Oh, Will . . .'

'Dude . . .'

'Now come on, son . . .'

All three of them spoke at once. Will would have bet that all of them were on the verge of tears too.

No matter that it was so long ago, that his name was never mentioned, Peter Hamilton still made his presence felt. Even in Sage's life, though she'd grown up knowing that she was loved and cherished by both her parents, not to mention her half-siblings.

It was Sage who reached Will first so she could throw her arms around him. 'You never have to worry about that,' she said, her voice thick and trembling.

'Well, I do worry about it. I'll always worry about it,' Will said, rubbing soothing circles on Sage's back with the hand that was still clutching the now entirely squashed pepper.

'You don't, because if I ever found myself in that situation, I know I could call you or Dad or Mum or even Rowan though she says I'm a brat, and you'd come and get me,' Sage insisted. 'It would be all right.'

Mary wasn't quite done either. 'I know I made mistakes in the past, but I found a good man second time around and we raised Sage not to take shit from anyone. Though maybe we were a little too successful,' she added with a watery smile.

Ian decided that this was worth putting down his oily rag. 'Sage has got lots of ambition,' he began. 'She's carving out new revenue streams that none of us could ever have imagined.'

'Oh God, I really am,' Sage said, rallying again.

'The way she's going with that flower crown malarkey and being a floral influencer on Instagram, if she did want to go to university at a later date, she could pay her own fees, isn't that right?' Ian prodded Sage who shrank back.

'Well, let's not be too hasty,' she said quickly. 'I bet Will wouldn't want me to pay my own tuition fees, not if he's already saved up.'

This was all getting derailed again. 'So, you'd better talk me through the golden window of opportunity that is Instagram,' Will said because he could be gracious in defeat. 'Be a shame not to take advantage of it while we can.'

'Well, yeah, so I've been doing loads of research on the festival circuit for my flower crowns and it's definitely viable,' Sage added. 'There's so much more you can do with flowers than, like, arrange them in vases. Spooky flowers for Halloween, wreath-making workshops for Christmas. There's so many Instagram users to exploit!'

Before pudding, they got Rowan on FaceTime and carved out the empire between them. Mary, with some input from Ian, would run the shop and the delivery side of things. Rowan would do the high-end weddings and events. Sage would take over all the social media channels and, overseen by Rowan and after taking some specialist floristry courses at Capel Manor, would continue in her quest to become the flower-crown queen of London. Also, the new logo would feature the same thirties font that they'd always used but would incorporate a photograph of a beaming Blossom wearing a flower crown.

Sage had also posited changing the name of the business to Bloom and Blossom, but Mary had put her foot down on that one.

And as for Will, one thing was obvious. 'You don't really need me, do you?' he pointed out cheerfully, though he had a feeling of all-encompassing dread lodged just below his gut.

'Don't be silly,' Ian said. 'Eighteen months ago, we were running about like headless chickens and were barely breaking even.'

'You're the one who really jump-started the events side of the business,' Rowan cried from the iPad screen propped up on the table. 'Not just because you invested in it, but because you've taken on all the boring stuff. Now I can focus on the flowers which I love, and I never have to look at another invoice or VAT return which I absolutely hate.'

'And all those women of a certain age love being served by you in the shop.' Sage winked at Ian. 'Stolen all your ladies, hasn't he, Dad?'

'Been nice to have another man about so I'm not completely overrun,' was Ian's contribution.

But it all confirmed Will's suspicions. Though deep down, he'd known this all along. 'You needed me a year ago, and now you don't, and that's as it should be.' Will tried to smile like it really was a good thing for everybody, himself included. He had to stop being so resistant to change. Change could be good. 'I knew that I couldn't stick around for ever. I had an email from a recruitment company ...'

Three pairs of eyes stared at him, and from the iPad, Rowan shouted, 'Turn me round so I can see Will!'

Now four pairs of eyes were staring at him. 'We do need you,' Mary said softly. She'd been loading the dishwasher, she never let anyone else help because she had a system, but now she placed a wet hand on Will's shoulder. 'Of course we need you, you're the glue of the family now Mum and Dad have gone.'

It was a touching sentiment, but no one could replace Bernie and Mo. It was as if there was a permanent fracture in the family that just wouldn't mend. 'I don't want to be glue. What am I? A human version of Pritt Stick?'

Rowan sighed so hard that it was a wonder the iPad didn't slide across the table. 'But glue is what puts everything together again, even when you think it's broken beyond repair.'

'Great. That's good. Everything's fixed and, like I said, you don't need me anymore, so it is time for me to get another job. Maybe think about moving out of the flat too. You're losing out on rent with me crashing there.' It was time to get his life on track. Work. Home. Relationships, because he wasn't just seeing Margot, he was in a relationship with her and he needed to find a way that they could both be happy without feeling compromised.

'Don't be ridiculous,' Mary snorted, turning to her husband. 'Ian, talk some sense into him.'

'Well, Mary, he's big enough and ugly enough to make his own decisions,' Ian said, because he wanted a quiet life and taking the path of least resistance was the best way to achieve that.

'You're not ducking out on us again,' Rowan piped up. Will hoped that the iPad would run out of charge very soon. 'Leaving when we all need you.'

Sage, who'd been quiet all this time, now felt the need to speak. 'Really, it's amazing that you've managed to commit to

Blossom. What's going to happen to her if you move away or get a full-time job? You can't take her with you. She's just as much ours as she's yours. And what about Margot?'

'Yes, where does Margot fit into all this?' Mary wanted to know. 'That girl is the best thing that's happened to you in years. Don't you dare ruin it.'

'I'm not planning on moving away,' Will said, because it was the truth. He was here to stay. He wanted to put down roots, have real permanence in his life, and not just because of Margot, but also he couldn't bear the thought of not having Margot in his life. He could feel his resolve weakening. Margot wanted so much, and she had every right to, but could Will give Margot what she needed? 'This thing with Margot, it's actually quite nuanced and complicated . . .'

Sage gave Will a good hard kick from under the table. 'Don't be ridiculous. What's complicated about it? Margot's amazing. What *is* wrong with you?

The same thing that had always been wrong with him: 'Maybe I'm just not good enough for her.'

39

Margot

'I am strong. I am independent. I am happy on my own. I'm doing just fine.'

Margot positively affirmed herself for the fifteen minutes it took to walk from her flat to their meeting point in Highgate Woods.

'I am cool. I am calm. I am collected. I am doing just *fine*.'

It had been a few weeks since Margot had last come here for an official handover and now it was June. Flaming June.

She'd only known the field when it was the domain of dog walkers and football players, but now it was living proof that when the sun shone in London, the inhabitants of that city would immediately find the nearest patch of green and load up on vitamin D. There were picnics and picnickers seeing off marauding dogs. Kids playing ball. Teenagers playing frisbee. At the other end, half of the field had once again been reclaimed by the cricket club.

Her father had played cricket and she had the dimmest memory, half-hidden in the shadows, of his cricket jumper and how it scratched when she hugged him. It wasn't a huge leap of logic to think that he must have batted and bowled on this very field, although Margot couldn't say for certain. She'd been so young then and where her father did and didn't play cricket had barely registered. It was a lifetime ago.

Margot was on time for once, but Will was already there, his eyes fixed on the spot where she emerged through the trees.

Her body gave a joyful jerk in his direction, but Margot forced herself not to hurry but to take her time.

She hadn't seen Will since that hurried morning when she'd felt wrong in her own skin. Margot had often known the frustration of being with a man who refused to commit, no matter how many hints she'd drop about moving in together or the narrowing of her fertility window. She hadn't done that with Will, but then she hadn't fallen in love with any of the other men. She might have wanted a family with them, but they'd never felt like family. And Will did. He felt like home.

But he wasn't home. He was a short-term let. So Margot had done the responsible, adult thing, and instead of talking to Will then mutually agreeing to end things in a civilised manner, she'd avoided Will for the rest of the week. When he'd asked to come over, she'd invented a sudden case of food poisoning ('It might not even be food poisoning, it might be something gastro-intestinal and horribly contagious') and had strung it out over several days.

It would have been at least a little validating if Will had looked a little wretched about his Margot-free week, but he didn't. Far from it. He was wearing jeans and a navy polo shirt, so Margot could appreciate that his skin was tanned light golden, even his hair was blonder, and for someone who didn't do CrossFit anymore, his arms were nicely muscled. Though Margot already knew that, she'd clung onto them often enough when Will had been driving her to dizzy heights of passion.

'Hi,' Will called when Margot was within distance and Blossom, who was a few metres away chewing ten shades of hell out of a tennis ball, eyes rolling back in ecstasy, decided that Margot was worthy of a greeting. She dropped her ball, got up, looked at Margot, looked back at the half-dismembered, soggy ball, then realised she could take it with her.

No matter how much Margot was hurting, Blossom could always make her smile. She came running towards Margot now, tail going like the clappers, and dropped the ball at her feet.

'I'm not touching that disgusting thing,' Margot told her, crouching down so she could kiss Blossom and gently tug at her ears.

'How are you? You look good,' Will said when Margot reached him. 'Are you fully recovered now? I wish you'd have let me come over with some soup at least.'

Margot was wearing a lot of make-up and the biggest, darkest sunglasses she owned, which obscured half her face and, in particular, the area that was swollen and red from the crying and the not-sleeping.

'I'm fine. Well, a little bit shaky still,' Margot said, which wasn't a lie though the hand she was stroking Blossom with was tremor-free. 'How are you?'

'All the better for seeing you, of course.' Will squatted down to rub Blossom's belly so their hands collided before Margot snatched hers back. He froze for a second, then quickly recovered, a bland smile on his face. 'Well, I've been doing a lot of thinking. About the future and about—'

'Me too,' Margot said, because they needed to find a way back to being co-pawrents and nothing else. Margot would just have to make her peace with that. Until that peace had been achieved, she couldn't bear listen to Will pontificating about a future that didn't have her in it. 'We've been seeing a bit too much of each other for two people who are simply having a little summer fling. Don't you think?' she added, her voice cracking slightly.

'Oh . . .' Will packed the entire works of Shakespeare into the exclamation. 'Is this about the other night? Because I thought that was what you needed.'

'That's the problem, isn't it,' Margot said, straightening up. A week of not sleeping properly had played havoc with her back. 'We need and want very different things, and even though we knew that, we still did what we did and now here we are.'

'If you give me some time, then maybe we'll discover that we do actually want the same thing,' Will persisted, which was sweet and conciliatory of him but if Margot had a pound for every time she'd heard a variation on this theme, she'd have an off-shore bank account in the Cayman Islands.

Margot was off her game. In the normal way, she'd launch into one of her trademark impassioned, forthright speeches. But nothing about this felt normal. She could tell Will that their affair was now derailed because she was pretty sure that she'd fallen in love with him, but she wasn't strong enough to hear that he didn't love her. And yes, he had good reasons for finding it hard to let people in, to love them, but Margot had good reasons to want to let people in, to be loved and love in return. Again, she couldn't believe that she'd deluded herself that love didn't matter at all.

'You're right. We both need some time to think.' Margot wanted this over because *this* was torture, but still she didn't have the courage to end things here and now. She hadn't managed to entirely snuff out that little flickering flame of hope. 'I mean, we can't go on as we are so let's see how we feel in a week or two.'

'Yes, but—'

'Anyway, let's talk about our blessed Blossom.' Margot thanked her god-given and annoying ability to ride roughshod over what anybody else was saying. Particularly when she didn't want to hear it. 'Has she been a perfect angel, as per usual?'

'She took a dump in one of my shoes,' Will said, red staining his cheeks, but that might have been because Margot couldn't help her very unattractive snort of laughter, even though her heart was currently fractured. 'It's just as well I discovered it before I put my foot in it. She's never had any accidents before.'

It was no accident. It was Blossom picking up on the stress in her co-pawrent's current relationship, Margot was sure of it.

'I think all this toing and froing with no proper routine must be unsettling her,' Margot said, seizing this damning bit of evidence like it was the last lifebelt on the *Titanic*. Will reddened even further. 'So it really does make sense to cool things for a little bit, doesn't it?'

'How long is a little bit?' Will asked, running a hand through his hair. 'I've missed you this last week.'

'I missed you too, but you were the one who just said you needed time . . .'

'But I thought we could spend that time together as we figure things out,' Will said.

'I'm sorry, but I can't,' Margot said, and she didn't have the emotional strength to look at Will any longer, to be so close to him but to feel as if there were continents between them. There was no point in prolonging this agony any longer. 'Let's catch up in the week, yeah? Come on, Blossom, time to go home!'

Margot thought that she heard Will say something, but she was already walking away, until she realised that Blossom wasn't walking with her. She turned round to see the dog standing at the halfway point between Margot and Will, hesitating as if she wasn't sure whose side she was on. Margot didn't want Blossom to take sides because she knew how much Blossom loved Will, and Blossom was about the only being that Will voluntarily loved. Margot wasn't going to deprive either of them of that.

But it *was* her week and Blossom had crapped in his shoe, so it was with a mostly clear conscience that Margot held out her arms and shouted, 'Blossom! I have chicken!'

Those were the magic words to get Blossom trotting obediently after her.

As soon as they got home and Margot kicked off her Birkenstocks, which surely hadn't been such instruments of podiatric torture last year, and said, 'Cuddles!', Blossom headed straight into the sitting room to jump on the sofa and wait expectantly.

Margot sat down and immediately Blossom draped herself over her lap, so that her belly was exposed, and her elbow was digging into Margot's thigh. 'I kind of thought that you'd offer me comfort, not cause me pain.'

She managed to get Blossom to shift her position, so that she was sitting between Margot and the back of the sofa and Margot could curl herself around her stocky form. Will had once sent her a newspaper report about scientific research into dog behaviour, which stated that dogs didn't like being cuddled because it made them feel claustrophobic and heightened their anxiety.

But as Blossom settled in Margot's arms with a contented sigh, it was clear that the scientists obviously hadn't polled any Staffordshire Bull Terriers. For every kiss Margot gave Blossom, she got an enthusiastic lick in return; it was so lovely, so uncomplicated, to show love and get love back.

Margot felt the first throb of tears. Love was the simplest thing in the world. Dogs had the emotional intelligence of an average two year old, but they still loved and loved very well. Whereas some people could have university degrees and yet were incapable of love.

'No! Blossom, don't do that. Let me love you,' Margot protested as Blossom struggled to free herself from Margot who now had her face buried in Blossom's neck, all the better to wipe her tears on Blossom's fur and inhale great whiffs of her biscuit smell.

But Blossom had had enough. She wriggled free, her front paws on Margot's chest to hold her off, and what looked like a stern expression on her usually soft, happy face. It was the same stern expression Blossom deployed when she saw other dogs behaving indecorously and felt the need to intervene.

'*Et tu*, Blossom?' Margot muttered, and she got another look from Blossom, like she wasn't angry with Margot, just disappointed, before she jumped off the sofa. Ten seconds later, Margot could hear the scrape of her empty bowl on the kitchen floor, as Blossom obviously felt that her need for food was far greater than Margot's need to be loved.

Margot couldn't mope for ever. Past experience had taught her that when she was in pain and unhappy, she always felt better for seizing control of the situation, exploring her options.

So, on Thursday morning, Margot had made an appointment at a Harley Street clinic that specialised in fertility services.

Their offices were in an elegant Georgian townhouse. The consultation room she was shown into was furnished in soft, sumptuous shades of grey and off-white so it resembled a boutique hotel rather than anything medical.

Margot's hands were sweating and she wiped them off on the skirt of her dress. She was meant to be having a fertility MOT. A chat with a specialist, then a blood test and a pelvic ultrasound scan, which was never going to be fun. Still, Margot might have to get used to unfun things happening to her pelvic region.

The door opened and a sleek blonde woman in a white lab coat entered the room. She looked more like she was about to perform tweakments on Margot's jawline than wielding an ultrasound wand in a few minutes.

'I'm Dr Draper,' she said, sitting down in the grey velvet bucket chair opposite Margot. Attached to her clipboard was the questionnaire that Margot had filled in earlier. 'But, please, call me Claire.'

It wasn't just her hands that were sweating. Margot could feel the sweat break out on her forehead and her upper lip. She took a couple of deep breaths and Claire smiled.

'I promise you, I'm not that frightening.' She finished with a tiny, almost bashful smile, which made Margot unclench slightly. 'Let's just have a chat about why you're here and how we can help you.'

'Well, I'm thirty-six, thirty-seven almost, and single. Very single. I desperately want a family, but I can feel my fertility dwindling with every day that passes, so freezing my eggs might take some of the pressure off.' Saying the words out loud was terrifying. 'I mean, I'm hopeful that I might find someone, but I need to be realistic.'

'I hear you,' Claire said, like she too despaired of ever finding The One, or a passable version. 'Now, let me just get a better picture of your reproductive health. Have you been pregnant before?'

Claire's voice remained soft and modulated as she grilled Margot on her sexual history, her contraceptive history and her periods, which of course Margot had been tracking on an app since she first got an iPhone.

Margot had enough friends with fertility problems to know that IVF wasn't a case of simply having your eggs taken out then popped back in once they'd been fertilised. It was physically and emotionally gruelling and not at all infallible. But she hadn't realised that she too would be injected with hormones, her fertility tweaked and monitored and enhanced, until the time was just right for her eggs to be harvested then frozen for up to ten years.

Margot couldn't even imagine being nearly forty-seven with her eggs still on hold while she waited for a man to want to start a family with her. Not in the usual way, but in a petri dish or test tube, though given how eye-wateringly expensive all these procedures were, Margot hoped that it would be a bit more sophisticated than test tubes.

And of course, if the man didn't turn up, then she'd have to use a sperm donor, and this wasn't how it was supposed to be. No matter how chic the soft furnishings might be, it was all so clinical, so cold. And there were no fucking guarantees that it would work.

Margot had always wanted children, to have a family with a man she cared for and who cared for her too, and now she had to acknowledge that it might not happen. It was increasingly likely that she'd be doing this alone, like she did everything else.

But even that wasn't the worst part. The worst part was when Claire asked Margot about her mother. Her fertility problems, which Margot only knew the vaguest details about because she'd been eighteen when her mother died, and there just hadn't been enough time to talk about everything they needed to. And of course, Claire wanted to know how Judy Millwood had died. Cancer. What kind of cancer? And Judy's mother, did she die from cancer too?

'Probably be a good idea to run some other bloodwork when we do your anti-müllerian hormone blood test, just so we have all the information we need,' Claire said. She tilted her head to one side sympathetically. 'Is that something you want to do today or would you like some time to think about it?'

Margot was here because she was exhausted from thinking about it. She'd been ready to have her blood taken, her reproductive organs ultrasounded and her signature scribbled on the dotted line.

'I just . . . I can't even . . .' Margot managed to get out. She thought that she might cry but she also felt as if she'd been encased in ice and wasn't capable of any movement.

Margot stood up, said she'd be in touch once she'd processed all the information, then fled along an airless corridor and down the stairs until she was out on the street, clinging to the wrought-iron railings and shuddering to breathe.

All the thoughts she skirted away from, shoving them ruthlessly away, were flooding back now. Back to the source. The last year of her mother's life.

In some ways those eleven months had been wonderful. Margot deferred her fashion degree for a year, hopeful that by that time, Judy would be better and the gnawing fear that clawed at Margot's stomach would be a thing of the past.

They spent all their time together. Yes, there was the relentless monotony of hospital appointments and chemo sessions, but Judy also wanted to set Margot up for the rest of her life: she taught her how to make a béchamel sauce, how to change a plug, how to weed out the good men from the bad.

Then when the drugs didn't work and diagnosis became prognosis, and treatment became palliative, Judy didn't fight on. She didn't decide to spend the last months of her wild and precious life ticking off items on a bucket list or reserving her strength. Instead she cleared out the house in Gospel Oak so Margot wouldn't have to do it, then sold it. Sorted out pensions and investments. Dealt with solicitors and accountants and estate agents.

It was why Margot didn't think she'd ever move, because her mother had seen her flat, had come to view it in between the last chemo appointment and going into the hospice. 'Yes,

I think you'll be very happy here, Margot. Very happy indeed,' she'd said, her smile shot through with relief that she'd done right by her daughter; had done everything in what was left of her rapidly depleting power to ensure that Margot would somehow cope without her.

She'd done all that for Margot and how had Margot repaid her? Margot was still standing outside the clinic, letting herself be buffeted by the merciless, hurrying Londoners pushing past her as she shied away from the memory of her mother's last weeks in the house in Gospel Oak before they moved out; Margot to the flat in Highgate and new beginnings, Judy to the hospice and the inevitable end. Those long, endless nights, separated from her mother by a wall and her own cowardice. She'd done something so awful that the shame of it made her shiver despite the sultry heat of high summer.

Margot would much rather think about her own uncertain present and future than the sickening secrets of her past. And what if she wasn't destined for longevity either? What if she ended up having children in her forties like her own mother, then left them before they'd grown up, before they'd had a chance to become the people they were meant to be?

When Margot thought of it like that, and she thought about it more and more often, then she might be better off not having children at all.

On the bus back into work, Margot concentrated really hard on not crying, on pushing down the fear again, the bitter bad memories. She was ready for them on birthdays, significant anniversaries, but they always managed to take her by surprise when she was at her most vulnerable. That last year. That awful, terrible, devastating year. Margot brushed back the single tear that had dared to fall and by the time she reached Ivy+Pearl she was dry-eyed. She felt shell-shocked and could barely blink at the news that the internet was down.

'Is it?' she asked without any interest.

'It is,' Tansy shouted from her office. 'Bloody Blossom chewed through the cable of the router.'

That shocked a gasp out of Margot. She'd left Blossom at work – she could hardly ask Will to look after her – knowing that Blossom was always a model employee.

'Are you sure it was Blossom? Maybe we have mice,' Margot said aghast. 'I can't believe you'd accuse Blossom. She never chews anything she shouldn't.'

'Caught her red-handed,' Derek said. 'Or red-pawed. Then I put her in a timeout in your office and she howled the place down.'

Blossom acting out? She wouldn't even look at Margot, but made a big show of turning her back on her devoted owner and doing one of her unsettlingly human huffs of annoyance. As if it were Margot who was in the wrong.

It was the last thing that Margot needed. But was it any wonder that Blossom was acting out of character when her routine, her happy little life had been completely disrupted?

It was time for Margot to get her house in order.

40

Will

'You've got a face like a wet weekend in Wigan,' Mary said on Thursday afternoon when Will got back from 'touching base offline' with Josh from Blue Sky Solutions. 'Was it a bad meeting?'

'It was all right,' Will assured her, but Mary also had a face like inclement weather had ruined a mini break in the Greater Manchester area.

'So, you're leaving us then?' She was in the back room of the shop and steadied herself on the worktop as if the prospect of Will's imminent departure had left her light-headed.

Will shook his head. 'No. I'm not leaving. I told him that I was interested in doing no more than thirty hours of consultancy work a month, I wouldn't work with any arseholes, then I wrote my hourly rate down on a piece of paper, added another nought to it, but he didn't seem that phased by the figure and said he'd be in touch.'

'Thirty hours a month is a lot . . .'

'It's four days . . .'

Mary sighed. 'But you have to do what makes you happy. Are you happy?'

Will grunted in response. He was far from happy. It was Margot's week. Because it seemed that they were back to simply being two people who shared a dog. No more walks together. No more hanging out together. No more holding her in the dark still of the night. No more sharing each other's secrets. Would there be a brief, terse handover every Sunday?

He looked up to see Mary giving him an assessing glance as if he were a bunch of flowers on the turn and destined for the half-price bucket. 'Well, I'll be happy if you can give me a lift home in the van. Marek from across the road is picking it up for its MOT in the morning.'

'Why can't Marek pick it up from the mews?' Will asked, but got a scowl by way of a reply.

Mary didn't say anything else until she was getting out of the van. 'Come in a second, I want to show you something.'

There was obviously some minor household repair that needed Will's attention while Ian was cycling to Paris for charity. The day before last it had been a colour-fast sheet caught in the washing machine pump. Will followed Mary up the garden path. Now that it was June, the wisteria bush that climbed up the outside of the house was in full bloom. Sage had gone completely overboard with the #wisteriahysteria pics on Instagram.

'Shall I go and get the toolbox from the garage?' Will asked once they were inside, but Mary shook her head.

'Said I had something to show you, not something to fix. Not anything in the house, that is,' Mary said, reaching up to tap Will's head with one finger. 'In the lounge.'

Mary made a beeline for the G-plan sideboard, bought by Bernie and Mo when they first got married, which had survived being hideously old fashioned for decades and was now bang on trend in all its mid-century splendour. Rowan was always dropping hints that she'd take it off Mary's hands if she fancied getting something more modern.

Mary slid open one of the cupboard doors to reveal a stack of photo albums. 'Now, which one is it?' she muttered to herself. There was a huge quantity of them in there. This was obviously going to take some time.

'I'll put the kettle on,' Will decided. When he came back with tea, Mary was sitting at the dining-room table, with a dark blue album in front of her.

'Did you remember my sweetener?'

'I never, ever forget your sweetener,' Will said, sitting next to Mary and placing the mugs down on the coasters, which were a permanent fixture on any flat surface in the house. 'What did you want to show me?'

'My wedding pictures. My *first* wedding pictures, that is,' Mary said, sliding the book over to Will, who had absolutely no interest in seeing mementoes of the day that his mother got married to a man who turned out to be a monster. 'Just have a look. Humour your old mum.'

With a tiny put-upon sigh, Will leafed through the first pages of Mary getting ready. Although she'd been twenty, she looked much younger. There was no contouring, microblading or any of the other things Sage and her friends did to their faces. Mary's make-up was minimal, her fine blond hair centre parted and left loose, a radiant smile on her face as Mo adjusted her veil.

There were more photos of pint-sized bridesmaids and a surly looking pageboy. Bernie and Mary getting into a vintage Rolls-Royce and, as befitted the daughter of a florist, a hell of a lot of pictures of the bouquet ('Pale pink amaryllis, white roses and baby's breath, we wanted to keep it simple'), the church flowers and the table centrepieces at the reception.

It took a lot of flicking until Will came to a picture of Mary and Peter walking back down the aisle, just married. They were in motion: Peter stepping into a shaft of sunlight slicing through the stained-glass windows, so his face was obscured. Even so, it was enough to make Will's stomach turn as if all the tea he'd drunk that day was sloshing about like a storm-tossed sea.

He had to force his fingers to turn the page to a photograph of Mary and Peter standing on the church steps, hand in hand. She wore a simple white dress, plain and unadorned. Peter was wearing a suit, flared trousers, and a shirt with shockingly big collars.

'It's amazing that anyone found love in the seventies, when you were all wearing such hideous clothes,' he remarked.

'Look at him,' Mary demanded. 'Take a good look at him.'

Will bit his bottom lip but bent his head and took a good look at the first photograph of his father that he'd seen in over twenty-five years. He could hardly focus at first, because he was seeing the picture of Peter that he'd had in his head all that time. Then he looked again, readjusting his memory, to take in this young man in his mid-twenties, smiling, eyes clear and adoring, as he looked at his bride.

He wasn't even that tall. Mary was about five foot, six inches, and he was only a little taller than her, his figure slim. Not the burly monster of Will's nightmares.

Will leaned in closer still to pore over Peter's face. He had mid-brown hair, a truly spectacular pair of sideburns, dark eyes. Not stunningly handsome, not unattractive either. He was wholly ordinary. The kind of man you'd walk past in the street without even noticing him; though Will would have sworn that Peter's face was imprinted on his mind forever.

Of course, a few years down the line, when Will had his first memories of his father, Peter's face was puffy with drink, his eyes red-rimmed and bloodshot, no easy smile on his face. Or was that just how Will had embellished his features so Peter looked more like the monster that he'd been?

Will stared intently at his father's face, searching for clues. The way you might look at pictures of dictators and despots, serial killers and suicide bombers, looking for signs as to who they'd become. A deadness to the eyes, a twist of the lips, a dark shadow cast over them, but in this case, there was nothing.

'He's not at all like I remembered,' he said to Mary, who'd left her tea untouched, her attention firmly on her son. 'He's just an average guy.'

'Average,' Mary repeated. 'Less than average. But I didn't know that then.'

'Was he good to you at the beginning?' Will asked though not sure if he wanted to know the answer, but Mary nodded.

'He was always telling me that he loved me. Not just at the beginning, when I thought, hoped, that it was true, but right through to the end.' She glanced down at the open photo album and covered Peter's face with her hand. 'Like love was a get-out-of-jail-free card. That his so-called love absolved him of all the terrible things he'd done. But I knew by then that he wasn't capable of loving or being loved in return . . .'

'That's how I feel. That I can't love or be loved,' Will said quietly.

'Which is bullshit, pardon my French, because you are loved, very much, and you love us back,' Mary said, tapping Will sharply on the knee.

'But I haven't amounted to much either.' Will felt like he was back in therapy, though Mary had a long way to go before she achieved Roland's impassiveness, because her face was scrunched into a frown.

'You might not have the fancy job anymore or the flat in New York with all the windows, but that's not important. What is important is that you're a good lad. Kind, caring. If Blossom was here, she'd agree.' She smiled, which made Will smile though he didn't feel like smiling. 'You're going to be all right, Will, but you have to let go of the past. I didn't begin to heal until I could do that.'

'Do you wish that you'd never met—?' Will asked, but before he could even finish his question, Mary was shaking her head.

'No. Absolutely not. If I hadn't met him, then I wouldn't have had you and Ro, and I love you both to death. But I also wish that you hadn't had such a terrible childhood. There were so many times that I thought about scooping you both up and getting the hell out of there, but I was too weak.'

'It wasn't weakness, Mum,' Will said, placing his hand over Mary's hand, which was still covering Peter's face. 'We know better now. We have words to describe what he did: coercion, emotional abuse. You were caught in a bad situation with a bad man and Ro and I have never once blamed you for what happened.'

'I blame myself, Will!'

'No, you were just as much a victim as we were. More, actually.' Will squeezed Mary's fingers. 'And now you're living the life you deserve with a man who loves you even more than his bike . . .'

'Almost as much as his bike,' Mary said, but then she slipped her hand out from underneath's Will's so she could stroke it down his face. 'Please don't give *him* so much importance in your life; he's not worth it. Look at him!'

Will looked again. This time he felt unmoved. He was looking at someone he hadn't seen or spoken to in twenty-seven years and would never have to see or speak to him again. Peter Hamilton had always been a stranger to him. And vice versa. Peter had never known who Will really was. Not even as a child. Will had merely been a reflection of his own failures and disappointments.

But also, he knew nothing about the man that Will had become, so why was Will still giving his petty words such weight? Allowing this man, this stranger, to have so much power over him?

His whole life had been lived as if he was still seeking Peter Hamilton's approval. The first-class honours degree. The jobs in Berlin, Paris, then those years in New York, earning more money than he knew what to do with, the apartment with all the windows, the latest gadgets, the designer clothes.

Not just the material things either. Every marathon run. Every mountain climbed. Every beautiful woman he dated. It was all a gigantic fuck-you to Peter, his father, the man who'd always told Will that he was useless.

But Will had still been unhappy, discontent, unfulfilled. Just like his father. As Will looked at Peter Hamilton, there on the cusp of life, his brutish, bitter future not yet written, he realised that he wanted exactly what Peter had wanted in that moment, frozen in time and captured by the wedding photographer.

He wanted to be loved. To love in return. Not to worry that love made you vulnerable because when you found someone who loved you, really loved you, it didn't make you vulnerable. It made you strong. You had a partner, a co-pilot. Someone who had your back. Someone who had your heart too. Someone just like Margot.

Peter Hamilton would say that Will didn't deserve a woman like Margot. That he wasn't worthy of that kind of woman. That kind of love. But just because Peter wasn't worthy of that kind of love, didn't mean Will wasn't too. He'd spent his whole life proving that he was nothing like Peter, so why stop now? Why not allow himself to have the happy ever after that would always elude his father?

Will put his head in his hands. Mary's landed heavily on his shoulder, in what was meant to be a comforting pat. 'It's all right, lovey. Crying's nothing to be ashamed of.'

'I'm not crying,' Will insisted, lifting his head so Mary could see that he was dry-eyed. 'I've just had a breakthrough, as they say in therapy. Not sure why I paid seventy-five quid an hour to a trained psychotherapist for a year, when you've sorted me out in ten minutes.'

'Seventy-five quid?' Mary, predictably, was appalled. 'Daylight bloody robbery. Now, enough of all this nonsense about not being good enough. You're certainly good enough for a nice girl like that Margot. She'd be lucky to have you.'

'I'm not sure she sees it quite like that,' Will said with a sigh, because that was the flaw in his masterplan. He'd thought that he'd be the one to pull back if things with Margot started moving too fast, but she'd been the one to withdraw, to stop returning his messages, to turn her face from him like she didn't want to look at him.

'Well, she should,' Mary said, like that was the final word on it. 'Have you got any exciting plans for tonight?'

Will was thirty-nine, lived in one of the most vibrant cities in the world and was going to go home and spend the evening alone. 'Not really, no.'

'I'm going to order us a Chinese and you can tell me why Margot's gone silent on the #TeamBlossom chat.'

'Do I have to?' Will asked without much hope of a reprieve, as Mary got to her feet to go to the drawer in the sideboard where all the takeaway menus were kept.

'If you won't think of yourself, then think of Blossom. It doesn't do her any good if you and Margot aren't on the same page,' Mary murmured, her eyes fixed firmly on Golden Valley's appetisers section. 'Now, stop pulling faces at me and help me decide if we should get a quarter of crispy duck or a half?'

41

Margot

Can't do our usual time for handover. Will meet you at 8 p.m. at the usual place. Margot

It was June twenty-first. The summer solstice. The longest day of the year.

Despite the fact that it was eight on a Sunday evening, a school night, the field in Highgate Woods was still crowded with people hoping for a little light relief, a gentle breeze, to cool the sticky heat. It hadn't rained in forever and the grass was coarse and bleached. Dogs were slowly walked around the perimeter, while courting couples sat on the ground, heads close together. A large group, which had splintered off into smaller groups, was having a picnic to celebrate someone's twenty-fifth birthday. Helium balloons of a two and a five swayed slightly, as the picnickers sipped Prosecco out of paper cups.

Margot never knew which direction Will would come from. Sometimes he appeared, a small figure in the distance, at the bottom of the field to walk towards them. Other times, he seemed to emerge out of thin air, taking the path that came out by the information hut, just a metre or so from where Margot was sitting on a bench.

Blossom had been quite frosty with her ever since the router incident, but this evening she'd deigned to climb on the bench and lean heavily against Margot. Her black dress would be covered in dog hair, but Margot was long past the point where she cared about that.

'Hi,' Will said, a sudden voice in her ear, which made Margot jump because she'd been scanning the bottom of the field.

Margot stared down at her pink polished toes. 'Hi,' she said, her voice a rasp, a scratch.

Blossom was up on her hind legs. With the added height from the bench she was just able to reach Will's throat with her tongue.

'Did you miss me? I missed you.' Blossom always got the better part of him. 'Nanna saved you some beef from Sunday lunch and said that I'm to give you a kiss from her.'

God, why did he have to make this so hard? She raised her head at last. Like Margot, Will was wearing black. Black T-shirt and black jeans. Though unlike her, he didn't look like a superannuated old goth; with his Ray-Bans aviator shades and Neil Barrett lightning bolt trainers (hopefully not the trainers that Blossom had christened), he was the kind of man who got second glances. Not just from the gaggle of teen girls congregated on the benches opposite them, but from two sprightly older women walking a herd of doddery old pugs.

It would have been much easier if he'd cut himself shaving this morning or was incubating a massive spot on his chin. If his hair needed cutting and the back of his neck was cultivating a thatch (something Margot particularly hated) or he was wearing his lilac shirt with the blue check that didn't suit him.

Not because Margot was shallow enough that any of those things really mattered, but because it would be some small consolation that she was doing the right thing in . . .

'Shall I take Blossom, then? But first, I really wanted to talk to you. I've been doing some thinking. Lots of thinking.'

'I'm sorry, Will, there's no easy way to say this, but I don't think we should see each other anymore. Not as friends, even. So, I'm also really sorry about this but I'm not handing Blossom over this week. Or any other week. I'm keeping her. Full time.'

. . . severing all ties.

Will's mouth fell open. If he hadn't been wearing shades, Margot imagined his eyeballs suddenly pinging out of his eyes on springs like in a cartoon.

'What are you talking about? What do you mean not seeing each other anymore? And you're not keeping Bloss. Don't be silly,' he said like it was just nonsense and he was shutting it down right now.

'I'm not being silly, I'm being deadly serious.' This was hands down the most difficult conversation Margot had ever had. But just because something was difficult was no reason not to plough on anyway. 'It was always a pretty experimental idea to share a dog and it's time to admit that the experiment hasn't been successful. Look, can you sit down and stop looming?'

'Can't do anything right,' Will muttered and he collapsed on the bench as if his legs couldn't hold him up anymore, Blossom between them as she always was, until she jumped down so she could claim another dog's abandoned tennis ball. 'What is going on with you?'

'I've realised that I was being an idiot when I said that I wasn't looking for love. And it's OK, I know that if you can't handle a serious relationship then you're not ready for love either,' Margot finished for him, because she didn't want to listen to Will extolling all her many virtues but concluding that they weren't enough to make him want to be with her.

'It's a bit too soon to be talking about love.' He sounded amused, and Margot was pleased because it made her hate him a little bit. 'I followed your advice and I've spent this last week thinking about us and sitting with my feelings. Really taking a deep dive to get to the bottom of them.'

If there was one thing worse than an emotionally damaged man, it was a man who used his emotional damage as an excuse for his shitty behaviour.

'Well, I'm sure that was hard and I applaud you for putting the work in, but I'm going to be thirty-seven in a couple of weeks and thirty-seven means I'm not in my mid-thirties anymore. I'm in my late thirties. I'm thundering towards forty. My fertility is—' Margot heard him sigh, and she had to dig her nails into her palms so she wouldn't smack him. 'Yes, I know, Will, I know that I'm every cliché in the book, I'm too bloody much, but my biological clock is slowing down and I need a man who's ready to commit.'

Blossom had been happy to lay spatchcocked in front of them while she destroyed her tennis ball, but at the sound of Margot's voice, high-pitched and agitated, she wandered over and placed her head on Margot's knee.

'It's been nine weeks, Margs,' Will said. 'It's not fair to put this kind of pressure on me, or on yourself for that matter, when we've barely started. And yes, I admit that I have I had intimacy issues . . .'

'You committed to Blossom within one week. A week,' Margot repeated, just in case Will hadn't heard her properly the first time. 'She smashed down all those famous boundaries of yours even though she's the dictionary definition of needy.'

He sighed for the third bloody time. 'Needy is different when it's a dog. It's actually quite endearing when—'

'*Really?* Are you fucking kidding me?' The vehemence of her delivery took all three of them by surprise. Blossom put a warning paw on Margot's leg, Will's shoulders stiffened and his face took on that shuttered look that Margot knew only too well, then he whipped off his shades, all the better to glare. Despite the heat of the evening, his eyes were positively wintry.

'So, let me get this straight. You never want to see me again?'

Yes, because it was too painful to see him week in and week out when she loved him and he loved sitting with his feelings; never reaching any kind of resolution. It occurred to Margot that Will didn't want to be happy and that made her heart hurt too, but she was actively seeking happiness and, though it didn't feel that way right now, she'd be happier without him. 'We should never have started having sex. We both knew it wasn't a good idea.' Margot stroked the top of Blossom's head. She was now doing a good impersonation of a meerkat as she watched two guys kicking a football back and forth, completely oblivious to the fierce custody battle that was waging. 'It worked much better when we were distant friends . . .'

'Distant friends, right,' Will echoed scathingly. Margot decided to ignore him. To say her piece and then leave with her dog and what was left of her heart.

'We knew that if we did become involved, it would complicate things. And now things are bloody complicated, and Blossom is completely unsettled and none of this is fair on her,' Margot said, impassioned now as she remembered the callous way Blossom had uncoupled from their cuddling. And the chewing! She hadn't confined her activities to a wireless router lead. She'd also chomped her way through the personalised Anya Hindmarch bag that Margot had gifted herself for her thirtieth birthday – in any other circumstances, it would have been impressive that Blossom had managed to hone in on the most expensive thing that Margot owned. 'There have been two incidents of wilful destruction this week; it's classic acting out.'

'She'll get over it,' Will said forcefully. 'She's got over much worse. We'll take her back to training.'

'Don't you get it? There is no "we" anymore.' Margot stopped stroking Blossom in favour of gesticulating wildly.

Pointing first at Will, then at herself, in case he needed a visual cue. 'I don't want to go to training with you. I don't want to spend time with you. I don't want to be in a WhatsApp group chat with you and Mary . . .'

'This is going to destroy my mother.' For the first time, Will sounded distraught, like he was beginning to understand the consequences of their actions. 'You can't do this to her. Or me. I love Blossom just as much as you!'

Why had she decided to do the honourable thing and tell Will face to face? A letter would have been so much better and then she wouldn't have had to see the pain cutting deep lines into his face.

'I doubt very much that you love Blossom as much as I do, when according to you, you're incapable of love,' Margot said, pushing the pangs of guilt as far away as they would go.

'And you know exactly why I believed that,' Will reminded her furiously. 'I can't believe you'd throw that back in my face. Is this your revenge because I'm not ready to get down on one knee while simultaneously throwing my condoms in the nearest bin?'

That was a low blow, Margot gasped from the impact. 'It isn't revenge. It's because Blossom is suffering and I'm suffering too. I'll admit it, I got my hopes up, even though I knew how you felt . . .'

'It's clear that you don't have any idea about how I feel.' Will's body was tense and coiled as if he were about to spring up from the bench and start pacing. 'And how come *you* get to have Blossom?' he demanded. 'We are equal owners, everything split down the middle.'

'But I saw her first. She was always meant to be *my* dog, until you muscled in,' Margot recalled.

'We both paid an adoption fee and you agreed that your lifestyle wasn't compatible with full-time dog ownership.'

'I didn't agree any such thing!' Margot said indignantly. She felt as if she should put her hands over Blossom's ears so she wouldn't be psychologically scarred from hearing Margot and Will really going at it, but Blossom wasn't sitting between them anymore.

'I'm pretty sure you did,' Will snapped back.

'Pretty sure I didn't,' Margot said, but her focus and heat were no longer on this horrible fight, of each of them taking the other one's innermost fears and using them as cheap shots. She cast her eyes over the playing field to see where Blossom had gone.

'When Blossom is with me, she's not on her own for longer than ten minutes, tops. Mary, who adores her, not that you seem to give a toss about that, spends all day with her and—'

'Where is she?' Margot exclaimed out loud.

'Where's my mother? She's at home, expecting me to come in with Blossom any minute now,' Will said witheringly. 'Don't walk away from me, Margot. This is not settled.'

Margot was standing up now. Her heart leaping at the sight of any vaguely small, vaguely white dog in her line of vision, but none of them were Blossom.

She turned to Will. 'Where's Blossom?'

He frowned. 'What do you mean? She was here a minute ago.'

'And now she's not,' Margot said, taking a couple of steps forward so she could properly investigate the birthday celebrations. There was an awful lot of picnic debris and Blossom had yet to find a food that she didn't like, except celery, but there was no small Staffy with her head in a Sainsbury's bag or tarting herself about in the hope of a belly rub. 'I can't see her anywhere.'

Will got to his feet and put a hand over his eyes to shield them from the setting sun as he too looked over the wide expanse of grass. 'Over there!' He pointed at the far end. 'She's giving that football a good shake.'

Margot's heart leapt.

'Oh no, it's a Jack Russell,' Will said.

Her heart sank again.

'Well, she can't have gone far,' Margot decided. 'She never wanders off. Unless there's a squirrel but then she always come back. Always.'

'Always,' Will agreed. 'The café's closed. So she's not scrounging food at the kitchen door. You don't really get a lot of squirrels on the field.'

'I read somewhere that if your dog runs off, they usually come back to the last place they saw you.' Margot scrutinised the bushes that lined one side of the green. 'She's going to come waddling back any minute now, looking very pleased with herself.'

They waited for a good five minutes. Margot could feel her heart racing faster and faster as each minute passed and there was still no sign of Blossom.

'Right,' Will said, standing up again. 'You stay here and I'm going to check out her favourite haunts. Squirrel alley, that place near the water fountain where we found the dead bird that time, and the clearing where they have the children's parties. Anywhere else?'

'I don't think so,' Margot said, because apart from Sunday handovers, she tended to walk Blossom on the Heath. 'Call me when you find her 'cause I'm starting to panic now.'

'Look, she has to be somewhere in the woods. It will be fine,' Will said, but his face was tight and he was already striding away, leaving Margot to sit there with nothing to do but fret and ask anyone in close vicinity if they'd seen 'My dog. A little fawn and white Staffy. She's very friendly.'

Nobody had, until finally! A middle-aged couple with a

majestic Bernese Mountain dog said they'd passed a Staffy about five minutes ago.

'Maybe it was tan,' the woman pondered. 'Would you say it was tan?'

'More brown than tan?' her companion decided. Margot wanted to scream, but instead she pulled out her phone and showed them her screensaver, which was Blossom wide-mouthed and smiling and unmistakeably fawn and white.

'Oh, no, not the same dog and this one was being walked by a young fella. Or rather the dog was walking him!' the man said with a smile because he really didn't know how to read the room.

They left. Margot wandered as far from the bench as she dared, calling Blossom's name. The sun was properly setting now. Then she heard the bell signalling that the woods would be closing in fifteen minutes. Because it wasn't the kind of wood you could just wander into. It had gates. Lots of gates. Gates that led straight on to the busy Archway Road, with buses and lorries thundering past. Gates that led towards East Finchley. Gates that led out onto Muswell Hill Road and more buses.

Blossom wouldn't wander out of any gate. She wasn't an adventurer and she hated to lose sight of whoever was walking her.

Any news? she texted Will, though if there was any news, he'd have texted her back.

Unless . . . for one awful moment, Margot wondered if Will had found Blossom and decided that if anyone was going to have full-time ownership of her, it was he. Then her phone chimed.

No news. Coming back to you now, Will texted back.

He was there a minute later. She knew that he didn't have Blossom with him, but even so, the sight of him coming back without their little shadow made Margot burst into tears.

Will's arms were around Margot in an instant, tightening as he felt her shake with the force of her sobs.

'We'll go to the woodkeepers' office,' he said, one arm still round Margot to guide her down a little path on the other side of the café, where there was one woodkeeper ten minutes away from finishing her shift.

Still, she was very kind, taking down their details and calling one of her colleagues. 'We have to do a complete perimeter sweep to lock all the gates, so I'll see if you can hitch a ride on the buggy.'

'She's so friendly that she'd go off with anyone,' Margot said, though her words were mangled by the shuddering sobs that she couldn't tamp down. 'She's a Staffy, so they'd want to use her for dogfighting. But she would never fight another dog, so they'd make her a bait dog instead.'

'Nobody's going to make Blossom into a bait dog,' Will said, but he didn't sound at all convinced. 'Shall I call the dog warden? Shall I call the police?'

There was a 'beep beep' as the little motorised buggy that the woodkeepers used arrived. Normally, Margot would have been thrilled to ride in the little cart, but not now when she was doing her best not to fall out every time they went over a bump and scanning the lengthening shadows for a flash of white.

It was impossible. There was so much foliage and night was coming in fast. Blossom could be anywhere and even though they called her name again and again, there was no sign of her trotting back towards them with that ridiculous grin on her ridiculous face.

The last gate to be locked was Gypsy Gate, which came out at the top of Muswell Hill Road, opposite Highgate Tube Station and, even at this time on a Sunday night, the busy and bustling Archway Road.

'I'm really sorry,' said the man who'd been driving them round with the patience of a saint; there'd been several false alarms when Margot or Will had thought they'd seen a sliver of white in the distance.

'Maybe I could stay in the woods overnight?' Margot suggested desperately, because she couldn't bear the thought of Blossom in there, all alone and frightened.

'You can't do that,' Will said very gently, and Margot knew that he was right, and even if Blossom was trapped in there until the morning, then it was preferable to her being out of the woods, in traffic, prey to someone without her best interests at heart.

There were a couple of benches at the top of the road. Margot sat down, her phone clutched in her sweaty hand. 'I'll call the dog warden, shall I?'

Will nodded. 'I'll call the twenty-four-hour vets. There's one in Hampstead, right?'

'I think there's one in Finchley, too.'

They were quiet as they both googled the appropriate numbers. When Margot got through to the dog warden, it went straight to voicemail. She left a message. Then she called the police who told her to call the dog warden. She could also call the dog wardens for all the neighbouring boroughs, Camden, Islington, Barnet . . . In the background she could hear Will giving his details to someone, then he stopped and frowned.

'You're beeping,' he said.

'Who's beeping?' Margot asked him.

'Your phone's beeping.' Will took the phone out of Margot's hot, sweaty grip. 'You've got a missed call and a voice message. How did you miss a call?'

'Because my phone is shit and I'm still three months away from my upgrade,' Margot said, snatching the phone back.

She didn't recognise the number, but whoever it was had left a message.

Please, please, please let it be someone who's found Blossom and she's all right. Even if they want a ransom, we'll pay it, Margot promised as she accessed the message.

'Hi, this is Sue from The Hat and Fan in Crouch End. Got your number off the tag of a little Staffy that we found. I think you ought to come down here as soon as you can.'

42

Will

Margot was crying again as they ran hand in hand down Shepherds Hill, but Will suspected it was more from relief than anything else.

'I hate running,' she hiccupped. 'And running downhill in Birkenstocks is like some horrible form of torture that I didn't even know existed.'

'We'll slow down,' Will decided, because while he didn't hate running, it had been a long time, but Margot shook her head and managed to keep going until she came to an abrupt stop.

'Now I've got a stitch,' she panted, clutching onto someone's gatepost. 'And all I want to do is get to the pub and see Blossom. But what if —'

'Stop talking and just *breathe*,' Will told her sharply, although he was the one who felt as if he'd forgotten how to breathe. He took Margot's hands in his and squeezed them in time with her shaky breaths, which calmed them both. 'You OK now?'

'I'm OK,' Margot confirmed, and he let go of her hands, because the hand-holding was all wrong, even in these extenuating circumstances.

'How about we don't run, we just walk very fast?' Will suggested.

Margot nodded. 'You know, to get to Crouch End, she had to cross at least two roads and that's supposing she went a direct route and didn't zigzag. I have this horrible vision of her trying to cross Archway Road when the lights were against her.' Margot came to a halt and shut her eyes. 'What if she's horribly wounded?'

'I'm sure she's fine. They'd have said if she wasn't,' Will insisted, but what if it was bad news that you could only tell someone in person? What if she had been hit by a car and though she looked fine, she actually had severe internal injuries? Or what if someone had tried to dognap Blossom and she'd somehow managed to escape but would now be traumatised? 'She's come through so much already.'

'I'll never forgive myself if anything has happened to her,' Margot vowed, as they finally reached the bottom of the hill and crossed over the road to the pub where Blossom, bleeding, injured, maybe even dying, had managed to find sanctuary.

Will followed Margot through the open door, his heart juddering, with fear and anticipation, only to see Blossom instantly.

Hard not to, when she was perched on an armchair and surrounded by a group of cheering and clapping drinkers.

'She is a bad, bad dog,' Will said in disbelief, because Blossom was very far from traumatised or dying. Instead, she was performing her entire repertoire of tricks in return for pieces of sausage, which had been cut into handy bite-sized chunks and put on a plate held by one of the bar staff.

'She is the baddest dog,' Margot confirmed.

'High five!' someone called out, and Blossom instantly obliged. Will noticed that several people were filming Blossom's hijinks so she was probably going to appear on LadBible before the week was out. 'Such a good girl!'

'That's our dog,' Margot said in a loud and terrible voice. 'Excuse me! Our dog!'

The crowd around Blossom parted, all eyes on them, apart from Blossom who turned her head like she didn't know either Will or Margot.

'Just wait until Nanna hears about this,' Will said, and it suddenly dawned on Blossom that she was in a world of trouble because she shot them both a panicked look then assumed the position: on her back with her paws in the air, tail wagging frantically.

'No belly rubs for you,' Margot promised sternly, but then her face crumpled. 'Oh, Blossom . . . you frightened the living daylights out of us.'

When Margot sounded like that, tearful and tender, it was obvious that she was going to let Blossom have everything that she wanted. Blossom scrambled upright so that she could launch herself at Margot, who staggered under her weight until Will came up behind her and put one hand on Margot's shoulder, another around her waist. 'I've got you,' he said, and Blossom paused from the tongue bath she was giving Margot to anoint Will's face with saliva too.

The crowd 'aah'ed and 'aww'ed, then melted away. Will was still standing behind Margot to support the weight of Blossom in her arms. 'Christ, she's heavy,' Margot muttered, which somewhat killed the mood of the touching reunion scene. 'I think I've sprained something.'

'Let me take her,' Will said, lifting Blossom out of Margot's arms. 'Sit down and I'll put her on your lap.'

Margot sank into the armchair with a grateful sigh then gave another sigh of resigned anticipation as Blossom plonked onto her thighs. 'She manages to skewer me with a pointy elbow every time,' she complained.

'Amazing that such a chunk can have any sharp bits,' Will said, because he knew everything about Blossom, had put her needs before anyone else's, even, *especially* his own. But the reason they were here, the reason why they'd been distracted enough that Blossom could run away, was because Margot wanted to take Blossom away from him. Because she wanted nothing to do with Will. Never wanted to see him again.

Will waited for the white heat of anger to overtake him again, but now all he felt was a bone-weary kind of sadness. He was shattered. It had been one hell of an evening. 'Do you want a drink?' he asked Margot, who had her forehead pressed against Blossom's forehead, her eyes closed.

'Yeah, I'd love one. I'll have a soft drink though. Whatever you're having,' she said, not even opening her eyes.

Though Margot hated him, wanted to take Blossom away, she was still attuned to Will's feelings, sensitive to what might be difficult for him. It would be so much easier if she were still hurling insults at him. 'You can have a drink drink. Honestly, it's fine.'

Margot opened her eyes. 'Really? In that case, I'd love a gin and tonic. A gigantic one, please.'

Will went to the bar where he was greeted by Sue, who accepted his profuse thanks with a gracious smile. 'Officially we don't allow dogs in the pub, but Blossom has a lifetime exemption. She's not shy, is she?'

'Doesn't know the meaning of the word.' Will glanced over to where Margot had her arms tight around Blossom, her face buried in Blossom's neck. Blossom had flopped her front paws over Margot's shoulder, so it looked like she was hugging Margot too.

Will didn't know why he'd always been so fixated on the supposed fact that he was incapable of feeling anything too deeply, because now he was pretty sure that his heart was shattered.

Margot only disentangled herself when Will came back with their drinks. He'd expected her to look blissed out because she'd got her girl back, but instead her face was concerned but resolute, as if she'd come to a decision.

He couldn't take a repeat of the argument they'd just had. There were a lot of things Will couldn't take but he was just going to have to somehow. He sat down in the armchair opposite.

'You can have Blossom,' he said. Margot smiled, but it was a tenth generation copy of her usual smile.

'No, you're going to have Blossom,' she said, and she gently pushed Blossom off her lap. Blossom wasn't going to sit on the floor when she could sit on a chair or, even better, someone's lap. She was already hoisting herself up Will's legs without any assistance, and he instinctively hooked his arm under her back legs so she didn't slide off. 'It's best that you have her.'

'I watched you when I was at the bar, like I've watched you all these months,' Will said in a throaty voice. He'd been on the verge of tears this evening at least three times. 'I've always said that you deserve to love someone and be loved back. You deserve it more than anyone I know.'

Margot raised her glass in acknowledgment of this truth, but she still had that grimly determined expression on her face. 'I can't do it, Will. Outside of your family, Blossom is the only being you've allowed yourself to love, so how can I deprive you of that? At least I'm open to love . . . to the possibility of it . . . whereas you've closed yourself off.'

Even if he didn't have such heavy emotional baggage to lug around, even if he'd devoted his life to battling climate change and eradicating world hunger, Will still wasn't sure that he'd be worthy of the woman sitting opposite him.

'I haven't closed myself off from love, but I've always been afraid to love someone in case I ended up hurting them.' Will kissed the top of Blossom's silken head as she settled herself in his arms. 'My dad wielded love like it was a weapon. When he was feeling sorry for himself, some small part of him ashamed of what he'd done, he'd cry and say to my mum, "But I love you", as if that made everything all right. Or he'd say, "If you loved me, you wouldn't dress like a slut. If you loved me, you wouldn't want to leave me on own when you go out with your friends. If you loved me, you wouldn't make me so angry".' Just remembering it, the threats, the excuses, made him cling a little tighter to Blossom. 'Love can be such a destructive thing.'

43

Margot

'And love can also be the most wonderful thing in the world,' Margot said simply. 'You are not your father.'

'I'm starting to realise that . . . or I hope that it's true, but it's taking such a long time to fix myself.' They were back in that tired old groove that they kept getting stuck in.

'But I don't have time,' she said wearily as Will shook his head.

'You *do* have time, Margs. We have time. Mary didn't have Sage until she was forty-two.'

'By rights, I'm allowed to smack you for that remark,' Margot said, but she didn't move her hands from where they were curled around her gigantic G&T. 'After years of trying, of being told that she was infertile and to just stop trying, my mother had me at forty-five.'

Her voice wobbled. She looked up to the ceiling and blinked a couple of times.

'But you're not your mother.' Will turned the tables on her.

'It doesn't work like that. There can be genetic factors to infertility, I don't know yet whether I am lush and fertile or if having a baby, starting a family, might take years, thousands of pounds, intrusive procedures and even then, there's no guarantee. And I lost both my parents before I was twenty . . .' Her face was still tilted upward, so the tears rolled straight down her cheeks.

'Margot. Oh, Margs . . .'

She managed a tearful smile. 'I'd have sworn I'd already cried this month's quota of tears.'

'You're allowed to cry but I wish you wouldn't, because I hate seeing you so upset, so does Blossom,' Will said, though Blossom was now asleep in his lap.

'The last year of my mother's life was the worst year of my life. Instead of focusing on her treatment or even enjoying what time she had left, she spent those last precious months fretting and worrying and buried in admin, all for my benefit, and I will never stop feeling guilty about that. Never.'

'She did it because she loved you. Any decent parent would do the same,' Will reminded Margot.

'To have to put my child through that . . .' Margot looked at Will with troubled eyes, her face tensed as if she was in pain. 'You think I'm a good person, don't you? People, my friends, do. That I'm caring, thoughtful, generous, the sort of person who would do anything for anybody, but actually I'm a selfish, shallow monster.'

'You're not, Margot. You're absolutely not. You are the kindest person I've ever met,' Will said swiftly, automatically. As if her alleged goodness was absolute, unequivocal.

But Will would say that because he didn't know about those nights when Margot had laid in her bed, in her childhood home, in her room that smelt of Angel by Thierry Mugler, covered with posters of Kate Moss, and listened to her mother crying through the wall.

Whether it was in pain or fear, Margot didn't know, because she was too scared, too cowardly to find out. She didn't want to see Judy's lovely face contorted, her elegant fingers clawed with agony. Didn't have the courage to listen to her mother's confession. She wasn't brave enough to push back her quilt, get out of bed and offer what little comfort she could.

'I would pull the pillow over my head so I wouldn't have to hear her,' Margot told Will, though she'd never told anyone this. Not even her therapist. Instead she kept going back for top-up appointments to heal the hurt, without ever being able to articulate that the hurt was actually shame that she'd wear like a crown of thorns for the rest of her life. 'You've never heard anyone cry like that. As if she was so scared, felt so alone, and I wanted to go in and comfort her, but I didn't know how because I felt so scared and alone too. I'm sickened when I think about it and I think about it *all the time.*'

'You were eighteen, you were a child,' Will pointed out, and instead of rearing back from her, his face screwed up in contempt, his voice and his eyes were soft with concern. 'What is clear is that your mother loved you and you loved her . . .'

Margot swallowed down another sob. 'I think this is why I can't find someone to love me. Maybe I'm unloveable. I don't deserve to be loved. I'm being punished for what I did – what I didn't do.'

'No! Sorry, Margs, but that's absolute rubbish,' Will said with such force that Blossom stirred in his arms. 'You can't really think that.'

But she did. How could she not? 'And what if history repeats itself? What if my family medical history repeats itself too and I'm in the exact same situation?' she demanded with a despairing shrug. 'Knowing that I'm leaving the child I so desperately wanted on their own with no family, no one to love them.'

'Margot, you have so many people who love you and who would love that child,' Will said, his voice catching. 'Also, you could live to be a hundred.'

'Or I could get knocked down and killed crossing the road.'

'But you just don't know. None of us can know,' he said. 'I've realised that I have to let go of my past too. I don't want it to define me anymore.'

Margot took a long sip of her drink. She didn't say anything for a while, her lips pressed together, her eyes downcast, as she tried to find the right words.

'Nobody gets through life without being burned. It makes us who we are. Do I wish I hadn't been orphaned by the time I was nineteen?' Margot looked up to the ceiling again as if she was searching for divine inspiration. 'Of course I do, but at the same time it did define me, just like your childhood and your father defined you. He's made you a difficult person to get to know, you're wary of letting people get close to you, but he's also made you someone who cares passionately about your family. He's made you someone who battles to do the right thing. There are a lot of people in this world who don't give a toss about doing the right thing, and I thank God that you're not one of them.'

'And losing your parents so young has made you independent, strong, your own person. You are not a monster. You have the biggest, most generous heart of anyone I know, you draw people to you, and I know that you'll always be all right, whatever happens. You'll be just fine, Margot.'

Oh God, she was crying. Again. Silently. Tears running down a face that was already marked by the tears she'd cried earlier, and a lot of dog slobber. She tried to wipe them away with the back of her hand. 'But I don't want to be just fine, I want to be much better, much happier, than just fine.'

Will leaned towards her as if he wanted to take her hand, but couldn't because his arms were wrapped around a still-sleeping Blossom, their conversation punctuated by her snores. 'I do too. I really do,' and when he said that, Margot felt like it might be an actual possibility. 'I know I don't always behave well—'

'Oh, I don't behave well either,' Margot assured Will, like he didn't already know that.

'. . . But you do keep interrupting me,' Will said a little sternly. 'Even today, I had this big speech planned about how I want all the things you want. Mary helped me with it, but I didn't get a chance to tell you because—'

'I blindsided you with my plans to keep Blossom and now I've interrupted you again because I *do* do that. It must be so annoying.'

'It is,' Will admitted, and Margot couldn't take offence because it had often been pointed out to her. 'But I can get used to it. And yes, neither of us have behaved well, but Blossom was much more badly behaved than either of us and we stuck it out because we'd made a commitment to her.'

Margot still felt quite teary, but she smiled into her drink. 'Should we get Jim to start positive reinforcement training with us?'

'If he was willing, would you still want to?' Will asked tentatively.

Did Margot dare to hope again? She leaned so far forward that their knees bumped against each other. 'I would still want to if you still wanted to. We've both hurt each other. We've both misunderstood each other, but we can get through that, can't we? People get through much worse. Look at Blossom.'

They both looked down at Blossom, whose jowls were fluttering with the force of her snores. It wasn't her most flattering angle.

'Actually, you kind of remind me of Blossom. She has secrets in her past that have made her who she is, but she soldiers on through. It hasn't stopped her from having a capacity to give and receive love,' she said throatily, but she was determined to hold the tears back.

'You remind me of Blossom too,' Will told her, though Margot failed to see how. Unless it was their mutual gluttony. 'You both share an unfailing optimism. She's been hurt, but it doesn't stop her from flinging herself at life. In Blossom's world, there are no strangers, just people she hasn't met yet who might want to give her a belly rub.'

'I definitely don't let strangers rub my belly,' Margot said, looking down at the belly in question, relieved that the mood had shifted and also that Will hadn't made his excuses and left. 'They have to at least buy me a drink first.'

'We have to stop using Blossom as a metaphor for triumph over adversity,' Will said, as, yes, hope fanned a tiny little flame deep within Margot, even as her expression grew grave. She'd been forgetting something. 'You don't love me.'

'I never said I wasn't in love with you.'

She closed her eyes for a second so she could pluck up the courage for one final confession. 'Because I love you. I do. I'm sorry, but I can't help it, and that's why I ended things because I knew love was the last thing you wanted, the very last thing you wanted to deal with.' Margot pouted a little. 'I was trying to do the right thing.'

'By breaking my heart?' Will sighed and he looked at her with his deep blue gaze, deeper than oceans and just as unfathomable.

'I didn't think your heart was something I needed to take into consideration,' Margot admitted. She shouldn't feel a thrill shoot through her at the thought of breaking someone's heart, but she couldn't help the little quiver. After all, Will had made her quiver right from the start. 'I thought you'd tucked your heart away so it wouldn't get hurt.'

'That was the plan,' Will said, leaning closer, their dog the only thing coming between them in that moment. 'I've always been scared of love, but a future that doesn't have you in it scares me even more. Not as co-pawrents. Or friends with benefits. I want all of you and all that comes with that, so yes, even children, who you will love, and I will spoil because we both know that I'm crap at establishing boundaries.'

It was as if the grief and guilt that she'd carried around, that had weighed heavy and ground Margot down, was suddenly prised off her and she wanted to gasp in relief. 'For someone who's all about the boundaries, you really aren't very good at them,' she said, because she would cry yet again if she tried to say something more heartfelt. But surely the love she felt for him was radiating from every pore? Still, it couldn't hurt to say it out loud, just because she could. 'I love you, Will. I tried not to, but I do. I love you.'

He nodded in acknowledgment and that was fine. This was new ground for Will. He'd said that he wanted a future with her, children, and that was more than enough to be getting on with. He didn't have to say it back just because she'd said it first and—

'You just said that you were unloveable, but if that were true, then I wouldn't love you as much as I do,' Will said softly. Their legs bumped against each other again and Margot had to blink back fresh tears. Not unhappy tears. Not this time. 'But you and I aren't the important ones here.'

'We aren't?' Margot begged to differ. Right now, it felt like they were the only two people in the world who mattered.

'No. It's Blossom who's really suffered.'

Margot looked across at the dog who would always have first claim on Will's heart, not that Margot begrudged her that. Even though Blossom's snores had reached a crescendo that could be called cacophonous and it was slightly killing the mood.

'So, we really are going to get back together for Blossom's sake?' Margot asked. She picked up her glass so half her face was obscured, but she was properly smiling for the first time that evening.

'We need to do something to stop her acting out. She did a poo in one of my limited edition, Gucci-inspired, Nike Air Force 2 trainers,' Will reminded Margot in scandalised tones.

'She chewed through my personalised Anya Hindmarch handbag,' Margot said sorrowfully. 'But more than that, she's already had a very hard life.'

'And we don't want to add to her trauma . . .'

'We really don't.' Margot sighed. 'Then I guess we really are stuck with each other.'

'I guess we are.' Will said, and he sounded very happy about it. With a groan of anticipation, he stood up and managed not to wake Blossom.

Margot stood up too, so now she could press more than just her knees against him. 'I should have known that you were the one right from the start,' Margot whispered in his ear. 'I mean it was obvious.' She picked up one of Blossom's paws, which was draped around his neck. 'Dogs are very good judges of character.'

'Hate to burst your bubble but Blossom isn't the most discerning of creatures. She'd love anyone if there was a sausage in it for her.'

'Blossom is an excellent judge of character,' Margot insisted. 'She picked us, after all.'

44

A year and a bit later

It was early September, one of those tricksy weeks when just as everyone thought autumn was here with its fallen leaves and *The Great British Bake Off*, summer decided to have one last hurrah.

It was a gorgeous day. Blue skies, a gentle breeze, and though it had rained earlier, there wasn't a cloud in sight, and the playing field in Highgate Woods was a glorious green once more.

Perfect cardigan weather, Margot thought with great satisfaction as she and Blossom entered the woods at the top of Muswell Hill Road. Blossom came to a stop because this was usually when Margot unclipped her lead, but today Margot shook her head.

'I'm not having you run off after a squirrel,' she said as her phone beeped in time with the frantic thrum of her heart.

Waiting for you. Usual place.

It was a walk Margot had done hundreds of times since Blossom came into her life. A walk she didn't give much thought to, usually her attention on Blossom as she trotted on ahead, but today it felt like the longest walk in the world.

Past the toilets, past the children's playgrounds, then onto the field. The weather had tempted out many, many people, but Margot had eyes only for the tall man in a suit who was standing in front of the café, the clock showing that Margot was running ten minutes behind schedule.

But then everybody always expected the bride to be a little bit late.

Aware of all eyes on them, Margot bent down to adjust the garland of flowers around Blossom's neck, then the crown of flowers on her own head, and walked slowly through the crowd, nodding at her dog-walking friends and Sophie from the rescue centre, smiling at her Ivy+Pearl family, waving at Daphne and Geoff from upstairs, and coming to a halt because she couldn't quite believe that there was Tracy, standing with Sarah and Jess, even though they'd agreed that it was too far and too expensive to fly all the way from New Zealand.

'Like I was going to miss you getting married,' Tracy said in Margot's ear as she gave her a quick hug, then a shove forward as people murmured impatiently.

Margot had said, to Will's surprise, that the 'getting married isn't as important as the being married. Really, I only have strong opinions on the dress and the cake. I don't suppose you know anyone who could do our flowers?'

'Possibly,' Will had said. 'I could make a couple of calls.'

But it had turned out that they both had a lot of strong opinions on getting married and, happily, most of those strong opinions had converged. They'd get married in Highgate Woods at the place where they'd met for those Sunday handovers, had sniped and argued and eventually decided that maybe they could be friends. Also, Blossom was Dog of Honour, and a surprising amount of wedding venues didn't have a dog-friendly policy.

They couldn't legally get married in Highgate Woods, so they'd done the actual deed the day before in the less than salubrious surrounds of Haringey Register Office, in front of Mary and Ian and Derek and Tansy.

So today, now, after pleading with the City of London

Corporation, was when Margot and Will would really come together. And everything was perfect.

Her dress was a blush pink duchesse satin, with fitted bodice and full skirt (which concealed the small but already pronounced curve of Margot's belly), three-quarter length sleeves, and pockets, as she later announced to delighted applause. Because her ankles were already swollen and because the terrain of Highgate Woods wasn't really suited to anything with a heel, Margot wore glittery trainers.

Will said that he'd wear trainers too, with his navy-blue suit, which set off the little sprig of pink-tinged marguerite daisies in his buttonhole. They'd had no say in the flowers whatsoever. Mary and Rowan had informed them that their wedding flowers would be sweet williams, marguerite daisies and orange blossom. When Margot had burst into tears, because she was bursting in tears a lot, Mary had patted her hand and assured her that the three flowers were a perfect match.

Margot gazed down at her bouquet, the delicate white orange blossom providing a beautiful backdrop to the vibrant cerise sweet williams, which in turn complemented the softer pink of the daisies. Then she lifted her head to where Will was standing with Ian, his best man, at his side.

Guests and onlookers clapped Margot and Blossom as they passed, so it felt a lot like a freedom walk with Blossom tugging at the lead until they reached Will, who had a soft smile on his face that she hadn't seen before.

'Hello, you look beautiful,' he said, taking Blossom's lead. Then he cupped Margot's cheek. 'You scrub up all right, too.'

'You don't look so bad yourself,' Margot said, as Blossom sat down rather heavily on her foot.

There was a cough, and Margot and Will turned to face Derek who had married loads of his punk friends back in the day, and had offered to do the honours.

'Ladies, gentlemen and honoured dogs, we're here to celebrate Margot and Will at a spot which has played a significant part in their lives ever since they first met at a dog-rescue kennels off the A41.'

There wasn't much for Derek to do, other than to set a light-hearted mood. They'd written their own vows.

'I promise that we'll always face the future together, whatever the future brings.'

'I promise that I won't just be your husband, I'll be your family.'

'I promise that I won't always stick you with that last ten thirty p.m. wee walk.'

'And I promise that I really will stop letting Blossom sleep in our bed.'

Then there were the final promises. 'So, Will, do you take Margot to be your wife?'

Will had never meant two words as much as the 'I do' he said quietly to Margot.

'And Margot, do you take Will to be your hus—?' Derek asked.

'Yes, yes, I do!' Margot said before Derek had even finished the question.

'And Blossom, do you take these two chancers to be your legally wedded pawrents?'

Blossom looked up with a huge grin on her face at the mention of her name. Will picked her up so that Derek could take her paw and Margot said, 'I do,' in the squeaky cockney accent that they'd both decided would be Blossom's voice if she were able to speak.

'Then I pronounce you husband, wife and doggo,' Derek announced to whoops and cheers.

Later there'd be photos, including a picture of Will, Margot and Blossom, with all forty-seven of their canine guests, which would go viral when it was simultaneously posted on the Blooms', Ivy+Pearl and rescue centre Instagram accounts with the caption 'Happy life, Will, Margot and Blossom. We wish you unconditional love, laughter and belly rubs. #relationshipgoals.'

There'd also be a slow, ceremonial walk down Shepherd's Hill to the pub that Blossom had wandered into all those months before where they'd dine on spaghetti Bolognese. There'd be toasts, speeches and dancing, then they'd get the bus home because what was the point of spending all that money on wedding cars?

But before all that, there was Will and Margot sealing their promises with a kiss, while Blossom, still in Will's arms, enthusiastically licked their faces.

At last the three of them were a family.

(Which had been Blossom's intention right from the start.)

Thanks

As the Beach Boys once sang, you need a mess of help to stand alone and I owe so much gratitude to the cast of (not quite) thousands who willed *Rescue Me* into being.

Huge and heartfelt thanks to my agent, the incomparable Becky Ritchie who always has faith in me even when I don't have faith in myself, Alexandra McNicoll rights queen, Prema Raj and all at AM Heath.

I'm so happy that *Rescue Me* found a home at Hodder and that Kimberley Atkins has enthusiastically and skilfully helped me turn it into the book that I always knew it could be. (Even if you did turn out to be a cat person, Kim.) Also, huge thanks to Amy Batley for her unflappable organisational skills, Callie Robertson for marvellous marketing and Veronique Norton for publicity. Natalie Young for copyediting, Kay Gale for proof-reading. Big thanks also due to Joanne Myler for designing the beautiful cover of *Rescue Me* and Abbey Lossing for the wonderful illustration.

I'm very fortunate to have so many writer friends who cheered me on through the lonely process of writing a book out of contract. I don't know where I'd be without Kate Hodges, the Lady Novelists Posh Lunch, High Tea and What's App Association. Ditto the Lord Peter Wimsey Casting Suggestions Lunch Club and The Wahaca Scrabble Ladies, especially Cari Rosen who often FORCED me to play Words With Friends when I should have been writing.

I'm also very fortunate to have Sarah Bailey, Jackie Hunter and Lesley Lawson in my life who never mind me jawing on about novelling, though it must be very boring for them.

Finally, no one tells you that when you get a dog you'll meet some pretty amazing people while you're out walking that dog. Eileen Coulter, I will always be grateful for that one day when Betsy and I bumped into you and Eric in Coldfall Woods.

In Memoriam

Miss Betsy 2009 to May 16th 2018

'You can't buy love, but you can rescue it.'

Six days after my father died, I was rescued by a little Staffordshire Bull Terrier called Miss Betsy (née Blossom.)

Betsy had been picked up as a stray several days after giving birth. Although she was roughly three years old, the vets said that she'd already had four or five litters. She was covered in bald patches and despite the fact that she still looked pregnant, you could see every one of her ribs.

She was broken, but I was kind of broken too and together we would heal. Right? Wrong! A thousand times wrong! The first six months with Betsy were an absolute nightmare. She went from shut down and submissive to holy terror; this book isn't so much a work of fiction but a faithful account of those long, long days when I thought to myself, 'Christ, what have I done?' as Betsy pulled on the lead, went berserkers if another dog came too close to her and yes, nearly got run over at Ally Pally when she chased a squirrel across the road.

But with a lot of patience, training and belly rubs, Betsy transformed into the dog that she was always meant to be. It was one of the most meaningful and rewarding experiences of my life to see Betsy become a smart, imperious, hilarious, very melodramatic little madam with an endless capacity for love and peanut butter treats.

For six years Betsy was my little velvet house hippo, the beat of my heart, and I'm so grateful to All Dogs Matter, a North London rehoming and dog rescue charity, who liberated Betsy from a council pound and brought us together.

Rescue Me, more than anything, is a love letter. Not just to Betsy, but to all those dogs who have been abandoned, neglected and abused but never lose their ability to forgive and to love again.

Sarra Manning, London
#adoptdontshop